PRIDELORD

GRYPHON INSURRECTION BOOK 8

K. VALE NAGLE

STET PUBLISHING

Cover art and map by Jeff Brown.

Interior artwork by Brenda Lyons.

Interior graphics by Crystal Gafford of Crafty as a Coyote.

Author sketch by Murphy Winter.

Editing by Dustin Porta and Tim Marquitz.

Published by STET Publishing, Denver

WWW.STETPUBLISHING.COM

WWW.KVALENAGLE.COM

Trade Paperback
ISBN: 1-64392-055-3
ISBN-13: 978-1-64392-055-9

BELAMURIA
ALABASTER EYRIE
REEVESPORT
WHITEBEAK
CRESTFALL PALACE
DUCKBILL
ARGENT HEIGHTS
ABYSSAL NAZE
CRA
NIGHTSKY
NEW EYRIE
ALWREN
C R
JADEBEAK MOUNTAINS
EMERALD JUNGLE
FLOWER OUTPOST
SUNKEN EYRIE
STORMTAIL
RAFTWOR
KING'S REACH
SUBMERGED FOREST

BLACKTALON
GLASSWORKS
MOTHFEATHER EYRIE
BLACKWING EYRIE
PITOHUI EYRIE
GLACIER PRIDE
POISONMAW
LING
A
CRACKLING SEA EYRIE
VER
CH
KJARR NESTS
REDWOOD VALLEY EYRIE
TAIGA
KJARR
WEALD
STRIX PLATEAU
LUMINAIRE

For Andi Privitere.

When I lay dying in the hospital the first time, you were the voice at the other end of the line, guiding me through one of the worst times in my life. May you be immortalized in these pages with soft paws...and a sharp bite.

ABYSSAL NAZE

The cave smelled of sour moss and trampled mint, bitter and clean in equal measures. Morning rainfall cascaded down limestone walls, distorting the chirrups and squeaks of the resident swifts. Zeph, once a small copperhawk gryphon from the weald on the far end of the continent, reached a tentative talon out of the cave, flinching when he saw its form in the light and pulling back. He'd hidden in the dark for too long, but he feared the illumination beyond the Abyssal Naze.

"It's okay, we can take it slow." Even without her opi trill, Kia's voice was a beacon drawing him into the sun-drenched world. Since he'd only seen the frozen seraph through the ice, he didn't know if they had softer beaks than opinici or if her new accent was a side effect of his blood.

When Mally's original Owlfeather Highlands laboratories were discovered in what felt like a lifetime ago, Zeph had feared the Nighthaunt's strange alchemy. The hills between the weald and Poisonmaw were littered with the graves of Mally's victims. After destroying the pools of Crestfall, turning the essential salts into the rarest substance in the land, Zeph had ceased worrying about becoming one of the Nighthaunt's strange experiments.

That had been a mistake.

The once-gryphon tried again, getting his talons out but wincing when the light hit his eyes. He pulled up a foreleg to block the sun's gaze, but with it came a copper-colored wing. Despite the nickname of copperhawk, he'd always been a dull brown in the past. Now, his feathers shone.

Nor were they entirely brown. Several of his primaries sparkled red, several of the primaries on all *three* pair of wings. In fact, splashes of blue and green covered his body, too—stolen from the opinicus who had saved him.

The *once-opinicus* who had saved him.

"Zeph..." Kia took his foretalons in hers. Motes of dust and speckled moths fluttered around her face. She spread her main wings to block the light, shrouding them in shadow.

Back Wings? Primary wings? He hadn't needed terminology for different sets of wings as a gryphon, and he grumbled to himself that he needed them now. *Totally adequate, not-needing-extra-help wings.*

The first week after his confrontation with Emin, the Seraph King, Zeph had refused to look at his reflection in the water. He hadn't just *liked* being a gryphon, he'd loved it. He couldn't stand the sight of the stranger staring up at him from the drinking pools.

Seeing Kia had also changed softened him. She'd gone into the vat healthy—gone into the vat to save *him*—and therefore recovered first, but the cave gryphons had kept her in another chamber of the Abyssal Naze. Only when Zeph was healthy enough to grasp what had happened did they let her in.

He took a misty breath and looked up at her. A wall of green wings, hints of red and blue, stood before him. Kia was just as beautiful as a seraph as she'd been as an opinicus. If some of her color had washed off on him, some of his beak had gone to her. Her short, red-shouldered parrot beak was now a raptor's countenance. Combined with the ear tufts and the lack of opi trill, he could almost imagine she was a gryphon.

He could almost imagine they were *both* gryphons.

He reflexively licked his paw and tried to clean his ear, forgetting it was gone. The seraphs didn't quite have or not have ears. They sported stiff, unexpressive feathers in the shape of ears, directing sound to the sides of their head. It was a strange sensation. He didn't like it.

But for Kia, he tried.

He took a step forwards, past Kia's wings and into the valley. His feet lacked their paw pads, and the ground's rough texture was like sharkskin against his digits. His foreclaws, once sharp enough to slice through a capybara, clicked against the stone walkways of the depths, dulling themselves into something more civilized but less gryphonic. For all the king's talk about how this was an improvement, Zeph not being able to retract his claws to keep them sharp felt like a step down.

His front feet weren't scaly the way an opinicus or a bird's were. Instead, all four were covered in almost owl-microfeather-like fur. Then there was the matter of the extra talon. His dewclaw had become like the backwards-facing talon that opinici used to grip tools or quill pens. He didn't know what to do with the extra digit while walking, but he supposed he could now learn to write sad journal entries about every time he started to run and tripped over his own feet.

Dear diary, today I fell beak-first into an underground river because I don't have paw pads. All of the crawfish saw.

Kia nuzzled him gently, bringing him out of his daydreaming. "Silky's pride covered the top of the valley in webbing, then lined it with thin leaves so no one will see us."

Her body was long, just like the Seraph King's, but neither of them were as large as Emin had been. The flameworks refugees brought rumors with them, rumors the world was full of seraphs now, but no word on their size. Perhaps the king's stature was a side effect of his long life, or perhaps the leftover salts had lost some of their potency by the time Zeph and Kia went into the vat.

Zeph may have grown the tiniest bit, but it was more like he'd been stretched thin and given too many feathers. In the medicine nests, he'd managed to curl up like a fisherfolk's knot and forget his new shape. Every time he got up to relieve himself, however, his new foreleg wings stuck up and reminded him he wasn't a gryphon anymore. His tail waged its own campaign for attention, knocking over supplies and gryphlets as he traversed the cave gryphon's thin corridors. No matter where he went underground, he took up too much space.

True to Kia's word, the top of the small valley was covered in silk. Leaves of yellow, green, and brown filtered the light. The limestone rocks, eaten away by rain, were covered in green moss, red ferns, and sprigs of mint.

That'll make this next part easier, he thought. He tried to leap atop a large boulder in the center of the valley, but his stomach hit the stone, and his back talons scrabbled for purchase.

"Careful!" Kia warned. She'd found a way to fold her—front wings? forewings?—so they didn't get in the way. Pieces of her scholar's harness had been modified with red cave silk to fit her new form. "Your body is longer now. You can't fling yourself at your target. You need to come in from the side and go around. Remember, your tail is your friend."

"You sound like Younce," Zeph grumbled, but he also wove himself around the top of the boulder, using his tail to keep steady.

His old tail had always bothered him a little as a gryphon. Outside of the fantails, it was rare to have a feathered posterior in the weald. His new one wasn't the same as Xavi or Hatzel's. With its thick size and flexibility, it was like a cross between Xavi's and the snake that had tried to eat him, and it gave Zeph a whole range of motion he wasn't accustomed to. Plus, it had decorative feathers at the end, which might prove useful for distracting goliath birds but otherwise had no purpose he'd found.

Not to mention he couldn't let them drag on the ground, having been told several times to be sure to keep the tip of his tail up, which felt a bit improper outside of mating season, in his opinion.

Kia gracefully settled onto her own perch. She kept her legs on top of the boulder and used just her tail to steady herself. "You need to learn to fly again."

"I know how to fly," Zeph snapped, but he quickly apologized. "I'm sorry. I just don't like being treated like a fledgling. You said the king flew away right after his change? Why can't I do that?"

"Because you were nearly dead when we put you in the vat," Kia explained. "When...*I* put you into the vat."

He couldn't stand to hear the guilt in her voice. "You saved me, Kia. I'm sorry I'm frustrated, but I'm not mad at you. I'd be dead if you hadn't."

He suppressed a flinch. When he thought of the king, he could *feel* Emin's talons going into his chest, crushing him. His scars twinged in protest, a reminder of how close he'd come to dying, but also a warning that if anyone saw Kia and him, they'd be killed. Outside of the Abyssal Naze, no one knew these two rogue seraphs existed.

Kia left her beak open a moment too long. There was more left unsaid, he could hear it in her words and tone. More she wanted to talk to him about, but she was waiting until he had fully recovered.

Well, no sense sitting around waiting for someone to dip me into a vat of gryphon. If I'm going to be a seraph, I'd better learn to be the best seraph the weald has ever seen. The best seraph Belamuria has ever seen.

He stretched his main, totally-adequate-on-their-own wings, pumping them a few times to get the blood flowing. Then he wrapped his tail around the boulder and shifted onto his hind legs, letting his forewings flap.

He took a deep breath, leapt off—beating only the wings on his back—and fell into soft moss.

"Not bad!" Kia called down. "Just remember that you need to use both sets of main wings together this time. You can ignore the feathers on your back legs for now, they're more for when you're soaring."

He gritted his tomia and climbed back up. Hatzel, Xavi, Younce, and everyone else waited for him back home. If he was going to return east, he needed to relearn to fly. Even if it made him feel like the world's oldest fledgling.

The *gryphonithing* leapt down, beating both sets of what Kia called *main wings*, and managed to slow his fall enough that it didn't hurt when he hit the ferns.

His landing set off an eruption of fluttering moths, attracting the swiftlets from the cave. The happy birds swallowed up the bugs in celebration before returning to their silky nests.

"That's great!" Kia said. "I know it feels awkward now, but wait until you get up into the open sky. Those funny long feathers on your back legs feel like their own little wings, and you can spread the feathers on your tail. You're never going to have a hard time on long flights ever again."

He launched himself from the boulder a third time but forgot to unwind his tail from the rock and went face-first into the peat moss.

Kia flew down after him, worried, and reached a talon to help him up. "Zeph...it's going to be okay. You know that, right? You're going to be just fine. *We're* going to be just fine."

He looked into her eyes, a hint of his taiga blue starting to show in them, then took her talon and climbed back up to try again.

1

BEYOND THE EMERALD VEIL

Nighteyes fluttered across the river separating her burrow from the rest of the Nightsky Pride's nesting grounds. The spring rains were out in full force, imbuing the air with the metallic tang indicating this storm had come down from the Argent Heights and not from the ocean side.

Having a burrow on a river island was great in the winter when the Emerald Jungle was dry, but currently, her home was underwater, so she'd slept on the roof.

She paused outside the nesting grounds proper, taking advantage of a ray of sunshine to preen some of the moisture from her feathers. Her mate would have teased her about her need to be dry, but Rudder had departed back to Stormtail territory after the eggs were laid, as was tradition. Since this was their third season together, he'd asked if she'd come stay with him along the coast.

She'd declined. Even though Lightningmaw's perpetual storm let up in late autumn, and even the

Winter Jungle was above water by then, she'd never had a truly dry experience in Stormtail Territory. There was only so much sand and spatterdock she could take, and she wasn't about to spend all winter with wet paws just to return home in time to get rained on all over again.

I'm sure even the desert has rainy seasons, but give me a dry place to lay my beak, and I'm happy. Enough with the water.

Something stirred in her from two years ago, a sandy smell where the salt marsh faded into dunes and desert, an army marching south from the Argent Heights, New Eyrie in danger—

And then it was gone, as though it had never happened, and she was left thinking of purple and gold squirrels. She had those moments a lot these days. She'd recall things so real she could taste them, then they'd fade back to nothing. She'd experience visions of her dream-self doing things she had no memory of, then snap out of it and forget what she'd just seen.

She finished drying off and headed back under the white-flowered canopy of the jungle. With the perfume of heat and sand fading from her nares, she caught the familiar scents of her sisters and Wendl up ahead. Her siblings' pheromones were similar to her own, though each had a slightly different floral hint to them. Wendl's natural scent was hard to detect, especially weak for a starling, but she used cassia to keep bugs out of her nest, leaving her with a cinnamon spice unmistakable as anyone else.

The Nightsky Pride was a sea of purple feathers beneath the jungle's shadows. Here, at the start of storm season, several violet-backed starlings abandoned their underground nests for ones in the trees. In the old days, they slept wet. But when Wendl joined—with her fancy opinicus talons and strange ideas—she'd set up a broadleaf overhang to keep her own nest dry. Not long after, every other starling in the pride had demanded a similar setup.

Wendl. I was talking to Wendl. We were at the edge of the jungle, near the ruins, and—

"Hey, Nighteyes," the only green starling in the nesting grounds chirped. Wendl wrapped her wings around the violet pride leader in an embrace, then pulled them back. "Oh, you're still wet. Do you need help drying off?"

Nighteyes gave herself another shake, purple and white feathers puffing up, but declined the offer. "There's no point. I'll be wet again by midday when the storms come back."

Wendl didn't look convinced but fell in step behind her leader. The jadebeak opinicus held a special role in the village. Where most prides had their hunters, their gatherers, their denparents, and sometimes two assistant leaders, Wendl didn't fit into the hierarchy at all. She existed outside of it, functioning as a medicine gryphon of sorts, similar to what the Ashen Weald had.

Nighteyes made her rounds, starting with the hatchery, the one place that had to be kept warm. This year's eggs were in nests of dried moss, kept safe by two denmothers. They nodded to her. All eggs healthy and accounted for.

At least they seem healthy, she thought. *We won't*

know if they have bloodbeak until they're a few months old.

Outside the hatchery, gryphlets and fledglings played. The gryphlets from last year still had so much fluff they were more white than violet, but the fledglings lacked any feathered down and should have left by now.

"They need their own nests," Nighteyes said. "They need to learn to be adults."

Wendl bowed her head. She didn't argue with her pride leader, not in front of the pride. Yet, many times in private, she'd let Nighteyes know she thought this was a mistake.

Wendl's thoughts had merit, even if Nighteyes didn't like to admit it. They'd lost half their hunters to green wing altruism, dead at the talons of the Golden Sky or Abyssal Naze. Altruism had a strange effect on the young, freezing them in place until it passed, so they hadn't joined the attack that devastated her pride.

With so many gryphlets and so few adults, they needed all the hunters they could get. The only problem was bloodbeak. Every hatch year, the fledglings grew up weaker, slower, and less capable—an epidemic that disproportionately affected the Nightsky and Sparkwing Prides. It seemed cruel to force them to hunt when they didn't have much time left.

Hence the current contention. Wendl wanted to coddle the fledglings for the rest of their brief lives. Nighteyes needed them out hunting to feed the gryphlets.

The pride leader waded into a sea of young. They

seemed reassured, like they'd never lost faith she'd find a way to save them. *But I didn't find a way. Not even with Wendl's help.*

Nighteyes licked the head of a fledgling whose beak and talons had a red sheen to them. She rubbed the youngling's face, leaving her scent behind. As leader, they were her duty.

"Any change?" she asked Wendl.

The green opinicus shook her head. "No. I must be allowed to talk to other scholars. I need to know what they're trying, and I need access to real tools, *opinicus* tools. Even to do the egg treatments, I need supplies from the Redwood Valley. And it's time to consider using our limited supply of salts on the oldest fledglings."

"The pridelord won't allow it." Nighteyes had never seen the starling leader so angry as when he discovered outsiders had used the Nightsky and Jade-beak Prides as weapons two years ago. The pepper scent of his anger had been so strong it had seeped into the stones of the temple itself, a lingering reminder to all who approached him of the past. He'd immediately pulled the starling prides back from the border and deployed the Newmoon Pride in their place.

To an outsider, the newmoon gryphons didn't seem to be any different than sparkwings or night-skies. But there was a reason the newest starling pride had been kept in the deepest recesses of the Emerald Jungle, away from the border glyphs and other star-lings. Moving them to the edge of the Agent Heights and Abyssal Naze was its own warning to those who knew what they did.

"It's just, if I could even leave a message for Piprik or Erlock..." Wendl began, but Nighteyes cut her off.

"The answer is no." The pride leader forced her hackles down. "I know you're worried about your friends. I'm worried, too. But think of what they did. The pridelord isn't wrong in his decision."

Wendl scratched a gryphlet's head with her talons like it was a pet. "Even if his *decision* is killing your pride?"

"I have full faith in you." Nighteyes reached the end of the nesting grounds and noticed someone was missing. "Was there another death?"

Wendl closed the gate behind her. It didn't do much to stop the gryphlets from climbing over it, but it gave them a place to gather when the denmothers whistled for them. "No, Sheen has joined the hunters."

"She's cured?" Both of Nighteyes' ears immediately faced forwards. This was the first good news she'd had in years. "Sheen recovered from bloodbeak?"

Wendl shook her head. "No, she still tests positive, but she seems to be doing better. She's stronger and more energetic than the other fledglings, even if she still struggles a bit. Don't ask me what it means. I don't know. With all diseases and disorders, there's usually one or two who get better even though death seems certain."

"Can't you use your salts? Make the others like her?" Nighteyes pushed. She could feel herself getting worked up, and she didn't understand Wendl's hesitation.

The opinicus always seemed to be looking

through Nighteyes, at her shadow. "Not until I know what's going on. Not while she tests positive. Maybe she just gets a few extra years, then she dies. Then, that's all the salts Khalim procured from Crestfall for us would let us do. Even assuming you could get me the supplies I need to *use* the salts. I've never done it before. I need to talk to someone who has."

Nighteyes sighed. The answer to all of their problems lay beyond the Emerald Veil that kept the starlings trapped inside. Inside, where they were safe from the Ashen Weald, the Blackwing Alliance, the Seraph King. Inside, where no one could reach them. Inside, where her pride's future was dying from a disorder the rest of the world had cured in eggs and may have already cured for the hatched.

Even if they have a cure outside the egg, it's entirely possible they'd try to destroy us to get our salts, given the chance. The salts were already rare when I spent my time befriending the Ashen Weald. The same friends who destroyed the glyphs, sacrificing my pridemates for their war.

Nighteyes and Wendl went to check on the hunters. Nighteyes liked to know where they were hunting so she could go off in another direction to search for prey by herself. In the old days, she could sense where every member of her pride was at all times, but the last few years, her senses had dulled. Perhaps her tenure as pride leader was nearing an end, and this was a sign she should pass the mantle to someone new.

She'd just about reached the first hunter, Sheen, the fledgling fighting bloodbeak. For a nightsky, the blue streaks in her plumage were unusual. Nighteyes was just about to comment on it when a familiar but unexpected messenger arrived from the sky.

Rudder, her old mate, caught his breath. Shiny, light blue feathers went from his spear-like beak down his long body and onto his even longer tail, giving it a dolphin-like appearance. She was happy to see him, but something was wrong. He loved swimming the streams and rivers crisscrossing the Emerald Jungle, and he'd only have flown if it was urgent.

"We have an emergency, and I need your help." The stormtail looked from Nighteyes to Wendl. "Both of you. Quickly, before the pridelord finds out."

Nighteyes shook out the last of the water in her fur and took to the air, letting Wendl catch up. Whatever the emergency was, they wouldn't have long before the pridelord learned of it.

B. Lyons. 2022

2

THE FRIGHTENED STORMTAIL

There was no timely way to cross the Emerald Jungle, the sea of green broadleafs, and also avoid the temple at its center. Nighteyes, Wendl, and Rudder could get to Lightningmaw quickly or secretly, but they couldn't do both.

The Stormtail Pride held the most unusual of the hunting territories. They controlled the entire southern coast, including Lightningmaw in the southeast and the Winter Jungle in the southwest. It hadn't always been that way, and the Jadebeak Pride still resented being pushed inland, but there was a reason the stormtails thrived here: They were made for it.

The trio of starlings followed one of the many deep, fast-moving rivers that filled the jungle. When they reached a waterfall at the start of Stormtail territory, Rudder chirped for them to land, then dove straight from the air into a small lake.

His body was muscular, somehow both long and squat, but still built for swimming. He wriggled through the water, coming back up on the southern shore as though dehydrated from the flight over, bright blue feathers glistening in the sunlight.

"Sorry." He grinned sheepishly, resting his forepaws on a giant lily pad rimmed with purple flowers, squishing a few in the process. The water shimmered green, a side effect of the rocks and moss beneath the surface. "I don't like to be dry for so long. I've been assigned to the Winter Jungle, but it's still in the process of flooding. I really missed the lakes and ponds around Lightningmaw."

To the east, dark clouds hid the Stormtail Pride's nesting grounds from view. Nighteyes was grateful they weren't going to have to get wet. She much preferred the Winter Jungle to Lightningmaw, even if her past experiences there left something to be desired. And she preferred being between the two, like now, to visiting either.

The Winter Jungle was so named because it was only a *jungle* in the winter. The tides submerged it in the spring, and it didn't dry out again until autumn. Nighteyes hadn't been out there more than a couple of times helping Erlock Startail search for clues about a missing weald gryphon.

Lightningmaw, meanwhile, was exactly what it sounded like: a tributary of perpetual thunder and rain, where any normal gryphon would not have built a home.

Stormtails, however, were prettier than they were smart.

"So what's going on? There's an injured gryphon here?" Wendl asked. Though Rudder had tried to explain it on the flight over, Nighteyes insisted they both keep their voices down lest a jadebeak overhear them.

Rudder motioned with his beak. An island sat to the north, at the base of one of the rapids draining into the lake. White willows framed the sight, the tips of their silvery branches swaying with the current. "One of my friends, Clamshell, is hiding out there. They had some sort of panic attack, and their scent just vanished. It's like they weren't part of the pride anymore. They started saying crazy things, like we weren't really who we were because they couldn't smell us. I don't want them to hurt themselves, but they're not the first. While I was gone this winter, five others had similar attacks."

"Why didn't you ask your pride for help?" Nighteyes asked. "If this is routine, surely there's an easy fix."

He looked down. "One vanished from the jungle entirely. The other four freaked out when the pride-lord arrived, and he had them killed. I don't want that to happen to Clamshell. And I remembered you saying you'd taken one of Wendl's elixirs that made you feel cut off from the murmuration, and I thought maybe you'd know what to say to them?"

Murmuration was one of the words Nighteyes had taught Erlock and Satra when she caught them calling a group of starlings a *swarm*. Referring to the packs of infected starlings roaming the bog as a swarm was one thing, but to use such a common term for the beauty of a murmuration was insulting.

Wendl was uncharacteristically quiet. Usually, these sorts of mysteries appealed to her. But at the mention of the pridelord possibly showing up, she'd withdrawn.

That's fine. I can handle this myself. Nighteyes looked at the island. The northern side's quick current kept the water there free and open, but lily pads butted up against the southern half. She never knew why islands sprang up below small waterfalls, but her home was built in a similar place.

She asked the others to stay back and gently landed on a section of the beach where a tree had collapsed into the water, making sure she was visible. She didn't want Rudder's friend to think she was sneaking up on them, especially if they couldn't sense her pheromones.

"Hello, Clamshell?" she called. "Rudder said you couldn't smell the murmuration anymore. My name is Nighteyes of the Nightsky Pride. I've gone through that, too, when I travelled beyond the Emerald Veil. Would you like to talk about it? I might be able to help."

A long, granite-colored beak poked out from the brush and sniffed the air. The feathers around their nares were teal, more green than Rudder's blue. "You don't smell like a starling. None of you smell like starlings."

Nighteyes made a point of sniffing back. Clamshell didn't trigger her altruism, at least not yet, but their identity marker was gone. "Neither do you. But here we are, both starlings. Let's find a way to help you."

NIGHTEYES SAT with Clamshell until the stormtail grew accustomed to her. It took some coaxing, but Clamshell finally allowed Wendl and Rudder to come over, too.

"What's wrong with them?" Nighteyes asked.

Wendl didn't like being called a medicine opinicus, but she filled the role often enough they treated her that way. She checked Clamshell from beak to tail, going so far as to check their claws and ask them invasive questions. It spoke to Clamshell's desire to feel better that they answered all the questions without hesitation.

It took the opinicus a few moments to offer her thoughts. "I don't know. If they were another gryphon, I'd say they're perfectly healthy. But clearly, if they're not part of the murmuration, something is wrong."

Nighteyes watched her former mate's whiskers droop in disappointment. "The Ashen Weald has elixirs that let them visit us. Could we give Clamshell something like that, just for now, while we figure this out?"

"It's not so easy," Wendl explained. "Those elixirs don't make them part of the collective. They just bypass the green wing altruism."

Clamshell and Rudder, both blue-plumed starlings standing next to Nighteyes' violet, gave Wendl a strange look at the *green wing* part of the name.

The opinicus sighed. "I didn't name it, okay? It's a reaction starlings have to other gryphons. It's hard to explain unless you've seen it from the outside. I have a few elixirs I can make, but it'd help me to know where you've been, Clamshell. Maybe you were stung by an unusual bug, or did you eat something strange? Did you go into the Jadebeak Mountains?"

Clamshell shook their head. "No, nothing like that. There were rumors of large crocodiles upstream from the nests, so I went to investigate. I relocated a few small caiman and caught a glimpse of something big hiding by the old Grasslake Pathway. Then...it happened."

"Wait, the Grasslake Pathway?" Rudder's tail swished back and forth in the water. "One of the others was up there, the one who vanished. Maybe that's where it happened?"

"We should investigate," Nighteyes said. "Wendl will know what to look for."

Wendl dug through her pouch for incense. "I'd rather stay here and try a few things on Clamshell. Rudder knows what plants and animals are usual for his territory, right? Just make note of anything out of place."

In the pit of Nighteyes' stomach, she felt a swirling of dread at leaving Wendl alone with Clamshell. She suppressed her instincts. Wendl had helped hundreds of sick starlings. Clamshell was as safe with her as anyone. If not for Wendl, Nighteyes wouldn't even be able to see.

But the pridelord often calls for Wendl, and she'd never do something to risk being out of his good graces.

"Coming?" Rudder prompted.

Nighteyes shook the invasive thoughts out of her head. "Yeah, sorry. Let's take a look."

3

SPATTERDOCK

The Grasslake Pathway wasn't a paw path, nor was it a flyway of pruned branches. True to the Stormtail Pride who named it, the *pathway* was a series of streams and rivers flowing down from the temple to Lightningmaw.

The *grass* part of the name came from the lily pads and aquatic plants covering every inch of water like interlocking scales. The pads came in every size and every shade of green, dotted with yellow and white flowers. With broadleafs blocking the wind off the mountains from reaching this far down, the path looked just like a field of flowers and groundcover.

Of course, when a stray gust broke through the wide leaves above and disturbed its surface, the foliage sloshed around, revealing the water underneath.

Nighteyes shivered at the thought of being covered in spatterdock, the tiny, vegetative slush that sat atop ponds and lakes. Her already-shiny violet feathers shimmered in the humid air. "Maybe you should go underwater by yourself and look for anything, um, unusual?"

Rudder rolled his eyes. "Still don't like getting wet?"

"Not really," she snapped, "but this time, it's more the green stuff I don't want to spend all night grooming out of my fur. I still remember what it tastes like from the last time you took me swimming in the southern jungle, digging for faerie shrimp."

He opened his beak to tease her, but something surged on the far side of the lake, sending ripples across the water lilies and spatterdock. "Did you see what that was?"

"No, it was underwater. Why don't you stick your head below and take a glimpse yourself?" she suggested.

The answer was obvious and exactly what drew Clamshell here in the first place: crocodiles. Large, angry crocodiles.

Spatterdock and algae weren't her favorite things, but they also weren't fatal. She'd flown over the Winter Jungle and had vivid memories of what she thought were downed trees floating in the water that suddenly opened their giant toothy maws and swallowed a swimming capybara whole. The stormtails had worked hard to try to clear the crocodiles out of the Winter Jungle, but nature had a way of overcorrecting.

If all the crocodiles had instead moved here, she didn't want to be in the water. She wanted to be back up north, where large crocodiles were not. For a dangerous crocodile to visit the Nightsky Pride, it would have to swim through a few other territories, and it'd probably get caught and eaten before it reached her.

Or so she told herself at night in her river-surrounded burrow when she heard a strange splash outside her nest.

"Can we just...throw a rock in? See if anything tries to eat it?" she pushed.

But Rudder had already smoothed down his tail-feathers and was slipping beneath a large lily pad to take a look. Unlike with the mystery surge, the slight ripples of his ingress were absorbed by the aquatic foliage.

Nighteyes moved away from the water. She'd seen rhea, sandy-colored flightless birds, pulled under by a variety of hungry reptiles. She pretended to look for any suspicious plants while she waited.

Thirty seconds passed, and her anxiety grew. The sweet-sour lily smell was so strong she could taste it. Crickets sang, filling the silence with their chirrups, while a pair of mallard ducks quarreled in the distance, their quacks at odds with the cricket melody.

Finally, Nighteyes had enough and flew back down to the bank. She'd just pulled up the closest, largest lily pad to see what the Grasslake Pathway looked like underneath when a scaly tail as long as she was broke the surface and thrashed. Lily pads fled from the scene as best they could, straining against their stem anchors. She heard the strange, squeaky bark of a stormtail, and a surge of displaced spatter-dock charged the shore.

She pushed off against the mushy ground with all four paws, alighting on a thick, moss-covered branch moments before a large reptile erupted from the water. Its snout was wide and deep, almost a pelican with teeth, unlike any crocodile she'd ever seen. Behind the twenty-foot beast was Rudder, nipping at its tail as the creature heaved itself onto land and fled north to the Jadebeak Pride's hunting grounds.

"Night?" Rudder called. He went to the edge of the grassway and used the relatively algae-free water under a lily pad to clean off. "Where'd you go?"

In the distance, she heard a splash and the protests of mallards.

"Up here," she replied. "I can't believe you let the crocodiles grow that large so close to the nests."

He barked a laugh. "That wasn't a crocodile! Didn't you see its itsy-bitsy teeth? It was just a caiman."

Nighteyes was used to iguana-sized caimans with mottled brown and dark blue patterns to their scales. She had no idea the southern variety grew this big. "Okay, sure the teeth were tiny, but there were a *lot* of them. And its mouth was still wide enough to fit a few gryphlets inside."

He shook his body, getting it dry, or at least what stormtails thought of as dry. A nightsky would call that *still very wet please do not come into my nest you are tracking water all over the dry moss I use to keep bugs out how dare you you're lucky you're so cute.* "We'd never let them get this big, but that particular waterway comes down from Jadebeak territory. They don't keep their rivers clear."

She looked up at the congested canopy, full of vines and wasp nests, and thought the jadebeaks probably felt similarly about how the Stormtail territory kept their lands.

Things were better when the prides were allowed to mix. Jadebeaks kept the flyways open, stormtails kept the waterways open, sparkwings kept the paw paths clear. I wonder why the pridelord started keeping us apart.

That was a problem for another time. At the moment, Clamshell and Rudder needed her.

"Now that our reptile guest is gone, let's fan out and look around," she suggested. "You check the water, I'll try on land. I think I see some talonprints along the shore."

4

THE CRESCENT MOON

After the incident with the caiman, even the crickets and prickly mallards had ceased their singing. The only sounds piercing the silence were Nighteyes' constant sighs of disgust every time she stepped too close to a floodplain and mud squished between her paw pads, followed by a bark of laughter from Rudder.

She'd remember all of this when it came time to find a new partner for this year's mating season.

Someone quiet and dry.

They tracked the talonprints to a glade where a flock of rhea were snacking happily on grasshoppers and other bugs. Since the stormtails enjoyed the taste of caiman and fish so much, the flightless birds in their hunting territory grew plump and slow.

Rudder, still wet despite not having stepped in any surprise puddles himself, came up behind her. His warm, damp shoulder pressed against her flank. He didn't say anything, but he made eye contact, and then looked at the rhea. Unlike his pridemates, his time with the Nightsky Pride had given him a taste for flightless birds.

Nighteyes' stomach rumbled, but she knew better and shook her head. "We don't know if Clamshell ate one of these. Or if a caiman did, then Clamshell ate the caiman. When they said they relocated a caiman, did they mean...?"

Rudder's small, rounded ears drooped as the tasty rhea heard the gryphons and ran off into the jungle. "Yeah, Clamshell relocated the caiman into their stomach. The reptiles mostly eat mollusks, fish, and crustaceans in these parts, but only *mostly*. They'll eat just about anything, so if something's wrong with the rhea flocks, it could cross to the caiman, and then to a stormtail. How do we test that?"

"I don't think you and I can. The best we can do is save our observations for Wendl and hope she has some ideas." Nighteyes sighed. Everything here looked the same as every other part of the Stormtail Pride's territory. Whatever she'd hoped to find, perhaps some strange red blossoms or a sinister opinicus, it wasn't here.

They walked back to the Grasslake Pathway to give it one more glance, and nothing stood out to Nighteyes. Nothing, except... "Hey, did we check over there?"

Rudder looked up. "Probably? We've been over this whole area three times. I'm sure we did."

"I...Hmm." Nighteyes tried to approach the thick vegetation. As per Wendl's request, Nighteyes was doing her best to note all of the types of flora. But the tangle here was so thick she couldn't make out any specific plant. It gave her a headache just to look at it for more than a few seconds.

She turned back to Rudder, but he hadn't stepped forwards with her. She pushed harder, trying to get close enough to identify any single species of tree, but the flight over must have taken its toll because her legs became weak from the exertion.

She was about to give up when she felt a pain in her left paw. She looked down to where she'd stepped on a freshly fallen spiketrunk, still charred from the lightning strike that felled it. She pulled up her bloody foot and licked at it. With the pain, her fatigue vanished and her focus returned.

Before her stood a strange row of spiketrunks, out of place among the broadleafs of the Stormtail territory. Dozens of silvery eyes stared out at her.

And then they were gone. The eyes, the trees. It was a tangle again, no single flora or fauna identifiable.

A smart or sensible gryphon might have turned and left, feeling she was seeing things and in need of food or a nap. Nighteyes could be sensible, and certainly she had her flashes of brilliance, but more than anything, she was a *determined* gryphon.

She stepped down hard with her paw again, driving more spines through her pads, and the spiketrunks came into focus, but the silver eyes were gone. She went to lick her foot and noticed a strange glyph on the fallen tree: a crescent shape.

She reached out, but Rudder pulled her back, stumbling over a rock in the process.

"Hey, what happened to your paw?" he asked. "Why did you do that?"

"I wanted to see..." she began, but it was gone now, replaced by mind fog. She'd wanted to see *something.* Or she'd *seen* something? All she could remember was the glyph. "There was a crescent design. Is that a new starling pride?"

Rudder shook his head. "Crescent like a moon? Maybe the newmoons?"

"No, they have a full ring not just the crescent." The farther she got from the tangle, the less tired she felt, but the more her paw hurt. "Ugh, figures I'd step on something sharp. All right, let's get back to Wendl."

There was another possibility. It could be an old, forgotten pride, too. Little was said about the ancestral starling prides. The only reason Nighteyes knew of them was because of her time in the temple having her eyes treated by Wendl.

The wet, tangy rocks of the lower levels were painted with what a young Nighteyes had assumed were hundreds of feathers. As her vision cleared, she realized they were paintings of starlings, their wings decorated with glyphs like the Nightsky's: a murmuration of prides.

By the time the treatments were over and Wendl was talking about taking Nighteyes back to her pride, she'd examined every carving on the wall, which had bled over into the hallway and nearly taken over another room full of jade statues. She'd located her own pride, the jadebeaks, and the sparkwings. And there, at the very end, she'd seen a painting of the stormtails and newmoons.

Since that day, since identifying all the prides she

knew, Nighteyes had wondered if every forgotten starling on the mural represented a dead pride.

WALKING with a hurt paw was a chore, so Nighteyes and Rudder flew back. They hadn't been alone in a while, not since he stopped dampening the threshold of her nest every night, and this was her first opportunity to ask an impolite but not unexpected question.

"So...did any eggs hatch violet at Lightningmaw this spring?" She tried to sound casual, but she was thinking about bloodbeak.

They'd traded which nesting grounds kept their eggs, an unusual setup that only seemed fair to her. The first spring, at Lightningmaw, there'd been no violet starlings. The second spring, at Nightsky, there'd been a mix of both, and she'd had Rudder smuggle the stormy floodlings down to Lightningmaw to give to the denparents, who were always discreet about such things.

She hadn't heard anything this season, though, and she was curious. The first year lacking violet-backed starlings could have been a strange fluke. It wasn't impossible, even with parents from different prides. She'd been forced to learn a lot about genetics from Wendl, courtesy of the bloodbeak outbreak that had hit her pride so hard.

"No, all the eggs that hatched were stormtails," Rudder said. It didn't seem to bother him any.

She was caught on the phrase *eggs that hatched*. "All of them? What about from any other prides? Were there any jadebeaks in the mix?"

Though the pridelord had banned other prides from breeding with the stormtails, little could be done about the long border the stormtails and jadebeaks shared. There were just too many opportunities for a lithe stormtail to touch whiskers with a lost jadebeak. Not even the pridelord could stop love at first sniff. A few even went on to be *summer friends,* the cozy term for gryphons who met up outside of mating season.

"Nope, all stormtails. Every egg that hatches at Lightningmaw is a stormtail. I don't think we've ever had to take gryphlets to another pride, not in my lifetime." Rudder didn't seem interested in exploring the issue further, which was normal for a gryphon.

Nighteyes was a pride leader and thought of all the gryphlets at Nightsky as her responsibility—second only to the denmothers, of course—but bloodbeak had made her very interested in the wellbeing of gryphlets in general.

Years, though, without a non-stormtail hatching there? That wasn't how eggs worked. "Okay, so back to the *eggs that hatched*, do you think it's too wet for eggs from other prides? If so, we should consider just leaving the eggs with the Nightsky denmothers next time."

Rudder started to answer, but a cry of alarm from below interrupted their conversation.

"That was Wendl!" Nighteyes switched to a dive, leaving Rudder to catch up.

ONLY HOURS SPENT PRACTICING HUNTING with the fledglings reminded Nighteyes to withdraw her claws and mind her beak when she crashed into Clamshell, knocking them off Wendl.

There was a wild look in the stormtail's eyes, like they didn't know who they were anymore. Even when she'd first approached Clamshell, they'd seemed to be aware she was a gryphon, just not the right gryphon. That was gone now, replaced by something suspiciously similar to green wing altruism.

Wendl pulled herself away to the safety of a nearby tree. When Clamshell turned on Nighteyes, Rudder caught them from above and pushed them against the soft, mossy floor of the island.

"Grab their beak!" Rudder commanded, and Nighteyes nearly lost an eye wrangling the long, bitey spear.

"What'd you do to Clamshell, Wendl?" Nighteyes asked. "Why did they turn on you?"

Wendl dug through her harness pockets and found a makeshift poultice. The right dried mosses could be used to stop bleeding and fight infection. "The medicine should wear off soon. It was just a small dose. I thought...well, I thought that they were already cut off from the murmuration, so a little dash of orange couldn't hurt. A dose that small on a healthy gryphon should just have dulled their sense of smell. The flowers have their own medicinal properties, but because of their unusual side effects on starlings, they're often a last resort."

Rudder knew a little of what Nighteyes had been through while taking the orange elixir. It was hard for her to talk about, in a literal sense. She'd become prone to migraines, and thinking about her time with the Ashen Weald for more than a few moments usually triggered one.

Didn't the pridelord order Wendl to destroy all of her elixirs, though? Nighteyes continued applying pressure to keep Clamshell's beak shut. "What does it mean that your little vial of goo turned Clamshell murderous?"

"I don't know. Just that they were a part of the swarm somehow before, even if they couldn't feel us and we couldn't feel them, and then I snapped that bond." With her bleeding stopped, Wendl reached for a handful of dried mint, crushing it in her talons and holding it against Clamshell's nares.

They coughed a few times, but the elixir was already wearing off, and they looked calmer. As the mint did its work, Clamshell dozed.

"You should be safe to let them go now," Wendl explained.

Neither Nighteyes nor Rudder did any such thing. Many a fish had been speared by stormtail beaks, and she had no plans on becoming a fish today.

Wendl changed her tack. "Okay, well, if you're going to hold them until the elixir fades, at least tell me what you two found. Any orange blossoms, by chance?"

"Nothing like that." Nighteyes filled her friend in on the caiman, Rudder's comments on how it could be in the fish—always a primary concern for storm-tails—and the flock of rhea. It took Wendl's pressing about every detail for Nighteyes to remember the strangest part of the trip. Like her desert dreams, it had nearly slipped away.

"There was a spiketrunk with a strange glyph,"

she recalled. "Maybe it was a newmoon gryphlet practicing? Though...I don't remember the last time I saw a newmoon gryphlet."

Wendl froze. "This seems pretty far from their territory. They're in the west, aren't they? Wait, I seem to remember hearing they were moved after the incident. Are they in the northeast now?"

"It could be old," Rudder offered. "The glyph was on a fallen tree. It could've been hidden by the vines and ferns for generations."

"I'd like to see this fallen tree." Wendl gathered her tinctures and poultices, putting them into the well-mended pockets of her harness. When neither Rudder nor Nighteyes let go of Clamshell, she added, "Fallen trees are hosts to all sorts of oddities. Fungi, mold: things that can be medicinal or poisonous. A fallen tree can do a lot to help...or hurt, depending on what we find there."

Nighteyes helped wrangle Clamshell's body so Rudder could hold their beak down. "Is that why we didn't recognize the glyph? It's a medicine thing?"

"Mmm." Wendl didn't elaborate further but allowed Nighteyes to lead her back.

5

MALLOW ROOT

The jungle by the Grasslake Pathway was different this time. Nighteyes couldn't put her paw on it, but something was off. The floodplains usually had a sour, lily stalk scent to them. And even when the rains came, they replaced the sour with a fresh, humid aroma. But this wasn't either of those. Now, the area almost felt coastal.

Nighteyes sniffed a few times.

"What is it?" Wendl's body tensed, like she was expecting the caiman to come back at any moment. Strange, as she'd been more relaxed next to Clamshell, who'd come close to seriously hurting her.

Nighteyes closed her eyes, letting the floodplains enter her nares, trying to ignore Wendl's cinnamon smell. "It's...salt? I smell salt. I thought it was ocean salt, but it's dry, maybe from the desert. Funny, I've been dreaming of the desert a lot. Maybe it's in my head."

Where she'd had a lot of trouble locating the spiketrunk, Wendl walked straight to it, even stepping around the rock Rudder had stumbled over previously.

The emerald starling pulled out an opinicus tool from her harness and chipped the glyph from the bark. Despite her claims about the tree's medicinal properties, she looked past it, into the tangle.

Nighteyes felt a migraine coming on, but she closed her eyes and used Wendl's cassia to follow her. The scent of salt grew, adding a hint of iodine and something more.

"Do you smell that?" she asked.

Wendl tapped her beak. "I don't have your nares. I get a bit of the salt now, that's it. Why? What changed?"

Nighteyes, still refusing to open her eyes, let the smell settle into her. "The bog. It smells like the bog. Like freshly harvested mallow root cooking down in a Crackling Sea ranger camp."

A starling's scent was made up of several things, and in her experience, a gryphon smelled like a gryphon no matter what pride they hailed from. But layered on top of a strong gryphon scent and a fainter starling pheromone was an individual's unique marker, which could be anything from cooked crab in Clamshell's case to cassia in Wendl's to the smell of citrus and afternoon thunderstorms for the pridelord. It was usually faint, just a hint.

That's why Nighteyes missed that the mallow root wasn't the actual plant. The scent grew and grew, overwhelming the damp of the floodplains, the tang of her blood on the spiketrunk, the dry salt, even Wendl's spice.

With her eyes closed, Nighteyes wouldn't have

known it belonged to an individual if the gryphon hadn't spoken.

"Hello there." The voice was soft with a slight scratch to it. It was the voice of two best friends or lovers speaking in the night, not wishing to be overheard. "And who is your friend, Wendl?"

Nighteyes tried to open her eyes, but the world spun this close to the glyph, and she closed them again. "Sorry, I'm Nighteyes of the Nightsky Pride. I have a bit of a migraine."

"So I see." The newcomer backed up a little, and the smell of mallow root narrowed. "Looks intense."

Wendl's wing wrapped itself around Nighteyes. "This seems very far out of your territory, Whisper. What're you doing here?"

"A few starlings got lost," Whisper said. "I'm bringing them home."

How does a starling get lost? Nighteyes wondered. *We can always smell where we are in relation to the pridelord.*

She forced her eyes open. The undefined vegetation was gone. Instead, she saw dozens of spiketrunks with the glyph, all close together. That in and of itself was strange: Glyphs mostly worked off scent, so they could be placed miles apart and still be effective. What's more, between the spiketrunks, she could see a paw path of sand.

Or salt, she realized.

"What is this?" She felt like a leafcutter burrowed through her skull. She turned to Whisper, seeing her for the first time, and stepped back with a gasp.

Whisper was a spotless starling, a species only the Newmoon Pride had, her black feathers and fur sporting the barest of grey stars hidden in them. Her tail was long and fluffy like a bog gryphon's. But what caused the reaction in Nighteyes was Whisper's eyes. They were grey. Silver goo, like the infected, had stained the fur around her eyes, her chest, and her paws.

"Wipe your eyes, Whisper. You're scaring her." Wendl used a wing to pull Nighteyes a little closer.

Whisper licked a paw and cleaned the silver out of her eyes. Unlike with the infected, her pupils were clear and focused underneath the shiny goo. "Apologies. We don't do much socializing with other prides. But what brings you here? This isn't your territory, either."

"A stormtail got disconnected from the murmuration." The smell of mallow root intensified, and Nighteyes coughed. "They were last seen in this area, so we were trying to figure out if they'd eaten something. Wendl heard about the glyph on the log and said sometimes poisonous fungi or bugs are attracted to rotting trees."

The newmoon gryphon circled Nighteyes. Where they brushed against each other, Whisper left smudges of dark featherdust. Nighteyes was too busy managing her migraine to scold one poorly socialized gryphon about etiquette. Not if the stranger could do something for Clamshell.

"Do you think you can help?" Nighteyes managed to ask. There was a hint of citrus in the cloud of mallow now.

Whisper ignored the question, addressing her response to Wendl. "Her smell is off. What did you do to her?"

The jadebeak opinicus kept her voice even and calm. "Nothing. Why would I have done something?"

"Hmmm." Whisper touched her beak to the tip of Nighteyes'.

Citrus filled the nightsky. "How...do you know Wendl again?"

Whisper's attention was on Nighteyes, but her words were for her old friend. "If you've done nothing, it shouldn't be difficult to reset her memories back a little. You have no objections if I tell her a little about the two of us, then?"

Nighteyes' vision was filled with silver, dripping markings. The leafcutter in her brain had friends now, but she refused to back down until she secured Whisper's help. "Who are you?"

Like the dull rumble of distant thunder hidden by rain, the sound of chittering came from the spiketrunks.

Whisper showed no sign of alarm. "I was a male mothfeather opinicus. I followed scholars Khalim, Mal, and Wendl into the Emerald Jungle. Where Wendl and my colleagues drank the blood of a jadebeak, I'd spent months transcribing Mally's notes, and I knew he'd run into problems with the blood of the old Newmoon Pride leader. When the blackwings, alabasters, and starlings converged on our camp, I took all of her blood from Mally's storage and became her."

"Careful." Wendl's warning was nearly lost by the chittering from the shadows.

"Why?" Whisper challenged. "If you did nothing to her, she won't remember any of this. Now, if you think that's interesting, you should hear what Wendl's friends have been up to."

Wendl, barely visible to Nighteyes through the pain, rifled through her packs. "Fine, I gave her this. A tenth of a vial in her cassowary stew once per week."

Whisper stepped back, letting the warm smells of the jungle return. Nighteyes shook her head, clearing the citrus and marshmallow. Her tongue was coated with featherdust, the white parts of her coat smeared like she'd fallen in charcoal.

Wendl opened the vial for Whisper, who breathed it in, her eyes closed. Her lids were dyed to match the markings on her face, creating wisp-like flames, as though Nighteyes stood before the god of the silver-eyed starlings wandering the bog.

"I see." Whisper focused on Nighteyes without bothering to open her eyes. "It's time for you to forget, new friend."

Nighteyes started to ask about Clamshell, but she only made it as far as, "What about..." before the citrus returned, mixed with four types of mint, and she collapsed.

6

CLAMSHELL'S ISLAND

Nighteyes awoke with a start on Clamshell's island, which now smelled strongly of gryphmint. Her migraine was gone, and she felt fully rested, if a little fuzzy-brained. A spotless starling, probably one of the Newmoon Pride, was sitting next to her on the moss. Clouds drifted overhead.

"How long have I been out?" Nighteyes wiped sleep out of her eyes. "What did you say your name was again?"

The stranger smelled faintly of the bog, of marshmallow and salt. Her scent was familiar even if Nighteyes couldn't recall who she was.

"You may call me Whisper. One of your migraines got the best of you, so we carried you back."

Nighteyes shivered. A storm was coming; she could feel it in the way the air moved. A distant splash pulled her from her thoughts. "Oh! Clamshell! Are you here to help them?"

"I already have." Whisper put a paw against Nighteyes' chest, stopping her from standing up too quickly. Across the newmoon's foreleg, just above the paw, was a half-circle of four dots in silver, the two in the middle a little thicker than the ones on the ends. Whether naturally part of her coat or dyed on, the design was strangely familiar. "I have some experience with lost starlings. I bring them home. Your mate will keep Clamshell here on the island overnight, just to be safe. You should head back before the pridelord notices your absence. You'll put them in danger if you stay."

Nighteyes untensed. "Thank you. I'm sorry, you seem so familiar, but I can't remember if we were introduced. Could you remind me who you are and how you helped Clamshell?"

"Just a newmoon starling." Whisper moved her paw from the nightsky's chest, leaving behind a charcoal pawprint. She stared Nighteyes in the eyes for a few moments, then added, "The Newmoon Pride's leader, so I suppose we're colleagues and even neighbors."

Colleagues and *neighbors* were not gryphon words, and in the back of Nighteyes' mind, she heard the voices of the Ashen Weald's scholars, though they quickly faded. The pleasant, minty feeling went with it, providing a little more clarity. "That doesn't answer my question. Clamshell is one of several gryphons to get separated from the murmuration. I need to know how to fix this if it happens with my own pride."

Whisper's eyes showed a mixture of pity and admiration, but both faded into a kind of curious mischievousness. "Fine, but you won't be able to replicate it. Do you know what role the Newmoon Pride serves in the Emerald Jungle?"

"I know you care for the sick." Nighteyes was privy to a little more information than the average starling as a pride leader, but she'd never inquired deeply into what the roles of the other prides were, as they didn't impact her day-to-day life.

"Yes, and no. It's more complicated than that." Whisper stood, scratching a paw on the ground, and the salty smell came back. "When the glyphs on the Jadebeak Mountains fade, the pridelord's flock sometimes stray to the bog and bring back infections. Small things, at first. The last few years, it's been... bigger things."

Silver eyes and chittering flashed through Nighteyes' mind again, and she finally placed the bitter desert salt smell on Whisper's paws: It had been all over the abandoned dig site she'd visited with Satra. It was the smell of the jars of parasite eggs harvested from the mummified opinithing.

Hidden in Whisper's thick, black fur was a medicine pouch. She pulled out some pale blossoms, licked them, then used a paw pad to crush them against the rocks and create a silvery substance. "Don't mind the eyeshine. It's calming to those I guide. As I was saying, without the glyphs to stop them, jadebeaks flooded into the bog, not knowing what waited for them there. They gorged themselves on capybaras, goliaths, and sailfins. They cleared out swaths of the bog, then they hid in caves and starved as their eyes turned.

"That's where I come in. I find our starving, gooey-eyed kin, and I bring them home. I reconnect them to their original pride as best I can. Or, if they're too far gone, I care for them."

"I've never seen an infected starling in the Emerald Jungle." Flashes of silver eyes and spiketrunks filled Nighteyes' mind, drifting away again as the scent of mint rose. "Do you kill them?"

Whisper laughed, a soft sound. "What a thing to ask. No, I keep them safe. And, as your question illustrates, I can't keep them near you lot or you'd want them killed."

"Do they recover? Recover fully? Can you fix them?" Nighteyes asked, but Whisper ignored her. The newmoon gryphon's eyes were back to a gooey silver, and she sniffed the air, searching for something.

"Too many questions, my new friend." Whisper seemed to find what she was looking for on the wind, then turned to Nighteyes. She moved uncomfortably close, putting her paw on the nightsky gryphon's forehead. The smell of mallow root returned, strong and clear. "There, you shouldn't forget my scent. Now let me make sure I don't forget yours."

Nighteyes had never heard of a gryphon increasing their own unique scent to help another memorize it before. That wasn't the strangest part, however. When a weak citrus smell entered her nares, she sweated through her paws. For the first time, she could smell her own scent, growing stronger by the second, like a sweet starberry syrup.

"Hmm, that smell brings me back home to the eyrie." Whisper inhaled deeply, then let Nighteyes go.

The nightsky starling immediately started wiping her feet on the moss, disgusted to feel so...fragrant. When she looked back up, Whisper had vanished, leaving behind only her charcoal pawprints.

What was that about?

NIGHTEYES FOUND her friends at the other side of the small river island, the stormtails playing in the water while Wendl wrapped doses of medicinal herbs into leaves.

"Hey-lo!" Rudder shouted. "Looks like someone is feeling better. Wendl said you were napping off a migraine?"

Nighteyes nodded, though Rudder's skeptical tone included a warning to be wary of Wendl. "I'm feeling much better now. I just saw Whisper off. I guess she's back to wherever the Newmoon Pride builds their nests."

"Oh, I thought she'd left an hour ago. I didn't realize she stayed to check on you." Rudder's tone was nonchalant, but he wagged his tail in agitation beneath the water, sending waves against the shoreline. "I'm glad she was able to help Clamshell."

Even with the clouds blocking the sun, Clamshell's form was visible beneath the water's surface. While hanging out in the bottom of a river swimming in circles wasn't *Nighteyes'* idea of relaxing, she'd seen Rudder retreat to bodies of water after an argument to calm himself.

Rudder lifted his tail up from the lake and slammed it down, sending ripples out. It was the stormtail way of reminding each other that they had nonaquatic guests.

Clamshell poked their face out of the water. Their whiskers were much perkier than the last time she'd seen them, and they even had a bit of a wiggle in their round ears. "Oh, Nighteyes, you're up! Thank you for helping me. And please, thank your dusty friend."

"I will, though she's more of Wendl's dusty friend." *Dusty* wasn't the first word that came to Nighteyes' mind when she thought of Whisper, but looking down at her chest, she had pawprints and smudges all over her white and purple coat. "So you're feeling better? Do you want us to stay with you?"

Wendl looked up with alarm. "We can't stay here overnight. We need to get north of the pridelord's temple before dark."

Clamshell shrugged their wings. "I think I'm okay. I don't know what the newmoon did, but I can smell where everyone is again. Actually, I think she maybe fixed things too well. You smell really, really fragrant!"

"Oh, Clamshell's right." Rudder took a deep sniff.

Nighteyes pushed his wet beak away from her feathers. "Save it for mating season."

"You need a swim. Wash all that scent off." Rudder swished his tail, spreading his tailfeathers to maximize their surface area. He splashed Nighteyes and forced Wendl to spread her wings to protect her leaf packets.

"You're all very dry," Clamshell confirmed. Light rumbling in clouds above made them change their assessment. "Though, perhaps not for long. If you're leaving, you should go."

Wendl made one of her famous broadleaf rain protectors to guard the medications she'd be leaving for them. "Take one every hour until after dark. Then wait until breakfast to return to your pride. If there's a problem, send for me. But keep Nighteyes out of it

this time. The pridelord learns of everything eventually. The key is to make it look like one strange day
long ago by the time he notices. That means keeping
her out of the south."

Nighteyes and Rudder said their goodbyes,
promising to seek each other out come autumn.
Wendl finished getting ready as a light drizzle began,
and they took flight north, back to the Nightsky
Pride's territory.

7

THE WORLD ABOVE

The heavy smell of ozone hung in the air like a thick mist above the Emerald Jungle. Nighteyes, with Wendl trailing behind, traced a path of spiketrunks through Jadebeak territory far below her, trying to take her mind off her worries. Clamshell and Rudder had a tough day ahead of them tomorrow. Had Whisper really fixed things? Or would the gryphons at Lightningmaw turn on Clamshell?

To the west, the jungle parted around a stone temple, though from the sky, the stone was only visible in patches. Green and blue moss covered broken spires, roots having eaten away at the architecture. Around the ancient temple, smaller buildings and towers, a similar verdant shade of green, spiralled out in every direction.

Several rivers converged here before becoming one larger body of water, and the city's layout paralleled the shape of the arriving rivers like the crown of a strange bird. Where they didn't match, Nighteyes wondered at the discrepancy. Perhaps the rivers had shifted over time.

A mossy courtyard marked the Nightsky River's terminus. Many pride leaders claimed a building around the temple for their pride, and the Celestial Courtyard was hers. She'd have preferred something taller. The past few times her pride had been called by the pridelord, they'd been forced to nest with the jadebeaks or stormtails because the courtyard was underwater.

It's a very wet constellation. I wonder if the stormtails would be open to a trade?

Wendl drifted left, keeping an eye on the Emerald Jungle's heart, and had to be reminded to give it a wide berth. "There are a lot of jadebeaks at the temple. Do you think they're after us?"

"Calm down, Wendl," Nighteyes chided. Her friend had always been skittish around the temple. "It's just a populated area. If not for the storm, we wouldn't be able to see the stone spires for all the jadebeaks in the air."

A heavy mist and light rain alternated on their flight. Nighteyes was wet and grumpy, never a fun combination, but at least it helped clear the starberry scent from her fur.

It could be worse. At least the lightning isn't bad, she mused.

Once they got back to the nesting grounds, there'd be a dozen small metaphorical fires to put out, plus a few real ones if the lightning was striking up there. For now, she had time alone with Wendl, and she wanted to take advantage of it to find out more about Wendl's strange friend.

"Hey, Wendl." When Nighteyes didn't get a response, she flew closer to nudge the jade opinicus into looking up. "Whisper said she retrieved lost starlings. If that's true, she could find the stormtail who went missing before Clamshell, right? She can cross the glyphs?"

Wendl's body stiffened at the mention of Whisper, causing her to drift down with a gust of wind and beat her wings to catch up again. "You shouldn't ask favors of Whisper."

Nighteyes didn't see why not and said so. "If she can cross the glyphs and bring starlings back into the murmuration, I think that's worth owing another pride leader a favor, isn't it?"

Wendl didn't reply for a long time. Finally, she asked, "What does the missing stormtail smell like? Do you know?"

"A sand rose," Nighteyes replied.

That gave the opinicus pause. "A floral-smelling stormtail? That's a new one on me."

"No, it's the leaves, not the flower. A poisonous smell that doesn't match his personality." Nighteyes went on to describe the sour smell as best she could. The lost gryphon had been one of Rudder's favorite hunting partners, and she knew his smell well enough.

It took Wendl a moment to understand. "Oh, like oleander? Whisper will know that scent. She was poisoned by it as a chick."

That brought Nighteyes to her second question, one that seemed to come from her subconscious. "You said she came with your friends to the Emerald Jungle. Why isn't she green like you?"

"Oh? Now you believe my 'crazy opinicus tales'?" Wendl chided, though she didn't seem interested in answering further until Nighteyes pressed her. "Whisper left the room when we took the blood. You've met Khalim, who used Piprik's blood. It's the same with Whisper. Most of us took whatever we could get before the camp was overrun, but those two were a little more purposeful in their choice."

They crossed into Nightsky territory, safe at last, and Nighteyes let the questions rest. If Wendl had wanted to dissuade her pride leader's curiosity, she'd failed. Assuming the stories weren't strange lies, Khalim had chosen his plumage for revenge. Why had Whisper chosen hers?

"Tomorrow, I want you to find Whisper and get her help for the Stormtail Pride," Nighteyes said. When Wendl pushed back, Nighteyes reminded her who was pride leader.

"As you wish," the opinicus replied, "but the pridelord keeps the newmoon separate for a reason."

He keeps the stormtails separate for a reason, too. I'm just not convinced it's for a good reason.

It was a traitorous thought, but she was too tired to care.

COOL WINDS FOLLOWED in the rain's wake. The last of the storm clouds rumbled as it shifted out of the moon's way, and a pale blue light made the Nightsky River glow. Crickets came out from hiding, unleashing their chirpy cacophony upon the jungle. Nighteyes took one look at the nesting grounds and

another at her home burrow and decided that whatever had gone wrong in her absence, it could wait
another day.

*I spent months across the Emerald Veil, and they did
fine without me. I'm sure they'll last the night.*

Flowers hung from the entrance to her burrow, a
sign someone awaited her inside. There was no way
Rudder would have left Clamshell's side, and she'd
seen Wendl fly to her own nest, so that meant it was
probably one of her sisters.

*Perhaps one has finally worked up the courage to chal-
lenge me for pride leader. That would be a welcome break.*

Inside her burrow, still airing out from the
winter damp, she detected the sour sage smell of a
surprise guest: Sheen, the fledgling who had
somehow recovered from bloodbeak. Nighteyes
wasn't keen on late night visitors, but it was well-
known she made an exception for those bearing
gifts of food.

Sheen was curled up in a nap behind an offering
of dead cassowary. She awoke as Nighteyes chirped a
greeting but didn't stand. "Oh, hello, Pride Leader!
You're back late. When I saw the sun going down, I
thought you might need food."

Cassowary meat was tough, so years ago, the pride
had decided it was better used for stew—a task that
fell upon Wendl with her talons. Generally speaking,
it was a good idea. Bloodbeak led to beak and joint
pain, so the sick preferred to drink their dinner. It also
cut down on the iron-blood taste of the meat, something the sick became sensitive to. That was unfortunate for Nighteyes, however, who loved the pungent
flavor of raw cassowary.

I'm definitely being bribed, she thought, but it didn't stop her from digging in.

"Are the cassowaries so plentiful you couldn't resist hunting them, or are we out of easier prey?" She meant it to be friendly banter, but she wasn't good at being casual when she was tired, hungry, and wet. She worried the answer was the latter.

Sheen preened a few dark purple feathers into place but didn't answer, which offered up another possibility. There *was* easier prey, but she'd decided to go after cassowaries anyway. Hopefully, she was at least smart enough she'd left most of the meat at the nesting grounds for stew and hadn't wasted it all on Nighteyes.

Unlike the rhea, which were an easy meal on two legs, the cassowaries that came down from the naze were vicious creatures with a nasty kick and a bad attitude. Killing one was a sign of bravery, desperation, or stupidity.

Really, killing one was a sign of bravery, desperation, *and* stupidity.

"You need to be careful, Sheen." Nighteyes' voice made it more of an order than a statement. "Cassowaries are deadly. Even caiman are safer."

Sheen broke her silence. "The fledglings like the stew, and if I kill the cassowaries, that leaves easier prey for the older hunters. I'm younger than they are. It makes sense that I should kill the cassowaries."

This brought up another issue: hunting alone wasn't smart when the prey could fight back.

Nighteyes sighed. "Do they not teach hunting smarts anymore? If you're injured and alone, you could die before anyone finds you. If you get hurt,

Sheen, you're catching no meat and helping none of your pridemates. Being a hunter doesn't mean taking greater risks for the sake of the pride, it means learning to take care of yourself because the stakes are higher. I need you to understand that."

"I remember what it was like to have bloodbeak," Sheen protested. "I remember the pain. I have a responsibility to my hatchmates because I'm better and they're not. It isn't fair, and I need to make it up to them."

That wasn't what Nighteyes had been expecting, but perhaps she should have. Selflessness led to stupidity as often as selfishness did. "You're not cured. Every test says you still have it. It's dangerous for you to assume you're always going to be okay."

"Exactly!" Sheen's voice raised. "I need to hunt as much as I can now before it comes back. Besides, Wendl is going to save us."

Wendl, who had a long list of things she needed from the other side of the Emerald Veil. Wendl, whose egg treatments Nighteyes had been forced to say no to when the pridelord closed off the borders and forbid communication with the non-starling prides. Wendl, who was convinced the rest of the world may already have a cure for bloodbeak, and without a way to communicate with them, nightsky starlings were dying unnecessarily.

Wendl, who was going to speak to the one gryphon who could apparently cross the Emerald Veil.

Hopefully, Wendl is as smart as Sheen thinks, and she sees the opportunity I've put before her.

Remembering how the opinicus would hug with

her wings, Nighteyes put one of her own violet wings over Sheen's. With the storm having passed, the moon's light shone on both wings, and it was clear that while Nighteyes' feathers were violet, her charge's had faded to indigo as she fledged into adulthood.

That's an unusual color. It should help her find a mate, though. Starlings love a stand-out. It's why the sparkwings used to be in high demand.

"Can I stay?" Sheen asked. "It's nicer here. I don't sleep well with the others."

"No." Nighteyes was sympathetic. Sheen was a lot younger than the other hunters. There were years of starlings missing from their ranks. It was usually the duty of each hatch year to train the one below them, leaving Sheen without a mentor. "You need to learn to be part of a team. Once you can hunt as a group, once you know how to work with the others, then I'll see about getting you your own nest. The worst part of being an adult is learning to work with others."

Sheen was angry, probably because Nighteyes had a burrow to herself, but she was smart enough to obey her leader. She shifted, revealing several cassowary eggs ranging in color from dark broadleaf green to fresh grass to a kind of blue-green that was a perfect match for Clamshell's plumage. She'd clearly been hoping to save them as a thank you for getting to stay, but she was smart enough to leave them anyways.

Nighteyes was polite enough not to eat them in front of Sheen. "When you leave to hunt in the morning, would you wake up Wendl? She'll be sore, but I set her on an important task before I knew she'd have stew to make. If she gets it started, do you think some of your hatchmates are well enough to keep the fire going?"

Sheen nodded, then made her departure.

Nighteyes sighed. She didn't like telling gryphons no, especially not ones she liked. And, despite the cassowary and eggs not leading to Sheen's intended outcome, Nighteyes did think fondly of starlings who brought her treats.

She alternated bites of pungent, iron-tang bird and rich, fatty yolks. She kept her eyes open just long enough to finish the eggs, then curled up and slept in the entryway to her nest.

As she dozed off, she realized she was going to smell like a dead cassowary in the morning. *Oh well, at least it'll mask the starberry smell.*

8

RUINS

Wendl dreamt of the plains east of Mothfeather on First Morning, the bee plants overflowing with purple flowers. The heat of the sun warmed her muscles, tired from hibernating. Despite an overabundance of blue-flowered flax, it was the aroma of fringed sage that filled her nares with its sweet and sour, herbal scent. She hadn't smelled that particular sage for years, not until one of the Nightsky gryphlets had been born smelling like she was secretly a sage grouse.

Wendl opened her eyes to see a dark purple face staring down at her.

"Hey, are you awake?" Sheen was visible only by virtue of the moonlight coming through the entrance to Wendl's broadleaf shelter. The leaves were sewn together and waterproofed with insect wax. Between the honey smell of the wax and the cassia of the nest, Sheen's summer prairie broke the illusion Wendl was living in a feral confectionery.

She pushed the young gryphon's face back and

groaned. "No, and I won't be awake for a few hours yet. Find me when it's light out."

Generally, Wendl liked to share the gifts of her talons with her adopted pride. Food, medicines, and tools were given freely. But she had one indulgence, warm hides she used as blankets, and she pulled herself under them now.

Sheen burrowed her beak into the hides, letting a draft into the warm sanctuary. "Hey, you in there? I need to talk to you."

The last day or two had put a strain on Wendl's nerves. She didn't like attracting scrutiny, and helping Nighteyes and Rudder's friend could easily bring down the ire of the pridelord. As much as random starlings becoming disconnected from the pride was a big issue that needed to be looked into, she knew her elixirs and research made her a suspect. She didn't want anyone poking into her work. And she really didn't want anyone looking into Sheen.

Hence the phrase *I need to talk to you* burned away Wendl's brain fog and pulled her out of her hideaway. "What's wrong? Are you feeling sick? Let me see your beak and claws."

"Oh!" Sheen said. "No, I didn't mean it like that. I feel fine. Sorry for the scare. I'm here to talk to you about making cassowary stew."

Wendl massaged her head to alleviate the stress. She'd seen the dead cassowaries on her way to bed, but she'd been too tired to make the connection. Of course Nighteyes would want Wendl to start the stew before she left. Wendl may be grumpy in the morning, but there was little she wouldn't do to help

Mally's victims, and if there was one thing they loved, it was cassowary.

She pulled on a well-loved harness, checking to make sure she had the basics—dry moss bandages, painkillers, a few things to fight infection, a pouch of mint that hid an incense bomb inside. Thinking back to Whisper's gooey eyes, Wendl pulled the lid off the crate where she stored her rarer medicines and added a vial of pumpkin.

Normally, she'd avoid carrying any orange vials with her. She didn't want the pridelord to think she was making more of the elixirs that helped starlings disobey him. Considering whom she was going to speak with later today, however, it seemed prudent.

Sheen, like most of the nightsky gryphons, watched the harness with fascination. "Can you make me a harness? Why do you need to carry so many things with you? Does it chafe? It looks like it would chafe. I tried to wear a bracelet once, and it chafed. I don't know if I could put on a harness with my paws. Do harnesses only work for opinici?"

"Fisherfolk wear harnesses, sometimes," Wendl started, but Sheen had already pressed in with more questions.

"What's a fisherfolk?" the fledgling asked. "I want to know about gryphons."

Wendl yawned, then pushed away the leaves protecting her home. "Some fisherfolk are gryphons. You just need to modify the clasp so you can work it with a beak."

"But where do you get a clasp from? How do you make it?" her indigo tagalong asked.

"Trade." It was an answer Wendl gave often, but it

wasn't one the starlings understood. She'd spent enough time with the jadebeaks post-altruism, and she'd discovered they didn't remember the Ashen Weald gryphons they'd nearly killed. Ultimately, even the starlings that left the Emerald Jungle on pumpkin expeditions all believed they'd never met a non-starling gryphon.

"Oh! I traded yesterday, just like you taught me." Sheen puffed up, proud of herself.

"Did you?" Wendl sharpened a knife scavenged from an opinicus who tried to poach from the Emerald Jungle last spring. "Who did you trade with?"

"Nighteyes." Sheen pulled the dead cassowaries closer to help. "I traded her a cassowary and some eggs to stay and sleep at her burrow."

Wendl cut the bird meat into strips, careful not to cut with the grain so it didn't get too stringy and tough when it cooked. Her grandmother had taught her better than that. "That was good of Nighteyes. Must be nice to sleep away from the snoring of the hunters."

"Oh, she didn't actually let me stay." Sheen deflated a little. "She just ate the cassowary and eggs and sent me home to sleep in my nest."

Wendl laughed in spite of herself. "That's not trade, little chicklet, that's a gift—or, arguably, an act of banditry. You have to receive something in return of comparable value for it to be trade. What's something you want? Other than Nighteyes' spare nest to sleep in."

Sheen thought this over. "I want to be allowed to hunt by myself."

"Good luck with that. Set your expectations lower." Wendl struck flint to tinder, more gifts from dead poachers, and got a fire started. The gryphons should be able to keep it going in her absence, but they were all rubbish with flint and tinder. Oddly, the stormtails were good with rocks, using them to break open clams. Not that fire was particularly useful for a pride that lived under a thunder cloud.

"A bracelet," Sheen decided. "I want a bracelet that doesn't chafe. And isn't just vines that rot and die. And that I can put on myself."

Wendl thought it over. She could probably make that happen. She had some strips of soft leather she'd taken from the dead alabasters near the Jadebeak Falls, back when she was allowed to visit there. She could figure out a way to dye them a prettier color and weave them together.

"Okay. I'll see what I can do." Wendl's fire was now hot enough, and the water neared a boil. Its heat felt good against the cool morning air. She idly wished for some rosemary or thyme, but the jungle was too wet to let her dry most herbs. She was desperate for the familiar flavors of eyrie life. If Sheen tasted as good as she smelled, Wendl would've tossed her in the pot. "In exchange, I want you to keep an eye out for any opinicus things you find while hunting. Paper, pens, ink, metal. You bring me enough of those, and I'll give you a bracelet."

Sheen perked up. "Oh! I like that."

"Now, go out there and make friends." Wendl patted her on the head. "Nighteyes is right, you won't get far without other gryphons to watch your back."

As the indigo starling left, Wendl watched her gait

for any signs of weakness. *Nothing. She still looks healthy. So why is she testing positive for bloodbeak? Maybe I got the wrong stormtail, but Rudder had Mally's mark on him. What am I missing?*

With the stew bubbling and her chaperone gone, Wendl went back to her leaf-shrouded nest and pulled out one of her few inkwells. Her advice to Sheen doubled as advice to herself. She and Whisper had been very close, even intimate, once. While Wendl didn't think Whisper would do a favor for most of their starling 'siblings,' she felt pretty sure Whisper would do a single favor for her.

Wendl hastily scrawled her message.

To Piprik of Swan's Rest, or failing that, to Biski of the medicine gryphons. Has there been any progress in treating bloodbeak? Attached are my findings with the Nightsky Pride's gryphlets.

AFTER ASKING AROUND, it turned out none of the nightsky who woke up early knew where the Newmoon Pride was located these days, leaving Wendl to head east and hope for the best.

The Nightsky Pride had always enjoyed a larger swath of hunting territory than it needed. After the incident with the Ashen Weald, Abyssal Naze, and Alabaster Eyrie, the pridelord had shrunk their territory, splitting it into east and west.

She assumed the Newmoon Pride had been moved into the eastern half and had nests there somewhere, but she'd have to cross into their territory and hope someone showed her the way. Assuming the

Newmoon Pride weren't busy guarding the border. Both the Ashen Weald and Alabasters would think twice before fighting a starling with silver eyes.

The loss of access to the northeast corner of the jungle was unfortunate for Wendl, whose hidden laboratory was in Mally's abandoned camp. She landed when she saw the circular glyphs of the Newmoon Pride and walked the rest of the way in.

Spiketrunks were more common in this stretch, and she watched where she stepped so she didn't get a shed spike through her foot. As Nighteyes was likely discovering this morning, the sap of the trees was toxic. Starlings were immune to the worst of it, but it'd be a few days before the aching stopped.

Despite the saying *only a starling would chase a squirrel up a spiketrunk* implying starlings were infallible climbers, Wendl spent a nontrivial amount of her time in the summer patching up wounded gryphons who hurt themselves doing just that. And the spikes weren't even the worst part. The pumpkin-shaped fruit of the trees had a tendency to explode on the hottest day of summer.

Out of habit, she looked up to make sure there were no spiketrunk fruit above her now. *Just squirrels, thank goodness.* The sounds of the fuzzy critters playing in the treetops and flightless birds roaming the underbrush did little to relax Wendl. Something was wrong, and it took her a moment to put her talon on what it was.

There aren't any gryphon sounds here.

Belatedly, she realized Whisper may not be back yet. She had a lot of silver-eyed starlings with her. Whether those were natural newmoons using eyeshine or infected jadebeaks pulled from the bog, Wendl wasn't sure. It was better not to ask. But if they were walking the hidden, salted paths of the jungle, they'd have had to march all night to get this far north.

Which presented her with an opportunity.

She let out a quiet call, nothing too loud.

No reply. There were probably gryphons here *somewhere*, most likely recovering from the parasite. But if none were by her old building...

She stepped closer, looking around. Someone had drug fallen trees from the spring storms and ringed them around Mally's dilapidated compound, the one hiding Wendl's workshop underneath. She examined the logs. They seemed fragrant even compared to the sweet-sour rotting smell of the wooden structure, but her starling brain didn't react to them. Whatever scent Whisper left, it wasn't meant for her.

I left my own safeguards to keep starlings out. I wonder why Whisper added her own?

One answer to that question posed a problem: Whisper could have gone in for herself and seen what was down there. It was unlikely Whisper would turn Wendl over to the pridelord, but it wasn't impossible. Unlike the rest of the Nighthaunt's former apprentices, Whisper had embraced being a gryphon, with all the loyalties that entailed.

Wendl went around back and found several branches laid across the entrance to the old cold storage area, her sticks of incense scattered. She reached to pick one up, but the hackle feathers on her neck rose, and she turned around to see who was watching her.

Whisper, quiet as her name, stood a few feet away. She was alone.

"Hey, I was looking for you," Wendl tried.

"I know." Whisper licked a paw but didn't groom herself.

It took Wendl a moment, but she realized Whisper was licking the pattern of four dots on her left forepaw. *I never took her for an anxious groomer.* The design was new. Wendl still remembered how her friend had looked stumbling after them into the Emerald Jungle: entirely black, the faint grey stars in her plumage only visible in direct sunlight.

When they'd arrived at the temple, escorted by very confused nightsky gryphons, the pridelord had dismissed them as half-starlings come home. He acted like this was a common occurrence, as though starlings didn't try to murder foreign gryphons they stumbled across. In the years since, they'd realized how rare such an event was. Only one outsider claiming starling ancestry had shown up: Erlock.

The reborn starlings didn't know how unusual their acceptance was then. But there was something that *did* seem strange, even at the time: The way the pridelord greeted Whisper. He didn't treat her as a half-starling newly arrived, he treated her as the starling whose blood she'd taken finally come home.

Whisper had been Mally the Nighthaunt's official scribe, and thus, she knew things about the elixir no one else did. She knew what chemicals he'd added to the salts and which he considered failures. And, most likely, he'd consider a change of sex to be a failure for the salts.

She hadn't. She'd stored away that information,

and thus, she'd had a very different reaction than the rest of them had. In fact, if Wendl were a little more paranoid, she'd speculate that Whisper had hidden away large quantities of newmoon blood and experimental salt mixtures just for this purpose.

Those four stars, though. They look like the pattern the rest of us got from the dead jadebeak. Does she wish she stayed connected with The Six? Of all the prides, the newmoons have the least freedom. She probably hasn't seen the others for years, not officially. Unless she's been spying on us from her hidden salt paths.

"I can't let you in the compound." Whisper's voice was always soft. "You were thinking loudly about me, and when your scent moved east, I knew you were coming. But the rest of my pride will be here soon. I flew back early to take care of someone."

Behind her were a pile of eggfruit, a few fish, and some other odds and ends. Wendl's scientific mind already knew what they had in common: none of the food could spread the parasite.

I wonder why? She'd have to ask another time, as she had more important matters at talon. "That's fine. It's just some old memories. I'm sure you've seen what's down there."

"Mmm." Whisper's nonchalance surprised Wendl. It was the kind of non-answer that, back when they were close at Mothfeather University, would have served as equivocation. If she'd gone inside, she'd have had some sort of reaction to seeing Wendl's paintings of all of them before their change. Of seeing herself before the change.

So she didn't go inside. Why? To protect my privacy?

There was another answer. The same incense

Wendl used to pull Nighteyes out of the murmuration might have a different effect on the Newmoon Pride. She'd never asked how the spotless starling caretakers kept the infected in line, but having seen Whisper treat Clamshell, she thought she knew.

Whisper seemed to have a fraction of the strange control the pridelord did. Not enough to challenge him, but just enough to fix things that went wrong. She also had to know where everyone was to sneak the infected through the other pride's territory, to hide their trail, and to erase their memories.

A trick she tried on Balthar once. I'm conflating Whisper the apprentice scholar with Whisper the Newmoon Pride gryphon.

Even her name, *Whisper,* wasn't entirely hers. It was the name the pridelord had called her when she showed up at the temple with the rest of them. She'd happily embraced it, claimed it as her own, and fought with friends who tried to use her old name. To Wendl, though, it was a role as much as a name. If the pridelord was a shout, a command no starling could disobey, her friend was a whisper, something intimate and subtle. Persuasive.

"I was wondering—Nighteyes was wondering— not all of the stormtails who left the murmuration died. One went missing near the border." Wendl moved away from the entrance to her old workshop. Two stories up, she could see where one of the balconies had collapsed. If she recalled correctly, it was near Whisper's old room.

The Newmoon Pride leader led Wendl away from the structure. "If they crossed the border, the Ashen Weald has probably killed them. They cower in their sunken eyrie, hiding from the pink reeve's patrols. As they explore, they find more outbreaks, so they're quick to deal with any infected. I'm lucky to have saved this last group for the susurration."

Susurration was a strange word, but Wendl knew what it meant immediately. It was a poetic word for the bond the infected had. A murmuration of the fallen. "He may not be infected. He'd probably only eat fish and hide in the water. He just needs to be brought back in."

"I can't leave yet. There is someone who needs my help," Whisper explained. Wendl started to protest, but the newmoon gryphon stopped her. "But I will go tonight. You ask a big favor of me. I do not normally cross the veil of my own volition. The pridelord will be suspicious."

Wendl pulled out a small scroll case, one scavenged from these very ruins. "I have a bigger favor to ask. The nightsky young are starting to die of bloodbeak. I need to know if the outside world has found a cure, and I need the equipment to treat any new eggs, if it can be spared. Can you leave this somewhere the Ashen Weald will find it? Then check for an answer the next time you're in the bog?"

Whisper looked at the case. She didn't answer, but Wendl could smell the calming mint. The newmoon gryphon produced a medicine pouch from her fluff and put the case inside. "You should go."

Wendl knew a dismissal when she heard one. She turned to leave and was nearly out of view, when she thought she saw a white shape reach for the eggfruit.

"Thank you," the voice began, before Whisper

hushed it and pushed it back into the cover of the broadleafs.

It could have been Wendl's imagination, or perhaps it was just that white was an unheard of color for a starling, but she was nearly certain she'd heard an opi trill.

9

IRI THE FIRST

With her main chore out of the way faster than expected, Wendl had time to scavenge for lunch. She'd never adjusted to eating the purple and gold squirrels that infested the Emerald Jungle but were unheard of beyond the mountains or naze, but she found some ripe eggfruit, caught a carp in one of the freshwater springs dotting the northern jungle, and had a nice meal before continuing on her way.

She'd spent her first year as a starling trying to map cave systems that connected starling prides, caves with entrances in one pride's territory and an exit in another pride's. She had one on the western edge of the Nightsky territory she used to meet with Balthar, her closest ex-scholar neighbor. But there was also one along the southern edge that connected with the Jadebeak Pride.

This was useful because it meant when one of the other prides was visiting the pridelord's temple, The Six could slip away and report to Wendl. It helped her stay in touch. One such meeting was coming up soon.

She flew low, looking for a break in the trees, careful not to fly too far south. The pridelord would notice if she came too close to his home.

She found what she sought next to a rocky outcropping of dirt she'd cultivated to grow Jadebeak Mountain bee plants. Not an easy trick in this humidity. They were not jungle plants. But it was sunny and high enough here she could usually get a few to grow, and that gave her an excuse to be this far south.

While they'd tower over her by the summer, here in spring, they were still small. It was a silly thing, but she delighted in seeing them as sproutlings. Growing up, she used to gather bags of their seeds, then she'd spread them around her ranch where the goliath birds had stomped away the foliage.

It was her little ritual before Last Twilight. Before she was tucked into her nest, she'd beg the pitohui vault guards to keep watch on her bee plants, painting them in her childhood equivalent of a scholar's journal.

The pitohui humored her, of course, but none of them were artists. By the time First Morning came and she collected her journal of scribbles, the plants were already up to her shoulders and starting to bloom. Getting to see them here, in the wild, growing from the tiniest of seeds, made her inner chick happy.

It also reminded her of who she was now: someone who was awake. Those who slept would not recognize her even if she could somehow find her way back to the family ranch.

With a sigh, she left the bee plants behind and searched around until she found the cave entrance. She lit an incense that matched her smell and gave it time to establish. Nightsky hunters searched every nook and cranny of their territory for food, and someone would fly by here while she was inside. What they smelled, the pridelord could pull from them later. This would make it seem like she was outside, tending to her garden, just out of sight.

Once she felt secure, she slipped beneath the earth. The cave here had high ceilings caked with smoke. Tenacious vines had grown through the passages until a particularly hot and dry summer caused them to catch flame. Starlings naturally avoided anything that smelled like wildfire, making it a good place to hide. She was supposed to be meeting with just Iri, so she was surprised to find a small group gathered around the fire.

"Wendl!" Balthar boomed. He'd been a loud blackwing opinicus, and he was now a loud starling. He resembled the jadebeaks and was often called in to work on the temple, but his actual beak was still as dark as a red-winged blackbird's. Where Wendl had distinguished herself as an adept medicine opinicus, Balthar made himself useful by modifying the jade opinicus statues into starling statues for the pridelord. Officially, he belonged to some small western pride, but his masonry skills kept him in Jadebeak territory most of the time. "Iri here thought you'd have to cancel again."

Iri the First was named so because she'd been the first of The Six to down the elixir when it became clear they were all going to die if they did nothing. Her beak had changed to jade, but she'd kept the warm-colored shoulders of a red-winged blackbird atop her green starling plumage.

While Balthar was a guest in Jadebeak territory, Iri lived here, though she normally kept to the east. In the damp closeness of the cave, even Wendl's weak sense of smell could detect Iri's festive, fermenting plum pheromones.

"You make it sound like an insult," Iri scolded Balthar. "I just know the Nightsky Pride keep their pet on a short leash."

Wendl rolled her eyes. Even without the red markings on her wings, there was no mistaking Iri for anything other than a blackwing with that arrogance. While Khalim had worked closely with Mally, Iri had bossed around the rest of the assistants.

Talli the Second, Iri's sister, pushed over a bowl of food stolen from the temple. With it came the scent of fields of sunbaked wheat, dredging up memories of Goldtree Gardens' farming communities. "I'm glad you could make it. We haven't seen each other in ages! I was starting to think you'd forgotten about me."

Despite having had a nice meal of eggfruit and fish, Wendl couldn't resist a few sweet berries. "It's too bad you're so far away. Does Balthar keep you up to date?"

"No, he's too busy hiding in the pridelord's root cellar," Talli complained. "I ended up having to take a mate just so I'd have someone to talk to."

Her comment downplayed how close she'd come to her pride. She'd had several mates, and unlike the others who used leftover red fern from their original expedition supplies, Talli'd had several gryphlets she played with so often she was an honorary denmother on top of leading her small pride. The others pretended not to notice, but

Wendl wondered if even Iri was starting to question Talli's loyalty.

When they'd first come to the jungle, the idea of befriending the starlings or even taking a gryphon mate seemed unbearable. Over time, most of them had done it. It started with the ones who had gryphon paws and were struggling to get used to losing their talons, such as Talli. Even Wendl had given it a try, though it was just the one time, and it hadn't gone well.

Love is overrated.

Balthar had been the last to give in. His dislike of gryphons was strong, but in the end, he'd fallen in love with a sparkwing, one of the fringe prides he'd been assigned to that had later been absorbed by the jadebeaks. They were only distinguishable from the green starlings by how the sun on their iridescence looked like lightning.

"What about you, Kism?" Wendl slid the bowl to the quiet starling across from her.

Kism the Third had been friends with their fourth, missing friend, who had died two years ago when the Ashen Weald and Abyssal Naze lowered the Emerald Veil. While his depression was stronger now, he'd always been a bit melancholy.

Assigned to a pride along the border with King's Reach, he'd been the only one of them to try to leave. Some of Wendl's earliest orange elixir let him break through the veil...where he succumbed to green wing altruism and killed an opinicus before returning.

The downside of the elixir was that it had made him aware of what he was doing, even if the potency at the time was too weak to allow him to stop himself from doing it. His actions had started Wendl down the path of trying to recreate the scent of forgetfulness the pridelord used.

"I see more of Balthar than I'd like." Despite Kism's mood, he seemed genuinely glad they were all together. "Though it's nice to spend time with the rest of you. Wendl, it's been too long. I'd forgotten what you looked like!"

Wendl chirped a laugh in spite of herself. Though the ears, forelegs, and tails varied a little, this meeting was a bit like the infamous Crestfall Hall of Mirrors. Each of them had the same four dots above their beak and the same shades of green feathers and brown fur, the most obvious reminders that their bodies had been stolen.

"Enough of that. This is serious. We were all called to the capital for a reason," Iri scolded. *Capital* was not how the starlings described their temple. It was an opinicus word, one that replaced the word they were all too afraid to use, *eyrie*. For that's what the abandoned temple really was, an opinicus city lost to time, now controlled by starlings. If not for the might of the murmuration, the Seraph King would have reclaimed it long ago.

"All? That's not entirely true," Wendl said. "The stormtails, newmoons, and nightsky weren't invited."

Balthar stretched his talons. "That's because you're under investigation. Well, the stormtails are. *You* were excluded because of your leader's choice of mate. And who cares about the Newmoon Pride? Nobody wants them out in public."

Wendl frowned. She let the comment on the Newmoon Pride slide, as that was just Balthar projecting, but this was the first she'd heard of such an investigation. "Is this because of the talonful of stormtails who went feral? That hardly seems like a big deal. Weird things happen all the time. Strange noises in the caves, dead blackwing scouts along the border. There was even that two-headed crocodile in the Winter Jungle four years ago. The Gourmand used its bones to decorate his nest."

"It's not just a pawful," Talli the Second corrected. "By my count, there's been two dozen now. The pridelord has been making the stormtails forget."

"Why didn't he do so this time?" Kism's irritation hung in the air as the scent of almonds, a sign of how gryphonic they'd become. "What's changed?"

"This time, there was a jadebeak, and my pride tore him apart." Iri's voice was cold. All eyes were on her, but her eyes were on Wendl. "Is this your doing? This is the exact same problem we had with the early elixirs."

Wendl had not expected an ambush. "Of course not. We've already perfected the orange elixir, partially thanks to the Merinkin bringing us the weald formula. There's no reason to make any of the earlier iterations. Besides, the pridelord asked me to destroy my stockpile, so I did."

"You shouldn't have told him about the elixir," Kism said. "That was a mistake, and it could cost us everything. We'd be better off if he didn't know about it."

"He was always going to find out. Better he think it was his idea to send Nighteyes to handle the Ashen Weald," Wendl countered.

The others often forgot about the scent trails and

memories they left in the minds of other starlings. They could hide what they were doing in the moment, but the pridelord would always find out at some point. Giving things like the orange elixir context was crucial to keeping The Six safe.

Iri was not convinced. "Wendl, you're playing with fire. If we get caught, they'll tear us apart. I need you to be honest. What are you up to?"

"Iri, Iri, calm down." Balthar came to Wendl's aid, a first for The Fifth. "Gryphons are mutating all the time. It's just evolution. They change quickly, and sometimes there are...mistakes. There've been lost prides before. There'll be lost prides again. The stormtails will stop being a problem on their own, or the pridelord will make them stop being a problem. That's just Belamuria for you. It's why the seraphs abandoned it in the first place, isn't it?"

It was a nice sentiment, and it did ease Iri's aggression, but it left Wendl wondering why Balthar was speculating on seraphs.

"I reached out to Whisper for help, and she was able to fix one of the stormtails." Wendl waited for the usual complaints about Whisper to die down before continuing, wondering at the speciesism at play with language like *feral* or *animalistic*. "With her help, we might be able to figure out what's causing it."

Talli the Second yawned. "If Balthar is right, it'll all work itself out. There's no reason to get grumpy whiskers involved."

Kism voiced his agreement, reminding Wendl that though eight of them downed the elixir, their group was called The Six for a reason, or had been until their fourth died. It made her sad, but then again, she didn't think Whisper or Khalim would want to be part of their group.

"Bloodbeak has gotten worse," Wendl continued. "I took advantage of the opportunity with Whisper to have her deliver a message to the Ashen Weald. We need to know what's going on in the outside world. If they've found a cure, we need to know what it is."

The First, Second, and Third disagreed with her statement again, mostly because they saw the Ashen Weald as a kind of small gryphon pride with no medical knowledge.

Balthar, ever full of surprises today, agreed with her decision. "Please, let me know what you find out. Things have gotten worse in the northwest, near the border with Alwren. A cure for bloodbeak could save the smaller prides there. Though be mindful of what you tell Whisper. If she knew what we were up to, she'd try to stop us."

"I worry about Whisper," Kism said. "I'm not suggesting anything drastic, but I think it's dangerous for her to be thinking about us. I preferred her better when she was on her own, happy to play gryphon with her gooey-eyed friends in the shadows."

"You don't need to worry about her looking into what we're up to," Wendl lied, specifically not mentioning the unusual barricade outside her workshop.

Iri stood and stretched, a sign their time was nearly up. "I'm not worried about Whisper on her own. I'm worried about you around Whisper. I'm worried you'll let something slip."

"You do tend to be a little loose-beaked around your old fiancé," Balthar added, swallowing the Crestfall é to make it more masculine. "Perhaps it would be better if you stayed away from the Newmoon Pride for now."

"Fiancée," Wendl corrected. "And I need to meet with her at least once more to find out what the Ashen Weald's response is, but after that, I have no reason to interact with her."

She did not tell them about the opi trill she'd heard at the ruins of their old camp. *Better to keep that information to myself, at least for now. With everything going on with the stormtails, they're already suspicious of me.*

"Well, that's one way to sour the mood," Talli the Second grumbled. "The first time in years we're all together, and Iri and Balthar can't help but turn it into an argument."

Iri *tsk*ed her displeasure, but Balthar let out a laugh.

"Now, now," he said. "I have come with gifts. Though our beloved Fourth was keeping the salts hidden away, I was able to sneak into his arboreal hideaway and acquire a little more. When the time comes, no one will be left behind. Here, here, everyone take one."

He reached into his harness pocket and pulled out six vials of Mally's essential salts, distributing them to the others. He paused when he realized he had six vials but only four friends here.

"I'll take the last one for Whisper," Wendl said, never afraid to stir up trouble. Under normal circumstances, all four of the others would have refused her. Since she'd been the one to acquire the salts from Khalim, they kept their beaks shut. "When the time comes for me to change, I'll leave her the vial so she can make her own choice. Will that make you happier?"

Iri let out an exasperated sigh. "Fine. I suppose we owe our wayward scribe that much. It's a waste, though. She's not going to want it."

"She may change her mind," Balthar said. "If everything goes off without a hitch, I don't know if there's any place for her *susurration* in the new Emerald Jungle."

"I'm more worried about the stormtails," Wendl countered. "If the pridelord believes they're causing the jadebeaks to leave the murmuration, I'm not sure there's any place for them in the current Emerald Jungle."

The Six said their goodbyes, and Wendl left the cave first, going north. They'd leave one at a time, slowly letting their scents establish themselves in new locations, just to be safe.

Still, Wendl was left with an uneasy feeling. She needed The Six to hold themselves together a little longer. What they did, they did for the good of all starling prides.

Though Balthar is correct, Whisper may not see it that way.

BOG THISTLE AND PUMPKIN BLOSSOM

Whisper waited for the evening patrols of jadebeaks to finish their chatting and night hunting before she left the Emerald Veil. Her path of salt and spiketrunks ended at the Jadebeak Mountains, but she wanted to be careful no one caught her scent before she left. She quietly suppressed her mallow root pheromones and absorbed the movements of the Jadebeak Pride.

They were loud when they talked about night hunting. There was a claim, often repeated, that rhea were easier to hunt in the dark. It was a lie, of course, as was the term *night hunting*. If night hunting were so lucrative, it'd be a year-long activity. Instead, it began in autumn and ended in the spring.

Two night hunters went off in search of an empty spot of jungle, chirping sweet nothings to each other.

Whisper rolled her eyes. Some starlings just could not let go of mating season. There'd been a rise in *summer friends*. If she didn't know better, she'd think she was back at the eyrie.

Once the jadebeak couple was gone, Whisper stepped off the salts, got a running start, and flew across the thinnest point along the Jadebeak Mountains. The stormtail would have crossed well south of here, but she didn't have a path that went deep into their territory. With all of the rains, she was lucky to have the one at the Grasslake Pathway where she'd run into Wendl and Nighteyes.

So long as there wasn't a perpetual storm overhead, spiketrunks grew close enough to keep her salted trail intact, protection against any of her charges spreading the parasite. She had a few jars of salt back at her nest, dug up from where she'd seen the bog crones hide them.

Most of them were harmless—or, in her paws, even useful. One jar, however, had included the parasite, and Whisper had brought it across the Emerald Veil by accident. That one she'd buried in a pit of salt until she could figure out how to dispose of it.

The rumble of Lightningmaw reached her in the mountains, and she was glad she had little reason to go down there. The infected shied away from the coast on either side of the Jadebeak Mountains. They loved the mountains, just not the water, and they especially hated the stormtails' perpetual storm. She'd seen an infected fall into a puddle of water once, and even with its mind mostly gone, it screamed a sound she'd never forgotten.

The mountains were clear of infected, thanks to her past efforts, and she'd nearly crossed them. The usual starling smells faded, and she searched out the border glyphs to study. She played around with matching their aroma, letting it fill her nares and trying to replicate it through her scent glands. This was Satra the Kjarr, the pridelord of the Ashen Weald, or whatever they called a pridelord. The glyph was pungent, courtesy of the paste it was mixed with.

Whisper sniffed again. It was *very* strong. The glyphs must have been renewed recently, sometime since her last trip across. That would pose a problem. She could cross and spend hours away from the Emerald Jungle, but her pride could not. If she ran into trouble far from the glyphs, she'd be on her own.

And if she brought her pride across, and they stayed too long, she might get them killed.

This would be tricky.

She licked her wrist absentmindedly, then massaged her paw. Featherdust was the easiest way to control other starlings, letting it carry her scent, but it was ethereal, especially when the wind worked against her. The scent glands on her paws were much stronger, and those pheromones would linger. She followed the border of jadebeak and Ashen Weald territory glyphs, continuing until she found the feathered shape of a stormtail glyph. Then she added her own pawprints along the way, stopping halfway between two sets of glyphs.

Once the scent trail was established, she found a dry mountain overhang and curled up, letting her fragrance fill the area and weaken the barrier between the worlds of the Emerald Jungle and the Ashen Weald. With such a strong Ashen Weald glyph, it would take her all day to create a small tear in the Emerald Veil, but she'd asked her pride to hold back before coming after her.

The starling she'd left in charge was timid, and

they'd wait here until she called. Hopefully, she wouldn't need them. But if she did, she wanted to be sure they could reach her.

She started to settle in, but as her nares adjusted to the Ashen Weald glyph, they picked up another aroma: dead opinici. Whisper stood, backtracking to locate the corpses. A dozen blackwings littered the forest floor. Their wounds looked inflicted by other opinici and not wild animals, so she shrugged it off.

The pridelord couldn't see incursions into his territory where there were no starlings, and the mountains were mostly left abandoned. Perhaps these blackwings had thought themselves safe just across the border and the Ashen Weald or Seraph King caught up to them. It wasn't any of her business.

Once an opinicus was dead, it was just a free meal for some sailfin or goliath bird. Or a cured jadebeak, if the parasite had eaten away enough of their brain, though Whisper was working very hard to fix the cannibalistic tendencies of the starlings she saved.

She returned to her makeshift nest, settling in. She would sleep away the last bit of night and the rest of the next day. She closed her eyes, settling her paws over her beak to keep it warm, and consciousness left her. While she slept, her scent glands and dusty feathers doing the work for her, she dreamt of the caves along the border of the Abyssal Naze and Emerald Jungle. She'd spent long hours there all winter, listening to the sounds coming from beneath the ground.

It was not her first choice of how she'd spend her time, but the pridelord feared the cave gryphons would come after them. In the bark beetles and swarm, he saw an attack on the murmuration. And so, Whisper split her time between saving lost starlings from Ashen Weald murderers in the east and safeguarding the border to the north against skulking, sneaky cave gryphons.

The clicks of the Abyssal Depths were interesting —and rare. Whatever had happened after the night the glyphs were destroyed had made them skittish. In their absence, however, she heard other sounds. Something was filling the absence held by the cave gryphons, something that might not obey the warning glyphs she put up along the cave mouths.

Save tomorrow's problems for tomorrow, Whisper, she scolded herself. *Today's are not yet resolved.*

WHISPER AWOKE IN THE EVENING. Her pride would be here soon. She used the last of the light to look out upon the bog while she chewed eyeshine, coating her tomia and gape in silver. She was familiar with the hidden paths and routes of the western bog, but familiarity was a dangerous thing. She found it was better to sit and wait, to take it all in.

The empty skies above the bog were a strange sight after travelling through the Emerald Jungle. What had taken root so deeply in this land that it reached up and claimed the skies for its own? The world beyond the Emerald Veil was a sad place, and she didn't understand Wendl's desire to go home.

Whisper had family at Mothfeather, too, but she was better off without them. She'd never been able to understand what her parents wanted for her. She'd never understood why her siblings were cruel. Among the starlings, among her pride, there was no such confusion. Wants, fears, hopes, and desires were all there in the pheromones. It took a lot to lie to another starling.

Misdirection, however, is easier. She thought of Wendl's strange scent trails that ended with a burst of smell that didn't move and wondered what her friend was hiding.

The sun descended, and Whisper moved from her spot. There was now a tear in the Emerald Veil. It would allow her to move through it. She could smell her pride approaching. They'd wait until they were needed. There was no sense alarming the Ashen Weald. Not with the pridelord primed to retaliate against the next incursion.

When Erlock Startail first came into our jungle and told us of the alliance of forest and bog gryphons, I thought them weak and ineffectual. I missed their danger the first time. I will not underestimate them a second.

Whisper felt her scent shifting to Erlock's and shook out her featherdust. For gryphons she saw only rarely, she had to recreate their scents regularly or she'd forget them, but it was dangerous to practice in the jungle. If her pride smelled her as a *not starling,* they could tear her apart before she had a chance to change her scent back.

There, I think that's how Erlock smells in case I need it later. Now to get back to myself. Once Whisper's pheromones were like herself and only herself again, she slipped down the Jadebeak Mountains, staying near an unnamed river. The sound of the runoff from the storms would hide her from owls, of which there were several. She'd avoided them thus far, but they'd killed an infected jadebeak before she could save him a month prior—the same one who had fallen into the water and screamed.

Spiketrunks faded to cypress and palm. The Ashen Weald believed themselves safe from the Emerald Jungle despite their crimes against the murmuration, and thus paid little mind to this border. The hanging moss reached the ground here, and she stopped to nibble at it.

There was little sustenance to be had, but she enjoyed new flavors. Where the grey-brown tendrils gathered were sprouts of edible green.

Someone else had the same idea, and up ahead, there was a break in the moss. Whisper stalked low, her underfluff brushing the ground. The wind came from the north, from the Crackling Sea, and she sniffed, taking it in. She could smell gryphons and opinici, but not close. She waited a few moments longer, and then she heard the sounds of confident strides from the east. She found a place where her silver eyes wouldn't catch the moonlight and watched the river.

"Do you see any kashow root?" The voice belonged to a bog witch with a missing eye. Her paint design was full of thorns and vines, and Whisper inhaled deeply, trying to isolate her scent.

"Not a one," another bog witch complained. This one had forgone all of her skulls and bones for something more floral. If she sat on top of the other gryphon, they could hide together as a rosebush.

Last, and least likely to remain camouflaged, a male witch trudged behind the other two. Though he had a few skeletal markings, and his wings had yellow star blossoms on top of them, his face was colored like a carved pumpkin. "I don't think we're going to find anything. I wish they let us come out during the day. I know they *say* it's not safe, but Blinky always seems to know when the 'mingos are sending patrols, so surely she could just...let us know? Hey, not so fast! Thistle, Petal, slow down!"

Whisper did not know who Blinky was, but she would not trust these three out during the day if they'd been newmoon starlings. To her chagrin, they hopped the smaller stream and headed in the direction of the largest river that came down from the Stormtail Pride glyphs, the exact place she planned to search.

Still, they leave a strong scent behind. They'll be easy to track.

Whisper decided to head back long enough to recover from being out of the Emerald Jungle, then follow them south. She was unsure what would happen if she were gone for too long. Nighteyes had been an experiment, and it had taken the pridelord to make her obedient again. Whisper wasn't sure she could fix herself if she lost the scent of the murmuration.

Whisper took a brief nap in her hideaway, the scent of her pride growing on the wind, then set back out. She was faster this time, gliding low where the trees gave cover, then stopping when she reacquired the scent of young bog witches.

Despite not smelling like thistles, petals, or pumpkins, she was able to keep them straight. They'd travelled farther south than she expected, reaching the mountain river the stormtails enjoyed. To her annoyance, they followed it west, into the mountains.

I do not want my scent showing up in Stormtail territory. That will make this more confusing than it already is if the pridelord asks what I'm doing here.

Thistle sang a song to herself. Whisper could tell her apart because she used blood in her bone paint, giving it a violent tint and an iron tang. To Whisper's nares, Thistle smelled like she had bloodbeak.

"Why did you come back to the bog?" Petal pressed the last gryphon. "I thought you liked The Wrecks."

"I needed to finish my medicine gryphon training," the pumpkin witch explained, the fishy smell of his breath reaching even Whisper's hiding spot. "I asked Deracho if me 'n Cielle could stay with his pride this winter, and he said only if I finished becoming a medicine gryphon. So here I am."

"Medicine gryphon, *pah*," Thistle scolded. "Being a bog witch is better than being a medicine gryphon. What do the feathermanes know about knife fish injuries or parasites? You should just stay here, Pumpkin. And who is this new pride leader, 'Deracho'?"

The prickly one is named Thistle, the flowery one is named Petal, and the pumpkin one is named Pumpkin. Is there no one with any imagination in this 'bog pride'? Whisper wondered to herself.

"Deracho is Thenca's mate, the leader of the new Hoarfrost Pride," Petal explained. "And don't scold Pumpkin. He just wants to be with his mate! Are you two getting back together, Pumpkin? He was really cute. Especially his tailfeathers."

"I hope so! But we'll see when the weather cools off," Pumpkin mumbled bashfully.

Whisper's patience was at its end. She was not risking her life to find out about bog witch dating lives. When Petal started to talk about how a gryphon named Soft Paws had taken two mates last season, a boy witch and a girl witch, Whisper was just about ready to give up. Thankfully, Thistle found something worthwhile.

"Hey, what's this?" Thistle beckoned them over. "Looks like a fish tail. Do you think it came from one of our Ashen Weald guests?"

Pumpkin and Petal both weighed in but quickly quieted. Whisper could smell their stress. They were worried, but not so worried they were going back for help or Blinkies.

"I think it's the infected jadebeaks," Thistle said at last. "We never got all of them. One must be hiding here."

Pumpkin started when a gust of wind rustled the hanging moss above him. "I don't know, this is close to one of our nesting grounds. Wouldn't they have attacked? Infected starlings aren't big on thinking. I wish I were at Hoarfrost now. They've killed all of their starlings. Most of the kjarr and taiga are free of them."

Thistle perked up. "How do they cure the wildlife, though? Even before the flamingos took over the old mummy dig site, the redspine sailfins seem to keep the bugs alive."

"Oh, you'll love this." Pumpkin seemed to have

forgotten about the impending infected jadebeak attack. "They fill pumpkins with meat and put them were the monitors live. The monitors play with the pumpkins and eat them. We got the idea from the way goliaths seek out pumpkins on their own to eat when they get sick. It seems to be working."

Petal nodded her approval. "We do the same thing by Bogwash, but we make peanut pumpkin mash and spread it on the trees for the birds. Sometimes I sneak out and eat some myself when Soft Paws isn't watching."

Thistle made a face.

"Oh, you can't do that with the meat pumpkins," Pumpkin explained. "We thought they were just snacks the first time we visited Hoarfrost, so Cielle pounced one and ate it. He was throwing up all evening, and the taiga gryphons laughed at him."

The witchy trio wandered off, and Whisper approached the fish tail. *Fish* was an understatement. This had come from a shark. There were a few options. Freshwater sharks did inhabit the bog, though they preferred the Jadebeak River in her experience. The long tail on this one looked more like a thresher shark, which was ocean specific.

If he's well enough to hunt from the ocean and bring the prey upstream, he's not too far gone. Yet.

Unlike Thistle and Petal, Whisper knew this wasn't one of the jadebeaks. She'd rescued the ones the owls hadn't killed, and they were recovering under the watchful gaze of her pride. The silver had mostly left their eyes, though one insisted on wearing a branch atop his head.

Sometimes, they come back...stranger.

Whisper searched the riverbank until she found a pawprint to confirm her suspicions. The webbed toes, the lack of retractable claws—both spoke to the presence of a stormtail in the area.

Moving water and three witches muddled the smell a bit, but she found a dryer pawprint and pushed her beak against it, inhaling. Her mind went back to the Mothfeather Eyrie's gardens, where she was showing Wendl the pink flowers of an oleander.

An orange caterpillar with black bristles fell on Wendl's head, and Whisper relocated it. She later chewed her talons idly, not realizing that the plants were poisonous, and spent several days getting nauseating medicines pushed down her throat.

Like most of Whisper's memories, it was pleasant except where it was toxic.

Okay, let's see where our 'Desert Rose' has gone.

She took a step or two, but instinctively sniffed as she passed some broken moss. The invasive plant had been freshly shorn, and not by the gryphons she was tracking. She sniffed again, and this time she caught a hint of owl.

Desert Rose is in trouble if the owl is tracking him. Not just the stormtail, Whisper herself was in danger. She could hide her scent, but owls had keen eyes and a keener sense of hearing.

She rested, letting the scents of the bog wash over her. Moss and thornvine were strongest, but she could make out the smell of her pride, waiting at the tear in the Emerald Veil. The witches were headed into the Jadebeak Mountains, but her pride was still upwind of her. It would be hard to get their aid if she required it.

She should not risk her life for a stormtail. She was too important for the health of both the murmuration and the susurration. She worried about the fate of the infected without her to champion their cause.

But that same worry meant she would hunt down this stormtail. Ocean hunting, hiding—if he was infected, there was time to cure him and bring him back. It was possible his mind would recover enough for him to rejoin the stormtails, but if not, he could always live with the Newmoon Pride. She could definitely use a stormtail.

Whisper shook herself, shedding the scents she was using to try to stay invisible to the Ashen Weald. Then she slowly built up a new scent, one that might confuse the owls. Had another starling followed her trail, they'd have found a dusty cypress that smelled strongly of moss, vine, kashow, monitor, and capybara.

Then, following the river northwest, the scent of Erlock Startail.

DESERT ROSE

Whisper followed the stream, worrying when she hit a waterfall. The infected jadebeaks she'd retrieved always shied away from the border with the Emerald Jungle, somehow repulsed by the glyphs. A starling moving towards them was unusual, but she'd never tracked someone who had been removed from the murmuration first.

Perhaps he clings to the Emerald Jungle, hoping to feel something.

Clamshell, Wendl's friend's friend, wasn't the first of their kind Whisper had fixed. As she skulked along the salted jungle paths, she'd stumbled across a dozen such starlings, hiding in caves, whimpering and contemplating desperate actions. She'd come to each of them with the calming scent of mint and reintegrated them back with their pride, careful to hide her involvement from the pridelord.

None of them had made it across the Jadebeak Mountains, however. This *Desert Rose* was the first. And common starling logic would say that a gryphon who was not part of the murmuration and not in the Emerald Jungle was no longer their problem. This was where Whisper differed from the others.

Idly, she licked at her left foreleg and the starry crescent.

Stormtails are always such trouble. It's too wet for a salt path in their territory, and they're very protective of their borders.

She looked from the waterfall to the cliffs above. A hidden den behind a waterfall felt like the sort of place a stormtail would hide, but checking it required her to get wet. The rainy season in the Emerald Jungle had taught her that being wet enhanced her scent while making it very difficult to change. And if she did go through the waterfall, there'd be no way to hide if the bog witches were on the other side.

Checking the stream above the falls felt like a happier, dryer use of her time. She unfolded her wings, then remembered the owl and folded them again. *Flying is too loud.* Instead, she crawled up the side of the mountain, trusting her fluff to keep her quiet.

Her muscles burned as she pulled herself up the last bit, but she enjoyed this kind of challenge. She examined the riverbank, finding more webbed pawprints, and continued her pursuit. The moon shone brightly, turning the mud a deep red. It was the sort of night the Mothfeather opinici would spend up late telling ghost tales to each other.

Stories of strange creatures that stalk the night, guiding the souls of the damned. I guess I've become such a tale myself. What would my siblings think if they saw me now? That I'm a monster? They never understood that true kindness wears a scary mask.

The first night she'd successfully cured an infected starling—in both body and mind—she'd sworn that she was never going back to eyrie life. There were gryphons who needed her here. She was the warden of the damned, and it was a role she took seriously.

The scent of excitement and worry came on the breeze down the mountains, and she quickened her pace. Several bog gryphons hissed loudly, their threat met by a loud bark, followed by chittering.

Whisper kept her Erlock scent as strong as she could while the smell of orange zest called out to her pride for help.

THISTLE TOOK THE LEAD. She was only a few days older than Pumpkin or Petal, but while they'd gone east to Bogwash when Soft Paws sundered the bog pride, Thistle had stayed behind and knew every inch of the borderlands like the back of her paw. It had been her jail for years under the crone.

The spiketrunks glowed red in the moonlight, their wicked spikes thrashing whenever the wind picked up. The pleasant smell of the river was mixed with the fetid aroma of dead fish and infection.

Where the moon's glow turned the mud and plants crimson, the infected's eyes shone silver.

"It's one of the long ones!" Petal cried out.

It barked at her, sending the flowery witch back. The sound ended in a chitter.

"Are there more?" Pumpkin asked. "It looks alone. Maybe we should try to capture it."

Thistle had spent hours flying over the ocean, luring *altruistic* stormtails into the Emerald Jungle in the past. She'd also fought them a few times with her wingtorn brethren before Satra strengthened the southern glyphs, and Thistle knew what they were capable of.

"No, it's too dangerous," she said. "These ones are fast, and they'll drown you if they get the chance. Don't let it pull you underwater."

Petal and Pumpkin stayed behind her, but they repositioned so they had their backs to the forest, not the water. Depending on who was asked, the infected were either perfectly predictable or completely chaotic.

To scholars, they were predictable, at least on parchment: The parasite would force them to hunt down the closest gryphon and try to bite it. It wasn't quite so simple, however, in the wilds. There were phases to the infection, and depending on where a starling was at, they could act in unpredictable ways.

For example, this stormtail already had one very unusual thing going for it.

"Shouldn't it be afraid of the water?" Petal asked. "I thought the infected hated water."

"Oh yeah, that's why the mummies were chained up under the water table," Pumpkin added. "I read that in a Darkfeather University book. Are we sure it's infected?"

It barked again, trailing into a bone-chilling chitter, removing any doubt.

"Maybe the infection is new?" Pumpkin prompted. "But the eyes are shiny."

Thistle kept her good eye on the stormtail. "I think if I'm closer, it has to go after me, right? You two get ready to attack. Go for the throat and neck, but if that fails, it can't flee if you take out its wings."

"That's cruel," Petal protested. "That's a cruel thing to do to anyone."

"It's going to have to die either way, right?" Pumpkin did not sound sure of himself.

"Then go for the neck. I don't care, as long as it's dead." Thistle feinted a few times, and to her surprise, the starling didn't take the bait. Instead, it crouched down and backed up, staying near the water.

"Aw, see? It's okay. I think it can understand us," Pumpkin said.

And Thistle could almost believe it, except the moment her gourd-loving friend put his beak down to go through his medicine bag for some bog blossom, the infected slipped between her and Petal like a doublejaw eel, grabbed Pumpkin, and dove into the water with him.

"Pumpkin!!" Petal screamed, but Thistle was already on it. She leapt on the starling's hunched back, biting at its neck, and she was just starting to get through its thick hide when something pounced from the opposite shore and crashed into her.

Thistle swore. Her first thought was that Petal had hit her out of some misguided attempt to protect the infected, but this was something new.

Of course, the infected never travel alone. Their altruism pulls them into a swarm.

The black starling hissed at her, a sound that did

not end in a chitter. It was the first of many contradictions. Even at night, it was clear this starling wasn't a dark green—it was true black—though Thistle had the afterimage of stars in her mind from being pounced. Its eyes were silver, but alert.

Its silver markings looked more artistic than anything else, and the same silver color created striped patterns in its coat of fur and feathers. When it hissed, the inside of its dark beak sparkled in the moonlight.

It looked like the afterimage of a bog gryphon. As though after staring at bog gryphon faces and fluffy tails all day, she'd closed her eyes, and images of this silver bog gryphon played across the dark night.

The final contradiction was what kept it alive. It fought the infected stormtail, something no two starlings should be able to do.

"Petal," Thistle gasped, "get Pumpkin out of the water!"

To her credit, Petal dove between the hissing and barking to retrieve Pumpkin, who coughed and vomitted up half a river and several minnows.

In their dance, Thistle began to see the starlings as gryphons again, not just monsters. *No one will believe this tale when we get back.*

The stormtail tried to drown the dark starling, but every time he moved in close to bite her, he pulled back as though smelling rotten eggs. He seemed confused, letting out several barks. There was a strange sound on the wind, and it took Thistle a moment to realize it was a soft voice. What's more, it spoke a version of common.

"Home, home, come to me, home, I can bring you

back, I am home, do you smell the storms, Lightning-maw, home, think of home..." the voice repeated again and again. It was all nonsense, but the river-bank *did* smell of a heavy thunderstorm.

This is mad.

The darker starling's eye goo had washed off in the water, and she no longer looked infected. Thistle had seen a few starlings lose their eye goo in a struggle, and their eyes didn't focus right behind it. The silver was almost a mercy, stopping the witches from having to look into those living-dead orbs.

The dark starling shook her fur, trying to dry it, and the water that splashed against Thistle had a strange smell to it, like a fantail.

She stepped to Pumpkin and Petal. "Are you okay? Be prepared. Whichever starling wins, the altruism will force the other to try to kill us."

The stormtail turned to flee, and the other starling let out a piercing cry that echoed across the canyon, coming back tenfold. The storm on the wind faded, replaced by a grove of gryphmint.

She stepped towards the stormtail, but it bit her shoulder and flung her away. Then it leapt across the river at Pumpkin again.

"Oh sweet floof—" Pumpkin began, but a new monster of moss and thornvine crashed down upon the stormtail from above, crushing it under her weight.

Blinky Reevesbane, protector of the night, had saved them. She dug her claws into the stormtail, but the other starling spoke up.

"Stop!" The voice was still soft and a little scratchy, but at a louder volume than before. "I can save him. Give him to me, and I will return him to the jungle."

Thistle'd known a few owls since the Ashen Weald had moved into her sunken eyrie, so she knew they were capable of showing surprise, but Blinky was unreadable.

"No," the Bane of the Crackling Sea Reeve said without moving her slight beak. "It is better two infected starlings die than he spread it to your swarm."

At the word 'swarm,' the clear-eyed starling's tail poofed up angrily. Thistle knew better than to distract Blinky, but she disagreed. Starlings without altruism? This was their first chance in years to find out what was going on in the Emerald Jungle.

"My name is Whisper," the newcomer tried. "He is Desert Rose. He has a family who miss him. I have enough pumpkin to cure him."

"I do not care." The owl gryphon did not blink, but she also had not killed him yet, a good sign.

The starling shook herself even though the first few shakes had already dried her off. "A trade, then. I have Erlock Startail. I will give her to you in exchange for Desert Rose."

Blinky cocked her head, listening. "I do not hear Erlock. She is very loud and says 'darling' a lot. No one has said 'darling' in my bog. I would have heard."

"She's unconscious," Whisper countered. "Nearby."

Thistle sniffed. "She's right, I can smell her."

"Are you a gryphon who lies?" Blinky asked.

It spoke to Whisper's dedication to the truth or her inability to know one answer would work better than the other that she replied with the affirmative. "I lie all the time. I have lied to you in this conversation several times. But I do it to keep my susurration alive, and hurting Erlock would not accomplish that."

Blinky's claws relaxed slightly, though she kept the infected stormtail pinned. Her tail twitched like she was a gryphlet playing a game. "What is one lie you have told me?"

Thistle thought she must be having a stroke, because the scent had moved on from mint to orange again.

Whisper relaxed a little. "I do not have Erlock Startail. She's fine, wherever she is. I just needed you to concentrate on me while my pride got into place. Your hearing was too good to leave you undistracted."

Blinky shook her head, then crouched and mantled over her stormtail prize.

Thistle looked at the spiketrunks. Though the Ashen Weald gryphons avoided them, she'd heard starlings knew how to navigate their long spines. And they were now covered by dozens of silver-eyed starlings.

Silver eyes, but alert silver, like Whisper's.

"Give her the stormtail, Blinky." Thistle approached the owl gryphon carefully, unsure how well she took commands. "If they leave or if we kill them, it's all the same, right? We kept this place safe."

The owl gryphon still seemed to be weighing how many starlings was too many to fight. "Approach close enough that I can kill you."

Whisper obliged, fluttering across the stream. The smell of citrus was stronger now, and Thistle's tongue felt coated with orange peel. Whisper shook herself again, but instead of water, Thistle felt featherdust coating herself and Blinky.

And the stormtail.

It went limp, and Blinky stepped back. "I will be listening for you, Whisper, if you come back."

The starling didn't reply but coated the stormtail in a thick layer of dust. It made Thistle itchy just to think about.

The Ashen Weald backed away as Whisper's pride flowed down from the trees and retrieved the stormtail, vanishing into the night until the only one left was Whisper.

The dark starling stared at Blinky long and hard, and Thistle wondered if they were going to fight or propose. Then Whisper turned to Thistle, pulled a scroll case out from a hidden herb bag, and tossed it over. "I will return to the border in a few days. Leave your answer hanging from a tree outside Wendl's cave at the Jadebeak Falls."

Whisper flew away, leaving Thistle to wonder what had just transpired.

"Who was she? *What* was she?" Pumpkin asked, getting to his feet now that the water was out of his system.

"The Newmoon Pride," Blinky said. "They were one of the starling prides hurt by us."

"How?" Thistle asked. To her knowledge, only jadebeaks came across the mountains regularly, so only jadebeaks *could* be hurt by the Ashen Weald. And the odd stormtail. It wasn't like the bog gryphons could hop into the jungle and say hello.

"That is not for me to tell." Blinky stretched her

neck, listening. "I am going to track them to the border. Take the scroll case to Soft Paws."

The owl gryphon vanished. There didn't seem to be a reason for haste now that the excitement was over and everyone had survived, so Thistle stayed behind and helped walk Pumpkin back.

Petal chatted on about how it would be a good story to tell Cielle, but Thistle couldn't get her mind off Whisper. They'd just spoken with a starling, and it hadn't tried to murder them.

How do we replicate that for next time? she wondered. *And what did Blinky mean by 'one of the starling prides hurt by us?'*

12

WATER LILY

He awoke with a start and the name *Desert Rose* on his beak. He shook his head a few times, licked a paw, and whittled away at the crust over his eyes and whiskers.

Where am I? Why am I dry?

He sniffed the air, coming back with mostly salt and spiketrunk. He instinctively dug his claws into the ground, expecting mud or grass, but instead finding sand.

A beach? He sniffed. *No, not sand, salt.*

He wiped again at his eyes, removing the last of the silver, careful not to fill them with salt. He was in a grove of some sort, a grove of spiketrunks.

His first thought was that he was in the Jadebeak Mountains, or perhaps in the Jadebeak Pride's territory. But where a lightning strike had felled a tree, he could see the wet grass and lily-covered floodplains of the Grasslake Pathway.

Rudder rounded the path from a nearby glen, chasing a flock of rhea near the water. Clamshell burst from the water and caught the largest of the flock, pulling it under. Several of the flightless birds balked, trying to turn back, where Rudder took care of them.

"Nighteyes was right, the rhea have grown slow and trusting." Rudder's voice was distant, as though Desert Rose were underwater and Rudder above the surface.

Clamshell plucked theirs, pulling out large chunks of feathers with their beak. "So it seems. You chose a good mate, if a bit dry. Though who else but a drypaw would ever think to eat things not in the water?"

Desert Rose barked a greeting, watching their small ears prick up, but they didn't look over. He started to walk out of the grove, but his body froze in place when he reached several crescent moon glyphs.

"Calm," a seductive voice came from behind him. The leader of the Newmoon Pride sat curled up, her tail under her chin and her paws on top of it. "If they hear you, it'll cause them distress. They cannot see past the glyphs. You'll be with them soon enough."

A cool feeling settled into Desert Rose's stomach, like when he'd dove too quickly through the sun-warmed ocean surface and hit the frigid depths. "I know who you are."

Whisper opened a silver eye, inviting him to go on.

"You ensnare the damned, stealing them away for your own murmuration." His hackles rose, but he knew better than to challenge the leader of a starling pride. Despite seeing his stormtail pridemates and flood plains, his mind was telling him he was somehow in Newmoon Pride territory.

"A little dramatic," she countered, "but you don't have anything to fear from me. The parasite didn't affect your brain much, and you should be fine to go back to your home pride. No need to join mine. We have enough beaks to feed."

He tried to exit the grove, but his brain refused to walk through the opening.

"Not so hasty. First, I need to know how you left the murmuration. Was it deliberate?" Whisper used her beak to open a medicine bag and began chewing eyeshine.

The newmoon gryphons prided themselves on their secrecy, and it alarmed Desert Rose to see one sharing the mystery of their silver eyes so freely. There were rumors, old greywhisker stories, that when you died, it was the moon prides who met you across the sky ocean and led you to your place among the stars. If true, the gryphon he saw before him now was just a vessel used by spirits.

It made sense to him that the Newmoons' ability to cross the veil between the living and the dead was what let them cross the Emerald Veil. These were tales so old, they predated the Newmoon Pride's formation to combat the parasite.

The secrecy of the moon prides did little to dispel the rumors, but Whisper looked real enough. Spirits would not have to apply their own eyeshine and stripes.

Though he didn't trust this gryphon not to kill him, the air filled with mint, and he calmed. "No, of course I didn't leave of my own accord. Why would any starling leave the murmuration?"

"Do you remember where it happened?" She politely offered him some gooey eyeshine, and he recoiled with a hiss. Some of his memories were coming back, and they included a silver-eyed reflection and chittering beak.

"Here is where Clamshell believes they became disconnected. Do you remember this floodplain?" she asked.

He told her he did not. "I spent most of my time up by the Greenscale Springs, do you know it?"

Whisper shook her head. Where her voluminous black fur moved, he saw the barest hints of her starling pedigree.

"Of course, a newmoon wouldn't. You live in the shadows of other prides." It was also possible the afterlife was so far away that little things like freshwater springs weren't visible to spirits. The soft mint intensified, encouraging him to go on. "Jadebeaks are bad at glyphs. They put theirs too high, far above the Greenscale Springs. It's hard to get down there, hard to get back up for the drypaws. Because the glyph is so high, I can slip in and steal their fish. The waters are treacherous but well worth the danger."

There was no point lying to a spirit, it was said they always knew the truth. The same strange tales suggested this was why no other prides took newmoon mates, though others claimed spirits didn't take mates at all. There were no newmoon gryphlets, yet the pride grew all the same by stealing the dead.

Perhaps it was the mint or some sort of spell, but he

felt like he was at the Greenscale Springs now, floating fifteen feet below the surface, large fish circling him. The play of light through the leaves, the cool water bubbling up from the ground, the way the cacophony of the jungle faded to silence—there was no place in the world he'd rather be than the freshwater springs. He didn't know what he'd do if the jadebeaks moved their glyphs lower.

The smells of the spring were coming from him, drifting to Whisper. She inhaled loudly, seeming to understand the location through his memories.

"Is that where you were disconnected?" she asked. He didn't know, so she added, "What do you remember after you left the murmuration? Where were you, and what was going through your mind?"

Mint became orange, and he flashed back to a different set of spiketrunks in the mountains. "Fear."

I'd always felt the will of the pridelord, his covenant of glyphs, but now my mind was silent. I ran through the Jadebeak Mountains, past rhea and caiman and the decaying bodies of yet more blackwings, arriving at the stormtail glyphs, but I felt nothing. Ahead of me, I saw a new set of glyphs, and I kept running.

Thick jungle vines and orchids faded away. Deep-rooted scrub grasses clung to the same loose scree of the Jadebeak Mountains that denied Desert Rose's paws purchase. Still, he pushed through, and the trees here grew farther apart, as though making room for him.

Where the air thinned, pine and aneda filled the gaps between stray broadleafs, becoming more common the higher he went. Eventually, even the hardiest of trees abandoned the stormtail. In their place, fuzzy cacti, rough on the paw but resilient enough to survive the altitude, clutched at his fur.

After he crested the peak, he located the last broadleaf before the murmuration's territory ended, and his paws finally allowed him to stop. The lost jungle remnant was wet with fresh paste. A black glyph with two golden feathers dripped down like silver from infected eyes. The smell had attracted a small burrowing bee, and the insect struggled to escape the viscous mixture.

Desert Rose refused to let the glyph stop him. A pressure built as he moved past, like a weak leash of vines from his nares to the center of the Emerald Jungle. By the time he left the Jadebeak Mountains, something inside his nares had popped, and blood leaked down his beak on and off for an entire day.

Food was the most important thing at that point. The bleeding would stop if he could keep up his strength. He could have eaten a whole beaked whale on his own.

With the cliffs behind him, the last remnants of plant and animal life he knew were gone. Cypress trees reached down to grab him, moss hanging off them like living decay. Instead of spatterdock and lily pads, small puddles were full of leaves, their leached tannin turning the water to acid.

He was used to ferocious rivers cutting through the broadleafs as they raced to fill the Winter Jungle. The water here crawled, skulked, and soaked. The entire land was a dead, bloated corpse, swollen with acid and neglect.

He'd crossed here once before, when the old kjarr's glyphs faded, but had followed a flying witch back to Stormtail Pride territory and been unable to cross a second time. During that visit, he'd seen the ocean and beach, not what lay north of it. This time, he stayed in the bog itself, sticking close to the rivers for need of running water.

A nasty run-in with a matamata made him wary, so he tried to reach the ocean, but it was full of rafts. He nearly stole the catch from a pair of blue heron opinici, but some sort of petrel fisherfolk dove into the water near the raft, and he decided not to risk it.

The easiest fish and alligators to catch were along the cypress ponds, where the water was slow. Alligators were much easier prey than the crocodiles of home. Unfortunately, the south was full of bog gryphons, and he was forced to search for new rivers, swimming north. The rapids made for tough aquatic travel, but kashow trees provided cover so no herons or flamingos flying overhead could find him. The sailfins, too, hid along the rapids, hoping to catch fish away from the turtles.

"Is this where you became infected? I heard the witches say the redspine sailfins carry the parasite," Whisper interjected.

"No," Desert Rose replied. "I'm much smarter than that. Where I got infected isn't a mystery. Sit back and listen. You'll know when we get to that part."

He was safe for a few days, but the Ashen Weald was low on supplies. Kashow, the same tree that kept him safe from patrols, brought the witches near his hideaways. He was forced to continue north, spending more time underwater scrounging clams and crawfish from the mud. That's where he found the stone puzzle.

"There were many like it, all over the strange canals around the sunken eyrie," Desert Rose explained. "They were carved into the bottom of the stone rivers, but most had become stuck. I enjoyed tracing their patterns to stave off boredom, but this one had come loose."

"Did you feel any violent urges towards the Ashen Weald gryphons? Had your nares healed?" Whisper asked.

He responded with confusion. "No, why would I? What does that have to do with the stone puzzles?"

When the bog witches were busy above the surface, he hid below, working at the mechanism. He scraped off as much mud as he could, revealing what he thought was a strange flower with six petals. He later realized they were wings, and each set could be moved, just a little.

The top wings pulled up. The bottom wings pulled down. That was simple. The middle set caused him trouble. Finally, with the help of a tree branch that had fallen into the water, he was able to get leverage to push them into the carving.

Then the stone panel collapsed, filling an underground chamber with water. The light revealed little except that one side had a gap at the bottom. If he swam under, then up again, he arrived in a dry room with no light.

He'd swum in many dark places in his life, so he had little fear. His nares *had* healed by then, and the musty, salty smell told him there were no other large animals in here. He followed the outside of the chamber, larger than any nest or burrow he'd been in, then walked lines across it, searching for anything in the emptiness.

There were moments in the blackness where he panicked, scurrying back to the wall. But he needed to know if it was safe in here. If it was, it would make the perfect hiding place to avoid the native gryphons.

He crisscrossed the darkness, never finding anything, until he decided to speed up the process and check the center. He counted his paces, locating the center of one wall, then he walked across the very middle, waving his beak back and forth so he wouldn't hit anything straight on.

He clicked against stone.

In the center of the room was a pedestal. Atop it was some sort of soft effigy, made of cloth or dried ferns. Perhaps strips of animal fur. He tried to picture the creature in his mind. He thought it could be a gryphon from the brittle ears, then perhaps an opinicus from the paws. But the shape was wrong. There were too many wings.

It was the strangest thing he'd ever felt, a soft effigy beneath the earth, hidden by water. Other than cave gryphons, who would make such a thing?

"I pushed my paw over its heartbone, and it writhed. Then I felt a flash of pain and fled. You found me a day later."

WHISPER LISTENED to the strange tale. Desert Rose's comment on heartbones was something the other starling prides thought of as metaphorical, but in serving as Mally's scribe, she'd had to sketch a stormtail heart, and they did develop ossifications in their hearts. Though stormtails assumed everything else also did, so she didn't trust that what he'd found had them.

It was an odd tale that told her nothing of how he'd become disconnected. He just changed the subject when she tried to bring him back to it, insisting on telling her about the parasite. She'd expected that part of the tale to be more mundane—Desert Rose had grown so hungry he'd been forced to eat a sailfin, got infected, and she'd arrived just in time.

Something he'd mentioned but perhaps did not understand the significance of was that he'd not experienced greenwing altruism, Wendl's borrowed weald word. Whisper had her own, much more dramatic terms for it which did not confuse what the word altruism meant.

"What happened after that?" Desert Rose asked. "How did I end up here?"

She considered answering him fully, but she could feel a citrus scent much stronger than her own pulling him back into the murmuration. "It is better if you don't know. The pridelord will search you for answers. It is better if there are none for you to give, beyond me rescuing you."

"If that's your wish. I suppose I owe you my life." He idly traced the six-wing emblem into the salt. "Why were the rivers around the sunken eyrie so square? Why create so many chambers hidden beneath the water?"

She didn't know. "In the Old Words, they call that

place the Plagued City. City is an old word for a small eyrie without a reeve."

"What do you know about them? Who built it? What happened with the parasite?" he pushed.

"If I tell you, I will have to make you forget." Already, her ability to speak candidly with him was fading. In the distance, Clamshell and Rudder wrapped up their hunting. She nuzzled Desert Rose towards the break in the grove, changing the scent to goldmint to neutralize the glyph.

He hesitated.

"Tell them you were hurt at the Greenscale Springs, and it took you a while to heal enough to return," she suggested. "They won't question it. They'll just be glad to have you home."

He moved a paw off the salt but didn't put it down. "Thank you for saving me, Mallowroot."

"My name isn't Mallowroot." She couldn't remember if she'd given him her name, but he must know it.

"Mine isn't Desert Rose, either." His eyes, clear of silver, sparkled.

She laughed in spite of herself. She couldn't remember the last time someone had teased her. He gave her a hug, a much more snaky affair than the ones Wendl gave, and Whisper winced, reaching a paw for the bite on her shoulder.

"Wait, did I do that? Are you infected?" he asked.

The answer was yes and no. She sniffed the air before answering. "The Newmoon Pride were created from a dozen other prides, each starling with bog ancestry so we would be immune to all but the most resilient strains of the parasite. So we could kill the infected. I'll be fine. You've been here for days, and we've both eaten a lot of pumpkin in that time."

He looked as surprised to get a straight answer from a newmoon as she'd been to be teased as one. He nuzzled Whisper, then stepped past her glyphs and into the Grasslake Pathway. The glyphs of the grove worked their magic, and he stumbled over a rock, confirming that he'd lost the ability to see the trees for the tangle again.

She couldn't help but watch him. She thought she'd done her job well, but every gryphon was different. She worried until she heard Clamshell's squeal of delight. Rudder rushed over, probably expecting the caiman to have returned, and crashed into both of them. They barked their strange stormtail cries of happiness, jumping and grooming like floodlings.

Clamshell led Desert Rose away, but Rudder lingered. He stared directly at the grove, moving his head back and forth like a serpent, trying to see the illusion.

She waited, knowing he wouldn't be able to, but surprised he remembered the grove at all. Stormtails were harder to work on. Ultimately, he grabbed one of the rhea and flung it in her direction, leaving it stuck on the spines of a branch above her.

"Why did you throw away our rhea?" Clamshell asked. "We'll never find it in that tangle."

Rudder paused before answering. "When good luck happens, you must throw a rhea to the forest spirits or the good luck will end."

Whisper could see a future where all of her spiketrunk hiding spots were full of impaled rhea. *I have made shrikes of starlings.*

The stormtails wandered off, and the cool smell of a moonlit night full of bloodvine blossoms wafted in from the north. She turned to see her pride's second-in-command staring at her.

"What's wrong?" Moonlit Blossom asked. He'd always been both suspicious of and affectionate towards her. She suspected the previous Whisper had been his friend, though she kept him at a paw's distance.

She told him what she'd learned. Of artificial rivers keeping mummies submerged, full of parasites waiting to flood out if their seals were broken and their rivers dry.

"Why is that any concern of yours, Pride Leader?" he asked.

She promised herself she'd be honest with this one starling always, because if something happened to her, she thought he would take over the pride. The work the Newmoon Pride did must continue after her death. "It's of concern to the pridelord, so it's of concern to all of us. The parasite has killed more starlings than any army, and worse, it killed his beloved jadebeaks. The day may come when it is too dangerous to leave the bog to its own devices. When a pridelord does not feel safe, that is when he is at his most dangerous. That's when entire prides vanish."

She didn't specify if she meant starling prides or outsiders. Instead, she reached up tall, retrieving the rhea and tossing it to Moonlit Blossom to carry home. The winds shifted, and she could smell happy stormtails coming out to hunt in celebration of Desert Rose's return. It was a day of happiness for their pride, thanks to her.

And Wendl, for setting me on this path.

"Pride Leader?" her heir prompted, but neither of them moved for a few minutes more.

"I need to speak to the alabasters," she said at last, and they disappeared down the salted path of the damned.

13

VIOLET WING ALTRUISM

Nighteyes walked among the young of her pride, her heart filled with joy at their squeals and play.

It filled with despair at how quickly they tired, how easily they bled.

There were moments where all pride leaders wished the mantle had fallen upon someone else. Moments when she'd approached her sisters and asked if any of them would rather lead the pride.

Their silence was an answer unto itself, one that should have been comforting but was not. They all had a duty to challenge her for the pride if they could lead it better. That they remained silent meant they didn't know how to save the gryphlets and fledglings either.

Her wanderings took her by a gathering of hunters, back from scouring the far reaches of their shrinking territory. Lizards, a few birds, and a pile of edible flowers that would do little to assuage anyone's hunger.

The older hunters were tired. It would be cruel to ask them to go out again today. Only young Sheen still had energy.

Nighteyes looked back at the nesting grounds, decided she could do no good by staying here, and approached Sheen. "Can you show me where you were finding the cassowaries? Let's give your friends here a rest. You and I will go find the birds."

Sheen perked up. "Of course, Pride Leader!"

Several of the older hunters looked grateful for the break. Others were keeping their beaks shut, which hinted at something Nighteyes already suspected—the cassowaries, who usually lived in the limestone forest above the Abyssal Naze, were right along the border, where they'd been dissuaded from hunting after the incident two years ago.

Nighteyes ignored the grumpy hunters, left her youngest sister in charge while she was gone, and then chirped to Sheen that it was time to leave.

The long walk beneath the canopy was beautiful, full of flowering vines. While it was possible to fly down and land in the middle of the nests, it was tradition to walk under the arch of flower constellations when coming or going.

It had been a while since she'd left the pride-grounds going west, since her burrow was on the eastern edge of the nests. Desiccated moss had been placed along the path, a nice way to dry one's paws when coming home after hunting. Wendl had continued her efforts to create a roof of broadleafs to keep the path dry, though the wax had given way in a few places, leaving some wet spots.

Once they were through the arches, Nighteyes and

Sheen took to the sky. Though the Nightsky Pride was known for such floral paths, it was beautiful from above, too. Waves of verdant green undulated in the wind. Birds and insects lent their song to the warm day.

I've missed this. I should go out hunting more often. Pridelord knows we need the help, and I'm doing little good as a leader.

Sheen led her to the northern edge. Though the glyphs would make the world fuzzy down below, from up high, she could see the broadleafs fade to new types of trees, trees that loved the rocky, mineral-rich soil.

"The cassowaries have been coming in here," Sheen said. They were right up against Nighteyes' glyphs.

Perhaps it was just that Nighteyes hadn't been here in a while, but she could just make out a path of some sort that ended at the jungle. Odd, as they didn't get visitors from the north. Perhaps the borders had shifted over time, and this had once been a goliath trail to move stone down to Alwren or King's Reach.

What was it like the day the Emerald Jungle cut them off from the north?

Nighteyes crouched low, sniffing for cassowaries. Sheen did the same, following behind like an apprentice. There were better hunters for the indigo fledgling to learn from, but Nighteyes would do her best.

She scratched at the soil a few times, and she detected fresh cassowaries. They hadn't gone far, either. The flightless birds had wandered down to a small pond with high rocks on all sides and only one way up or down. They'd be easy prey, or at least as easy as cassowaries got.

"This way, but stay quiet," Nighteyes cautioned. "If we do this right, we'll have stew for a week."

NIGHTEYES DRAGGED the last of the cassowaries to the stone path. Sheen was already plucking hers, pulling out mouthfuls of feathers with her beak. The angry, flightless birds had drunk their fill, discovered no other way out, and had been slowly working their way back up the path one at a time. It was a rare opportunity, and the Nightsky Pride would eat well.

Maybe that's the answer to feeding so many sick. Just depend on large quantities of food wandering in from the Abyssal Naze, frightened.

If she'd been less tired, Nighteyes might have taken more time to wonder what had driven cassowaries out of their homes. They liked to kick first, bite second, and flee third.

Pridelord protect us if the titanoboas come down next, chasing the cassowaries, she thought. The southwestern prides may complain of crocodiles, but nobody liked the idea of titanoboas slithering into their territory. It was a cause for celebration if they only ate one gryphon before they were killed.

She concentrated on plucking the cassowaries. Now that the hard part was done, she should send Sheen back to fetch the other hunters while she guarded their kill. Even if the others hadn't been part of the hunt, it would be good for the pride to see them return carrying food.

It might help them warm up to Sheen, too, if I let them think it was her idea.

Nighteyes scraped cassowary feathers from her tongue and turned to Sheen when something struck her. There was a scent on the wind. An oily scent she couldn't quite place.

She stood and walked to her glyph, staring out at the misty world beyond. There was something there, she could feel it. There was *someone* there.

"Sheen, we need to go." Nighteyes' voice was a soft growl. Surely, no gryphon was stupid enough to cross into the Emerald Jungle. But if they did, what happened next would be a bloodbath.

"But the food!" Sheen protested. "We can't leave it unguarded. The gryphlets need it."

Nighteyes swatted Sheen, and they'd nearly gotten into the air when an opinicus burst through the Emerald Veil.

It's a...duck? The intruder's green head shone in the sunlight. His brown body was covered in a strange harness marked with a fiery lamp that smelled of oil and smoke.

One outsider was unfortunate, but through the shimmer came ten more; gryphons this time. Some sort of cave gryphon, though not one of the oilbirds. They were small and black, covered in soot and carrying large, coarse sacks with their forepaws while they landed on their back paws and set them down.

As they turned and shifted, their tails were visible. They had both the long fuzzy tail of a gryphon with the feathery, fanned tail of an opinicus over top of it. The feathers ended in long, deadly-looking spikes.

Not ten, twenty. One of the sacks wriggled, and a

chubby, adorable oilbird gryphlet poked her head out with a squeak. Well, it was more of a hellish cry, but the *cute* version of a hellish cry.

The altruism hit Sheen first. She turned, let out a hiss, and attacked mindlessly, latching her tomia into the duck opinicus.

The bristle-tailed cave gryphons worked to divest themselves of their gryphlet packages, running to pull Sheen off their guide.

That was when Nighteyes' own altruism kicked in. Or, rather, it kicked her out. She felt like she was in one of those dreams where she was seeing through the eyes of a purple squirrel, able only to watch and not act.

She rushed straight for one of the crying oilbird gryphlets, praying the entire time someone stopped her. One of the bristles tackled her, and now she had a new fear—for her own life.

Sheen was small and fast, and she'd wriggled free of her attackers and was leaving them bloodied. The nightskies had an advantage over the refugees, who looked like they'd been on the run for days carrying heavy gryphlets.

As Nighteyes clawed and bit, pounced and hissed, she shouted inside her mind to let her free. When she'd watched the jadebeaks go into a frenzy during her time with the Ashen Weald, they'd seemed completely unaware of what they were doing. But Nighteyes was far too aware.

Don't let me watch Sheen kill a baby gryphlet. Don't let me watch someone kill Sheen, our darling Sheen. Don't let me watch myself kill....

The words echoed inside her prison, along with

an accusation. Wendl's elixirs had done this to her. They'd made her aware in the altruism, aware of what her body did while her mind was away.

Would it be better to wake up to several bodies, perhaps even Sheen's, and not know what happened?

Nighteyes struggled against the altruism, but the best she could manage was a moment's hesitation that allowed a bristletail to save a gryphlet from her claws. She could do nothing to save herself, and nothing to stop Sheen, who was lost to the frenzy and growing bloodier by the minute.

The mallard swore. "We need to go back! They'll bring the rest of the swarm down upon us if we kill them."

"No!" one of the bristletails countered. "There were fifty alabasters on our tail. If we turn back now, we're dead. We have to get east first. Otherwise, they'll kill the gryphlets. You think the sort of opinicus who could run a lampworks is going to show a traitor like you mercy?"

The mallard, perhaps the only opinicus who would argue against killing starlings, even if he did it out of a place of self-interest, caved in. He reached in his pack for something, some opinicus weapon, and Nighteyes tried a new tack.

Instead of trying to hold back her altruism, she channelled it, focusing on him—the only opponent without a child. Her body stood up from the bristletail it was mauling and pounced the duck, knocking the satchel out of his talons.

It's hopeless. Two starlings cannot stand against so many.

Her beak caught on his lampworks badge, saving

his life. She bit again, certain the mallard had used up the last of his luck, when an explosion wracked the Emerald Jungle.

The ground beneath the bristletails collapsed, and only their quick thinking and fast wings kept the oilbird gryphlets safe.

"Slate!" the mallard cried with relief. The starlings were no longer outnumbered five to one, they were now outnumbered twenty-to-one as adult oilbirds joined the attack, crawling out of the ground and shaking off dirt the same color as their fur.

Nighteyes' altruism did not care. Sheen, foreleg clearly broken by one of the bristletails, did not care. They would die, courtesy of a strange quirk of their biology.

With numbers on their side, the new gryphon, Slate, took a different approach. He screeched to disorient Sheen while the mallard tossed a net over her.

They managed to knock Nighteyes down, then retreated back into their hole. She stood, unsure if her own bones were intact, and gave chase.

It was dangerous to pursue cave gryphons into their burrows. Depending on how deep they were, the aboveground glyphs may not repel a starling. She begged her paws to stop, but she was running into the abyss.

A flash of light revealed the shape of a long, lithe creature, its vibrant red, green, and blue out of place in such darkness. Then another small detonation collapsed the tunnel, breaking Nighteyes' line of sight and smell from her targets.

The altruism released her, and she collapsed into

a pile of injuries, despair, and relief.

THE EXPLOSION KNOCKED something loose inside Nighteyes' mind. It began with a strange scent, one her brain refused to place, and she saw a room of opinicus paintings. Beneath one of two brown opinici with their wings around each other was Wendl.

"*You understand now, don't you? That's why there can't be a pridelord,*" Dream Wendl said. "*You will never be free while he controls you.*"

A stranger to her own mind even in the dream, she heard her own voice reply. "I agree. When the time comes, I will do what needs to be done."

Nighteyes snapped awake, her ears ringing, and coughed up smoke from the colorful creature's explosive exit. Her consciousness took a while to settle back down into her body. She wasn't sure if this was the altruism's doing or the dramatic way it ended.

She tried to move, unsuccessfully at first. Finally, she felt herself raise a paw to her beak, lick it, and groom the soot out of her ears. It was another fifteen minutes before she tried to stand, and a full thirty before she succeeded. Sheen was already on her feet, or at least three of them. She held her broken paw against her body.

"Oh, look," the bloody fledgling said. "There are some opinicus things! Wendl said she'd trade me some bracelets for them."

Nighteyes limped over to Sheen, unsure of how to proceed. Once they were beak to beak, however, she saw something in the indigo gryphon's eyes.

Awareness.

Nighteyes looked from Sheen's broken paw to the abandoned lampworks supplies and back again before she spoke. "You remember it all, don't you?"

Sheen jumped, wincing at the paw movement. "Yes. Some."

When gryphlets were in distress, there were a few tried and true methods to make them feel better, no matter how intense the despair. Nighteyes picked the easiest, and she groomed the blood, soot, and smoke from her pridemate, purring softly to reassure her.

Sheen was not so old that this was unusual, and she relaxed immediately. Though Nighteyes felt better than Sheen looked, thoughts were stirring in her brain. For a moment, she'd thought she could see the whole picture, then it had vanished when she woke up. But she remembered her conversation with Wendl. She remembered what she'd said.

Nighteyes had long suspected that months of taking Wendl's elixirs while in the Ashen Weald had done something to her. It had left her aware in moments where other starlings had blank eyes. The pridelord, the altruism: everything was just one degree off from how other starlings experienced it.

Sheen, though, remembers what happened during her altruism, too.

There were several possibilities. Perhaps the explosion, or something in the soot. Nighteyes found herself dismissing them all out of paw, as there was a much more likely explanation.

Wendl had done something to this fledgling and not told Nighteyes.

If another oilbird explosion erupts beneath me, will I

have a new vision of myself agreeing to let Wendl experiment on Sheen?

Nighteyes searched deep within herself, and she knew the answer. *Maybe.*

Maybe, because Sheen was alive and healthy. *Maybe*, because she tested positive for bloodbeak, but she wasn't dying of it.

Rage welled up like altruism inside Nighteyes, but she pushed it down. If Wendl had found a cure, why hadn't she shared it? What was going on?

She thought back to the starling opinicus sending a message to the Ashen Weald. Perhaps it would be better if Nighteyes showed up at the Newmoon Pride's home and demanded to see the reply herself, without Wendl.

First, however, she needed to make sure Sheen was okay.

The smell of distressed starlings pulled the Nightsky Pride and several blue and green starlings from the northwestern jungle to their location to help, the sky fluttering in a rainbow of colors.

The first gryphon to land was one of her own pride, who looked from the cassowaries to the smoking crater and asked, "Did one of the birds explode?"

The second gryphon who arrived was an unusual one, as his pride was supposed to be visiting the capital. The second *gryphon* to land was actually an opinicus, Wendl's friend Balthar, who scooped up the mallard's things as if he thought Nighteyes couldn't see him, then fled into the Sparkwing Pride's old territory.

14

―――――

FIREFLY

After sleeping and eating to recover from her bite wound, Whisper decided it was time to visit the southeastern edge of newmoon lands. She'd asked Blinky to leave the reply at the Jadebeak Falls, but Whisper hadn't visited it before and only knew it from the scent trails left by others.

She perched atop the Jadebeak Mountains, at the top of the waterfall, and took it all in. This place was a strange scent anomaly, a location with both Ashen Weald and Nightsky smells. Technically, the top of the falls were Emerald Jungle, but the pheromones on every tree warned starlings to stay away.

I wonder if I can convince the Ashen Weald to call it the Newmoon Falls since it begins in my territory now.

She descended the mountains, landing above a cave. The fragrance of owl gryphon was too fresh, so she didn't go inside. Instead, she waited for one to materialize.

Blinky stepped out from the entrance, dropping the scroll case. Whisper had asked them to leave the scroll case on its own, but she wasn't surprised by the turn of events. The glacier owls who visited Moth-feather had also been bad at taking orders. It was something she'd admired about them during her rebellious phase, and it highlighted a small problem with her current pride. No one ever told her no.

"There is a traitor in the jungle." The owl gryphon did not explain where her information came from. "I do not know how, but it is true. The Nighthaunt knows what is going on with the starlings while we do not."

Whisper expected this to be the precursor of asking a favor, and she tried a soothing gryphmint smell to dissuade the owl.

Blinky immediately put both forepaws over her small beak and glared at Whisper, who laughed and gestured for the owl gryphon to move upwind.

As Blinky passed by, Whisper inhaled the owl's essence, memorizing it. The last time they'd met, thornvines and hanging moss had made it hard to tell what her true scent was.

"You should tell us what is going on," the owl continued. "The Nighthaunt knows. We should know."

Whisper tilted her head, curious at the owl logic. "I can't disobey the pridelord. He wouldn't want anyone to know. The solution is to kill the spy, not for me to spy for you."

Blinky considered this. "That is fine. Promise you will tell Wendl."

Whisper didn't have time to answer, as the owl gryphon vanished. Rather, she flew off, forgetting Whisper was downwind from her, and hid in a tree.

Now that Whisper had Blinky's scent, she could tell where the owl was.

The newmoon gryphon shrugged, took the new scroll case, and returned to the mountains. Near the Jadebeak Falls was a Nightsky Pride glyph. Though Whisper's scent had overridden most of Nighteyes' old markers, she'd forgotten about their physical appearance. She licked her paw a few times, transferring the eyeshine to it, and put her silver pawprint over the nightsky purple.

Now that Desert Rose had been recovered, and Wendl would soon have her scroll, Whisper could go back to tending to the susurration. She was ready to relax. What she'd heard from the alabasters had worried her, but not enough to act.

The winds coming from the north reeked of carrion, and she adjusted her flight to look into it. Fresh was better, but meat was meat, and the recently cured jadebeaks were ravenous, having wasted away to nearly nothing. They ate like mothfeathers approaching Final Twilight.

I haven't thought about Final Twilight in years. Where did that come from?

She solved the invasive thoughts problem the way she solved most: by landing and sniffing around. Her focus narrowed to just smell, and she realized where the memories had come from.

One grove north, her eyes confirmed what her nares already knew: more dead blackwings, forty or fifty of them. Unlike at the southern edge of the border, there were no signs of struggle. They'd just been dumped here, though the reason why eluded her.

The perfume of rotting meat and blackwing soldiers wasn't what had given her thoughts of Final Twilight, however. She searched the bodies until she found what she was looking for: a scratch toy in the shape of a giant teratorn.

Approaching Final Twilight, it was common for the inhabitants of the Sleeping City to leave their scent on trinkets to give to their non-mothfeather loved ones who would have to brave the winter with eyes open. One of Whisper's older siblings had a spouse from the neighboring Goldtree Gardens, and they exchanged blankets.

A teratorn scratch toy wasn't the sort of thing exchanged from one lover to another. There was a chick or fledgling who would awake on First Morning with one fewer parent.

A small voice in Whisper's head, masculine and with a mothfeather ranch accent, told her to bury the dead. All it took to drown out that voice was a whisper.

Meat is meat. Whatever befell these blackwings, their bodies will sustain my charges. She adjusted her scent for the next gust of wind, and her featherdust carried word to her pride that there was food to be had here.

Despite herself, she was shaken up by the thought of the mothfeather chick. She only snapped out of it when she flew past one of her jade pridemates, the one who insisted on wearing a leaf hat, and she was struck by an alarming scent, citrus so strong it pulled her out of her own mind, forcing her to land and curl up.

The pridelord's messages arrived in bursts of

information. The scents came in three: *You, gryphon out of place, explain.*

She waited for the citrus to clear. The message came via a dozen jadebeaks in the jungle southwest of her who didn't even realize they were relaying the commands of their leader before the message echoed through her pride. Starlings had a way of not understanding a scent meant for someone else.

When the smell of lemons drifted away, she sent her own reply, relayed through the jadebeaks: *Yesterday, lost gryphon, united, today, forty kills of food for pride, rest, tomorrow, repair, Emerald Veil.*

The pridelord didn't ask more questions. He'd never once asked her to explain or rephrase. He always assumed every starling replied honestly, as they could not lie to him.

Two more scents overtook her. The first was *problem,* the second was the unique smell of a specific jadebeak. Then he was gone, back to whatever it was he did in his temple.

Whisper queried the nearby jadebeaks. They all know the smell, could tell her specific information about their problematic pridemate, but none knew where she currently was.

The newmoon gryphon sighed. Had more jadebeaks left the murmuration? The pridelord would take that personally. But then, faint, to the southeast, just on the jadebeak side of her border with them, came the barest flicker of a scent.

Ah, there you are, little Flicker. Not gone yet, are you?

It was an interesting opportunity. This could be a jadebeak in the process of leaving the murmuration. There was much to learn.

While her pride went north for their feast of blackbirds, Whisper requested entry into Jadebeak territory. Scent communication was a mix of conscious and subconscious for other starlings, and sometimes they didn't seem aware they were doing it. Her hidden salt paths would be too slow for this project.

The responses were instinctual and spoke to how jadebeaks felt about her personally. As the message was relayed, she got back a hundred scents that boiled down to *no, mallow root pheromones, go away*. They reached Iri, the new leader of the Jadebeak Pride after the previous one became disconnected and was torn apart in the winter, whose *no* and *go away* were particularly pungent.

Whisper laughed. Some things never changed, though she appreciated the honesty and straightforwardness of pheromones over family dinner back home any day.

Then the pridelord's overriding response came in, and every starling, including Iri, sent back a *yes*.

A gryphon with silver eyes, silver markings, and black fur casually walked across her southern border and into the land of jade sparkles and bad attitudes.

Where are you, little Flicker? I am here to save you.

Being in the Jadebeak territory, the true Jadebeak territory and not her hidden salt path, was a strange experience for Whisper. The glyphs and spiketrunks helped shield her from the *quotidienne* thoughts of her green neighbors.

She quickly learned that the most popular pieces of information shared throughout their pride were about squirrels. Everywhere she went, she'd hear an echo across the pride that someone had stumbled upon a popular squirrel. The jadebeaks even had names, or at least unique scent markers, for each of them.

Once the pridelord had commanded his favorites to let Whisper in, the jadebeaks warmed up a bit. Their version of friendliness was a kind of scent list of all the squirrels they'd seen that day. She thought, at first, they were sharing this information to hunt the squirrels for food. It quickly became apparent that no one was allowed to hurt the named squirrels, and this reinforcement of where they were located was to deter accidental squirrel deaths.

It was as endearing as it was useless.

She flew past a hunting party of three, and when they chirped, she felt obliged to land. She asked them about Flicker, but they ignored her. She modified her approach, instead telling them about a particularly acrobatic squirrel she'd come across by a pond, one who was very good at hopping across tree branches.

Squirrel came the scent from each of them. They told her about the squirrels they'd seen on their hunts. Apparently, they'd nicknamed a particularly large, territorial fiend the *squirrel pridelord.*

They'd best hope he doesn't find out.

She tried again, asking about Flicker, and this time they gave her all the information they knew. Mostly, their knowledge was about Flicker's past life, growing up as their pridemate. One of her parents had been from the western starling prides, the same one Talli was now a member of, and her plumage was red despite the fact she'd decided to stay as a jadebeak. There were enough small prides who had been absorbed by jadebeaks that a red, blue, or even grey gryphon didn't look out of place among them. Sadly, this set of jadebeaks didn't know her current whereabouts.

Whisper thanked them and continued on. She decided to use her specialized sense of smell to avoid further interruptions. She'd last caught Flicker's scent somewhere in the east, along the border. Whisper began her search there, hoping to stumble across signs of distress. Instead, she disturbed the squirrel pridelord, who chased her away.

The flicker of scent appeared again, somewhere nearby, and Whisper replied with her own pheromones, but it vanished.

That's what happened last time. What if I remain true to my name?

She suppressed her own pheromones and waited. The squirrel pridelord threw an acorn at her, bouncing it off her head, and she wondered if she could eat the purple rodent or if the jadebeaks would notice it was missing.

When Flicker returned, this time Whisper didn't respond but narrowed in on the scent. She tracked it like a gryphlet chasing a firefly on a moonless night. The jadebeak was moving, but not far. She appeared a few times at a stream. Perhaps whatever was wrong with her had made her thirsty. Either way, Whisper would have her soon.

The newmoon gryphon crawled through the jungle, between the ferns and broadleafs, until she came to a clearing. The soil had been turned, grass and fern removed from it, and a jadebeak hummed a song to herself while digging in the dirt. Several long, waxy leaves full of water sat by the holes.

The malfunctioning gryphon wasn't green but instead the bright red of a tomato.

No, not a tomato, a strawberry.

Her white speckles completed the look, small dots across her berry-colored feathers. Mud obscured much of the gryphon's lower half, but when she scratched her flank on a tree, the fur beneath was red, though a duller shade. Her tail trailed behind her at twice the length of most starlings, more akin to what the cave gryphons had.

Whisper had seen red fur before, or at least orange, from travelers staying overnight at the Mothfeather Eyrie. Orange was the color of pitohui or motmots, always paired with rosettes, stripes, or spots. Flicker's hindquarters lacked markings, at least as far as the dirt let Whisper tell.

Flicker was an unusual starling. Whisper allowed her mallow root marker to resume, and the jadebeak vanished from her nares again.

Curious.

The newmoon pride leader walked loudly through two palm bushes, not wanting to startle her quarry. Reactions to her from the lost ranged from relief to fear, depending on if they expected her to fix them or take them away.

The jadebeak, however, shouted at her with annoyance. "Hey, watch my pumpkins!"

Whisper blinked, taken aback. She stepped off the

dirt, walking around the perimeter, and approached the jadebeak again.

"You think it's easy growing bog plants in the jungle?" Flicker protested.

Whisper did not. She'd attended university to be a scholar, sure, but she'd come from the stretch of farm-lands east of Mothfeather. She'd grown up around berry farmers and goliath ranchers, and she had an appreciation for how hard the work was. It had been part of what connected her to Wendl, who'd grown up with capybaras and crops, when they'd met as apprentices.

Whisper just hadn't been expecting to find a gryphon attempting to grow pumpkins in the middle of a jungle. Other than Wendl's hidden herb gardens and Balthar's mislaid attempts at growing squirrel-brush, the starlings didn't seem to have much interest in agriculture.

The jadebeak chattered on about soil conditions and how hard it was to get her pridemates to save the seeds from the pumpkins they'd stolen from the bog.

Whisper cleared her head. "You, Flicker. Stop speaking. We have things to discuss."

The farmer paused. "Well, discussing *requires* speaking. Wait, why did you call me Flicker? Is that a pet name? Are we mates?"

The newmoon gryphon wasn't sure if she were being flirted with, if this gryphon had actually forgotten she had a mate, or if this was just a weird side effect of whatever condition was disconnecting her from the murmuration. But she was pretty sure the jadebeak had no conscious idea what she was doing when she hid her scent.

"Do you feel the murmuration?" Whisper asked.

"What? Of course I do," Flicker said, and in that moment her scent reappeared, queried the other jadebeaks, all of whom then sent messages to Whisper that roughly translated to *Oh hey, we found that gryphon you wanted us to find, she's right next to you. Also, we found that jumping squirrel you like, he's going south.* Then Flicker's smell vanished again.

"Come here," Whisper commanded, pushing the citrus.

Despite the urgency of the command, Flicker ignored her.

"Flicker," Whisper said, and the jadebeak's scent reappeared, and the citrus kicked in enough to bring her across the pumpkin patch.

Whisper examined Flicker's eyes. There was no sign of infection, no sign of sickness at all. She tried a few scents, but Flicker was gone again, the firefly vanishing in the night. Citrus made starlings obedient, but this strange pumpkin farmer was the opposite of compliant.

In fact, Flicker looked curiously into Whisper's eyes, then began critiquing the newmoon's silver paint markings, complimenting her medicine bag, and recommending several types of nut oil that would clear up her featherdust problem.

"Flicker, stop talking," Whisper commanded, pushing the citrus again. She stared very intently into the jadebeak's eyes.

Flicker licked Whisper's beak.

The newmoon gryphon was taken aback. Flicker's scent appeared again, but the mallow root of surprise had already drowned out the citrus.

"Oh! I'm so sorry. *Is* Flicker your pet name for me? I *thought* maybe we were mates. I didn't *remember* having a mate, but then I thought, well, maybe that's because she's a newmoon gryphon. Maybe I've been neglecting her this entire time, and then she had to come all the way down to my pumpkin patch! That felt very embarrassing, and now I can see how flustered you are."

Flicker's scent remained while she spoke, sending emotions to Whisper, and vanished when she stopped speaking.

"Isn't mating season over?" the strawberry jadebeak continued. "Or...No, there's still a day left for newmoons, right?"

Flicker was a curiosity. Most starlings were constantly receiving and sending information through smells. And when Flicker spoke, she did send out that underlying information. When she seemed worried about Whisper, she could also take in the information. But there was no way to order her or force her to answer questions in between those moments.

Whisper remained quiet, trying scents that just bounced off Flicker, gathering information when she spoke. She was, by every metric, a healthy starling. No hint of Wendl's alchemy or any environmental causes showed up in her smell. Using the jadebeak network to answer questions about Flicker's past, it seemed that she had grown up normal. This *firefly effect* had started last year. She had few friends, so no one had really noticed until now.

The scent of the word *friends* happened to get through when Flicker was talking. "I'm pretty sure we are friends, now that I see you up close. Oh! I love your paw decoration. Were we mates last year, too? I'll bet we were."

"No," Whisper said at last. "We were not mates last year, and we're not mates this year."

She emitted a scent of finality, but Flicker was dark when it hit and wasn't affected.

"Hey, not with *that* attitude!" Flicker protested. "But there's a little time in the season left, right? It's not every day a pretty newmoon takes a stroll down my pumpkin patch, if you know what I mean. Oh! Do I have a cute nickname for you, too?"

"Whisper," the newmoon gryphon began, but she didn't have time to explain it wasn't a cute nickname before Flicker's beak opened, filling the air with her loud vibrancy.

"Ah, that's really adorable! Because you're so soft spoken, right? That's just the sort of name I'd think of. Hey, *Whisper,* want to go back to my place and be mates for a day?"

The pridelord's order to fix this problem clung to the forefront of Whisper's mind. But there was another voice, too, that came from within her. Part of holding a susurration together required a lot of strong smells and stronger orders, especially for the gryphons who had lost their minds to the infection and couldn't take care of themselves without her gentle reminders. She had to set compulsions every few days to keep them going so they didn't die from neglect.

Having a mate who could just choose to ignore her held a certain appeal.

And besides, it's one day. Judging by how often she

forgets mates, she's not going to come looking for me in the autumn.

"Fine." Whisper sighed. She needed at least another day to figure this out, anyways. "What do you require from a mate?"

Flicker gestured to the fields. "I *require* help planting all of these seeds! And getting water from the creek. That, too."

Whisper's father had always said, *Son, you should settle down with a nice mate and grow crops.* It was strange that, in the end, he was getting his wish.

Whisper tossed the herb bag and scroll case next to a makeshift nest, presumably Flicker's, and got to work digging new holes and fetching water while Flicker planted seeds. Every time her new mate spoke, which wasn't often as pumpkin planting was hard work, Whisper got a little more information from her pheromones.

By the time the planting was done, they curled up under the stars and slept.

15

THE WHISPERER AND THE DARKNESS

The next morning, Whisper rolled herself out of the nest and onto dirty paws sore from digging. She could feel her grace period in the Jadebeak territory fading, and she had yet to do anything about Flicker.

She looked down at her mate, snoring softly, and considered her options. Whisper could try to overwhelm Flicker with scents and rewrite the abnormal part of her brain to stay on. Flicker had spent most of her life as fully part of the murmuration, so she was capable of it, or at least had been.

She seems happy, though. Perhaps just a little nudge, so she connected with jadebeaks more often? It seemed to go against Whisper's overriding goal of making the murmuration happy and healthy to mess around inside another already content starling's identity.

She slipped the herb bag over her head. The rope, stolen from dead opinici in the bog on a rescue mission, had once been white. After spending so much time with her, featherdust had turned it black, and now most gryphons didn't see it against her fur.

Flicker, too, was covered in featherdust. Just a little, just a night's worth, so it would wash off. Then she'd forget Whisper had ever been here.

The newmoon gryphon weighed her options. Often, her choices came fast, more of a reflex, without the luxury of sitting and thinking through things first. None of the starlings she dealt with allowed her more than a moment to make a call—Desert Rose had taken a bite out of her shoulder, after all, and he was far from the only infected starling to try to murder her.

She nuzzled her single-day mate. "Flicker, it's time for me to go home."

The red jadebeak looked up at Whisper, who almost expected Flicker to have forgotten she had a mate by now. "Oh! You're right. Come back next autumn, won't you?"

I was pretty sure she wouldn't want to be mates again, Whisper thought, then realized what Flicker was getting at. "Ah, you'll need help with the pumpkin harvest."

Flicker slow blinked. "Yep! You save lost starlings, right? The calming eyeshine makes you look less scary to them? I'll have a lot of pumpkins ready for you by then, and you can use them to save more. We make a great team."

Huh. Whisper had underestimated Flicker. "I need you to do something for me. As one mate to another, at least until the moon fades."

The jadebeak rolled over and stretched. Her white

tummy had been smudged dark grey. "I'll probably forget, you know. I have a lot of things on my mind."

"This is important." Whisper put her paws on Flicker's cheeks. "The pridelord can't always sense you, and that makes him nervous. I'm going to teach you to massage your scent glands, and I want you to put a pawprint on the tree outside your pumpkin patch while you're here. That's enough that he won't bother you."

To her credit, Flicker said she would. If she didn't, Whisper would hear about it and be sent back. *No sense worrying about something that hasn't happened yet. I almost envy Flicker. She's the only starling who can get some peace and quiet.*

The newmoon gryphon began her trek north. Despite her best efforts to avoid any jadebeaks, a few caught her scent and hurried to tell her about the latest squirrel drama.

Squirrel, pridelord, squirrel, leaper, big fight.

By the time she reached home, she had a mental map of how the squirrel territorial markers had changed. The squirrel pridelord was out, overthrown by a small jumpy thing with a bad attitude.

By the time Whisper was back at her nest, she'd completely forgotten about the scroll case and its contents. Had Wendl been nearby, perhaps she would have remembered, but her friend's strange burst of aroma had come at a cave on the far side of Nightsky territory, so it was unlikely she'd visit anytime soon.

Whisper closed her eyes and ignored her

second-in-command's words while she let his pheromones catch her up on what had happened in her absence. Moonlit Blossom remained suspicious of Whisper, but he wasn't trying to hide that from her. She subtly sent him a message that combined a peppery *danger* with the smell of marshmallow, and he stopped talking long enough to laugh before continuing.

Still, everything was fine, mostly. Their new territory had enough to eat thanks to the *donation* of meat from the Blackwing Eyrie. They'd located some safe winter caves not full of oilbird gryphon scents that disappeared into the darkness below. The susurration had held together in her absence. No one had died.

In the early days of saving starlings, she'd nearly given up. The ones she caught and brought home were mindless. They didn't remember who they were, and they'd wander off cliffs and forget to fly or eat. They were empty shells, husks hollowed out by small red bugs.

She shivered involuntarily. She'd seen some things on the other side of the Emerald Veil that couldn't be unseen. She'd found emaciated starlings a breath away from death, a pack of twenty of them. Many had died just upon smelling her. She'd crawled through their bodies to retrieve the one starling who could still be saved, feeling the parasite-carrying bugs crawling over her the entire time.

It was why she'd started spending more time away from the Emerald Jungle. Why she'd stolen as much of the salts as she could from abandoned dig sites. She'd spent hours with dying starlings, querying the murmuration to see if anyone remembered their name, giving them a new name if they were too far gone to be remembered.

It was hard work, and many died. The ones that survived became the susurration, starlings who were not safe to reintegrate into the murmuration, but which the pridelord permitted her to keep alive.

And, over time, hope had returned. She started catching starlings when the infection was new and she could return them to their home prides. It was a good feeling. The jadebeaks, knowing the glyphs would soon be restored when Nighteyes finished her task with the Ashen Weald, became more desperate, raiding the bogs for pumpkins to save their kin. Ironically, that led to more of them becoming infected, starting the infection-pumpkin cycle anew.

Even now, once per season, she'd bring the jadebeaks from the susurration to the border to see if anyone remembered them. It became less likely as time went by, but she held onto hope and told herself that, overall, things had gotten better.

And I expanded my search, finding...new things.

She'd hoped the caves along their border with the Argent Heights would give her new shelters, places to hide the stranger parts of her susurration. Unfortunately, the caves out here were not as empty as she'd expected, which the Nightsky Pride would have known if they'd patrolled their borders better. Oilbirds, wild beasts, even some ornery ptarmigans had taken over the caves, along with pheromones she'd never smelled before.

The scent of starberries reached Whisper's nares, and she stood, reapplying the silver sheen over her eyes. Eyeshine made it harder for her to see, certainly, but she had her sense of smell. And it was worth the decoration to dissuade nightsky starlings from coming to visit, as one was about to do now.

She shifted her scent to something bitter, warning the susurration to get out of sight. Then she moved away from the old expedition ruins. She suspected Nighteyes had been part of whatever had gone on there.

The violet-backed, starry-eyed leader landed inside the Newmoon Pride's territory without invitation, and Whisper felt the pheromone equivalent of a *hiss* come from her pridemates.

"Hail, Nighteyes of the Nightsky Pride, most violet of all starlings," Whisper drawled. She kept her scent at the proper level of respect but took liberties with words since most starlings didn't listen to them.

"Whisper." Nighteyes did not look happy. Upon closer inspection, she'd been attacked. Blood stained patches of her white fur Flicker red, especially around her stomach.

Whisper sniffed. Some of it was Nighteyes' own, but others were from opinici and cave gryphons. She was angry, but something simmered under the anger. Whisper resisted the urge to fluff her tail up large and imposing in response. It was unlikely Nighteyes was upset with Whisper specifically.

"Have you heard back from the Ashen Weald?" Nighteyes asked.

Whisper slipped the scroll case off her neck. "I was saving it for Wendl."

She wasn't protesting, of course. The message would have ended up with Nighteyes all the same. But it was a shot in the dark that because Nighteyes only knew Whisper through Wendl, her friend may be the real target of the other pride leader's anger. The scent she got in response to her barb confirmed it.

Interesting.

Nighteyes opened the scroll case. Inside was vellum. Whisper found herself reaching for it out of scribal instinct before pulling back. Most days and nights, she didn't miss being an opinicus. The one thing she missed was being able to write. She could scrawl out short messages with a long claw if she dulled it a little first to keep it from cutting a leaf or some lost paper from an Alabaster Eyrie scout, but it was slow going.

Nighteyes unrolled the vellum, and Whisper put a paw at the top to hold it open, smudging it with her featherdust. While the author of the message was unknown, where it had come from was unmistakable. It was written—by a claw much more deft than her own—in bog blossom blue.

Oh, not an unknown author. Someone named Soft Paws signed it at the end.

The introduction was a plea to reopen diplomacy with the starlings, as though either Nighteyes or Whisper had that power. Whisper skimmed to see if there was anything interesting, finding a note about Piprik being unavailable because he'd gone back to Blacktalon, but Nighteyes went straight to the end and read it aloud.

"We are, through careful use of weald medicines, able to keep them alive just past fledging. But no one with bloodbeak is doing well. Kia hoped to study the New Eyrie refugees Mally reactivated the disorder in.

They, too, are starting to die off. As of now, there is no hope. Signed, Soft Paws."

Nighteyes' despondency was a powerful perfume. "So that's it. Even when they keep them alive long enough to fledge, they're weak and near death, without exception. Just like here."

"Mmm." Whisper could detect a slight deception, though she didn't know what that meant. "We don't know if there are exceptions here. The other starling prides were more careful about who was allowed to have gryphlets. And without Wendl's help, their gryphlets died before fledging. The Nightsky Pride owes her much."

Nighteyes didn't reply, but instead shook out the scroll case. Scraps of missives fell out. All of them had owl bite marks on them, probably stolen from unwary Argent Heights messengers. They didn't mean anything to Whisper.

Whale attacks on the rise in the southern ocean.

Famous gourd thief strikes again.

The Fanged Beast of Poisonmaw.

WANTED: Reeve Rybalt Reevesbane and Iony. Long believed dead, but recently spotted near Blacktalon.

A vague sketch of something called a seraph in brown and red, inquiries into whose offspring they are, with a reminder that all seraphs must be registered with Hi-kun.

Bloodbeak on the rise, are you doing your part?

Padfootery afoot near Reevesport! Reward for information regarding bandits calling themselves the 'Tree Cobras.'

The Starling Menace, a pamphlet on how to keep yourself safe from 'wild starlings' when visiting Alwren or King's Reach.

Warnings not to come within 50 miles of the northern blood coast on pain of death by order of the Portmaster.

Whisper shrugged. She'd expected to care about Blacktalon, but that life was so far away, she couldn't bring herself to. She wondered if it would be different had there been an article about the Sleeping City.

I should warn Flicker about the gourd thief. It says here he's pink. Maybe a flamingo?

Whisper cast a suspicious glance at Nighteyes, but her violet visitor continued to be mad at something Whisper couldn't pinpoint.

"Why do you smell like fire?" she asked at last.

Nighteyes didn't answer. "What's it like being the only outsider to become a pride leader?"

It was an odd question. Not even Whisper's colleagues considered her an outsider to the starling murmuration anymore, she imagined. "I'm not the only one. Iri the First took over the jadebeaks when the previous pride leader became disconnected and was torn to pieces. Balthar's dead mate was the pride leader of the Sparkwing Pride. Had the pridelord not divided them among the other prides, he could have taken over. The sparkwings loved him. Same with Talli."

"What was that about the jadebeaks?" Nighteyes asked, but then her demeanor stiffened.

Whisper could smell the altruism welling up within Nighteyes and several of her own pride, too. She waited to see what happened, where the danger was coming from. Nighteyes struggled, trying to fight the rising urge.

If Flicker can will herself out of the murmuration to garden, perhaps this starry-eyed gryphon can do the same.

It occurred to Whisper that she could give a slight nudge to suppress Nighteyes' altruism, but Whisper decided to wait a little longer. The aroma on the wind, coming from the caves on the border with the Argent Heights, had an oily texture to it.

"No...not again!" Nighteyes managed between gritted tomia, but it was too late. She spread her wings to fly at the invaders.

Whisper pounced Nighteyes. Generally, starlings wouldn't hurt each other during the frenzy, but it was still dangerous for the newmoon gryphon to get in the way.

She held Nighteyes down and covered her in thick layers of featherdust, her white fur becoming a dark grey.

"The...altruism?" Nighteyes coughed a few times, spitting up dust.

"This is a temporary solution. You should leave before it wears off." Whisper flew to the caves with their strange scents and sounds, annoyed to hear Nighteyes follow.

A rockslide had opened up a new cave, and voices came from inside, along with the smells of fear and blood, gryphon and opinicus.

And something else.

"We have to find the satchel and get out of here," one cave gryphon shouted. He stood over a bloody white opinicus. Dark brown and grey markings wove through his thick fur and long tail. His eyes were all black, though he didn't seem to struggle seeing in the light, and his whiskers were the most pronounced Whisper had ever seen.

"Wait, I know that one. The duck opinicus called

him Slate," Nighteyes explained. "I saw him yesterday."

Another cave gryphon, this one smaller and lighter in color, nuzzled the unmoving body. "She doesn't have it. I don't think she was running *at* us, I think she was running *away from* something else."

Whisper sniffed again, and the unknown cave scent had grown. She'd smelled many things in her life, but this was unique to the old Nightsky Pride territory, something from the blackest depths, from the inverns. "This is it. This is what I've been smelling."

It was undeniable now, and even the oilbirds had its scent. The sound of something scraping against the cave walls echoed out of the loose scree and black.

"What is that sound?" Nighteyes asked.

Before they saw the creature, they saw the dead body of an oilbird gryphon come flying out of the cave, nearly torn in two.

The monster stepped into the light; it must have been ten feet tall. It stood on two legs—or stooped on two legs inside the cave, considering it didn't look that spacious. A wiry, shaggy coat covered its entire body and came down over its eyes. A long beak like a goliath bird stuck out of the fur. At the end of its forelegs were claws nearly a foot long. Thick, wicked things for burrowing through limestone.

That wasn't the strangest thing about it, however. On its back weren't the feathered wings of a gryphon or opinicus, but something much more leathery.

"What *is* that?" Nighteyes asked.

Whisper thought back to university. "That's why pregnant gryphons aren't allowed to eat bats."

The beast let out a cry that both deafened and disoriented, echoing off trees and gryphons alike, and turned to look hungrily at the body of the unconscious opinicus.

For once, the wind was in Whisper's favor. She dug her paws into the ground, thought very hard about all of the members of her susurration, and shook, sending her dust across the Nighthaunt's old ruins.

16

THE THING IN THE CAVE

Nighteyes' first thought was the creature couldn't be real. She'd seen many strange things in her time, including the Ashen Weald's sketches of the mummified opinithing. She'd never heard anything about this.

Except there were stories. Stories of what hid deep in the earth. Stories she'd assumed hinted at their northern neighbors, the gryphons of the Abyssal Naze.

That Slate and his friend were right in front of her, and they seemed just as frightened as she was, suggested they were not the origins of those myths.

Just as frightened, though not nearly as surprised.

She took a step forwards, but a terrifying sound rose up from the Newmoon Pride's nests—chittering. Newmoon gryphons, dark of coat and fluffy of tail, sprinted into action. Behind them came a legion of cured jadebeaks. Not all of their eyes focused, though at least none were silver.

One had a leaf on his head.

The jadebeaks rushed forwards, attacking the cave creature. Its claws sliced through them like chalk, and when an emaciated jadebeak finally drew blood, the beast's roar drew out two more of its kind from the caves.

Nighteyes reflexively extended her claws. Whisper's paws were still, but she shook out her coat, filling the air with a slight sparkle. Where the pridelord needn't expend any effort to control the entire murmuration, the newmoon leader struggled to control a single pride of starlings.

But it wasn't just starlings. Beyond the jadebeaks came new gryphons. Some still had silver stains under their eyes, perhaps the same bunch Whisper had been escorting when Nighteyes found her days ago. And behind them came opinici. Nighteyes recognized an Alabaster Eyrie harness. A contingent of the white-tailed kites had chased Khalim into the jungle, where Erlock Fantail and the jadebeaks ambushed them.

And it looks like some tried to hide there, succumbing to the infection before being collected by Whisper. How has she hidden this from the other prides? Surely they'd be very interested in non-starlings inside our jungle.

Nighteyes' brain wove a different tale, however. Their pheromones told her they were newmoon gryphons even as her eyes showed her alabaster opinici. There were more gryphons, too, that her eyes warned her could not be part of a murmuration.

No cave gryphons—though Whisper could be hiding them from Slate—but there was a gryphon in the shape of a frost chicken or ptarmigan. Nighteyes had met the taiga pride during her time with the

Ashen Weald, and the snowy gryphons of the eastern mountains didn't look like that. There were even a few argent hawks with the murmuration.

Not murmuration, susurration. She's controlling them all, starling and non-starling alike. If she can control ptarmigan gryphons and silver hawks, what's to stop her from converting the entire Ashen Weald into 'starlings'?

One of the new creatures lumbered from the cave at the oilbird gryphons. Slate's friend seemed to have a hurt wing, and Slate flew up and harried the clawed beast to slow it down, only just pulling up his paws in time to keep from having them swiped off.

I wonder if those bat wings let it fly?

Nighteyes chirped a warning to Whisper to help, but the newmoon gryphon appeared as mindless as her susurration. Nighteyes tried something new, trying to give off specific warning pheromones before rushing to the cave gryphons' aid.

She didn't know if it worked or not, but the frost chicken and more cured jadebeaks appeared to help the cave gryphons.

Hopefully, she dusted her pride with anti-altruism smells or this could get messy.

Slate was swatted out of the air, landing hard on his forepaws. When he saw her rushing towards his friend, he hurried to intercept, using his back legs and wings. "Chert, be careful! It's the pink one from earlier."

It took a claw to the face from *Chert* for Nighteyes to realize that, to a gryphon from beyond the Emerald Veil, a rushing starling could never mean a friend. They could only mean danger.

"Stop!" she protested. "The altruism is gone for

now. Can we drag your friend to a cave? Do you have a safe way out?"

Slate was nonplussed by her speech. "You're...not altruistic?"

"Hey, yes! Kia said one of the purples could leave the swarm sometimes, right? There's a hidden path to the naze northwest of here, through the heavy ferns," Chert chirped. "If we can get in there, we'll be safe. It's a straight shot to the naze, no alabasters or clawdiggers know about it. I don't know if I can walk *or* fly. That darkstalker got me good."

Whatever a *darkstalker* was, Nighteyes had no idea. Presumably the bloody opinicus body the inverns clawdigger had nearly eaten. "Yeah, get on my back. Your friend doesn't look great either. Slate, was it? Can you help me carry her?"

When the older cave gryphon landed, he could only walk with a limp. "Wings're fine, but I hit the ground too hard. Already had a smashed paw from when a tunnel collapsed on us. Must have been those clawdiggers. I'll try to help Chert get on top of you."

Though the monsters were large and deadly, there were only three of them. The susurration was starting to beat them back. One already lay dead, and even though Nighteyes knew Whisper's gryphons had all been cured, their brains still acted infected. Several jadebeaks were eating the deceased cave monster.

"Chert's heavy. Where are we going?" Nighteyes asked.

Chert protested the assessment of her weight. "I filled up on water before we left, like the safety guide said to! Um, through the break in those trees there."

Slate flew short distances, landing carefully on his

back paws. "The cave's on the other side, beyond the jungle's edge. Can you cross? It's past those limestone spikes up ahead."

"I'm not sure." Nighteyes used to inspect this land when it was part of her hunting territory all the time, but she'd never seen limestone spikes. Nor had she noticed the scent of monsters, but perhaps they had come in later. She followed Slate's gaze and was surprised to see a path and what appeared to be thin spires rising up out of the ground like a caiman's teeth.

Did Whisper's dust protect me from the glyph markers, too?

There was only one way to find out. Nighteyes carried Chert across the Emerald Veil and into the treacherous landscape of the Abyssal Naze.

By the time the monsters had been fended off, Whisper was a mess. She shook, covered in sweat and barely able to stand. Moonlit Blossom carefully helped unbury her paws from where she'd stress-kneaded them into the dirt and guided her to a trough of water they kept filled for the cured.

She drank deeply, threw up, then tried again at a slower pace. She tried to send reassuring scents to her pridemates, but nothing came. She'd practiced controlling the infected in the past, teaching them to hunt as a pack, but it had never been this difficult. Suppressing their altruism and stopping them from attacking the cave gryphons or Nighteyes had taken all she had in her.

That she'd even had to persuade some of the jade-beaks not to attack Nighteyes had frightening implications. The susurration was ceasing to be a subset of the greater starling community. It was becoming its own murmuration.

It's the same ones I let eat the dead blackwings. Maybe they're just not cured enough yet? She didn't have the energy to query them, and it left her wondering if anything like this had happened in the past. Spiketrunks of the sort that lined her salted paths took generations to grow as large as they currently were.

Even the previous Whisper wouldn't have been around when they were planted and glyphed, though it seemed like she was the one who started salting the path. Starlings didn't conceive of long periods of time the way eyries did, and the current Whisper couldn't find information on how long the moon prides had been around. She'd seen the crescent glyphs along the path, and some of the older jade-beaks she'd acquired had memory of a Crescent-moon Pride.

Did the final leader of the Crescentmoon Pride find themselves in a similar situation, watching their susurration strain to break free of the murmuration? If so, where did the susurration go afterwards? Whisper was left with visions of black fire ant colonies being wiped out by red.

Moonlit Blossom slipped under one of her wings to hold her up, sending the calming scent of mint her way and calling to their pridemates. Thankfully, the other spotless starlings knew how to manage the susurration and wrangled their more colorful pridemates back to the nests. They'd also tend to the wounded as best they could.

What I wouldn't give to have Wendl here now with her talons and bandages.

Moonlit Blossom, using a trick she'd taught him, tried to use his pheromones to force her to sleep, but she rustled up enough of a scent to override him. If they were going to live in this stretch of the jungle, she needed to know what she was up against. She did, however, permit him to guide her to the dead bodies.

Three cave beasts, two dead. The third had retreated, leaving a trail of blood behind it. One had been chewed beyond recognition by jadebeaks, specifically those she'd pulled out of a den that had nearly starved to death. They were the reason she'd been forced to convert the infected snowfoot gryphon and alabaster eyrie opinici into starlings. If she hadn't, the jadebeaks would have torn them apart and eaten them before they were cured.

She looked from the chewed monster to the mostly intact beast to the dead body of an alabaster stranger. The opinicus didn't smell dead, but Whisper's senses were too tired to function properly.

"Call the alabaster starlings here," she ordered Moonlit Blossom. She was careful to use *starling* after their name, and had she the strength, she'd have used her featherdust to reinforce that. Sometimes the cured jadebeaks still looked at them like they might be food.

She nuzzled the paw of the cave beast, flipping it over so she could get a good look at its claws. She'd seen the interior of the caves here, and she'd assumed the weird striations along the walls were the result of erosion or an underwater river that had long run dry. Now, she saw where these foot-long claws could have carved through the softer rock.

They didn't invade my territory. I was living in theirs. Or perhaps they came in after the incident with the naze and weald?

The bite marks bothered her. "Tell five others, the least wounded, to go pick castor plants. Find the starlings who ate this creature and force them to eat the castor until they vomit. Then bury the meat. No gryphon eats...whatever this is."

Moonlit Blossom gave the olfactory equivalent of a frown. "Why? You had no problem letting them eat the opinici, and the prey out here won't last forever. There's a lot of meat on a creature so large."

She *tsk*'d. "Do male gryphons not know this? You do not eat bats, squirrels, capybaras, or whales while pregnant. This season's eggs are already laid, but I do not want to risk it."

Several female members of her pride who'd come to gather the castor plants nodded.

"Is this some sort of bat?" one asked, examining the wings. "I've seen carvings of them at the temple, but I didn't know they were real."

There was a time when Whisper hadn't known about avoiding fuzzy creatures or whales. She didn't know if the elixir's transformation would let her bear offspring, but she knew better than to risk it. As far as she remembered from keeping the Nighthaunt's notes, the sex problem was the first thing he'd solved.

It wasn't even a problem that needed solving. He'd added an alkaline mixture to the salts to try to increase their potency, and the sex change had been a side effect. He'd discarded the mixture then and there, and she'd had to pull it from the trash.

No sense tempting fate. I have my own adopted gryphlets now. With silver eyes, chittering beaks, and a murderous streak.

Whisper realized they were staring at her. "Looks like bat wings to me, though I've only ever seen their skeletons. I think this was once a gryphon who fed upon bats and..."

"Capybaras," Moonlit Blossom chimed in. "It's fuzzy like capybara fur."

Whisper had never seen a capybara with foot-long claws, but she supposed anything was possible. "Drag the other one to the Newmoon Falls and push it over so no one is tempted to eat it."

If the outsiders can toss blackwings over our side of the fence, surely they won't mind if we toss a dead...whatever this is...to their side.

The alabaster starlings arrived, worse for wear but still alive. They weren't happy to be here, in the Emerald Jungle, as starlings. Still, if not for her, they'd have died in the bog. She'd pulled them from a cave near the Jadebeak Falls, expecting them to be jadebeaks. While she couldn't control, say, an owl gryphon beyond overwhelming their senses, the infection had emptied out parts of these opinici's minds, and she'd been able to fill it. She'd done one as a trial, and he'd begged her to go save his friend, too.

She decided to give them a little test and brought them to the body of the alabaster. Up close, she could see it was still breathing, if barely. She needed to know if she should save it or not.

The alabasters hurried to the body like a starling

rushing to the aid of another starling. But when they saw its—*her*—face, they recoiled.

Whisper could smell fear and respect from them. Disgust and subservience. She was intrigued. She examined the eyes of the wounded, and it was like looking into a twisted mirror.

The stranger's white-tailed kite markings dripped like black ink, to the point where Whisper wiped them to see if they were painted on like hers were.

They're not. The feathers are growing in dark.

The opinicus' eyes were black, and there was stubble where long whiskers had been trimmed. She wore a sturdy harness, thick and practical, but the metal talons over her natural ones were a swirled silver the craftsmanship of which rivaled anything Whisper had seen.

She sniffed the talons. Oilbird blood. The design of the metalwork appeared to be the style of the best blacksmiths at Blacktalon, but the ore was too pure.

The Seraph King captured Blacktalon, and the metal-works serve him now. That's the only explanation. If he took Blacktalon, Mothfeather is next.

She willed herself not to care, instead checking the wounds of the stranger. There weren't any signs of internal bleeding, though it could be hard to tell. There was a good chance she could save this opinicus.

But should I?

She tried to query the alabaster starlings, but her scent was too weak, and they refused to answer. She asked, out loud, about the metal talons. They didn't know about that, but they recognized the darkstalker's badge. The one with six wings was obvious, but she had a smaller one beneath it.

"The bloodworks," an alabaster starling said, only a slight chitter remaining in his voice. "She works for the Nighthaunt."

Voices and memories stirred within Whisper, including her own old rasp. When she'd last seen Mally, he'd been a pale falcon opinicus. She'd heard —from these two alabasters, in fact—what the Nighthaunt had become post-expedition. This *darkstalker* must have been one of his prototypes. This could have been Whisper. She shook out the dust of fear, refusing to give in to the past.

"Take her to the caves atop the Newmoon Falls," Whisper said at last. "We'll let her live or die on her own."

It was a lie, but Whisper had said it out loud, so it wasn't a *starling* lie. The strange, in-between nature of the falls would let her nurse the Nighthaunt's pet back to health. It would take all of Whisper's current energy to mark the area and keep starlings out while deterring the Ashen Weald's owls from investigating. After that, she'd consider her options.

"Now, where'd Nighteyes get off to?" Whisper asked.

The Newmoon Pride looked around. None of them had an answer. Moonlit Blossom tracked Nighteyes' scent to where the cave gryphons had previously been, but it vanished against the border glyphs.

What did they do, kidnap a starling pride leader? When the pridelord finds out about this, it will not go well.

17

THE NAZE

Nighteyes pushed through the thick, feathery ferns blanketing this new forest, surprised at how strange things looked on the other side of the border. Large limestone deposits, split open by the roots of broadleaf trees, sparkled wherever stray beams of light struck them.

The broadleafs were rarer the farther north they trekked. The forest here was made up of birch, pine, and even some maple. She was so busy staring at the trees, she stumbled through a fern and startled a group of flightless birds who ran away.

She let out a slight laugh.

"What is it?" Slate asked. "Is it the altruism kicking back in?"

Nighteyes cleared her throat, suddenly reminded that whatever Whisper did to her could wear off at any moment. "No, it's just that I've never been north of this border before. This is the land of cassowaries and titanoboas. I've travelled the southern continent from the Winter Jungle to the Strix Plateau, but I've never stepped two paces north of my home."

The cave gryphons exchanged a look. It was clear they were wary of bringing a starling home, even a starling who was *pink*, as Slate had put it.

Fortunately for her, they didn't have a choice. Slate's leg injuries were getting worse, and Chert alternated dozing off and waking up in pain.

"How long until the Naze?" Nighteyes asked. "It'll be dark soon."

The oilbird gryphons didn't seem bothered by the idea of losing the light, and it occurred to her that she may find herself in some very dark places the longer they travelled together.

"Shh, quiet," Chert mumbled between her gasps of pain. "We're not safe yet."

Through a break in the trees, Nighteyes saw a huge hole going deep into the ground. Streams and rivers from all sides collapsed into waterfalls, vanishing into the black. On the far side of the pit was a large cave opening, completely covered in what looked like the web of a giant spider.

Nighteyes froze, a primal fear welling up from within her.

"Oi, keep walking. Stay out of sight," Chert warned.

Nighteyes proceeded despite her instincts. "What made that? What manner of creature needs a web that big?"

Slate gave a short, rumbling laugh. "That's the Silkmouth Pride. Scary, ain't it? The alabasters come in every so often to burn it and look around, but they ain't keen to look too close. Sometimes, Silky will wrap up dead opinici and hang them from the web."

Nighteyes was starting to have regrets and wanted to turn back, but Slate located a familiar design on a small boulder. The rock was lighter than it looked, and someone had scraped the moss off to create a subtle glyph design.

She set Chert down and pushed the rock aside. Then Slate held it in place while they went down, following after. The stone fell into place, and the light of the tunnel vanished.

Nighteyes froze, afraid to go deeper, but unable to see where the boulder had been behind her. The quiet, the cold, the darkness: all three seeped into her fur and left behind a chill that sapped her strength.

"Hey," Chert chirped. "You're okay. I'm right here. It's pretty big, isn't it? But just follow the path and you'll be fine. Maybe a wet paw or two, but that never hurt anyone, did it?"

The path? Nighteyes wondered. She looked around, or at least she moved her head in several directions. There was nothing to *see*, so calling it looking was misleading.

She sniffed a few times, but her nares kept sending alarms to her brain, warning that there were no starlings here. It smelled wet, fungal, oily, and still had a hint of guano.

"Hmm, your eyes will adjust." Slate's encouragement fell on deaf ears. "Chert, can you guide our starling friend?"

Chert put her beak against the top of Nighteyes' head and directed her. True to the earlier warning, Nighteyes stepped in a few puddles. Her internal sense of panic grew and grew, focusing into a small, fiery dot.

She blinked, and the dot went away. She opened her eyes, and it returned. She moved her head, but the dot wasn't in her imagination. It was a light source.

Her footsteps became surer. This wasn't a moonless night. Or, rather, it wasn't a starless night. She walked from star to star, passing slow-burning candles and rushlights.

She'd expected light to shrink the cavern, but it had the opposite effect. The Ashen Weald's braziers had lit caverns and eyries alike. The bits of flame here did little to tell her how large of a space she was in. As she wove between them, she was left feeling like she really was walking across a cloudy sky.

Slate gave guidance from overhead, adding to the vastness of the cavern. "The next one is dim. Watch your step, there's water ahead, high enough to clean your tummy fur."

I hope this doesn't wash off all of Whisper's feather-dust. I'd hate to find out what happens when it's gone. Something wriggled past Nighteyes' paws. She didn't look down, just kept going. At times, her ears picked up clicks. She passed by a waterfall and felt the droplets splash on her wings.

When she finally thought to wonder why cave gryphons would need light at all with their echolocation, she reached the last rushlight.

Oh no, please don't make me go back to the darkness.

With a rustle and a click, Slate pushed aside a thick curtain, and light flooded in, blinding her. As her eyes adapted, she saw that she was in a narrow tunnel. *Huh, the size was a trick of the light all along.*

She almost laughed, thinking it had all been an illusion, but she looked back over her shoulder and the light opened up and vanished into a cavern. She could see water sparkling on the ground, and it disappeared into the vastness that stretched back behind her.

"You're okay to put me down and go in," Chert encouraged. "We'll find someone to carry me the rest of the way."

Behind Nighteyes, the *nothing* surprised her. But going forwards, it was the *everything* that caught her off guard. Beyond the curtain, she was in a large, well-lit room that smelled like gryphons. Nests five high were stuck to the walls with more silk, and even more hung precariously from the ceiling. The squawking, chirruping, meowing, purring, and shouting of too many voices to count filled the cavern. It was a rockslide of fuzzy cave gryphons, and more. A lot more.

The oilbird gryphlets from a few days ago were packed into a nest and screeched their abyssal cries, answered by the squawking of an equal number of osprey opinicus chicks. Crow gryphons squabbled with woodpeckers. A tropical gryphon, greens and blues and oranges with a long tail, puffed up her feathers to intimidate the same mallard opinicus Nighteyes had nearly killed.

And this was just one chamber—she saw a dozen side passages, some blocked off with curtains, others left open.

"There're a lot of refugees these days," Chert explained. "At first, we struggled just to feed everyone. But then one of the reds got us organized, and we weren't just *surviving*, we were *thriving*. We found ourselves able to hit the lampworks and silkworks to free even more."

Nighteyes shook off her amazement. "One of the reds? A Redwood Valley opinicus?"

"Eh, not an opinicus," Slate said cryptically. "Come on and see. She'll be back with the medicine gryphons."

"No, wait. I need to talk to whoever is in charge of all this. I need to talk about what happened two years ago." Nighteyes only had so long before the altruism kicked back in, and she wasn't going to waste it. She'd waited years to yell at someone for the deaths in her pride.

Chert started to speak, but Slate interrupted her. "Ay, I can make that happen. Let me fetch someone to take Chert in, and I'll lead you to the gryphon in charge."

Two clicks was all it took to get the attention of a trio of osprey who lifted Chert off Nighteyes. If they knew she was a starling, they didn't show it. Maybe violet was too strange a color.

"All right, come with me," Slate said, guiding her away from the crowd.

NIGHTEYES ALLOWED herself to be led away, and she belatedly remembered Slate was wounded. "Do you want me to get someone else to show me the way? You should be with Chert. You need someone to look at your forelegs."

"I'm afraid there's a very good reason I can't do that," he began, "and that's because I'm the one in charge of the cave prides. I'm not a pridelord as such. It's more like I'm in charge of the Abyssal Naze itself, the cavern I mean, so I speak first, and the others get to argue with me. Not really an honor, per se, and as I was the one who could have stopped the plan to remove the glyphs, it's a bit of a dishonor."

Nighteyes hadn't grown so close to the strange duo of oilbirds that she was above yelling at them, but also, they were so...small and unassuming. She'd expected to stand before the Pridelord of the Abyssal Naze, a thousand black eyes following his every move, and scream ineffectively at the darkness about what it had done to her pride.

This was one gryphon, all alone, who regretted his decision. Who might be dead at the claws of a strange beast if she hadn't intervened.

"You okay there?" Slate asked. "I mean, physically. Emotionally, I get that you've got a lot going on between the ears."

She didn't have time to consider her words carefully, so she spoke her mind. "If I had done nothing, you would be dead at the claws of that monster. My kindness for someone outside of my pride brought me here."

"Is that what you want? Someone to pay for what happened with their lives?" he asked.

"Yes." Her reply was cruel but true. She wouldn't kill him now, but with the truth settling over her like

Whisper's featherdust, she wished she'd left him behind or let the susurration get him.

He stayed quiet, which annoyed her more.

Time was running out, so she asked what was on her mind. "Why?"

"A mixture of things," Slate replied. "It was our only shot at killing the Seraph King. He was hunting us across most of the continent, thanks to the Nighthaunt and his darkstalkers. If we'd succeeded, we could have made the world a much better place overnight. Nearly got Hi-kun and Mally, too. With them gone, we could easily have freed all of our kind while the alabasters were in disarray. I'll bet some of the eyries would have broken free again, too."

She just stared at him.

"Do you know the skies above the Abyssal Naze used to be full of gryphons coming to visit?" Slate asked. "Now, those same prides are broken and lost. They don't live free on the surface. They've been forced underground. When's the last time you heard of an opinicus and gryphon living together in an eyrie. I say it again, but the world would have been a much better place if we'd pulled it off."

"But you didn't," she countered.

He bowed his head. "We didn't."

"Because you didn't think about the other prides," she started.

But he wasn't cowed by her words. "Can you honestly tell me that if our roles were reversed, the starlings wouldn't have done the same thing? You're telling me the *pridelord* cares so much about us other prides that he'd give us one feather off his tail to make our lives better? I ask you, how many innocent lives has the Emerald Jungle claimed under the guise of altruism."

She didn't know, so she changed the topic. "What was in the sack the mallard carried into Nightsky territory?"

"Research." He cleaned his whiskers, some sort of oilbird calming ritual. "There's a high-ranking official in the Seraph King's inner circle we're after. The king is hiding his fleet and resources in Alwren and King's Reach, we think, building boats and who-knows-what. None of *us* can get there because the Emerald Jungle's in the way. You act like you're neutral, but your altruism is the armor worn by our enemies. You do a better job of protecting the king than the royal guard and Golden Sky Army combined."

She ignored his insinuation. "What does the research have to do with the king?"

"This official is a traitor," he answered. "Someone at the lampworks figured out who it was. Some overheard conversation, something in the paperwork, we're not sure how. The lamplighter was loyal to the Seraph King and planned to turn the traitor in, but thankfully, they died before they could share that info. A chimney swift was watching them, so we grabbed their research and torched the place. If the king figures out who the traitor is, he'll kill that opinicus. But if we find out who they are, they can tell us what the alabasters and Nighthaunt are up to. What's more, they can tell us where every lampworks and silkworks is located. If we hit them all at the same time, we could free every cave gryphon in one go."

"The satchel's in the Emerald Jungle, so it's lost to both sides." She didn't offer to get it for them. She did not plan to have another conversation like this in the future.

He sighed. "Well, as long as no opinicus ever gets their talons on it, there's hope we'll figure out the traitor another way, I reckon."

"Yes," she said, but in the back of her mind, she remembered a green set of opinicus talons taking the satchel.

"There's one more thing," she began, but her vision turned grey, and she felt a literal need to bite someone even stronger than her metaphorical need to do so. "I...need..."

A roar came from down the passage, and the smell of a clawdigger filled the path.

"What? How did it find us?!" Slate shouted, ignoring her.

"I need to...get away...from other gryphons..." Nighteyes tried to tell him, but even wounded, he was gone—into the darkness.

Slate reared back, wings open, and let out a screech that may or may not have deafened the clawdigger but definitely did so to her. "I won't let you near the gryphlets!"

A shadowy shape charged down the corridor, but it was a lot smaller than the clawdiggers from earlier. Strangely, it didn't just smell *like* the one who had given Slate his injuries, it smelled *exactly* the same.

The tiny shadow hit a patch where the ground was just webbing covered in a thin layer of dirt and fell.

"Ha!" came a new voice, hidden down one of the endless side passages. "Got one. *Can't build a web big enough to catch a clawdigger, Bristlespine told me. Well,*

I showed her! If I can get a snake, I told 'er, I can catch some overgrown bat."

"Good job, Silky," Slate commented.

Nighteyes felt her vision grey, but she crawled to the webbing and looked down to see the monster.

In the trap was Whisper.

18

COCOON

Whisper had tracked the strange cave gryphons through the forest, evading alabasters and giant snakes alike, searching for a way in. Ultimately, she'd followed something called a *silkmouth* until it showed her how to access the side passage.

From there, the strange underground winds had brought her Nighteyes' scent. While the silkmouths, oilbirds, and other gryphons were plentiful, starberry nightsky fragrance was rare.

Whisper's only mistake was in thinking that a clawdigger smell would frighten them away from Nighteyes. It had not, and in her weakened state, she'd been unaware of the silkmouth hiding above her—or the silkmouth's trap below Whisper's paws.

And so, I find myself wrapped up like a moth in a cocoon. How embarrassing. At least Flicker isn't here to see this.

"You should let me go," Whisper commanded. "The pridelord will descend upon the Naze like a swarm of locusts to save his two favorite pride leaders."

"Eh, it can speak," Silky said. "Thought for sure it was infected with those peepers. First no altruism, then they learn words. Well, I'll wrap her up in the cave maw and let the alabasters wonder what she is. They're terrified of the parasite, so those shiny eyes might help keep 'em out of our tailfeathers a little longer. Maybe we'll get a whole month without another burnout."

Slate seemed to be weighing her life. Whisper tried to send calming mint his way, knowing mint was calming to even non-starling gryphons, but getting featherdust out of a hole in the ground while wrapped up like a spider's dinner was beyond her.

For now.

"Hmm. They saved me and Chert," he said at last. "I reckon we should keep this one alive. What do you think, Nighteyes?"

The smell coming off the Nightsky Pride leader was a mixture of rage, *other*, and self-preservation. She'd nearly lost herself.

"Her altruism is kicking in. Release me, and I can stop it, at least temporarily," Whisper ordered.

They didn't listen to her until Nighteyes nearly took a chunk out of Silky, but then quickly changed their minds before their violet guest managed more than a nip.

Whisper, exhausted, dry, and sore, used some of the last of her energy to calm Nighteyes. "We need to get you back to the Emerald Jungle. Now."

"No can do," Silky said. "A flight of alabasters just descended, conducting their own search for the satchel. Your best bet is to depart in the early morning and make a mad flight for it."

Whisper could feel her paws shaking while she took stock of the situation. *This isn't good. If the pridelord catches us out here, he could decide our prides are too dangerous. We could be the next Sparkwing Pride. Or Crescentmoon.*

"Just leave me here," Nighteyes managed between breaths. "I got what I came for. Tell Wendl what happened...and my sister will take over."

Whisper shook her head. "It's dangerous to come back without you. You're not some lost jadebeak. You're a pride leader."

"What can we do?" Slate asked. "I know Nighteyes said she wished we were dead for what we did to your prides, but believe me when I say we're here to help. What do you need right now? We'll carry you to the jungle ourselves through the alabasters, if that's what it takes."

"You might, Slate, but I won't," Silky protested. "I won't risk one silkmouth for a starling. What has the Emerald Jungle ever done for us? Name one thing a single starling has ever done for a gryphon who isn't a starling. I'll wait."

Before an argument could break out, Whisper had an idea. "I smell emerald broadleafs. Fill a room with them, and seal it closed. Is there someone who can make the glyph paste? Get me as much as you can. I think I can trick her mind into thinking we're in the Emerald Jungle."

The cave gryphons rushed off, leaving the starlings alone together. Whisper held Nighteyes' head in her paws, calming her. The Nightsky Pride leader looked sick, as sick as she'd been when Whisper and the others joined the murmuration.

Wendl had stepped out of line to help Nighteyes. It was why she had so much leeway with the Nightsky Pride these days. Her first act had been kindness.

What was my first act? Whisper wasn't sure. Where the scent from the others had been panic and despair, she'd been overcome by euphoria at her change.

Slate and Silky returned with a lot of leaves, a pot of paste, and an old oilbird medicine gryphon.

"Will this do?" the elder gryphon asked. "Which of our glyphs do you need?"

"None of yours," Whisper said, causing Slate to stop massaging his paws. "Get food and water, then we need an enclosed space about this high and this wide. Sealed off with silk."

They looked at the hole they'd just pulled Whisper out of.

"Yes, fine, that will work. Line it with the leaves, then seal it up top," she said. "Nighteyes, I know you're fading fast, but see this paste? I need you to glyph one side of the chamber, and I'll do the other. We need to trick your senses."

Nighteyes blinked. "Into thinking we're at the border between our territories. Will it work?"

"Yes, absolutely. I've done this before." Whisper knew her faint scent told a different, more terrifying tale. She'd nearly stayed away for too long once and lost herself. While the pridelord had several 'specialists' hidden among the starling prides—the Gourmand of the Winter Jungle being the most terrifying, and therefore the farthest away—only he and Whisper could fix the psychosis that took over a starling lost for too long. And she didn't know what would happen if he started rooting around in her mind.

Silky and a chimney swift called Bristlespine finished wrapping up the walls and leaves before settling in to spin the roof. Whisper hadn't given much thought to where the webbing came from, but it made her feel a little better to see that it came out of their beaks.

They were nearly done when a flash of long red and green tail crossed over the slit in the roof.

"Are you sure this is safe?" the newcomer asked. Her voice had the barest hint of opi trill to it.

Slate stumbled over from where the medicine gryphon had been working on his legs. "Aye, we owe it to them. That's Nighteyes down there."

"Nighteyes? The Ashen Weald's starling?" the newcomer asked. "Is she able to speak to the Ashen Weald? They'll be worried about us. We sent Cherine back ages ago, but we never heard anything."

The silk sealed Whisper and Nighteyes in, and they hurried to put up as many glyphs as they could before they passed out.

NIGHTEYES AWOKE in the middle of the night, or so she assumed. Someone had left a scentless brazier outside her strange chamber, so there was a flickering light that kept the level of illumination the same as when she'd gone to sleep. It felt like night, though.

"Whisper?" she asked. "Are you awake?"

The Newmoon gryphon opened an eye, revealing

they were a mossy green when they weren't silver. "You need to sleep and regain your energy. We'll make a dash for the border tomorrow."

"It's just..." Nighteyes chose her words carefully. "Thank you. Thank you for coming to get me. I know you said if we didn't come back, the pridelord might hurt both of our prides, but that's only the case because you left to come find me. I'm not one of your infected, but you still put your pride at risk. You owe me nothing."

Whisper closed her eye again, then adjusted herself so she faced Nighteyes. "It's not just the infected I was created to save. Before the Newmoon Pride was the Crescentmoon Pride, who sought out starlings who became lost in new territory, before the glyph markers existed, back when starlings could roam the continent. And before that, the Fullmoon Pride, who...well, who can say, but I imagine they had a similar purpose."

That sounded ominous, Nighteyes thought. "There's something else. Between your featherdust and being so far away, I-I remember something. No, that's not right. I remember *everything.* Clear as day. The migraines are gone."

"Everything Wendl hid in your brain?" Whisper asked.

"Wendl *and* the pridelord," Nighteyes replied. "I remember everything they both wanted me to forget. And I remember everything he told me not to do. All this time, I thought it was Rudder's voice that was giving me a headache, but no, that was what it felt like to disobey the pridelord."

Whisper opened her eyes, giving up on rest. "I did

wonder how you were able to take a stormtail mate. When the first stormtails left the murmuration, the pridelord ordered them to stop breeding with other prides to stop the spread of, well, whatever was wrong with them.

"There were a few non-stormtails who broke the rules and took them as mates, but your compulsion was placed on you by the pridelord himself. I could not have disobeyed an order like that myself."

"Rudder has a really cute tail," Nighteyes opined, surprised to hear Whisper's genuine laugh, ending in a snort. "What, you've never done anything stupid for love?"

"I once took a mate on the last day of mating season," Whisper said.

Nighteyes gave her own brief laugh. "Well, if you're not really one for conversation, that has its perks. I don't know if that's so weird."

"I was also once engaged to Wendl," Whisper added. "Back when we were opinici."

That caught Nighteyes off guard. With all of the compulsions removed from her mind: pridelord, Wendl, and even Whisper's from when they first met, Nighteyes was able to believe this silver-eyed, silver-stained female gryphon had once been a male opinicus. It still felt strange to hear Whisper talk about the before time.

"What was it like being an opinicus?" Nighteyes asked.

Whisper looked lost in thought. Then she sent the smell of honesty. "I hated it. Maybe it would be different if I'd been a female opinicus? But there was a casual cruelty I was able to ignore so easily. You don't end up as the Nighthaunt's personal scribe if you aren't easily led astray. I look at all of my life leading up to the Emerald Jungle, and I wish I could have stood up for myself just once. I feel better now. Kinder. I know how to help gryphons, and I do it. I know how to help myself, and I do it. There is no Nighthaunt on our side of the jungle. His bloody talons do not pierce the Emerald Veil. Starlings are safer and kinder than any other gryphon or opinicus I know."

"I'm not so sure," Nighteyes said. "I said some horrible things to Slate, but I'm starting to think the same words could fairly be lobbied against all starlings. Just how many gryphons and opinici have died at the paws of the murmuration? The Nightsky Pride? Myself? The worst part is realizing we don't know when it happens, not even who we've killed. I don't understand why we need the altruism."

"Khalim was an idiot to spread that word across the veil," Whisper grumbled.

Nighteyes didn't let the conversation fade. "Tell me why, though. Tell me why we have altruism now. Clearly, we haven't always had it. Erlock Startail came searching for a Merinkin gryphon, some sort of harpy eagle who had visited us. I have only the faintest memories, but I also don't remember him leaving. Who was he? Did altruism kill him?"

"Merinkin? A wealder, like Erlock? Show me what you know of him." Whisper's scent grew stronger, a mix of hazel and nutmeg this time that made Nighteyes feel nostalgic.

"I remember...I remember him coming to trade at the temple." Nighteyes' memories came into focus with Whisper's olfactory prompting. "We still had the altruism then, I was wrong. He had some sort of yolk-bloom elixir he'd gotten from starlings in the past. He was happy to be here. He said he had elixirs that would let a starling take a non-starling mate. He passed through the Emerald Jungle, to the Winter Jungle, and…I lose the trail. I was just a gryphlet. He never came back through my territory; I have no memory of him there."

Whisper stayed quiet for a while. "I can track him when we get back, possibly. Maybe. It depends upon the pridelord. The Winter Jungle is not where you would send a weald gryphon getting ready to return home. There is one strip of land at its tip that stays above water, and no gryphon should cross its glyphs."

"Wait, what?" Nighteyes said. "So he could be there now? Is that like our version of an opinicus prison…?"

Whisper's scent had the word *gourmand* before it quickly vanished. "I will see if he left there. But do not go there yourself, and do not send Rudder there. It is where the pridelord can best hide things. He does not like that the stormtails control the Winter Jungle, but what other gryphon is so well adapted to do so?"

"We should sleep." Nighteyes felt the weight of the day come down upon her. The glyphs had done their part. Despite the flickering brazier light, she felt like she was at home. But whether or not they'd get back to the Emerald Jungle tomorrow might honestly depend upon her ability to hold back the altruism. She closed her eyes, but she felt Whisper adjust herself so she hovered over Nighteyes.

The newmoon gryphon put a paw on the violet's

forehead. "I can make it so you keep remembering, but it could place you in danger. I couldn't ask you before because you weren't your true self. I suspect Wendl hid away your memories so the pridelord wouldn't hurt you. I cannot make it so the pridelord can never find out what you know, but I can make it so he won't suspect. And I can show you how to control what memories are hidden. If you, Nighteyes-who-remembers-everything, wish me to."

Nighteyes considered the gift offered to her. She'd nearly died in the Abyssal Naze today. This could get her killed in the Emerald Jungle tomorrow. Still, the answer came easily. "I want to be able to remember."

"So be it," Whisper said. "I'll do it while you sleep. But this will grant me access to a lot of what Wendl has hidden. Be sure you want me to know. Your pheromones will not lie like your beak can."

"Spying on your ex-mate?" Nighteyes asked.

Whisper just shrugged. "Wendl is just a friend now. But I know she keeps secrets. I am giving you the opportunity to hide that from me."

"No," Nighteyes said. "I'm done with secrets. Fix my brain. I want to know it all."

19

METAMORPHOSIS

Flashes of color came to Nighteyes in her dreams. She saw herself in the abandoned expedition ruins, past the lines of incense meant to block out the murmuration, next to Wendl.

"You need to understand that what you saw in the bog, the jadebeak's succumbing to altruism, isn't an isolated incident," Dream Wendl explained. "Do you know how many innocent gryphons I've seen you all kill? And every single one of you forgets. Well, most of you do. When a starling can remember, they vanish soon after. I'm offering you a chance to break the cycle."

Dream Nighteyes nodded. "We need the pride leaders to control their own prides directly, not for everyone to be controlled by one starling."

"No, that's not quite what I'm proposing." Wendl pulled out a map of the jungle and pointed at the center. "I'm proposing that no gryphon is controlled by anyone. I think every gryphon should decide for themselves what to do."

"But what happens if someone attacks the Emerald Jungle?" Dream Nighteyes knew the outside world was dangerous. Only by acting as one had the Emerald Jungle remained safe where the Ashen Weald had nearly been destroyed several times in its brief existence, and even then, many free prides eschewed membership. How much stronger would the Ashen Weald be if the fisherfolk, taiga gryphons, and Strix Pride were forced to join it?

Wendl shrugged. "Then you learn to work together or you perish. There's a better way to live, a way full of diplomacy and love and friendship. But you'll have to fight for it."

"I don't know," Dream Nighteyes admitted. "What if this Seraph King invades? He fears the murmuration. He does not fear the Ashen Weald."

Wendl didn't have all the answers, but she made a compelling case. A lot of what Nighteyes needed was beyond the Emerald Veil. What stood between her and the rest of the world was one gryphon.

"It's not enough to just kill the pridelord," Wendl continued. "When that happens, the other pride leaders struggle for control. Then a new pridelord is created. What we need to do is to capture the pridelord and use the salts to replace him with someone who can disconnect the starling prides one at a time. It worked for Whisper, so it should work for us. We can just...slip a new gryphon in using his blood."

Dream Nighteyes wasn't persuaded that time. It would take many more sessions of talking to Wendl, many more dead gryphlets, many more strange commands from the pridelord, before Nighteyes agreed. But, at long last, two years ago as she lost more of her pride to altruism, she *had* agreed.

"Fine," the Nightsky Pride leader said. "How do you propose we capture and hold the strongest gryphon on the continent? And who are you going to replace him with?"

Wendl held an inky talon up to a wall with the glyphs for all of the prides. "You."

NIGHTEYES JERKED awake to find Whisper holding her down. She struggled against the newmoon's grip, expecting to get covered in mint or some other weird smell, but nothing came.

Whisper was sweating and finally collapsed to the side. "I think it's done. If the pridelord sends a pheromone inquiry into your brain, you will temporarily forget. Otherwise, you should always remember."

"Th-thank you." Nighteyes' head swam. "Did you see what I saw? In the smells or whatever?"

Whisper hesitated. "Yes, or enough. Wendl is trying to assassinate the pridelord. And I believe she's working with The Six to do so."

Before Nighteyes could ask who The Six were, several scents and information filled her nares, and she just *knew*. "But did you see who they want to be the new pridelord?"

"Yes." Whisper avoided commenting further by scarfing down some of the cave fish left uneaten from last night.

Nighteyes gave an exasperated sigh. "Okay, so...

how does that make you feel? You're standing next to your enemy, it seems."

"You should not do it," Whisper said simply. "During the clawdigger attack, I tried to control the susurration. When I give them a simple command, like *hunt*, they do it. But when I give a complex command, such as *stop the strange claw beasts from killing the oilbird and don't eat the darkstalker and don't hurt the nightsky starling,* it takes everything out of me. Pridelords need years of training before they can take over. We need a strong pridelord like the one we have. One who can hold the murmuration and susurration in equilibrium. Otherwise, those adopted into my pride are in danger."

Are in danger, or do they become a danger? Nighteyes thought, keeping it to herself. "If I'm the pridelord, I can do that work, right? I can, like, separate out other prides but also help you with yours?"

Whisper switched from cave fish to chewing eyeshine. "If you do so, you will be betraying The Six, and they will simply kill you and change one of them into the new pridelord. Iri the First, most likely. I do not think it is a coincidence she rules the jadebeaks—nor that her predecessor died mysteriously to make it happen. She has more experience ruling large numbers of starlings than you do. Your reaction to being told you will be made pridelord is very different from my own in such a situation."

"Oh?" Nighteyes asked.

"Yes. If someone told me they were going to make me pridelord, especially one of the Nighthaunt's old apprentices, I would assume it was a trick and they were trying to get me killed." Whisper reapplied four dots to her wrist, though she hesitated as she did it. Then she added silver stripes to her tail before moving on to her face. She must have practiced adding the dripping markings without using a pond's reflection, because she was very good at it.

Nighteyes did her own grooming. "I'm not going to hurt anyone. Except maybe the pridelord. But can't we switch him to a different gryphon or something? We have a lot of salts."

"I will confront Wendl when we get back," Whisper said. "I'll persuade her to try something different. But be warned, the original Whisper was created to save the susurration, to bring back lost starlings. As the new Whisper, I cannot do that without a pridelord, perhaps not without a murmuration to lend me strength. If you continue down Wendl's path, you will find us at claws."

Nighteyes understood what Whisper was saying, but she'd also just relived every conversation with Wendl over the past few years, all of which had been persuasive, too. "Is there a way to disconnect the other pride leaders? Like, to ask them what they think, then make them forget the way Wendl did to me?"

Whisper let out a scent that made Nighteyes dizzy, then began adjusting it and watching her reaction. "Wendl will already know how to do it, but let me see if I can recreate what she used on you. It's a strange blend of chemicals. I am stuck with the smells starling scent glands normally make. With her stolen opinicus alchemy kits, she is not. I think I can pull off a close approximation. Yes, there we go. What do you hope to gain from talking to the other pride leaders?"

"Perspective." Though Nighteyes was aware that if

she truly wanted to know what every pride leader thought, she'd be required to talk to Iri the First. "Is there a way to make one of The Six forget?"

Whisper considered, then opened the dusty medicine bag. Inside were eyeshine petals, charcoal, a small journal, and various opinicus trinkets. It was less a medicine bag than a collection of keepsakes. The newmoon gryphon reached into the bottom and pulled up a tiny fish skeleton, wrapped a leaf partway around it, and carefully groomed some featherdust all over it before sealing the leaf closed and wrapping it in cave gryphon silk. "Be careful you do not use this on anyone else, but it should work for one of The Six."

Nighteyes had more questions, but a tapping sound came above, and Whisper quickly covered the violet starling in dust to suppress her altruism for the trip home.

20

GOODBYES

Awoodpecker couple led Nighteyes and Whisper away from their webbed broadleaf nest and down a set of corridors going the opposite direction from the domiciles. Water dripped from the ceiling and disappeared into the grooves of the floor. There wasn't enough to splash, but there was enough that Nighteyes' paws never stopped feeling damp.

The path alternated wide open caverns with thin, cramped sections the locals referred to as *crawls*. The woodpeckers traversed them as easily as if they were the sprawling, flowery arches outside the Nightsky Pride's nesting grounds, but Nighteyes' head was decorated with a few new bumps.

"Got another crawl coming up," a woodpecker warned.

The path was strange. Their group would cross a dozen caves without seeing another soul, then, without warning, a pack of twenty oilbirds would come running, tapping each of them as they passed.

The woodpeckers brushed a talon or paw on the oilbirds, so Nighteyes and Whisper joined in, not wanting to seem rude. Despite their name, the oilbird gryphons were soft and warm, like fuzzy lamps.

Where the caves were large, the packs of cave gryphons rushing by weren't a problem. When Nighteyes was attempting to squeeze through a crawl, the packed bodies nearly drove her into a state not dissimilar to altruism.

She was the last one out of a particularly bad passage when a team of seven oilbirds squished themselves into the tiny space, their whiskers brushing against her face, and said a hello with their tap.

"Pretty plume."

"Nearly there!"

"Coming through."

"Stay left, please."

Even once they were past, the corridor didn't feel any larger. She still had trouble squeezing out of the small space and into the next cave.

"Sorry about that." The taller woodpecker reached a talon in to help pull her through. He sported woven bracelets on both sets of talons, a mixture of the same colors as his plumage.

The other woodpecker, a gryphon, wore a matching set on his paws. "This is their home, so we don't say anything, but you handled that a lot better than I did my first time. I actually screamed until I couldn't breathe."

"He did," the opinicus confirmed. "Right before he fainted. We had to pull him out by his tail."

The gryphon did a little twirl, showing off his long

red tail. It looked sturdy enough to use as a safety leash. The spin also highlighted the differences between both woodpeckers. The opinicus had joked, *You can tell us apart because he's red, black, and white while I'm black, red, and white,* and it was a silly joke— the talons on the opinicus and very long tail on the gryphon were better indicators—but it was also true that they weren't quite the same species of woodpecker.

A new set of oilbirds squeezed into the cave, running to a wall with water trickling down it to drink. The woodpeckers didn't join in, but Whisper lapped at the vertical stream, then pulled her head back.

"It's very sour," the newmoon gryphon hissed, her only words since the woodpeckers arrived.

"I used to carry a flask of fresh water just to avoid needing the waterfalls myself, but it kept catching on the rocks," the opinicus said. "It's not much further. Sorry for the long trip, but we have to keep the pyre away from the lampworks rescues. If you think *he* can scream, you haven't heard anything until you've heard what the rescues are like around any flame bigger than a rushlight."

The woodpecker gryphon rolled his eyes. "At least I don't cry when I find a whip scorpion in my nest. Okay, I think that's the last of it. I'll go first and make sure no more cave gryphons squish you this time. Just wait for my call."

It took so long for the go-ahead to come that Nighteyes nearly tried the wall water. Only Whisper's open-beaked disgust, as though she were airing out her silvery tongue, convinced Nighteyes to wait.

Still, the water gave her something to look at. Behind it, someone had scratched diagrams of clawdiggers into the rock face. Either the artist hadn't seen a living one, or perhaps there were different varieties.

"Okay, come on through!" a woodpecker called.

Nighteyes sighed, took a deep breath, and pushed herself into the last cramped space before the so-called pyre.

THE PASSAGE EMPTIED into a circular chamber of flickering pink light. Where most of the paths felt discovered by cave gryphons, this room had been sculpted, albeit poorly.

Not that I could do much better, Nighteyes admitted. The fact anyone had built something underground was an achievement.

The pyre was made up of two main areas: the fire in the center, then a ring around the outside. The pyre was for cooking, and a team of Alwren fisherfolk were searing very salty meat on the flames, which was then taken to a dry room for storage.

Between the pyre and the outer ring were panes of flame-resistant glass. Nighteyes had seen a little of the strange material, a kind of warm ice, resistant to melting that came from the desert, during her visit to the Ashen Weald. The Abyssal Naze must have stolen this glass, as the panes were all different colors and levels of opacity. Hence the sparkling pink entrance.

"Do you need something to eat?" a woodpecker asked.

Whisper shook her head. "We ate last night and can't afford to stay much longer."

Nighteyes' stomach rumbled dissent. Salt, meat, and heat tricked it into believing she was at the storm-tail's summer feast. One of the naze's cooks slipped her a strip of salmon spiced within an inch of its life —then beyond. The pepper coating crunched when she bit down, earning Whisper's quiet disapproval.

The violet starling ate as they were led halfway around the outer ring, passing through rooms of blue and green before reaching a chamber with trans-parent glass. Dozens of egg-filled nests formed rows starting a gryphon-length from the barrier. Denmothers from different cave and refugee prides watched over them and made sure none overheated. Slate rested in the back, on his side with his wrapped forelegs splayed out straight. It was a ridiculous pose for a pride leader.

"You made 'em walk all the way here?" Slate asked the woodpeckers. "Shoulda just sent a messenger."

"They asked to see you," the opinicus explained.

Slate grinned. "And you explained I was a dozen caves away and our guests would have to squeeze themselves tighter than a diamond to come see me, and they still insisted?"

The woodpeckers had left that part out.

"Eh, well, no harm done. Right?" Slate looked to Whisper.

The newmoon gryphon hesitated before answer-ing. "No, no harm yet. Her altruism is still suppressed."

The faint scent of citrus reminded Nighteyes she was the danger and lessened the burning feeling on her tongue. Had her altruism kicked in, things would not have gone so well. The woodpecker couple apologized to her, then vanished back the way they'd come.

"I wish I had an easier way back for you." Slate spoke as though they were alone, but denparents wandered between them, checking eggs. "After hearing about our run-in with the clawdiggers, the Silkmouth Pride took it upon themselves to start closing up tunnels and setting more traps. We're going to have to send you back the long way."

Nighteyes would have preferred familiar terrain and a shorter trip, but Whisper seemed to approve.

"This way, our old scents will not give us away," the newmoon gryphon said.

Nighteyes rolled her eyes. "I don't think they can track our scents. They're opinici. Do opinici even have nares? I'd rather not see how long you can keep the altruism at bay."

One of the osprey denfathers gave her a look, and she realized she'd forgotten what it was like to be in the company of opinici—or, well, even other prides. The Nightsky had been her focus for so long now.

She looked through the smoky glass, down to the pyre below. She had to shift her beak as the heat built up, turning the side facing it away when it got too hot. This underground catacomb was the same vision the Ashen Weald had. Prides, eyries, and even fisherfolk working together for something better. Were they in contact with the Ashen Weald?

It was almost admirable, except for the part where they'd used the starlings as a weapon. That was something she'd never forgive.

I was out hunting with Rudder. He was teasing me

about hunting on land when my burrow overlooked a river stocked with fish. The skies filled with jadebeaks, then nightsky, then newmoons. I looked up, and then I saw a parrot leading them to the break in the glyphs and the altruism kicked in. We were just about to fly when an explosive went off.

No, an incense bomb? Wendl dragged me to the nesting grounds. She followed with Rudder much later, though he was bleeding. Then she took Sheen and—

Whisper sent the olfactory equivalent of a nudge, snapping Nighteyes out of her lost memories. "I've regained control of her, but we should leave soon."

Nighteyes blinked to refresh her dry eyes, unable to do anything for her toasted nares. She wanted to protest that she hadn't been lost to altruism, but the bitter scent of aniseed told her to keep her beak shut. She accepted the warning not to talk about what she'd seen but still spoke. "Will you or Chert be joining us?"

"I'm afraid I'm not much for walking for a while." Slate showed off his bandaged forelegs. "Chert'll be fine soon enough, but better safe than snake bait, like my denmother used to say."

Several denparents made knowing *mmmmm* sounds from the nesting room. If someone had told Nighteyes she'd feel worse going alone than with the gryphon who had ordered the border glyphs removed, she'd have called the speaker a liar. His barbed words still clung to her hide like burrs, however, and she wished she had time to process them.

"Before we go, may I visit Chert?" she asked. "I'd like to make sure she's okay."

Slate looked from Whisper's silver eyes to Nighteyes' beak, which shook the slightest amount. "Make it fast, and don't wake her if she's asleep. I'll have your overworld guides collect you from there."

He called for a handful of cave gryphons to lead them out. With all of her silver makeup, Whisper was unreadable. Nighteyes assumed if a few minute delay could put them in danger of altruism, the newmoon gryphon would let her know. Then again, Whisper had turned out to be a lot less inscrutable after spending a night in a leaf-wrapped cocoon with her.

Whisper and Wendl, who would have guessed? Nighteyes snorted, and some nearby cave gryphons leapt back, feathers and fur poofing up.

"Keep it under control," Whisper hissed. The firelight's reflection danced in her silver.

Nighteyes apologized to the oilbirds. "Sorry, got some pepper up my nares."

Their escorts did not calm down but did continue to lead them through the nests, the larder, and several passages. Nighteyes had seen versions of these rooms yesterday, and she half expected Whisper to be overcome by the sights. Instead, Whisper kept sniffing every gryphon she came across.

"Don't embarrass us," Nighteyes teased. "You're representing the Emerald Jungle here."

Whisper hissed slightly. Though her fur was raised and her tail was almost as big as her body, her ears were forward and inquisitive. "There's...a lot going on here. Every gryphon and opinicus scent is a new language I'm trying to learn, but I only know the words for fear, anxiety, hunger, and relief in their nomenclature."

Nighteyes didn't have to ask what *fear* smelled like. Every time they stumbled across someone in the winding corridors, they'd get a confused look when they saw Nighteyes and then an alarmed one when they saw Whisper.

21

FEATHERSNAKES

Nighteyes and Whisper's guides abandoned them at the medicine gryphon caves, after explaining to a new pair of woodpecker guards that Slate had given them permission to visit Chert. Away from the heat of the pyre, the woodpeckers wore a kind of metal armor designed to protect their beaks.

Nighteyes' first thought was of mining equipment, but the tips had been sharpened and the detailed lattice-like engravings suggested a more sinister target than rocks. They wore opinicus harnesses with the badges removed. An attempt had been made to stain the grey leather a darker shade, but the winged decorations on the metal bits spoke of the guards' previous allegiance to the Seraph King.

Nighteyes was happy to move past them and into the medical wing, whose clean stone floors reminded her of the Crackling Sea Eyrie's interior. Though some of the patients were awake, Chert snored softly, and drool leaked down one side of her beak, coating her long whiskers and dripping down onto her wrappings.

The bitter smell of aneda brought back memories of the taiga and weald for Nighteyes. Wendl's bandages smelled of moss and cassia, a much more calming combination than aneda poultice. While aneda trees grew in the Jadebeak Mountains, they were rare. Nighteyes suspected they were probably more plentiful up in the Argent Heights, and the ones growing on the jungle's border were anomalies.

Though the nesting areas where she'd first come in were warmed through body heat, mostly from intense discussions and carers chasing chicks and gryphlets around, the majority of the tunnels in the naze were uncomfortably cool for a jungle denizen like herself.

The cave where the wounded were kept was as warm as the nests had been, but the exact method for warming them was lost on Nighteyes. She suspected it involved redirecting heat from the pyre in one way or another.

"Can you leave her with, like, a calming scent that says we hope she recovers?" Nighteyes asked. With the eyeshine, she couldn't tell if Whisper had rolled her eyes or not.

Small apprentices flitted about like butterflies landing on flowers. As with the rest of the naze, they weren't just oilbirds. In fact, they seemed to be reporting to an osprey opinicus at the far end of the ward. She'd mix the appropriate herbs together, then send a gryphon apprentice to the patient.

The ospreys bothered Nighteyes in a way she couldn't put her paw on. She'd overheard someone saying they came from Alwren, a set of islands with one mainland coastal settlement divided from the Emerald Jungle by powerful glyphs. If these were refugees from the Seraph King, had they somehow fled over the jungle to the Abyssal Naze?

Nighteyes shook her head. Most of the memories had come back, but the ones lost to altruism were the hardest. Those could wait until she was back home. She hadn't asked to come here to inquire about ospreys.

Nor had she come here to see Chert, not really. She wanted to know about Slate's red, green, and blue friend. "Do you smell anyone...different?"

"Different?" Whisper sniffed the air. "Everyone here is different. None of them share a smell. Even with twins, each develops..."

Nighteyes cut her off. "No, I mean I saw someone. They said they had a *red* here, and I thought they meant a Redwood Valley opinicus. But I caught sight of someone green with red tailfeathers. If there's someone here from the Ashen Weald, I'd like to speak to them."

"I'll see what I can do." Whisper braced herself, entering a trance not dissimilar from the one she'd used while controlling the susurration. Rather than draw attention to them, Nighteyes remained with Chert, grooming the oilbird's head feathers.

After several minutes of grooming, Nighteyes finally asked, "Any luck yet?"

"I'm not sure." Whisper's posture relaxed. "There are two strange scents in this room. One is fresh."

"You can stop licking my head," Chert said, causing Nighteyes to jump back.

"Er, sorry," the violet starling apologized. "I didn't mean to wake you, I just got carried away there. I hope I didn't cause you any pain."

"No, no, you'll save Xin grooming me later." Chert didn't explain who Xin was. "Thank you for saving me."

Nighteyes didn't respond at first. She was glad Chert had made it home safe. Nighteyes hoped she'd make it home, too. But she held onto a lingering anger for the Abyssal Naze she wasn't ready to shake yet.

Whisper pushed past Nighteyes and put a paw against Chert's face. "This smell here. And that one there. Who is that?"

Chert's forelegs were wrapped, so she needed Nighteyes to remove Whisper's paws from her face. "You're looking for Zeph and Kia. They're probably practicing their flight. Head down the corridor, third left."

Whisper lowered a decorated black and silver paw. Even the tips of her claws had been tinted with eyeshine. "Our escort will be here soon. If we're going, we should go now."

Nighteyes considered her options. They could get into real trouble if they were found wandering the naze. Then again... "Stay with Chert. Try to keep them calm. I'll be back as soon as I can."

Whisper stared at Chert, a gryphon she had just met, and shrugged. Though she didn't speak, Nighteyes thought the calming mint was meant as a yes.

"That is quite a nesting grounds, there at the pyre," Whisper said as Nighteyes slipped away.

"Yes," Chert replied. "These days, all cave gryphons are born of fire, one way or another."

THE UNDERGROUND PASSAGES of the Abyssal Naze held a lot of curiosities, but perhaps the biggest surprise—after the cavern of darkness and stars—was an enclosed valley with enough room to fly.

Nighteyes gazed upon a ceiling of gryphon silk. Leaves covered perhaps a quarter of the web, but even though it wasn't transparent, it let the weak light into the valley.

Moss, grass, and ferns coated the valley floor. Where a strip of silk had been torn and a slice of sunlight bled through, snakeweed bloomed gold on the valley wall. There were several high perches, and spans of cave silk formed a kind of safety net over the far end. It resembled the flight school at the kjarr nesting grounds.

How are Satra, Erlock, and Biski? Nighteyes wondered if they'd ever found the ingredients for the Merinkin's elixir. *Not that it would matter with the current pridelord. But maybe...*

From the patch of snakeweed above, loose scree tumbled past Nighteyes. She crouched, spreading her paws and preparing for an attack. When she looked up, she didn't see what had dislodged the stone. Below the golden flowers were just fern-covered stones, some granite and limestone, and then a vein of copper.

The vein of copper slithered higher, and the part of her brain that feared titanoboas screamed for her to flee. The only thing keeping her in place was that the copper had been covered in feathers.

Do snakes have plumage now? With the dim light, she only got the general shape, but she couldn't quite make out what she was seeing. It was long, very long —longer than a stormtail, even. She thought she recognized the tail end, with a strange split feathered appearance. She looked up to where she guessed the head should be, but the light wasn't good enough for her to make out details.

"Okay, one more time. Zeph, to me!" came the Redwood Valley voice with the slight opinicus trill from the far side of the silk valley.

From the location of the unseen voice, a leather ball covered in green feathers and painted with the face of an angry kakapo ground parrot was tossed in a long arc across the valley.

The coil of copper unfurled and flung itself from its perch. *Unfurled* was the right word: first one set of wings spread out, then a second, then the feathered back legs formed a kind of rudder. As though bowing to her previous complaints, the sunlight intensified, and the feathersnake glistened.

Within its plumage were streaks of red and green. Nighteyes got a good look at them as it flew overhead, four large wings beating until the feathersnake caught the parrot ball in its beak. Then the forewings folded in, revealing talon-like, fuzzy forepaws that took the faux-kapo from its beak and transferred it to the back paws.

The creature landed on an outcropping in the middle of the clearing. Its lower body curled around the stone, clinging to it for balance, and its tail now held the prize.

"Great job! That was really good." From across the valley, another of the creatures glided down from a perch. This one's wings were green and blue with hints of red. When Nighteyes saw the crimson tail, however, she knew this was the mysterious opinicus from the cave.

Opinicus was the wrong word, but the word choice and faint accent had hints of eyrie-speak. She didn't know what this was. She started to back up, but the coppery one twitched an...ear? A long tuft? and turned to look at her.

"Hey, we have a guest. Is this one of the new refugees, Kia?" he asked.

Seeing them side-by-side, their beaks shared a similar, hawkish look. There was a blue sheen to both of their eyes, as though they had their own shade of eyeshine. Body-wise, the slashes of color on the unnamed, coppery one matched Kia's plumage. Similarly, Kia had her own bits of copper.

Nighteyes wondered if that was their natural plumage, or if they'd decorated each other to match the way the woodpecker couple had with their woven bracelets. "Oh, hello. Sorry. I took a wrong turn. Just need to get back to the Emerald Jungle. My guide will be waiting on me."

Kia leapt from the outcropping, gliding over Nighteyes and landing between the starling and the exit. The move wasn't a hostile one, but it did leave Nighteyes in a precarious spot. The copper one followed after, landing next to Kia and letting the kakapo ball roll away. His long, feathered tail swished back and forth, but when it touched Kia's, hers naturally wrapped around his to stop it from moving.

First clawdiggers, now feathersnakes, Nighteyes mused. Despite having better questions to ask, she stuck with the expected one. "What...are you?"

"Zeph," the copper one replied, then he glanced at the discarded kakapo toy. "Zeph Parrotsbane, of Hatzel's pride."

"Kia Reevesbane," the other said. "Friend to many prides, but none are currently my home. Though I think I left my favorite journal at Poisonmaw."

Nighteyes shook her head. "No, not *who* are you. *What* are you?"

The feathersnakes shared a look.

"I guess you'd call us seraphs now," Kia explained. "Have you never seen one before? Where have you been for the last two years?"

Zeph stretched his long body towards Nighteyes. "That's right, you said you were going to the Emerald Jungle. You're a starling? I guess there are no seraphs in the Emerald Jungle."

Being around Whisper so much had made Nighteyes aware of her pheromones, and the scent she was giving off was fear. She'd heard the names Zeph and Kia before. She'd even met Hatzel the Saberbeak during her time with the Ashen Weald. But by all accounts, they were just a gryphon and an opinicus. Not a...whatever a *seraph* was supposed to be.

"Well, it was nice meeting you two feathersnakes. I can tell that you're busy flying. I'd love to stay, but I really need to get going." Nighteyes scurried past Kia and into the corridors, feeling precisely like a squirrel attempting to escape a serpent.

She slipped past several young medicine apprentices who paid her no mind. She walked past the woodpecker guards, who seemed uninterested in starlings or feathersnakes.

She arrived back at the medicine caves just in time to hear Whisper talking to their new guides: "She takes a very long time to pee, she should probably see a medicine gryphon, but you know how things are at the Emerald Jungle—Oh! There she is now. We can go."

22

RETURN TO THE JUNGLE

Where have you been for the last two years? was the question that stuck in Nighteyes' mind as she departed the Abyssal Naze with Whisper and their two guides, a cave swiftlet named Silky and a chimney swift named Bristlespine.

In the past few years, Nighteyes had been in two places. One was the Nightsky territory, her home. That had, until recently, included Wendl's hideaway, where she'd helped plot to kill the pridelord. There'd been brief sojourns to Stormtail territory, but they were few and far between. During all that time, she hadn't done anything to help another pride until Rudder showed up at her doorstep and begged her to come save Clamshell.

Now she was escaping the Abyssal Naze with Whisper, having seen a dozen gryphon and opinicus types she'd never heard of before.

Not even counting the clawdiggers and feathersnakes.

Whatever Whisper had done to her had made her more aware of the way scents formed...not words, but a kind of knowledge. She must have been thinking loudly, because Whisper echoed back indescribable smells that made Nighteyes think of the words *feather* and *snake.*

She thought the word *later* and hoped Whisper got the idea. She really had no idea what she was doing, just that something had opened up inside of her, the subconscious turning conscious. She didn't know how scents formed words, but she suspected whatever block had been there was gone, and she could figure it out if she had the time.

Belatedly, she realized this was probably what it would be like to become a pridelord. Whisper had warned her that it took years of training. Perhaps the newmoon gryphon had kicked off something inside Nighteyes just in case Wendl's schemes came to fruition.

Bristlespine pushed up another light rock disguised with moss to resemble a boulder, and Silky slipped outside. A few moments later came the all-clear. Away from the flickering brazier light of the depths, the small differences between the two swifts were visible. Silky's spines extended well past the end of her tailfeathers, whereas Bristlespine's were like tiny, pointed tips, easy to miss.

The chimney swift also smelled like a lampworks, though it was tough to tell if that was her natural aroma or if she picked it up by raiding the sinister buildings to rescue oilbird squabs. Beyond that—and the eponymous mouth goo—they could be sisters.

Though the silk roof of the feathersnakes' valley had given the impression of a cloudy day, the world above the naze really was fairly misty. Droplets hung in the air, and every time Whisper took a deep sniff, she sneezed water.

"This is good," Silky said. "If it stays misty, we can get to the border without being detected. There's a network of caves from here to there. I think we're going to have an easy time of it."

Whisper wasn't big on asking questions, leaving Nighteyes to make a fool of herself by inquiring why they were aboveground if a system of caves led straight to the Emerald Jungle.

Bristlespine clicked, a habit she'd apparently picked up from being around the oilbirds. It was meant less as a means of echolocation and more as a reminder to stay quiet and on topic.

Still, she answered Nighteyes' question. "Most of our routes are a mix of tunnel, surface, and sky for safety. You can't just walk wherever you want underground. If a particular tunnel sees a lot of use, the darkstalkers set up an ambush there. And if a cavern is large and deep enough, you can bet your primaries it has clawdiggers. Using a bunch of small, independent cave systems that don't feed into any existing network is just smart thinking. You just skitter from one to the next and nobody bothers you."

"Lone caves are great," Silky added. "You can hide in caves. Or cover the entrance in silk and take a nap. And if one cave fills up with scorpions, you just change the route to use a different one. Honestly, I think you're going to find you'll miss caves once you leave."

Whisper was unreadable, so Nighteyes couldn't wager a guess as to whether or not the newmoon gryphon would miss caves, but Nighteyes was looking forward to having open skies again. Even the mist felt like an insult, hiding the world above the canopy from her.

The swifts alternated who was in front and who brought up the rear. Despite Bristle's name, the spines on the feathers over her tail were short enough that the starlings preferred when she was in the lead. Her lampworks smell, while ominous, made it easy for them to follow in her wake.

Bristle's beak clicks were also crisp and clear, unlike Silky's, well, *silkiness*. Whenever a bird or squirrel made noises, she'd tap her beak together, creating more of the gooey silk used to seal off the maw of the Abyssal Naze.

Nighteyes wasn't good at estimating how long it took to traverse a distance by paw, but her heightened senses told her the density of jungle trees had increased. The maples were gone now, and even the birch grew scarce. They paused at several caves, taking the time to eat—and for one of their members to spit out extra silk.

"We're close now," Bristlespine whispered. "Just one more cave. It's probably safe to fly for it if we get spotted."

They had not warned Nighteyes that it was *unsafe* to do so before, which would have made for a bad situation if something had attacked. Every so often, they heard the sound of creatures larger than a jungle bird flying overhead. Possibly, the naze had its own version of giant teratorns. More likely, there were teams of opinici searching for the satchel.

The satchel Balthar took. What good is information on an opinicus spy network to a starling?

The final cave was shallow, and they had to dislodge some large frogs to make room for everyone. Silky warned that while they *could* eat the frogs, they'd probably regret it later. The mist coalesced into soft rain, and Bristlespine struggled to seal the cave entrance with a broadleaf.

"Do you need me to do it?" Silky asked, but Bristlespine hushed her.

"Something landed!" came the chimney swift's quiet hiss. "To the back of the cave."

The broadleaf barrier drooped, giving Nighteyes a view of rain falling on the small glen outside their shelter. True to the swift's warning, several opinici landed, mostly ducks.

"This is the place," the leader quacked. "Coulda been cassowaries, but I saw more than one plume color. Spread out and look around."

Unlike the mallard Nighteyes had nearly killed, these seemed to be in the employ of the Seraph King. None came towards the cave, which was good. With the leaf in front of it, it probably looked less like a cave and more like an eroded boulder. Luck might be on their side.

A white-tailed kite, golden armor dripping in the rain, stood next to another mallard in a fancy brown-and-green leather harness and a peafowl. Nighteyes couldn't see who they were talking to, but they were talking to someone.

"You don't look like much of a fighter," the mallard told the hidden opinicus.

"She was sent here by Silver," the peafowl said. "Delivering messages."

The white-tailed kite shook water out of his wings.

"That's *Reeve* Silver. We respect the Argent Heights in these parts. If not for her, more of our friends would be buried in the naze, food for cave gryphons."

"Sure, whatever," the mallard groused. "*Reeve* Silver. What I mean is that our new friend here doesn't look like she's any more of a messenger than a fighter."

"Aw, that's not nice," Silver's unseen opinicus said. "Here, and I even brought you a message."

Nighteyes couldn't tell what happened next, but whatever was on the letter the mallard had been handed must not have been very nice. He shouted angrily while the other opinici laughed at him.

"Okay, enough riling the duckbills up," the kite ordered. "We've got a job to do. Check the caves here, then we'll move on. You know darkstalkers. They don't like to be in the light."

Both the starlings and swifts tensed, though Whisper's reaction preceded everyone else's. Nighteyes was in the front. With her white and violet plumage, she'd be impossible to miss. *I wish we'd thought to hide me in the back. The swifts resemble rocks. Maybe they won't see this cave.*

Fortune was not on her side. There came a rustling, then the leaf was pushed aside and the hidden opinicus messenger revealed.

Foultner? Nighteyes couldn't believe it. Nor could Foultner, it seemed. The Redwood Valley opinicus stared into Night's starry eyes for several seconds without making a move.

Finally, Foultner slow-blinked like an owl. Nighteyes and Whisper reflexively returned the gesture. The opinicus replaced the leaf, then shouted,

"Nothing except cave toads. I thought I heard something flying east. Let's head that way and check."

As the patrol's leader grumbled outside, Nighteyes relaxed a little.

"What was *that* about?" Whisper asked quietly.

What was *that about?* Nighteyes wondered to herself. Aloud, she said, "I have no idea."

Once the Seraph King's forces—and Foultner, Satra's right-paw opinicus—departed, the party made a dash for the Emerald Jungle's border.

Silky and Bristlespine wanted to draw out the goodbyes, but Whisper cut that short. "She's going to lose herself to the altruism at any second. Thank you for the help, but we need to go."

Hidden in Whisper's auditory response were the scents for *hunter of night*, which just confused Nighteyes. She stepped through the Emerald Veil, into her jungle home once more. Her last return, the one from her visit with the Ashen Weald, she'd been met by a hundred starlings and the pridelord himself. This time, no one waited for her.

A frisson of guilt sprang up, like when she used to go star-watching with her sisters and had to sneak back into the nesting grounds without the denparents catching her.

Nighteyes turned to look back, expecting to find the same misty jungle that blocked her vision in times past. Whisper's changes held, however, and Nighteyes could see the two swifts arguing stickily with each other.

"Hey," Nighteyes began, "I just wanted to say—"

Whisper cut her off. "Say nothing. Hurry home. If anyone asks, the monster pulled us into its cave, and we only just escaped. Do not mention our new friends. Do not come visit me. Our scents must stay separate. We have nothing to talk about."

The newmoon gryphon flew east, leaving Nighteyes alone. They *did* have a lot to talk about, but that would have to wait for another time.

For now, Nighteyes saw more clearly than she had in years. She needed to find Wendl and have a long chat about what was going on. About the pridelord, about what Wendl was up to, about what she'd learned, about her friend who had stolen the satchel.

But if I do that, am I betraying Whisper? Whose side am I on?

Nighteyes felt pulled in three directions, pulled apart into three gryphons. One was a mindless leader, reset by the pridelord, loyal to the murmuration. The second was an insurrectionist, beaten down by the procession of dead nightsky gryphlets, who agreed to take over the murmuration by force and subterfuge. And then there was herself, in this moment, free of altruism and memory loss.

This Nighteyes smelled of clawdigger, feather-snake, newmoon, cave gryphon, and even wood-pecker. She'd stood in the depths of the Abyssal Naze and accused the ruler of the depths of killing her pride. Then she'd been accused of being just as heart-less, and those barbs tore at her heart because she knew they were true.

Whose side am *I on?*

She hesitated. She could decide tomorrow. Right now, she only needed one thing: to see Sheen.

23

HOMECOMING

The Nightsky Pride had held together in Nighteyes' absence, not that she'd had any reason to think they'd miss her. She'd spent months away with the Ashen Weald, after all, and no one had attempted to take over. She could take that as a compliment, but it also worried her. What if she hadn't come back?

The leader of the Nightsky Pride settled down and let her sisters preen her dry while one of the denparents tended to her wounds, mostly just her prior wounds having reopened. Her spiked paw had not enjoyed all the walking. Wendl was suspiciously absent. Or perhaps Nighteyes was just feeling suspicious these days.

She listened to the gossip and let the gryphlets and fledglings visit her. The younglings wanted to tell her about their epic battle with a particularly ornery squirrel who had snuck into the hatchery, but the adults were in a tizzy about the *invasion* into the Emerald Jungle. She reminded them that it was a pawful of gryphons and opinici who had quickly retreated. "Hardly an invasion. Just a few lost souls who paid the price for crossing into our territory."

"The jadebeaks and stormtails have the same problem," her youngest sister said.

Nighteyes perked up. "I haven't heard about this. They've had cave gryphons and alabasters in their lands?"

"No, not those," her sister replied. "It's the red-winged blackbirds. They find them dead all along the border. They must be trying to sneak in, then get killed. Maybe it's the creepy Newmoon Pride leaving the dead everywhere."

Nighteyes wondered if that was the work of clawdiggers, though the ones she'd seen were pretty intent on eating their quarry. She let the conversation move on to more pleasant subjects, not saying what she thought had *really* killed those opinici: greenwing altruism. It was curious that they were all blackwings, however.

The feathersnakes were right. She had no idea what had happened outside the jungle in the past two years. But as best she remembered, the Blackwing Eyrie was on the opposite corner of the continent. *Gryph-a-corner*, as Foultner used to say. The last time blackwing opinici had wandered into the jungle... Well, that had been the same expedition that had given them Wendl and Whisper.

"Say, has anyone seen Wendl?" Nighteyes asked at last. She suspected the answer was one of the usual excuses. Wendl was probably stealing sap from trees to make tinctures or something opinicus-y.

Her older sister's reply caught Nighteyes off guard.

"Wendl? Oh, she's been watching Sheen ever since you left. Won't let her out of her sight. I guess she wants to make sure Sheen's leg heals straight."

Nighteyes stood, startling a napping fledgling who was wrapped around her tail, the same one who had ultimately fended off the squirrel and earned the admiration of his peers. She apologized to him. "Er, sorry, li'l paw. I'm a bad pride leader, I totally forgot about Sheen. I should go check on her myself. Thanks for the grooming time, everyone. Have a good rest of the night!"

She slipped out of the common area, towards Wendl's hideaway. She hadn't forgotten about Sheen, she just hadn't realized that's where Wendl would be.

Despite not having any reason to believe Wendl would do the fledgling harm, Nighteyes broke her *no flying near the hatchery* rule to cross the nesting grounds.

Nighteyes landed to find Wendl standing over Sheen's unconscious body. Nighteyes' heart missed a beat while she waited for Sheen's chest to rise and fall. Any other day, seeing a medicine opinicus watching over a patient would have reassured her. After her awakening, however, everything Wendl did looked sinister.

"Oh, you're back!" Wendl said, as though she wouldn't have been able to tell by starberry scent alone when her pride leader returned.

Or maybe she can't? Nighteyes wasn't sure. "Yep, there was another incursion on our border with the

Newmoon Pride. Some sort of infighting between the naze gryphons. I got stuck in the caves, and it took all day and night to get back."

"Mmm," Wendl said noncommittally. She applied a sticky paste, probably made from the same plants she was always tending to, on Sheen's wounds.

Except for her breathing and a bit of light snoring, Sheen remained unmoving in the late morning light. The mist had burned off, and she glowed indigo beneath the sun's rays. Nighteyes examined the fledgling's wings. Along their outer edges, they were a deep blue. She picked up a paw and inspected the pads and claws.

They'd been a light brown when Sheen was a gryphlet, losing color from bloodbeak every day, but they'd gotten darker as of late. What Nighteyes had taken to be a sign of returning health looked different with eyes unclouded by Wendl and the pridelord's interference. The pads had a blue tint to their brown.

Sheen's claws were the same. What appeared to be a healthy, dark color returning to them was really a dark blue deposited where bloodbeak had previously turned them red. The same story played out across her beak and eyes.

Wendl watched Nighteyes closely. The pride leader knew what was going through the opinicus's mind, so she removed any doubt.

"Whisper had to bring me back to the jungle." Nighteyes kept her statement simple in case anyone else heard, but Wendl tensed. "What, exactly, did you do to Sheen?"

Wendl put away the sticky resin treatment. "She

has stormtail blood in her. It's keeping her safe somehow."

"No." Nighteyes let the word sit. Sheen had been born sick, and the denparents had codes to keep track of who the parents of each egg were ever since blood-beak had taken over the pride. Sheen didn't have a stormtail parent—her real parents were a nightsky and jadebeak who had both died over the Abyssal Naze—and she'd only started to recover in the last couple of years. "You took Sheen, did something to her, and she got better. Don't lie to me now. I don't just remember our conversations, I remember *everything*. I remember you taking her."

Nighteyes didn't really remember everything. Bits were still coming back. She remembered enough to convince Wendl, and very specifically, she remembered Wendl taking Sheen away the day the Emerald Veil was pierced by Slate and the Abyssal Naze.

Unbidden, the memory of a parrot gryphon, a mix of reds, blues, and greens, flying over the Emerald Jungle that day came back to her. The details matched the Ashen Weald's description of Kia. The colors matched the feathersnake who used the same name.

"There's no lie. Sheen has stormtail blood in her," Wendl answered. "I put it there."

Nighteyes pushed aside her personal feelings. "Why did you think stormtail blood would work? And how did you get blood from the Stormtail Pride?"

Wendl's answer about how she got the blood surprised no one. "I took it from unconscious storm-tails using Crackling Sea jelly toxin I stole from dead rangers when I'd help the jadebeaks raid the bog for pumpkins. I grabbed stormtails who came through our territory looking for mates. I suspected it would work because I'd tried everything else. I had Mally's research on the other prides. He took most of the stormtail research with him, or perhaps it had been lost. Either way, the void is where you search for hope when you can't find it in more conventional places."

"Is it all stormtails, or just Rudder?" Nighteyes had spent long hours lying next to the stormtail, and she knew about the scars hidden beneath his coarse fur—presumably medical codes in some opinicus language. She also knew that not a lot of stormtails were swimming around her pridelands except for him. "And if it isn't a cure, what is it?"

Wendl shrugged, not bothering to deny it was Rudder's blood she'd infused Sheen with. "If I knew, I'd have told you during our...private chats. It isn't *all* stormtails, but it *is* at least him. Whatever is in his blood inhibits bloodbeak. I think the blue pigment is a side effect. Based on how some stormtails are more blue or green, others may have it, but not the few I tested. And this could just be temporary. We still don't know."

There was so much information Nighteyes needed but had no way to find out. Wendl had made a case for sharing knowledge across the Emerald Veil with the Ashen Weald to find a cure, but Nighteyes lacked even much more local information. Had any stormtails died from bloodbeak? She didn't know of any, though they were one of the prides Mally had experimented on.

And how does that fit in with all of the eggs hatched at Lightningmaw turning out as stormtails? And is it related to stormtails and jadebeaks breaking out of the murmuration?

Nighteyes wasn't scholarly, but she was shrewd. Before the pridelord had banned the stormtails from breeding with other prides, they'd often searched out mates from the Nightsky, Sparkwing, and Jadebeak Prides. The Jadebeak Pride made sense, they shared a border—which was apparently a dumping ground for dead blackwings, which they both had to bury.

Gross.

But the Nightsky and Sparkwing Prides were far from the southern coast. The stormtails had avoided any other prides.

Those three prides shared one thing in common. They'd all had members taken by the Nighthaunt who returned and bred with others, infecting the prides with bloodbeak.

What if it's some sort of defense mechanism? Every egg that could have hatched with bloodbeak instead hatched as a stormtail. Could the pridelord somehow influence which eggs hatch or what type of starling the egg becomes? What if the command to avoid the stormtails was a ruse, and he secretly put a compulsion in my brain forcing me to mate with Rudder?

No, that doesn't make sense. I'd be dead by now if I had bloodbeak. Although, Wendl said it's more complicated than that, some gryphons can have offspring with blood-beak, otherwise it wouldn't spread.

Can the pridelord sense which ones of us have the potential to give our gryphlets bloodbeak?

She was back around to worrying that the pride-lord had secretly orchestrated her attraction for Rudder. These thoughts made her mad because she couldn't test her theories. The only starling who had the full knowledge of the murmuration at his claws was the pridelord. The pridelord, who'd specifically forbid the stormtails from breeding with the other prides for fear that they were somehow causing starlings to get cut off from the murmuration.

Better to leave the murmuration than die of bloodbeak.

There used to be a little voice in her head that stopped these errant thoughts from straying into blasphemy, but that voice was gone. If the stormtails had a natural resistance to bloodbeak, the pridelord was stopping that resistance from being transferred to other prides. In which case, perhaps he *didn't* know about it, perhaps *he* was the problem. Every path her thoughts travelled down to find a way to save her gryphons, one starling stood in her way.

If the pridelord didn't know, the murmuration was in danger. If he did know, he was forcing certain gryphons to mate, meaning he'd forced her to fall in love with Rudder against her will. He was a tyrant either way.

This is why it was so easy for Wendl to persuade the other me. I didn't need her help at all. Left to my own thoughts, I end up at the same conclusion.

"Er, pride leader? Did you hear what I asked?" Wendl waved a talon in front of her friend's face.

Nighteyes had not. She stared down at Sheen. "We have the Crestfall salts from your friend, Khalim. I can convince Rudder to give more blood. That's enough to save my pride from death. Maybe it doesn't last, but we're losing gryphons by the season. If we wait much longer, there won't be anyone left to save. Now is the time."

Still Wendl hesitated, looking down at the sleeping Sheen. "I don't have the salts here. And this isn't the cure-all you think it is. We just don't know enough."

"I'm your pride leader. I order you to save my pride's future." Nighteyes held Wendl's gaze, and she could catch the scent of emotion coming off the opinicus in a way she hadn't been able to before Whisper's interference. There was fear and distrust, and something that equated to heartbreak without any context for whether it was for their friendship or the dying nightsky fledglings.

"No." Wendl didn't move.

Nighteyes had been surprised to find out that disobedience to pride leaders was fairly common in the weald, taiga, and kjarr prides. The severity of the action had different tiers of associated punishment out there, but in some cases, it was possible to face no repercussions.

In the Emerald Jungle, pride leaders were careful about their demands, as it was understood no starling could say no to them. The exact punishments were never spoken about because no one ever broke the rules. The murmuration was too important. The two times it had happened in Nighteyes' lifetime, it had led to a starling challenging the current pride leader for control of that pride.

Something Wendl also seemed to recall. "Do you want me to fight you for the Nightsky Pride? I'll do it, and you won't have to kill me to win. Then...what? At best, I get assigned to another pride. Is that any better for you? Is that any better for the fledglings?"

Nighteyes didn't reply. In the back of her mind,

she'd known Wendl and the others weren't really star-lings. This just confirmed it.

But is this real? Perhaps because of Whisper, Nighteyes was getting several scents off Wendl. Her faint, true scent hidden beneath the cassia, but that wasn't all. There was something layered underneath it, a memory of a different scent. Presumably, a moth-feather smell, never forgotten by her friend.

Friend.

Wendl wasn't a starling, but she was a friend. That part was true, or so Nighteyes chose to believe.

"If you really remember everything, you remember agreeing that this plan is the right one." Wendl stepped away from Sheen's sleeping form. "I'll happily use all the salts and Rudder's blood to treat your fledglings and the others, but I want to know there isn't a better, safer cure already out there. The moment you're pridelord, you can free us from this jungle prison and let me find out."

A pang of guilt twitched in Nighteyes' gut. She hadn't even thought to ask the cave gryphons or feath-ersnakes. Kia was supposed to have been a scholar. "A message arrived for you at the Newmoon Pride. The Ashen Weald knows of no cure."

"I see." Wendl paused. "Well, it was unlikely. The Ashen Weald was never our best shot. If not for the Redwood Valley's *scholarship*, we wouldn't be in this predicament, and without their university, they're probably struggling just to treat the eggs. Our best hope lies with the Blackwing Eyrie. Or...with Khalim infiltrating the Alabaster Eyrie."

Nighteyes thought back to the comments she'd overheard.

"Any word of the Ashen Weald? We sent Cherine back a year ago..."

"Where have you been for the last two years?"

It was possible there were answers outside the Ashen Weald.

"I hear the jadebeaks and stormtails are finding dead blackwings along their border," she casually remarked. "If you want to know about your home, you should ask them."

"I'm mothfeather, not blackwing," Wendl protested, reinforcing Nighteyes' opinion that she wasn't dealing with a starling. "I'll see what I can find out, but I can't question a dead blackwing. There's only one answer that will save your pride, Nighteyes."

The leader of the Nightsky Pride didn't trust herself to respond.

"The only way out is through." Wendl departed, leaving her friend alone with Sheen.

Nighteyes longed to talk to Sheen, to tell her what was going on. But Sheen was still part of the murmuration in a way neither Wendl nor Nighteyes were. It would be too dangerous to speak to her about this. Even discussing it with Rudder would put him at risk, something she hadn't considered during her argument with Wendl.

A rumble of thunder brought back the rain, not bothering to block out the sun first. Nighteyes idly groomed Sheen, gagging a little when she got a tongueful of medicinal resin. For all of her efforts antagonizing Wendl here tonight, she didn't disagree with the *mothfeather*.

"If the Nightsky Pride is going to survive, something needs to change," she spoke to the sleeping fledgling. "No one was strong enough to step up when I left. I'm the leader. This falls upon my wings and my wings alone."

And if we fail? she wondered. *What happens to my pride if I strike at the pridelord and lose? That's the more likely outcome.*

Sheen stirred in her sleep, and Nighteyes cooed a calming lullaby about a cassowary who pecked at the ground so long trying to catch a worm that it created the Abyssal Naze.

There was still one more loose end.

I owe a lot to Whisper, but the Newmoon Pride can afford to leave things the way they are. That's a luxury my pride doesn't have. I'll just have to hope whoever becomes pride leader next will take care of the susurration.

24

HUNTER BY NIGHT

Exhaustion clung to Whisper like bog moss, weighing down her every step since the Abyssal Naze. Once she was in the Emerald Jungle and Nighteyes had been sent on her way, the newmoon gryphon curled up to take a short nap. There was a strong breeze coming down from the mountains, the last bits of the mist she'd travelled through to get here, and she spread her wings and paws, letting the wind carry away the scent of her trip.

Then she massaged the oil glands on her paws, hoping to find the rights scents to tell her pride she was home, but nothing came. When she'd changed from opinicus scribe to gryphon, pheromones had become her words and her scent glands the ink. Now she'd run dry.

That's troubling.

Her time as pride leader had sent her into the bog, heights, and even border eyries to recover lost starlings. No matter how exhausted she'd been, no matter how daring the rescue, her paws had never come up empty like this. Though something had been bothering her even before the naze.

Did it start with Desert Rose? she wondered. *No, it was the clawdiggers.*

The newly cured had fought against her control, acting more like they were infected, seeing everything as food. It wasn't just the oilbirds, alabaster, and clawdiggers. They'd wanted to eat Nighteyes the same way they'd consumed the dead blackwings on the border. Holding them at bay had left her drained, though the overnight trip into the Abyssal Naze had certainly made things worse.

And then I left them to retrieve Nighteyes from the depths.

She considered flying back and making sure Moonlit Blossom was okay but stopped herself. If her pheromones were this faint, someone could attack her before they identified who she was. She needed to find a safe place to hide until she recovered.

Whisper licked a paw, rubbing it against the scent glands on the corner of her mouth, but all she smelled was saliva. Then she went to the northern border, where she'd warned her pride to stay away from, and began walking back towards her nesting grounds.

Birds of paradise called to each other, their cries barely audible over the other songbirds of the jungle. Rhea chirped happily as they fed on fallen eggfruit. Squirrels fought over an acorn from a lost northern oak. Despite the jungle chorus, Whisper was overcome with her own thoughts.

The rhea chatter as though there are no predators, so I should be grateful no snakes or goliath birds are in the area. Yet why am I ill at ease? She stalked past the flock, and while the birds eyed her, they didn't run. That's when it clicked. *No predators—gryphons are predators. The local birds must have adapted to our smells and use them to avoid us. I'm so out of scent, I'm invisible to their nares.*

It could make for a new hunting strategy, a way to sneak up on the elusive northern rhea who loved to hide across the border when gryphons came calling. Of course, even if a starling could willingly force their scent to be this faint, which she doubted, they'd run the risk of being hurt by other starlings.

When the Nighthaunt's expedition arrived in the jungle, they'd believed the northeast empty. These days, Whisper suspected her predecessor had been watching them, keeping her pride hidden. The camp was established and fortified before they encountered their first starlings. Of course, when the gryphons arrived, it was...memorable. She'd been a moth-feather then, and she'd never forgotten the sounds of altruism, of nearly being gored by a green beak.

Those thoughts came back to her now, but she tried to push them down. She *was* a starling. Her pheromones were faint, but if anyone got near her, they'd know who she was.

Right?

The rhea flock spooked, fleeing north, and Whisper crouched low. Her scent glands may not be working, but her nares were—and they detected starlings.

A fallen broadleaf provided her with visual cover, and the smell of fungus helped conceal any lingering stench of Silky or Bristlespine. Whisper debated wiping clean her eyeshine to improve her vision, but in an emergency, it might help the infected recognize her.

The canopy above had yet to fill in the hole left by the missing tree, and the sun shone down upon three starlings, led by the one wearing opinicus talons as a hat. This *Taloncrest* led them to the border, sniffing at something.

Loud sniffing might betray her position, but she had a good head for what every part of her territory should smell like. To the west, the way she'd come from, was a glyph marking the buried jars of salts she used to form the paths through the jungle. Past it was her next glyph, marking some of the hills of the Argent Heights that bled into her territory. The infected jadebeaks were halfway between.

She inhaled deeply. One of Nighteyes' old glyphs was here, helping shore up the border with the Abyssal Naze. Whisper had decided to leave it, as she'd wanted to mark the clay jars and the hill. Bark beetles had eaten away a few of the nightsky glyphs marking this as their territory, but some ivory-billed woodpeckers had snacked on the beetles before they ate the section marking this stretch as the murmuration's border.

Taloncrest stood in front of the remaining nightsky glyph and moved his head back and forth, looking like a Crestfall hooded cobra. She'd seen elderly squirrels use this strategy as their eyesight failed, but in a starling, it was more about scent.

She wasn't worried. The Emerald Veil would make the Abyssal Naze and Argent Heights beyond look like nondescript jungle. Whisper didn't know how the pridelords had originally discovered this ability, but she'd been taught how to replicate it. Taloncrest's eyes were mostly clear now, but they didn't show signs of focusing beyond the tree.

Everything is fine. Just the newly cured being weird. This is just like with the hats. Or the cannibalism. It's a phase they grow out of.

Taloncrest stepped one paw forwards. Then another. He looked disoriented, unable to see what was around him, but he passed Nighteyes' old glyph like it wasn't there.

Okay, that part isn't normal.

Five paces in, the veil overwhelmed him. He ran back to the jungle, shaking his head, but his two friends began their own forays, running past the glyph, getting disoriented, and returning. Taloncrest tried closing his eyes and trusting his nares, and he reached the crossed feathers of the Argent Heights marker.

Whisper did not approach. During a terrible storm, she'd once watched a ranchtalon approach a goliath he'd raised as a chick, claiming the beast would never hurt him because he'd raised it from an egg. The bird was in a frenzy, terrified by the lightning and howling wind. The ranchtalon hadn't survived the encounter, and it had served as a reminder that animals, gryphons, and even opinici were all prey to their own nature.

If Taloncrest tore her apart, it would be because he didn't know who she was. It would be her fault if she got hurt here.

And if I lose three starlings? What will the pridelord do to the susurration then? I need to help them. Though the ranchtalon probably thought the same thing, right before he was stomped to death.

Quiet as her name, she slipped her medicine pouch off her head, opened it, and pulled out one of Wendl's incense bombs, liberated from her underground laboratory and wrapped in enough leaves so Whisper hadn't been able to smell it. Just being near it had caused problems.

She didn't trust her shaking paws to light a flint and tinder fungus, but she hoped if she smashed it on the ground, the smell would be enough to incapacitate them.

Then Moonlit Blossom finds us hours later, when my pheromones are working again. Hopefully.

She crawled towards the trio. They'd begun to mark their path to freedom with pheromone trails like leafcutter ants. The Emerald Veil still made them blind, but the infected no longer depended on their sight. She waited until just Taloncrest was recovering in the jungle, then approached.

He opened his eyes and stared at her.

She tried calming words, the same ones she'd spoken when she found him in the bog, eating an Ashen Weald ranger. Other than chittering, the infected weren't very auditory. It was part of what made them so dangerous. They would lie in wait, silent, until an opinicus stumbled over one. Then the chittering and screaming began.

Taloncrest sniffed loudly but didn't call for the others. He hadn't regained his voice yet, probably wouldn't ever recover it considering how little was left by the time she got the bugs out of him.

He recognized the faint remains of newmoon

scent on her but was still skeptical. He sent out queries, demanding she identify herself.

Now to find out if I've recovered at all from those hours of walking.

She concentrated very hard on the pheromone marking someone as part of the murmuration and massaged her left paw, the easiest place to get a scent. To her relief, she could smell the weak pheromones. She rubbed it into her face, the first place most starlings would sniff. It translated to *Whisper of the Murmuration.*

Much like the murmuration marker on the nightsky glyph, it was lost on Taloncrest. He queried her again, demanding she identify herself. She could hear his beak starting to chitter quietly. The parasite was long gone, but its ghost haunted his mind, coming out in his rewritten instincts.

Whisper had little time to act, but a thought occurred to her. What if this wasn't a result of his infection, what if it was something else? Taloncrest didn't recognize the murmuration, but neither had Desert Rose—or Clamshell, who hadn't come into contact with the parasite at all. Starlings had been disconnected all along the eastern jungle. Except for her pride, or so she thought. But now these starlings hadn't recognized Nighteyes as being part of their pride, either.

If an infected was disconnected from the murmuration, would my own compulsions still bind them to the susurration?

She expected she had one last shot at this. Taloncrest's beak clacked, and his two friends turned back to see what was going on. The farther one still had black feathers around their beak.

Dead blackwings dropped along the Stormtail territory. Dead blackwings dumped along the jadebeak border. Dead blackwings along our border. When Desert Rose told his story, he didn't know when he'd become disconnected, it was a blur. But he said he'd passed by more *dead blackwings. That means he'd come across them before. The stormtails and jadebeaks would have buried the dead. But my pride ate them.*

She was too tired to do anything about her revelation, but it told her what her next gambit should be. With the last of her pheromones, she rubbed her right paw's scent glands, then groomed them into her fur.

I am Whisper of the Susurration.

Taloncrest relaxed. She could smell the others querying him, being too far away to catch her faint scent. He relayed the information, and they, too, relaxed.

Whisper, leader, their pheromones confirmed.

They abandoned their attempts to break free of the Emerald Jungle and fell in line behind her.

Exhausted as she was, she didn't trust herself to sleep until Moonlit Blossom had control of them for her, so she began her trek south. The three starlings she'd been afraid would eat her minutes ago nuzzled her encouragingly, leaving behind their pheromones on her, a sign of affection. Everyone carried a little of their pridemates' scent on them, and other starlings often judged someone's importance by whose pheromones they wore.

Though she tried to keep her mind on the walk,

she couldn't help but think of how close they'd come to disaster. Most likely, every jadebeak she'd let eat a blackwing—*a blackwing corpse laced with some sort of new anti-starling poison, tossed over the border*—had been disconnected from the murmuration.

She'd have to spend the next week slowly fixing them as she had Desert Rose before anyone outside of her pride caught on, but it raised a lot of questions. Her tired mind worked on the *how*, but once she had rest, it would be time to figure out the more important question.

Why were the tainted corpses tossed over?

A TROUBLING SENSE of dread haunted Whisper after returning from the Abyssal Naze. She was valuable to the murmuration, but she wasn't irreplaceable. The pridelord could remove her abilities and raise Moonlit Blossom up in her place. Or he could decide enough infected starlings had been saved from the bog and her services were no longer required.

Still, like a gryphlet playing too close to a ledge, she couldn't help but aid Wendl, Nighteyes, and even Flicker. She liked being a starling and knew better than to take such risks. Yet here she was, surly and unable to get in a good nap due to the stress she'd brought into her life.

She purred a little. Not the happy, content purr of a gryphlet. The purr of a gryphon who was trying to calm herself down. Her surly, sour scent brought in Moonlit Blossom, who was supposed to be watching the murmuration-removed starlings until she had enough scent to fix them herself.

Moonlit Blossom is a good name for the pride leader of the Newmoon Pride, she thought to herself. *He was born to take over for Whisper, by all rights should have done so, and yet here I am, Whisper reborn, taking that from him.*

"Taloncrest and his friends are sleeping, and your new...acquisition is doing better today," he prompted, ignoring the fact her eyes were closed, and that meant she was pretending to sleep. "Perhaps you should pay her a visit before she's well enough to wander off and get eaten by our pridemates? You set a bad precedent by letting them eat the dead opinici."

Had I known they were laced with strange chemicals, I wouldn't have.

Whisper sighed and stood up, not bothering to groom her plumage. Particles of dry featherdust floated through the air around her, lit by the sun. "Are you sure you don't want to be pride leader?"

"Noooo thanks," he laughed, but it was a short sound.

She stared at him, waiting for a more honest answer.

"Oh, are you serious? I'm sure I will someday, when you die, if no one better comes along before then. Why, are you sick?" He sniffed her. "You smell healthy, if...overdue for a bath. Where were you that smelled like smoke and cave mushrooms?"

She didn't answer his latter question. "I'm not sick, but you'd be a more conventional leader than I am. I don't believe you'd do a bad job."

"I'm not sure *conventional* is what this pride needs." He used a wing to gesture at where her escort home had left offerings of meat next to her nest while she pretended to sleep. "Do you remember our conversation before the blackwings captured you?"

"No. I have few memories before being taken." Whisper had none, of course, of her namesake's former life. Whisper had her predecessor's essence and shape, that was all. In a way, Desert Rose's accusation that Newmoon Pride were spirits put in new shells was true, at least for her. "All that remains is... something else, almost a compulsion. No, that's not right. It isn't an obligation or even a duty, but a sense of purpose. I am driven to help the susurration, and I can't do otherwise."

Moonlit Blossom pawed idly at an unripe eggfruit. "Yes, it figures that's all you'd come back with. I knew you'd changed, I guess I didn't realize how much. We were, well, close before you were captured. Back then, you asked me to be ready to take over the pride in your absence, but who was I? I didn't lead the hunters. I wasn't a denparent. I was no one. The only gryphon who saw something in me was you; I didn't even feel that way about myself. And then you vanished, and I did nothing. I didn't step up and fill your wings as leader."

"And now?" She'd wondered why Moonlit Blossom looked at her the way he did. What she'd taken for suspicion had, perhaps, been longing...or loss.

Or even shame.

He stood taller, his ears forward. "If you had not come back from saving the nightsky gryphon, I would have taken over. I can lead this pride. I'm ready."

"Excellent. Then we fight!" Whisper puffed up her

fur and tail, looking twice her normal size. With her feathers spread out like that, the faint grey starling spots were just visible.

"What, no!" Moonlit Blossom started to protest, but then he caught the teasing scent of her renewed featherdust, a mix of rose and sunbaked sage used to denote playtime among gryphlets. "Oh my *feathers*, you almost gave me a heart attack."

"Yes, you did appear about to faint. Another time, then. Our battle for control of the susurration can wait." Whisper looked down at the pile of offerings from Taloncrest and the infected. She didn't have the appetite to eat any of it. Still, she didn't want gryphons to *stop* bringing her food while she slept, so she ordered Moonlit Blossom to clean it up for her.

He happily ate the treats while she flew east to the border, where the so-called *darkstalker* was kept. She'd suppressed the altruism in several of her pride just enough that they could keep watch on any infected non-starlings she brought home. Two of them chirped greetings as she flew past. In the sunlight, the iridescence in their black fur sparkled a rainbow of colors.

Whisper, too, shone when clean, but she needed her featherdust to survive. All three times she'd nearly died had been after she'd cleaned herself to a shine, and she now resigned herself to a dusty life. Idly, thoughts of Flicker's strawberry-red fur stained with black pawprints and eyeshine came to her.

Those thoughts could wait until the darkstalker and Taloncrest were dealt with. Whisper chirped a greeting to her pridemates, and they departed. She felt their scent shift closer to home, an anxiety lifting from their small, spotless forms.

Despite having room to spread out in their new territory, the Newmoon Pride only felt safe around each other. They'd grown shy of other starling prides, something that would worry Whisper if she hadn't seen the susurration hold together even when the murmuration fell apart.

She landed a good distance from the Jadebeak Falls. *Newmoon Falls,* she corrected herself. There was no sense letting the Ashen Weald's owls catch a glimpse of her. She walked the rest of the way in, pausing to groom her feathers and check her scent.

Moonlit Blossom was right, she smelled like everything that had happened the past few days: clawdiggers, silkmouths, oilbirds, and Nighteyes. She didn't know if the opinicus's sense of smell would be enough to detect it, but she was too tired to care.

She approached a small hideaway in the Jadebeak Mountains—she wasn't quite ready to try to get them renamed to the Newmoon Mountains while they were full of clawdigger monsters—and stepped inside the burrow, chirping a calming sound as she entered.

The darkstalker was not reassured to have a starling come into her den. She stood up, reaching for a pair of metal talons the pride had already confiscated. They wouldn't fit over gryphon paws, but they were shiny, and gryphons liked shiny things. Taloncrest would be unlikely to part with his new hat.

The newmoon leader emitted calming mint out of habit. "Your friends are looking for you. Several patrols have come up against the edge of the Emerald Jungle. Do you want to go back?"

"Yes." The darkstalker's words said one thing, but her scent showed deception with a hint of curiosity. She'd just been saved from becoming clawdigger lunch, but she had the stench of someone who'd spent months terrified. The fragrance of relief was faint, incomplete.

Whisper tried not to sniff too loudly, but there was something else. The opinicus felt safer here than she did back home.

Fascinating.

"Perhaps it would be best if you took a few more days to recover," Whisper prompted. "I did not realize you were so weak. You will be safe so long as you follow a few simple rules. Stay within two miles of the den. Do not eat any meat that isn't fish. And do not go to the waterfall itself."

"...thank you." The darkstalker stepped into the light, and it was like looking into a pond's reflection. Her dripping black marks on white feathers mirrored Whisper's own silver on black. Whisper was so busy inspecting the opinicus that it took a few moments before she realized that she, too, was being inspected.

"We're a matched set," the newmoon gryphon joked. "Perhaps we balance each other out."

The darkstalker had realized Whisper's markings were all paint, though, and dismissed her. "Mine's not something I can take off. You wouldn't understand what it's like to be one of the Nighthaunt's experiments."

"Ah." Whisper didn't correct the darkstalker's incorrect assumptions about her. "Would you go back to the way you were if you could?"

For Whisper, the answer was simple. No, she

would never go back to the way things were. She was happy now. She imagined for Wendl, Balthar, Iri, and the others, the answer was also quick but in the other direction. Especially the ones who had traded talons for paws.

Talli might be the only exception there.

The darkstalker paused for a long time before answering. "I'm not sure. We're getting to go home soon. How could my sacrifice not be worth that?"

"Who's getting to go home?" Whisper was unclear what *home* meant in this context if it didn't refer to the Alabaster Eyrie.

"All of us," the darkstalker replied. "All opinici. A gryphon wouldn't understand."

"Well, now that you've won and are going home, would you change back once you got there?" Whisper pushed. She'd heard the Alabaster Eyrie was religious, but that bit of trivia had come from blackwings. She didn't trust either side at this point. Her time with the cave gryphons had made her curious, though, about the outside world.

"No, I-I mean..." The darkstalker looked up, and Whisper could see her own silver eyes reflected in the opinicus's dark orbs. The scent had changed, unsure with a hint of self-deception. "You wouldn't understand. What the Nighthaunt does...if you haven't been through it, you could never understand who I am."

Whisper had never felt so tempted to tell an outsider the truth about who she was. The so-called Six had gone through what she had, but they were different. They hated being gryphons. Even Wendl and Balthar resented their forms. With this darkstalker, however, there was a real conflict inside of her. Perhaps Whisper's joy would give her peace.

The winds shifted, and scents of hundreds of nearby starlings reminded Whisper of the other side of the equation. She finally decided to answer, trusting an opinicus couldn't smell the lie. "That's not entirely true."

The darkstalker's face was unreadable, but her scent was not. She didn't believe Whisper.

"The Nighthaunt had a camp not far from here. He began with eggs, but once he gained access to the salts, he tested them on starlings first." She gestured vaguely west, deliberately not pointing directly at the camp ruins. "You'll find a lot of starlings have gone through something...if not similar, similarly disturbing."

Now the darkstalker's face was as readable as her scent. "You...didn't start out looking like that? All of the silver dye, I assumed it was to hide how normal you are. It didn't occur to me it might hide what he did to you."

"Well, the paint has other purposes," Whisper protested, a little offended, "but yes, this is nothing like how I looked before I met the Nighthaunt."

The darkstalker looked at Whisper anew, perhaps trying to guess who she'd once been. "Would you go back?"

"No," Whisper said. "I've never been happier than I am now. I wouldn't give this up for anything."

Despite her protests to the contrary, the look on the darkstalker's face was just as revealing as her scent. She did not believe Whisper any more than Whisper believed her. "I see. Well, thank you for your…hospitality. I'll depart the jungle once I've recovered."

Whisper bowed her head slightly, then left the burrow. These were dangerous times. She doubted the Seraph King posed any real threat to the Emerald Jungle, but she had a day or two to decide if she wanted to trust this stranger with her story. It wasn't like every day needed to have its own emergency.

25

CLAWGRYPHLETS

Having spent the previous night painstakingly restoring Taloncrest to the murmuration while having Moonlit Blossom dig ditches for the little that remained of the blackwing bait, Whisper slept through the morning. Daylight she could ignore, but chittering and the spicy aroma of alarm pulled her out of dreams of gardening with Flicker.

She untangled herself from her unusual nest made by every other member of her pride. It remained big on symbolism, community building, and leadership—though not comfort.

The infected were not the best builders, even once cured. If there was a nesting instinct, the parasite ate away that part of their brains. So while Moonlit Blossom slept nearby on his carefully crafted bed of maple, soft leaves, and dried herbs, Whisper often awoke to find herself at the bottom of a pile of twigs.

She managed to right herself, dislodging a log far too cumbersome to be used for the nest of anything smaller than a teratorn, and untangled a spiketrunk branch from her tail fur. Taloncrest, grateful to be able to serve the murmuration again, had attempted to add his metal spiked hat to the bedding, requiring Whisper to remove at least one prong from her posterior.

She forgot about the panic and chittering for a moment while she chewed the long spines off the spiketrunk branch and licked her wounds. The opi weapon was new, but the spines were a common enough occurrence. She wasn't sure which of the infected was doing it, but every time she de-spiked the branch, a new one would show up in her nest.

Was it a practical joke by one of the rare newmoon gryphlets, some sort of passive-aggressive protest to her remaining leader so long, or just the strange antics of the cured? She had no idea, but she was getting tired of being poked in the tail.

Moonlit Blossom, awake before dawn to lead the hunters, looked on with amusement. "You could always forbid your pride from building nests with spiked branches, you know."

"If I thought for a moment it would stop our rescues from filling my nest with spines, I'd do it." She dislodged a few more sticks, then shook herself, getting a feel for how dusty her feathers were. "Unfortunately, I think it'd be more likely to cause infighting from silver-eyed jadebeaks who no longer understand what they're doing wrong. What's all the excitement?"

Hopefully, not more dead blackwings. I need to warn the jadebeaks and stormtails not to touch the bodies. What's the point of killing a few starlings, though? Do the mysterious corpse-tossers really think they can thin out our numbers in a way that matters?

He shrugged his wings. "I don't know, they wouldn't talk to me. I think they've got something cornered by a cave."

"Cassowary scat, I hope it's not a dead clawdigger. Those can't be safe to eat." She got a running start and flew to the source of the commotion.

Silver-eyed jadebeaks stood in front of a cave along the mountains separating the Emerald Jungle from the Argent Heights. She returned the metal talons to their jade owner, who placed them back upon his head before turning to express his displeasure at the cave again, something echoed by his pridemates.

Based on the length of recovery time, some starlings chittered while others hissed. Whisper shook her feathers a bit, cautiously querying her pride to see if her attempts to suppress their altruism a few days earlier were in play. That would help her decide if it was a starling in there or something else.

Her scent still held. For the jadebeaks she'd spent all night fixing, it was strong. For the others, just barely. She'd panicked during the clawdigger attack and rescue of the darkstalker and sent a stronger message than intended.

So it could be anything in there.

Ordering starlings, especially the newly-cured, to go away and ignore something was a futile gesture. Instead, she refocused their efforts, ordering them to stay back and guard her flank from any surprise attacks. They fell in line behind her like a long, feathered tail.

She sniffed at the entrance to the cave. The mysterious aroma plaguing the northeastern jungle had been clawdigger, as they'd recently discovered. This was similar. In fact, it smelled a lot like two of the beasts her pride had torn apart.

Too bad we don't have the darkstalker or an oilbird with us. I could use their sight now, she thought. And the dark part of her brain replied with, *There's still time to add one to the susurration.*

She shook away such thoughts and stepped into the darkness, following the miasma of fear. Moonlit Blossom hadn't mentioned any surviving clawdiggers. Then again, she'd been so busy fixing Taloncrest, perhaps he hadn't had the opportunity.

She sniffed again. The tang of gryphon blood was strong, but it was from a few days before. They were near where the earlier fight had occurred, and as the passage twisted, she suspected it was all part of the same structure. She passed by dead cassowaries, capybaras, and even a few blackwing bodies.

Better they eat them than we do, I suppose.

Her ears twitched, some sort of fear reaction, but she pushed on, giving the dead opinici a wide berth. Then she heard the squeaks. Faint, inquiring even, at first. More alarmed as she neared.

She swore softly, then adjusted her scent, trying to mimic the clawdiggers her pride had killed. Not precisely—she didn't want anyone to think she was one of the dead returned to life—but something close.

Familial.

She continued her approach, reaching the edge of a giant nest in the darkness. The smell told her there were five, maybe six gryphlets. The way the air currents moved as they shifted to face her told her that, even as gryphlets, they would tower over her. She had flashbacks to the pointy, toothed beaks of the adult clawdiggers. Even a gryphlet could kill her with a single bite.

The cave here was warm, uncomfortably so. She wondered if there were more adults nearby, or if the reason her pride had found these was that they were noisy or letting off smells of distress. She didn't know. Instead, she backed up slowly, retreating to the entrance of the cave.

Moonlit Blossom waited for her there, holding back the others. "I thought it'd be better if you went in alone. Is it more opinici like the darkstalker?"

"No, it's gryphlets. Clawgryphlets." She weighed her options. When a predator became so dangerous it threatened a starling pride, sometimes the pridelord would order them to destroy the nests. That had happened with a particularly nasty set of crocodiles once, though there were often unintended consequences. In the case of the Winter Jungle, without saltwater crocodiles, juvenile serpentine whales had taken over.

On the other paw, which had her starry crescent dyed into it, what would happen if she tried to root out all of the clawdiggers who nested in the mountains? The glyphs alone would keep most of her pride from going deep enough to reach all of them.

A cool wind descended from the heights, and she fluffed her feathers, sending out another inquiry. Sparks of individual scents came back, informing her of how many opinici were in the ranks of the susurration.

"I can kill them if you don't feel up to it," Moonlit

Blossom offered, though his perfume made it clear that he didn't believe himself capable of the task. "Are they a type of cave gryphon?"

"Of a sort. No, I won't need you to do this for me. Just head to the pride stash and fetch all of the opinicus things we have. And fetch the darkstalker while you're at it." The past few days had put her in a strange mood, but she wanted to exhaust her non-lethal options on the clawgryphlets first.

WHISPER STOOD atop the ruined workshop, above her old room, and surveyed her pride's efforts. The Sleeping City had weather barriers it used during the cold months, designed to secure passages against wild animals. In the modern era, assuming it hadn't changed since she'd left opinicus society behind, blackwings and trashbirds stood guard above the Great Seal. But in the old days, predators would sometimes scour the abandoned eyrie, looking for hibernating mothfeathers to prey upon.

It still happened, from time to time, that a poorly made barrier would fail and a starving goliath would kill a family that chose to sleep away from the eyrie. It wasn't common. It might not happen for five years in a row. But it wasn't just an old gryphon tale, either.

Heh, 'old gryphon tale.' Listen to me. I hate this plan already.

She'd helped her family construct their barriers several times, and she thought she remembered how to make them. If she could close off the caves along the border of the jungle, the clawdiggers might move elsewhere. Based on what little information she'd gleaned about them from overheard conversations in the Abyssal Naze, they usually lived in the deep places, but when the oilbirds and cave swiftlets abandoned the tunnels, they rose up once again.

That meant they had another home to go to, and Whisper intended to push them away from her pridegrounds. Unfortunately, *someone* had gone through this opinicus research camp and taken all of the useful tools for her own use.

Wendl just can't leave well enough alone. Not that Whisper was without blame. The first thing she'd done when the pridelord moved her pride was to search for some of her old things, too. Which was how she'd discovered Wendl's burrow and the deadly incense below.

Deadly was a strong word. Even when lit, for most starlings, it would just disconnect them a bit, leaving them like Clamshell or Desert Rose for an hour. This was probably where she'd worked on Nighteyes.

For the Newmoon Pride, who required specific scents and instructions at all times to hold together, that kind of interruption could be deadly. And when Whisper had wandered in here upon first arriving, not realizing what the smell was, it had sent her pride into disarray.

So none of the Newmoon Pride were permitted down there. The stench of incense was too strong, even unlit. The corridor into the old cool storage area reeked, and all of the best tools were down there.

Thankfully, Whisper had one out-of-pride gryphon she could rely upon, one who would probably be happy to do something to stem the tide of clawdiggers. An opinicus, in fact.

The darkstalker looked nervously at all the gryphons. Several of the new starlings, still a bit silver in the eye without needing eyeshine, sniffed her, including the one wearing her talons as a hat.

Whisper kept their killer instincts at bay.

"You requested my presence?" The darkstalker did not ask if it was safe for her to be out. Perhaps she worried this was some sort of cruel trick.

Whisper pointed to the pile of wooden planks below her, the best she'd been able to do to keep her pridemates from wandering in there. "There's a hidden passage below. I need you to go through it to the cold storage at the end and bring out everything you find."

"That's it?" The darkstalker raised an eyecrest, which looked funny above her inky markings and eyes. "I'm grateful not to have been eaten by the clawdigger, of course, but don't you have some rabid fiend that can play fetch with you already? Maybe the one with the deadly headwear?"

Whisper was well-acquainted with the levels of recovery a gryphon—or opinicus—could go through. A spike in sarcasm was a sign the worst was over. Then, based on the individual, the snarky comments often decreased in frequency once they were back to themselves again. "The incense in there is designed to hurt the murmuration. When I went down last time on my own, it sent everyone into a frenzy. It's better to have an outsider do it."

The darkstalker didn't reply, but she got to work removing the broken planks and sticks, eventually finding the entrance. "There's a brazier here. Am I safe to light it? This isn't saltpeter storage or something, is it?"

"No," Whisper said before correcting herself. "Well, I don't think it is. Could be."

The darkstalker left the brazier unlit, instead emitting a clicking sound that echoed across the jungle. Whisper released a calming mint and felt her pridemates settle down.

Several clicks later, and her new assistant entered the darkness, leaving Whisper behind to monitor her pride's efforts. One of the alabaster members of the susurration needed her, but she sent Moonlit Blossom in her stead. She wanted to keep an eye on the darkstalker, and she really didn't want the stranger seeing she had some of the Seraph King's subjects in her pride.

The darkstalker returned, and Whisper moved upwind for her own safety. The opinicus laid out several glass vials, needles, quill pens, art supplies, and a partially rotted scholarly notebook full of sketches.

"Any of this what you want?" the opinicus asked.

Perhaps Whisper should have been more specific. "We're hoping to build some weather barriers to close up the caves along the edge of the Emerald Jungle. There're some clawdigger nests on the other side, and we'd rather they retreat back to where they came from. I'm thinking more along those lines."

"Ah." The darkstalker grabbed the portable brazier and slipped back into the tunnel. Despite her avian forelegs, she moved in silence, her talons never touching the ground—a predator from the deep places.

Whisper walked over to the notebook, using a silver claw to open it. The first drawing was of Wendl. Not as a jadebeak starling, as a mothfeather. She didn't quite look the same as she did in Whisper's memories, but enough time had passed that the newmoon gryphon wasn't sure which one of them got it wrong. She flipped through a few more pages. Though nine sketches of every ten were Wendl, Whisper recognized attempts at recreating Talli, Kism, and the others.

Around twenty drawings in, she reached several of Wendl and Whisper, back when Whisper had been her former self. Before seeing the inky orbs of cave gryphons and darkstalkers, she would have called mothfeather eyes black. Still, they were darker than most. Where a blackwing might have drawn the ex-couple as a solid brown or grey, basically a boulder with a beak, Wendl brought out the browns, greys, and black in the texture of their plumage. A mothfeather looked like a mountainside, not like a single rock.

Whisper had trouble looking away from the familiar stranger on the page, unsure of what to think. She wasn't repulsed, exactly, so much as it was surreal to think anyone associated that opinicus with her. The opinicus with his wings wrapped around Wendl in the sketch looked content, even if he was a fiction of her mind.

Whisper extended her other claws, ready to shred the page, but then reconsidered. She'd let Wendl have her memories. Whisper retracted her claws but brought the book up with her and dropped it down a hole in the roof into her old room in the rotting building.

The darkstalker returned again, this time with metal tools. Whisper shivered a little at the bonesaw, remembering what it had done to a dead ptarmigan gryphon that attacked the Nighthaunt's expedition in the mountains east of here, but thanked the darkstalker all the same.

"There's some of Mally's old research down there." The darkstalker spoke softly, which was endearing. It wasn't as though most of the starlings here had any idea who the Nighthaunt was.

"Oh?" Whisper had suspected as much. Though if there were anything useful, Wendl probably had it on her.

"I burned it." The darkstalker smelled faintly of smoke. It was a good ruse. The smoke helped hide her scent, making it harder for Whisper to get a read on her. The opinicus really had burned *something* down there. Of course, she could also have emptied her harness pockets and stuffed them full of any notebooks first.

Mally's notebooks...or even Wendl's.

Whisper had a lot of practice reading starling mannerisms and scents, and most of those carried over to opinici. Within the smoke was the gentle perfume of deception. She'd either taken the research, or she'd read and memorized it.

Do I care? Whisper wondered. Knowledge was most dangerous in the talons of the Nighthaunt, who presumably already knew it all. Did it really matter if his minion brought a few old notebooks back? It was unlikely the cure was here.

The darkstalker's scent now included fear, and her black eyes searched Whisper's own silver for hints as to what the Newmoon Pride leader was thinking.

Whisper decided she didn't care. "It seems like you're feeling better. Would you rather leave now, while my pride is distracted? I can escort you to where the patrols were searching for you."

The darkstalker looked north. "With the entire Abyssal Naze between me and Duckbill? No, thanks. I'd rather hit the Argent Heights and go from there."

That filled in another piece of the puzzle for Whisper. If the Argent Heights were safe, that meant the blackwings weren't sieging it and providing the Seraph King with a lot of convenient dead blackwings to toss into the jungle. Any type of meat could be laced with the anti-murmuration poisons; gryphons weren't picky eaters. But blackwing corpses specifically had been brought to the border for this morbid experiment.

Not corpses—the bodies were fresh when I found them. Live blackwings were brought here to be killed and tossed into the jungle.

Whisper felt sure about the who and how, but the *why* still eluded her. If the stormtails and jadebeaks hadn't buried the dead opinici, they may not have been affected at all. Whyever they were doing this, they were either too stupid to know uninfected starlings wouldn't eat opinici, or they were smart enough to know the bodies would be buried.

She let her featherdust spread among the susurration, warning the alabasters among them to hide from view, then flew with the darkstalker to the north-eastern edge of the jungle. Spiketrunks fought for purchase in the rocky soil of the Jadebeak Mountains, often tumbling down when they grew too large. The only aneda trees in the starling's territory were here, though they were too scrawny to have much medicinal use.

Gryphon and opinicus landed among the aneda, and Whisper waited for the darkstalker to leave. The dark-eyed opinicus did nothing, a hint of fear and deception still in the air. The fear, however, didn't seem to be for Whisper.

"Thank you," the opinicus said at last. "I've been lucky in the depths, but I was sure the monsters or the cave gryphons were going to kill me that day. I was sure *you* were going to kill me when I woke up."

Whisper nodded.

"We're not allies. Who can be allies with a starling?" The darkstalker quoted it as fact.

Whisper continued to not reply.

The darkstalker looked around to make sure no one else might overhear her. "But I think you're in the same position I was, and you just don't realize it yet. The Nighthaunt knows about the Newmoon Pride. Be warned."

And with that, the dark-eyed opinicus Whisper had saved from certain death departed for the Argent Heights. The newmoon gryphon watched and waited to make sure no owls appeared to murder the opinicus, then started her flight home, stopping to sniff around any caves she found.

The warning seemed strange, weak, and perhaps a little absurd. Everyone knew the starlings existed.

She'd even seen a few alabaster and Ashen Weald scouts using some sort of contraption of Crestfall glass to spy on the jungle from just outside the glyph markers.

It was likely they'd seen the newmoons once the pridelord moved them to guard the border. He wanted them to be seen, wanted the murmuration's enemies to see silver eyes and be afraid.

But the darkstalker made it seem like there was some intent behind this knowledge, and that's what made no sense. The Newmoon Pride simply minding their business inside the Emerald Jungle wasn't a problem anyone else had to worry about. Really, they should be thanking Whisper for taking care of the infected. She was doing a service to starling and outsider alike.

She let her mind wander back to the darkstalker, the way she'd looked around before speaking, trying to detect any deception or meaning in her smell, but there was nothing.

Could it be related to the blackwings? If so, they failed. I reconnected Taloncrest, and I can warn the other prides.

The opinicus clearly intended for Whisper to do something with that knowledge, but it meant nothing to her.

Still, she couldn't shake the feeling that it mattered, so she went south, close to the border with the jadebeaks, and waited. The faint fake glyph she'd taught Flicker to make was doing its job. It took a full hour, but her one-day mate's real scent appeared and vanished again just as quickly, reminding the murmuration—and the pridelord—that she existed and was fine.

I really need to remind her to update the scent glyph now and then like I taught her.

Once Whisper had that confirmation, she continued back to manage the alabaster opinici's craftsmanship. A nest of clawdiggers was certainly a much bigger danger than her old mentor.

26

WENDL AND BALTHAR

Wendl downed a tincture to calm her nerves and paced back and forth in a border cave, incense lit, waiting for Balthar. Droplets fell from stalactites into pools as sour as her mood, and she hissed under her breath at the occasional newts who moved between them. The newts stared back with black eyes, pink bodies, and broccoli ears, unconcerned at the irritated opinicus in their midst.

Nighteyes had been fine, and Wendl's plan had been moving along slowly but, more importantly, *safely.* Then came the explosions that wounded Sheen, followed by cave monsters. Strange things did happen in the Emerald Jungle, but usually the starlings chattered for a week and returned to their usual routines, forgetting the drama. What was different this time was, as best she could tell, Whisper.

When Nighteyes had depended upon Wendl's incense for freedom of thought, the green opinicus had been able to set the timetable. Now that Whisper had interfered, Nighteyes was impatient and in control. What's more, Wendl had no idea why Whisper had done it. Was this some sort of ploy to stop The Six? Or was it, as Nighteyes had said, just a strange side effect of Whisper retrieving her from the naze?

Nighteyes' demands weren't unreasonable, either. She might even be right.

Maybe I should get half the salts, save as many nightsky gryphlets as I can. Then, once we know more about the other eyries' efforts in fighting bloodbeak, use the other half.

It sounded reasonable when Nighteyes said it, but the danger to Wendl was real. Nighteyes might be willing to risk her own life for her pride's gryphlets, but Wendl wasn't. At the moment, the pridelord had a vague idea the salts could be used as a medicinal treatment. They were stored the way an eyrie might stockpile aneda resin or pumpkin extract.

Once he understood exactly how they worked, however, it would put The Six in a precarious position. Starling brain chemistry seemed designed to stop them from understanding who—or *what*—Wendl and the others were, which had probably saved their lives. But if he saw the salts in action and made the connection...

Wendl thought back to the way Nighteyes had treated her after Whisper's interference, as an outsider. That eschewal had hurt, but the pridelord wouldn't use harsh language if he found out. He'd order The Six all killed. If Wendl acted now, she'd put the others at risk.

She heard paws on slick rock coming from the

other end of the cave and tensed up, ears back and tail poofed out.

"Calm your tail," Balthar grumbled as he shook out a back paw. He looked worse than even she did. They hadn't met in this particular cave in two years, and the plentiful burrs stuck to his fur suggested he hadn't bothered to keep the entryway clear. "What's so urgent it couldn't wait?"

She took a deep breath, let it out, and lied. "I need more of the salts and one vat to run some new tests on bloodbeak. I had a breakthrough while treating one of the wounded nightsky hunters, and it bears a second look."

"It can wait." Balthar echoed Wendl's own view to Nighteyes back at her. "We're too close to take that kind of risk. When we control the murmuration, you'll have as much freedom as you want to experiment—back at the Mothfeather Eyrie."

"When *Nighteyes* controls the murmuration," Wendl corrected. "We agreed a starling should rule the starlings, and she understands how important this is."

Balthar's pause worried her. "Of course. Do you think she's still up for it? What did she say the last time you pulled her out of the swarm?"

"She's still on our side." Wendl hadn't told the others that her makeshift lab had been taken over by the newmoons. "But her pride's children are starting to die off. If you don't want her to resent us, sooner would be better."

"Mmm." Balthar's talons went to his harness pocket, the one where he kept his own vial of salts. "I saw one of the young hunters during the kerfuffle at the border. Sheen, I believe. She looked healthy. Didn't she have bloodbeak?"

Wendl didn't remember telling Balthar Sheen's name. "No, you're thinking of someone else. Sheen is Nighteyes and Rudder's offspring. She hatched with the stormtails, and the denparents brought her back up when they saw she resembled a violet-backed starling. Since liaisons with stormtails were forbidden at the time, it was kept a secret. She's not one of the bloodbeaks; she had a different childhood disorder."

"Hatched at Lightningmaw? Is that so?" Balthar's tone hinted he knew something she didn't. "The stormtail denparents must be quite stealthy, to have hatched and relocated the chick in secret."

Lying wasn't part of who Wendl had been before she joined the Emerald Jungle expedition. She hated that it had become necessary for her own survival. She felt less guilty lying to keep Nighteyes and Sheen safe, but she looked forward to a day when she could leave this life behind.

The vial in Balthar's harness clinked against another, and he looked up, startled. "We could just leave, you know. Take the salts to the border, change, and don't look back. If you're so concerned about interfering with the starlings, isn't that the best option?"

"Where would we find the blackwing and moth-feather blood?" she asked, pushing aside her curiosity at Balthar's second vial. "I hear there are blackwing bodies lining the Jadebeak Mountains these days, but I've heard no word of mothfeathers. I'm not even sure any are awake yet."

How strange, she thought. *Once, I lived by the calendar. Now I can't remember when First Morning is.*

Indignation showed around his eyes. "Surely, you aren't comparing being a blackwing to being a gryphon. You'd be in the right body, at least. Even Whisper, if she'd the option to become a female *opinicus*, would surely leave this gryphon nonsense behind."

"I'm not so certain about Whisper." Wendl wondered if Balthar's surprise was at her comment or finding out about the bodies. She wished she'd thought to partition out that information better. "I realize I won't get my own body back, but I'd still like to be mothfeather again."

"Even sleeping away large portions of the year?" he pressed. "Even with how you're treated by the other eyries? With one vial of purple salts, every eastern eyrie would treat you well. You could attend a real, *blackwing* university, not just the one at Mothfeather."

Wendl'd had similar conversations with herself since Khalim delivered the salts. She'd even wondered if she could become a Crackling Sea or Redwood Valley opinicus and join the Ashen Weald, leaving the northern conflicts behind. Unlike Whisper, however, Wendl missed her friends and family dearly. She wanted to be with them again, even if that meant sleeping through the winter.

There was one other thing that bothered her. "I don't think you realize what being a blackwing has done to you. It's not just the arrogance, Balthar. There's a poison inside you, a cruelty. I hear it in the way you talk about the starlings, the way you talk about gryphons. You blackwings are so far on top, you can't imagine what it's like for the glacier pride or motmots."

Wendl had a theory the Blackwing and Alabaster Eyries were two sides of the same coin, that the blackwings would have attempted to conquer the continent themselves if the alabasters hadn't beaten them to it.

To her surprise, he didn't protest. "You're not wrong. I thought my time with the sparkwings had changed me, but perhaps I'll always be a blackwing at heart. Our own hubris brought us here, didn't it? Iri acts like she was born to lead the jadebeaks, like she's superior to them. Talli and Kism are the same, just with smaller prides. That's all the more reason for the two of us to leave. We don't belong."

"You know we can't do that." Wendl was off balance, but they'd both danced around the real worry: their altruism surviving the change.

He shrugged, turning subtext to text. "How many jadebeak expeditions did you join in the bog? And you were fine. Nighteyes spent months with the Ashen Weald without incident, and she's a real starling."

"Nighteyes felt the elixir's strength wane over time," Wendl countered. "And I still feel the altruism, deep inside me. I think if I woke up away from the jungle, I might hurt someone before I got it under control."

If I even could get it under control.

"Kism was a fluke, and we've fixed the recipe since then. You'll be fine once you're in your own skin again, I promise. Don't let fear get the better of you." Balthar's words did little to assuage her worry.

A squirrel scurried past the cave entrance on the Nightsky side, and Wendl's ear twitched. "Our own transformations can wait. We need a new pridelord. Do you have any salts you can reach? It would go a long way towards building goodwill with Nighteyes."

"This is all I have." He rummaged through his harness pockets, unwrapping two vials from a nest of singed vellum and making her wonder at their original purpose if each of The Six already had their salts. "You're right, though. Between the stormtails and jadebeaks, the pridelord is going to find us. We need to make our move. It'll take me a few days to get ready. How many of your incense bombs do you have ready to go? I tested them on the others. Iri and Talli are immune. Kism is too far gone, he'll need to stay away. Can you be ready in four days?"

Wendl had called for this rendezvous hoping to slow Nighteyes, but instead, she'd accidentally sped up Balthar. She thought of the dying Nightsky gryphlets. Her olfactory weaponry was under the expedition ruins, but if this was the only answer, she'd find a way to get past Whisper. "It'll be tight, but I think so. If I leave the incense along the jadebeak border, can Iri pick it up for you?"

"That's fine," he replied, "but Wendl? You'd better make sure Nighteyes stays out of trouble for the next few days. Whatever you do, she stays put. No contacting her old mate with the stormtails. No talking to Whisper. Don't let her do anything that might make the pridelord more suspicious than he already is. While working on the statues below his meditation chamber, I've heard him grumbling about the new blackwing invasions and stormtails vanishing from the murmuration. Something big's going to happen sooner or later."

Nighteyes wouldn't like keeping a low profile, but it was just a few days, and Wendl didn't see an alternative. "Fine. We'll stay out of the pridelord's gaze for a bit. Then, on the fourth day, I'll make a formal challenge to take over the Nightsky Pride, and we'll demand the pridelord oversee it. That'll give us a reason to visit him at his temple. Have Iri come ahead with the weapons to cut him off from his guards, and you be ready in the temple with the salts at the right temperature."

"Four days and not a moment sooner." Balthar turned and left. His steps were shaky, but Wendl's weren't much steadier. It was one thing to talk about overthrowing a pridelord, it was another thing to actually do it.

WENDL'S WORDS were not met well. Sheen was doing much better and was thus awake, so Nighteyes brought Wendl to her island home for their plotting.

"I sent you to buy us time for my gryphlets, and this is what you do instead?" the pride leader hissed. "Call it off. I need more time to think."

"You already said yes. This is a plan you agreed to several times," Wendl pushed.

Nighteyes' hesitation concerned Wendl. In their private meetings away from the fog of the murmuration, there'd been no reservations.

"The preparations are already in motion," the opinicus continued. "To stop now would require contacting everyone a second time, which would surely raise suspicion. We have a plan in place that just requires a few fires and stray scents to commence. We didn't think we'd need a way to call it off."

The pride leader paced inside her burrow. Wendl had given her the two vials of salts, and she'd hidden them behind a piece of caiman-shaped driftwood. Her circuit often passed by the wood. "We should use the salts and try to save as many gryphlets as we can in case things go wrong."

"With all due respect, we shouldn't, and we can't," Wendl countered. "It takes time, resources, and privacy to get a vat of salts going. With Whisper parked over my hideaway, there's no easy way to treat just one or two gryphlets. Even were Whisper to let us in, if both of us cross into another pride's territory, the pridelord is going to notice. This plan requires secrecy. I need you to stay put until it's time to go to the temple."

"We should at least let Rudder know his blood could help," Nighteyes protested.

Wendl cut her off. "That's the *last* thing we should do. The stormtails are under constant watch, and the pridelord is a feather's length from removing them from the murmuration already. You wanted to save your gryphlets *now*, and that requires drastic actions. Once you control the murmuration, then you can do whatever you want. All you need to do is sit tight and don't get into trouble for three days, and on the fourth, you can cause all the chaos you want."

The pacing continued, but the protests stopped. Though Balthar had mapped out this plan years ago,

Nighteyes' pushing had forced them to take the first real steps.

"What was it like?" the nightsky gryphon asked. When Wendl looked confused, she added, "When you changed, what was it like?"

Wendl was tempted to tell a soft lie to make it easier for Nighteyes to enter the vat when the time came but decided it would be better to brace her friend for the reality of what would happen after. "You burn, inside and out. You feel sick and wrong, like you're dying, and you're sure the salts are melting you away to nothing. I don't know how to describe the sensation, exactly, to someone who hasn't gone through it. But you have this sense of the way your body feels, and suddenly, your face is not your face. Your talons are not your talons.

"I became obsessed with my beak. Every time I wasn't in a panic, I could *see* it was wrong. We found some berries on our way into the jungle, and I couldn't bring myself to eat them because of how they felt against my beak. The edges were wrong, the shape was wrong, the feel was wrong. Even my tongue had changed."

Nighteyes stared at Wendl's beak. "What helped you recover?"

"At first, nothing. Later, it was the scars." Wendl changed how she was seated, pulling forwards her back leg, which had a nasty scar by the ankle. Then she used her talons to push away the fur to show another on her chest. "With the salts, my new wounds healed. But some of my old scars remained. They're not quite the same shape, but they're mostly in the right places, and that helped ground me. I got the one on my leg from a nasty goliath bird my family owned. He got out and was running after one of my brothers, still a chick. I got between them and gained two scars for my trouble. The bird bit my leg, and my brother's beak was buried into my chest as I lifted off with him, giving me the second."

Nighteyes licked a paw and pulled down an ear, revealing a small scar. When Wendl told her it was too small, the salts would probably erase it, she rolled on her back, careful to show her stomach in a non-submissive way. "I suppose these'll have to do."

Most gryphons' stomach skin was tough and evolved into a network of scar tissue over hunts and fighting. It was another way Wendl didn't fit in. The flowers she picked occasionally had thorns, but none left marks like a cassowary's kick. Even the other members of The Six had earned their scarred stomachs after so many years here. Balthar's was like Nighteyes', a leaf shape on his stomach where a cassowary had kicked him while he was saving his sparkwing mate from the ill-tempered bird.

Wendl traced a talon along Nighteyes' matching maple-shaped scars. "That'll do it. Now if I can see your stomach, I'll know it's you. Though...Hmm."

"What?" Nighteyes asked. "Oh, the pridelord...he won't have any scars. He took over as a fledgling. Well, I doubt anyone will notice."

"Let's hope." Wendl had planned to appeal to Whisper's better nature to collect a few things, but the sun was setting.

Nighteyes stopped her pacing and turned pensive. "It's strange, I never realized you had any siblings. Or raised goliath birds. I saw the Ashen Weald's variety.

They're monsters for anyone to take care of. What was your gryphlethood like? Er...chickhood?"

"Good, actually." Even when Wendl had pulled Nighteyes out of the murmuration to talk rebellion, they'd never spoken about Wendl's past. "I had friends—Vilessa and Khalim—siblings, a nice ranch, and we made enough that, eventually, we could hibernate at home instead of returning to the Sleeping City. We had neighbors we trusted to watch the animals, which made life a lot easier in winter."

"Do you regret becoming a starling?" Nighteyes asked.

Wendl paused to think. "I regret every decision that led me to join the Nightsky Pride, but I regret nothing I've done since then. Besides, when I get to go home, I'll have left the Emerald Jungle a better place by putting you in charge, right?"

Nighteyes' reply came in the form of a hesitant, "Yes."

"Here, do you have some food? There's a game we played at the ranch, but it requires food," Wendl said. "Now, I'm going to tell you two truths and a lie, and you're going to guess which is the lie. If you guess correctly, you get a bite of the tart. We'll use dead squirrels instead of tarts. Okay, I'll go first..."

27

THE WHISTLING KITE

Wendl waited until Nighteyes was busy checking on Sheen the next morning before departing. Despite Balthar's warning that Wendl should avoid all contact with Whisper, she found herself flying to the Nightsky-Newmoon border.

Better I visit Whisper than Nighteyes does, I suppose. There's no one else we can trust.

She went through the plan several times. In her head, she rehearsed her wording and posture for when she'd challenge Nighteyes for the pride. It had to sound sincere if they were going to be granted an audience before the pridelord.

When the Newmoon Pride's territory came into view, she set her mind on a new task: deception. Or, really, *focused honesty.* She couldn't lie to Whisper. The newmoon leader would be able to smell the truth or lie behind Wendl's words. There wasn't even room for equivocation where starlings were concerned, not exactly. But if Wendl had a specific, focused request that was true, she should be able to get what she wanted.

Or so she hoped. There was only one way to find out, and she needed those incense bombs. The pridelord was willing to hear grievances in private, especially the ones that would require his blessing, such as the changing of a pride leader inside the murmuration. The moment he sensed danger, however, the swarm outside his private halls would come in. That's what she needed the incense for.

She located a newmoon glyph and landed next to it, taking a few steps into their territory. The silvereyed fiends must have been occupied elsewhere, as it took the better part of an hour before anyone acknowledged her presence.

Wendl was expecting Whisper. What she got instead was a generic spotless starling, a flower dipped in eyeshine tucked behind his ear.

"Nice to meet you," Wendl said. "I need to speak to Whisper."

The gryphon glared at her. At least, she assumed he did. With the eyeshine, it was hard to tell. Finally, he turned and left, which she took as an invitation to join him.

I'd have assumed a floral scent based on his love of flowers, but he smells like pepper to me. Is his scent naturally angry, or did I do something wrong?

The Newmoon Pride's nests remained hidden from view, but its members were located north of the old expedition ruins. Whisper stood over several makeshift weather barriers. At least, they resembled the barriers Wendl had seen at the Mothfeather Eyrie when her family sometimes went there to hibernate with relatives. The only difference was they were reinforced three or four more times than necessary. Whisper perched above them, inspecting their quality.

"Expecting a blizzard?" Wendl asked. While snow did sometimes come down from the Jadebeak Mountains, there was a joke in the jungle that the sound snow made was *drip, drip, drip* as it melted the moment it landed on anything.

Whisper looked up from the barriers. "Of a sort. What I certainly wasn't expecting was anyone from the Nightsky Pride. Why're you here?"

"I left some things below the ruins," Wendl replied. "I'd like to retrieve them, if that's okay."

The flower gryphon made a noise too close to a chitter for Wendl's tastes, and several silver-eyed jadebeaks crawled out of the jungle and dragged the weather barriers northeast.

Belatedly, Wendl wondered how they'd managed to craft such expert opinicus doors without talons. It seemed unlikely they'd stumbled across pre-built weather barriers in the jungle, unless some Argent Heights traders had stolen them from the east and were attempting to bring them home when they met starling misfortune. "So...I can get them on my own, if you're busy."

"Moonlit Blossom, go see that the barriers arrive at the right caves." Whisper waited until he was out of hearing range before she spoke to Wendl. "What exactly are you after in storage?"

Here we go, Wendl thought. *Time to tell the truth as best I can.*

"Well, there are some old medical notebooks. The

bloodbeak situation is getting desperate," she began. "I'd really like to remove all of my incense from the ruins. Obviously, thanks to whatever you did to Nighteyes, I don't need it anymore. It'd be safer away from your susurration, I think you'd agree."

Whisper gestured a silver-striped wing at where the hole leading beneath the ruins was filled in. "My pridemates will help you carry it to the border."

"Is that wise?" Wendl asked. "Considering the effect it could have on them."

"Make it safe." Whisper sat down and watched Wendl as she worked to clear the way down. Apparently, the carrying help didn't extend to clearing debris.

Wendl searched her pockets for flint and got a brazier lit halfway down the passage. It provided just enough light for her to search through her old crates and journals. To her surprise, someone had been through them. It hadn't been a squirrel, or they'd have chewed through the bedding material to make their own nests. Instead, everything was tidy, but several journals and tools were missing.

Did Whisper come down here? Or was it someone else? It seemed unlikely anyone could get in here without Whisper knowing. *Perhaps it was Nighteyes.*

The incense bombs were mostly untouched, though one appeared to have been taken apart and inspected. The knots holding it together were in a style Mally had insisted his assistants use for stitching up wounds, not Wendl's usual Mothfeather style. She wrapped a few in waxy broadleaves, hoping they'd dull the scent, and tied them Mothfeather-proper with strips of leather and string she'd scavenged from outsider corpses—saving the brightest pieces for Sheen's bracelet. Once she'd brought up the first dozen, Whisper was waiting with water and food.

"They're quite large." Suspicion dripped from the newmoon leader's words. "I was expecting something smaller, intended for subduing a single starling."

Wendl had grown used to meat with the Nightsky Pride, but the offerings here were mostly eggfruit of questionable ripeness and early season starberries. "I do have some smaller pouches of incense, but I combined them into the broadleaves to make them easier to carry."

That was true, and honest, and incomplete. One of the broadleaf wraps had twenty of her smaller incense bombs like the one she'd used to save Nighteyes and Rudder from the Abyssal Naze years ago. Most of them were, in fact, very large incense bombs. The sort that would have allowed her to carve a path out of the Emerald Jungle if the pridelord ever figured out what she was up to.

She got the eggfruit down and thanked Whisper. "I ran into Balthar a few days ago. We scavenged a little of the salts, and he asked me to give this to you. Do you think you'd ever want to go back home?"

"No." Whisper took the vial of salts, leaving Wendl to wonder why she'd do that if she didn't plan to use them. "Though if you have access to them, you should leave now. The jungle has no need of starlings who don't wish to be here."

As though greenwing altruism would let us. Wendl didn't verbalize her reply, going down to get the last of her incense. Whisper must have guessed something was up, or else Nighteyes had told her. Either way,

Wendl should leave before her pheromones accidentally revealed anything.

As she brought up the last of her incense—some of which was tailored for quieting bees so she could steal their honey instead of being used on starlings—she saw that someone had dropped her old sketchpad on the ground by the leaf wraps.

Ah, the one with my sketches of her in it, Wendl thought.

Whisper was nowhere in sight, perhaps having gone back to overseeing weather barrier construction. Instead, Moonlit Blossom and several cured jadebeaks, one of whom wore an unusual hat, stood behind the wrapped incense.

Wendl could smell the flower gryph's pepper irritation before she saw him. "That's the last of it. Let's get it over the border."

THE NEWMOON GRYPHONS escorted Wendl to the nightsky border but didn't cross it, leaving the broadleaf wraps on the border. Wendl wasn't sure what to think of that, but she dragged them from the newmoon glyph to the nightsky glyph. When she reached the last one, Moonlit Blossom dismissed his pridemates but remained.

"What's with the jadebeak with the metal claw on his head?" Wendl asked. When she got no response, she continued, "Well, thanks for the help. I guess I'll be going."

Moonlit Blossom finally spoke. "Once you cross

the glyphs, don't come back. You're not welcome in Newmoon Pride lands anymore."

"Is that an order from Whisper? Why didn't she tell me that herself?" Wendl asked.

"It's an order from me," he countered. "Whisper has a soft spot for you, and it clouds her judgement. I don't need her nares to tell me you're bad for her."

Who is this gryphon? Wendl wondered. *I just met him today.*

"What's your problem?" She sized him up. She didn't feel like she deserved to have a gryphon with a flower behind his ear try to intimidate her.

"Have you heard of the whistling kite?" His eyeshine made him unreadable, but he didn't wait for her reply. "The whistling kite flies before a wildfire, and so the other birds believe the kite is there for them in hard times. But they fail to see the truth. The whistling kite carries a burning branch. It brings the hard times in its wake. We do not need your fire here, Wendl."

With that, he turned and flew away, leaving her at a loss for words.

"Whatever *that* means," she grumbled to the squirrels and trees. She'd been called a few things in her days, the worst coming from the beaks of black-wings, but whistling kite was a new one.

28

KISM THE THIRD

Wendl's incense bombs were too heavy for her to move alone, and she was forced to leave them behind by the newmoon border and return to the Nightsky nests. She'd have to return in the morning and conscript Nighteyes to help her move them to Balthar's drop location. That was one day gone, three to go.

When she awoke the next morning, Nighteyes was absent. Wendl grumbled, but it was probably better if her friend stayed busy. The more scent trails showing her doing normal pride leader things, the better. Unfortunately, that meant Wendl would have to fly all of the incense to the border for Iri to pick up.

She'd finished moving half when an unexpected visitor showed up.

"Wendl!" Sheen shouted, scaring the green starling out of her skin. "What're you doing?"

Unlike Whisper, Sheen couldn't tell when someone was lying, which made Wendl's work a lot easier. "Oh, the jadebeaks are having trouble with hornets this spring. Several of their nesting grounds are overrun, and they begged me for help. You know the incense we use to steal honey from the bees? I'm sending some their way."

"Oh, neat. I'll help you out." With her injuries, Sheen couldn't carry anything, but she insisted on keeping Wendl company. "So you don't get bored."

Boredom was the least of Wendl's worries, but she figured her own scent trail would look a lot less suspicious if it was mixed with Sheen's, so she let the indigo gryphon tag along.

"I think something's wrong with Nighteyes," Sheen said. "She keeps preening her feathers even though they're already preened. If she keeps doing that, she might preen them away. Do you think she's mad at me?"

Wendl had never been good at reassuring fledglings, but she did her best. "I don't think it's you. She and I had it out last night. But even if it was you, I don't think she could ever be mad at you, though she could be worried. You gave us all quite the scare! Once she sees you're okay, she'll feel better."

"Why me?" Sheen asked. "I'm no one special."

"That's not true. You're special to me. You're the one who gathers relics for me from the northern jungle," Wendl insisted.

Sheen poofed up, pleased with herself. "I'm looking forward to my bracelet reward. I tried to fly out to where the strangers were, but I think someone got there first and cleaned up their stuff."

"Probably just a stray rhea flock. You know how they like shiny things and string," Wendl said, though she wasn't so sure. She'd gone out on her own to look around the next day, and the hunters were complaining of strange scents.

With Sheen's version of help, Wendl brought the last of the wraps to the Jadebeak Pride's glyph. She didn't dare go into the cave with Sheen here, so she waited next to her bee plants. A few had started to blossom, their faint purple flowers luring iridescent green bees from their underground burrows.

Similarly, Sheen's chatter lured another creature out from its underground burrow.

Even with her opinicus nares, Wendl smelled his bitter almond before she saw him. "Kism? You're not supposed to be here."

Balthar had specifically warned her that Kism was too gryphon to be safe around the incense, to give it to Iri. A point Wendl couldn't raise with Sheen here.

Kism had settled in with a pride of lighter-plumed starlings and taken to sunbleaching his feathers to fit in. It took a lot to lighten feathers, but she could smell bleaching powder on him, a strange addition to his cyanide perfume.

"Iri was busy, so she sent me in her stead." He shook some of the cave's dampness from his fur. Despite his words, he made no move to take the wraps.

Wendl tried to will her hackle feathers down, but they refused to oblige. She didn't mind Kism when The Six were all together, but she'd been deliberate about not being alone with him since his escape attempt. "Are you sure that's wise? You know the effect *apiary* incense has on you."

"It seems you've done a good job of wrapping

them up. Or perhaps that was your friend here?" Kism bowed to Sheen.

The indigo starling bowed her head, but only slightly. Opinici and gryphons were the same in that there was a season of their lives when they were adults, but they lacked the discretion and danger instincts they'd develop a few years later. Perhaps Sheens' recent injuries had aged her, because despite her wounds, she was halfway into a hunter's crouch.

Wendl tried another tack. "You shouldn't be across the border without Nighteyes' permission. The pridelord will not be kind if he catches you."

Kism's stare unnerved her, partially because she'd remembered what it had been like when his eyes were kind. They'd spent hours together in the early days when they shared a border, talking about what it would be like to go home. He'd been the one she'd first entrusted with the knowledge she'd perfected an elixir to suppress both altruism and the call of the murmuration—or so she'd thought.

For a year or two, she'd blamed herself for what happened next. In the end, though, she *had* been confident the elixir would work, and she'd planned to test it herself. It had been Kism's decision to slip the juice of a rare berry into her drink, and as she slept through the night and the next day, take her elixirs and try to flee on his own.

What happened next was on his head, not hers. She just didn't know if he saw it that way.

Is he trying to sabotage the plan? He's getting his scent trail across Jadebeak and Nightsky territory, tying it to mine and Sheen's.

"Sheen, we need to get back," Wendl ordered.

"Kism, I trust the jadebeaks can help you carry the wraps to wherever you need them. Give Balthar my regards."

Kism didn't reply, watching as they left. It was always unnerving to have his gaze on her, but she was more disturbed by the fact that it was really Sheen he was tracking.

What does he want with her?

THE SILENCE WAS the worst part of the next two days. Left alone with her thoughts, Wendl reconsidered Balthar's offer to run away several times. With the vial he'd given her, she didn't even need him. She could just leave and figure out the logistics of changing from the safety of the Ashen Weald's hideaway.

While Moonlit Blossom seemed to have it out for her, Wendl was pretty sure Whisper would let her fly to the border and past the barrier. Wendl even had some orange elixirs hidden near the Jadebeak Falls, enough to buy her a few days without altruism.

I wonder what the fisherfolk villages are like? Is there room for a scholar down there? The shoreline north of Mothfeather and Blacktalon had been too close to the blood coast for fisherfolk settlements.

Despite Nighteyes' barbed claim that Wendl wasn't a true starling, it was her worry for the murmuration that held the opinicus back. She'd done her part to keep the Nightsky Pride's bloodbeak at bay. Even without the salts, she thought with contraception she could keep those who had it from passing it on to more offspring. But other prides still suffered, prides she had no sway with, and that meant they weren't tracking who could pass it along to their offspring.

Mally's interference had become a pandemic, and unlike in the Redwood Valley, no one was treating the eggs. The outside world seemed to be worrying about a few lost hatch years, but Wendl was staring down a curse that would span generations.

And she could fix it! She just needed someone in charge who would let her.

Balthar and Iri must have begun preparations for their coup by now, and if Wendl vanished, they'd get caught. The pridelord always found out what his gryphons were up to, it just took time. Once he focused on a thread, however, that was that.

Even Kism—emotionally scarred Kism—would get his wish if Wendl went through with it. Much as she told herself she owed him nothing, that his actions had been his own, she still wished for him to have a happy ending.

I can do this.

She settled down in the center of the nesting grounds. Nighteyes glared at Wendl from across the common area, all part of the ruse.

Sheen flittered back and forth between them, trying to make peace. It broke Wendl's heart to see the fledgling try so hard, but it meant she really believed Wendl and Nighteyes were fighting.

If they could have their confrontation tonight, they could visit the pridelord in the morning. Iri would have the incense bombs planted outside the pridelord's private chambers. Talli had come up with an excuse to visit the capital by now, or else she was hiding, waiting to flee if things went south.

Good luck with that. Knowing her, she'd seek asylum with King's Reach. How quickly we turn to enemies when our allies abandon us. Wendl could imagine a starling walking into the port eyrie and how well that would go.

Balthar had the hardest part of the plan. He needed to get the vats and salts going. Beyond the pridelord's private meditation chambers were the vaults, where the starlings kept old opinicus treasures, carvings, and murals. She'd visited them several times, and it was stunning what knowledge had been lost down there.

She could spend hours examining a map of Belamuria that showed the Emerald Jungle, bog, and kjarr as once having been a major center for opinicus trade. The stone animal carvings defied description. Wingless gryphons without beaks, standing on two legs with long claws. Thin, noodly capybaras with sharp teeth and tails the length of their bodies hunting crocodiles.

Nighteyes stood, dislodging a gryphlet sleeping on her tail, and began her choreographed march to Wendl.

This is it. It's time. Muster your angry voice, Wendl, you've got an audience to convince.

Starry eyes glared down at Wendl. "I know you think I'm mishandling the sick, but that's the decision of a pride leader, not a lazabout flower-picker. If you have a problem with how I'm leading, you can leave and join the green plumes down south. I'm sure *they* don't mind having adults who don't hunt in *their* pride."

"And leave the sick to die under your care?" Wendl put as much venom as she could rally into her accusation. "A medicine gryphon's place is with her patients. If you don't have the strength of will to save this pride, maybe *you* shouldn't be in charge."

Sheen whimpered in the corner, and both Wendl and Nighteyes stumbled for a moment, before the green opinicus caught herself.

"You don't see what needs to be done!" Wendl shouted, emphasizing sight while looking into Night's scarred, starry eyes. "Of course, without me, you wouldn't see anything at all, would you?"

Nighteyes' paw came fast, slashing Wendl across the cheek. Blood flew across the pridegrounds. Even knowing Nighteyes had half-retracted her claws as they connected, the impact left Wendl stunned. Though similar in size, she lacked the muscle of gryphons who had to hunt to survive.

"Leave or challenge me," Nighteyes quipped. "I have better things to do than waste my time on you."

"I demand mediation before the pridelord." Wendl spoke the magic words that would get them the audience they needed without her having to fight here and now.

Nighteyes fully retracted her claws, then flicked blood from her paw into Wendl's face. "We leave before sunup for the capital. I'll send one of my sisters tonight with word to expect us."

Wendl stomped off to her den. Sheen looked lost, unsure who to follow. She kneaded the ground, forgetting the pain in her injured leg. Wendl made it easy, closing the hide flap behind her to make it clear she wouldn't be accepting visitors.

Once she was inside, she let her guard down and felt hot tears fall down her cheeks, burning against the cuts on her face. It was all for show, but it had *felt* real because of their past arguments. That was what made it believable.

Wendl took a few deep breaths, searching her supplies for dry wound-moss. She shoved a few pawfuls of it onto her nest, then rested the bloody side of her face against it while she slept.

Today had been draining, but it was a drop in the bucket compared to what would happen in the morning.

I can do this. We've all made sacrifices, all had burdens to bear. This is mine.

As she drifted off, her thoughts turned to Khalim. Had his own path ever given him pause?

29

PRIDELORD OF THE EMERALD JUNGLE

The pridelord surveyed his temple grounds. A cool, dawn breeze whistled through cracks and crevices in the ruins, playing the melody of the jungle. Post-storm renewal hung in the air, bringing with it the scent of the murmuration across the pridelands. A gust blew past, and the temple itself rustled.

Wherever a gryphon couldn't perch, sweet moss grew in shades of blue-green. Wherever a gryphon *could* perch, however, one did. He moved through them like a boa swimming through spatterdock, feeling their scents brush against him, gifting him their story.

In return, he granted them calm and purpose, mint and orange, and sent them on their way. He didn't need to stroll among them to check in on his starlings, but he enjoyed the movement. A temple could just as easily be a tomb as a place of worship, and he preferred to be the skipping rock on the pond causing ripples.

He increased his pace for a few steps, then

stopped. The gryphons around him stumbled to keep from crashing into each other, successful in all but one place. He followed the ripples and found an old sparkwing.

The Sparkwing Pride was gone, and layered into her identity was one of jadebeak, too. But the same way his scent told her she was a jadebeak, her scent told him she still thought of herself as a sparkwing. Some changes were instant. Others, like *sparkwing*, had to be bred out over time.

The pridelord wasn't a large gryphon, but she was so small and frail he still knelt to check on her. The sparkwing's coat was worn, but she held herself like a denparent. She shivered in fear at his scent. Her memory was starting to go, and the subtle commands that turned his murmuration into a sky of living water didn't always make sense to her. He increased the mint until she calmed.

His father had sometimes talked to other starlings. He'd ask them questions, getting back the answers he wanted to hear. It was such a useless endeavor that he began to talk to rocks chipped away to resemble gryphons instead. Perhaps, had he lived long enough, the pridelord's father would have become like this elderly sparkwing.

Instead, he'd died of a different disease. Something Balthar, another once-sparkwing, called cancer.

If his father were here, the pridelord would have asked him what to do with the frail creature before him. His father would have responded about the health of the murmuration, saying something about how all predators ultimately became prey in the end, and letting nature take its course.

His father had not dealt with the silver-eyed.

The pridelord carefully preened the top of the sparkwing's head, more a ceremonial gesture than grooming, and put a command into her mind. *Newmoon, Care.*

She'd make her own way to the northeast, and once she crossed into the Newmoon Pride's territory, she'd forget she'd been a jadebeak. Though her brain refused to let go of the Sparkwing Pride, Whisper would sort that out. The newmoon gryphons understood nuance and care. Together, they'd navigated the silver-eyed, giving them a home.

Starlings didn't serve the murmuration, the murmuration served starlings. Nothing more than an ideal at its core, it kept them safe. They were hungry, scared, or lost. He gave them a home, fed them, and protected them from harm. He was good at what he did because he'd had no choice.

Times were simpler when his predecessors ruled. The old pridelords had dealt with outside threats. They'd forged hard borders with other prides, closed them off, and when other starlings sometimes forgot the rules, they took the frenzy instinct only used when a starling was in danger and turned it on all the time.

The threats the old pridelords faced and conquered were not the threats the current pridelord faced. The same way cancer had taken his father from him, the murmuration now faced its own sickness.

The Emerald Veil held. The prides were strong, yes, but that could change in an instant.

The parasite from the bog was just the start. He'd handled that. With his starling-opinici who knew medicine, with Whisper who pulled back some of the lost strength of infected jadebeaks, with Nighteyes' teaching the new Kjarr how to fix her father's glyphs, he'd stemmed that tide.

Then something new had risen up from an otherwise healthy pride, the stormtails. He'd been too kind there, having felt guilt about using them to combat bloodbeak. He hadn't cut out the rot, and it spread to the Jadebeak Pride. Something that made a starling a not-starling, something more dangerous than silver eyes or red beaks.

He sighed, and the gryphons in front of him spread away from his breath. Perhaps that was enough exercise for now. He returned to the center of the temple and its broken throne, crossing down into a hidden passage revealed by the erosion of time, and left his hive behind.

A room large enough to allow flight, a cathedral decorated with a thousand carved wings, spread out before him. It was where he handled private mediation, like what awaited him with Nighteyes and Wendl later in the morning. The glyphs marking this place were so old, they'd been forgotten.

The name, however, had been passed down between the leaders of the starling prides. The glyphs, according to his father, called this the *Sky Beneath the Earth*. A dark place of meditation, a location where starlings learned to navigate by scent instead of sight. It was where he solved problems. It was where the Newmoon Pride had been created.

And the Crescentmoon Pride. And the Fullmoon Pride.

With the addition of the talon-pawed starlings returning home, the pridelord had taken to keeping one around to add some illumination to this second sky. The scent of the candles, stolen from a shipwreck outside Alwren, calmed him. The needs, desires, and frustrations of the outside world dimmed. He'd been young when his father died. Most pridelords took on the mantle as adults.

But all the starling pride leaders had seen the toll being pridelord had taken on his father, so they declined, deciding instead to put the weight of the Emerald Jungle upon the wings of a fledgling.

He inhaled, letting the candles dull his connection. He'd sent a faint command to the starlings to relay between themselves, which would reassure them he was watching over them. Until it echoed back to him from across the jungle, no one would notice his absence.

While the Nightsky Pride deserved his attention, his mind had latched onto the Stormtail Pride. Who ruled the nightsky mattered little to the murmuration, but the stormtails presented a problem he hoped to solve today. Small starling prides often disappeared; the moon prides were proof of that. But they were absorbed into other prides, like with the sparkwings. To take a whole starling pride and remove them from the murmuration, that would take some doing.

And then there is the matter of the traitor.

From the far end of the Sky Beneath the Earth, new candles burst to life, revealing his guest.

"Ah, Pridelord?" Balthar the Talon-Pawed said. "You asked to meet with me in private...?"

30

AMETHYST

It was dawn by the time Nighteyes and Wendl left for the Jadebeak Pride's territory. Sheen had gone to plead with Nighteyes to forgive Wendl. They'd expected that, however, and Wendl had given Nighteyes some medicine to help Sheen sleep. Nothing strong, but just using the leaf to hold water to sip out of was enough to get Sheen to doze off after she'd had her say so Nighteyes could rest.

By sunup, the whole pride was in a tizzy. A strong breeze came from the ocean, bringing with it strange eyrie smells from Alwren. Not uncommon, but it stirred up the pride, and some of Nighteyes' sisters tried to convince her to wait, taking it as a bad omen.

The new scents had played tricks on the hunters who stalked the midnight jungle for prey. They all reported strange sounds along the border, things moving just beyond their vision in the Abyssal Naze.

Problems for the feathersnakes and cave gryphons, Nighteyes thought privately. *We have to clean our own nest before we can look to others.*

Neither Nighteyes nor Wendl wanted to keep the pridelord waiting, but he could always sniff out where they were if he was worried. Once they were far enough away from the hunting grounds, Nighteyes asked about the scratch marks on Wendl's face.

"They hurt, but thank you for retracting your claws," the medicine opinicus said. "Remind me not to get on your actual bad side."

Nighteyes pushed down a little guilt, reminding herself this was for a greater good. "I just worry I've set a bad example for the gryphlets and fledglings. They already have problems with fighting."

A grouse burst through the jungle below them, pursued by jadebeaks, and the nightsky duo finished their flight in silence until they reached the temple.

One of Nighteyes' first mates, a gryphon who had been far too sure of himself, had claimed there was a jadebeak starling for every leaf in the jungle. Generally speaking, his poetry left much to be desired, as did his personality. Rudder had bad puns, but even a bad pun had a certain level of enjoyment bad poetry did not. Still, seeing every inch of the temple covered in jadebeaks, she could believe the leaf claim.

Despite the sea of green, Nighteyes didn't see—or smell—any sign of Iri or Talli, whom Wendl said should be here. Hidden in the scent trails was a hint that Talli might be *near* Jadebeak territory. Iri was harder to place, as she controlled the Jadebeak Pride, so her scent was present everywhere and strong nowhere.

Nighteyes pushed down her hackles when they reached the back of the temple. A ramp led down to the lower levels, where the pridelord met in private. On either side of the door were broadleaf wraps.

Well, at least one thing I was told to expect is here. That's a good sign. Wendl tried to look inside the broadleaf, but Nighteyes swatted her with a white and purple tail, bringing her attention back to the present. *No sense drawing attention to ourselves, I guess. But if Talli and Iri aren't here, who's going to light the things?*

Soft moss coated the path down, leaving Nighteyes to wonder what the stonework had looked like when the temple was new. Though she firmly believed starlings were the best gryphons and all gryphons were better than opinici, she couldn't imagine who the original architects had been. The size of the temple, rising above the tallest broadleaf, was impressive enough. But the fact it had survived this long without falling down left her in awe.

If only whoever had built the Celestial Courtyard had built it just as tall so we didn't get soggy nests every time my pride has to visit here.

They left the morning light, descending into a darkness lit by burning braziers, another strangely opinical touch. Either the pridelord was as dexterous with his paws as Askel the Phoenix, or he'd had a starling opinicus light them for him.

Considering Wendl was here and Balthar was supposed to be getting things set up in the depths with the salts, Nighteyes figured the pridelord spent his free time practicing with a flint and tinder fungus pulled off the blackwing corpses littering the eastern border.

Though the stormtails are pretty handy with their

rocks. If they weren't soggy all the time, I bet we'd see a lot of singed tummy fur.

Nighteyes paused to gawk at the room. A thousand wings were carved into the stone, and it always took her breath away. When she was pridelord, this would be her meditation chamber. This was where she would do her thinking. This was what it felt like to stand at the center of the murmuration, the eye of the hurricane, and command it.

It was humbling.

"You know, they call this chamber the Sky Beneath the Earth," Wendl began before getting interrupted.

"I do know that," Nighteyes snapped. "What I don't know is where the pridelord is."

Outside, his commands echoed among the murmuration in his absence. Within, his scent was everywhere, but as a presence rather than a message. His smell alone was enough to bring back up his command to her and Wendl to be here now. Yet the chamber was empty.

Maybe that's how these things always go? Perhaps he likes for the fighting gryphons to spend time alone beneath the splendor of the murmuration to think on the needs of all starlings and not just their petty squabbles.

Wendl sat in the center of the chamber, still, her breathing even. She made a good assassin that way.

Nighteyes found herself unable to resist pacing, unable to keep irritating thoughts out of her mind. "Can you just...move over a little? If you're in the center, and I stand next to you, then it's not even. So if you move over a little, the room will be equal."

The green opinicus didn't comment, but she did

take three steps to her left, helping balance the room. It was enough to calm Nighteyes, who closed her eyes. They sat there for another fifteen minutes, waiting patiently, without interrupting the silence.

With her mind calm, her hunting instincts settled over her. Something was wrong.

Nighteyes started to say, "Do you smell that?"

She was interrupted by Wendl's, "Do you hear that?"

The smell of blood came from the corridor across the Sky Beneath the Earth. So did the rhythmic echo of dripping.

The assassins shared a glance. Wendl wasn't good at danger, so Nighteyes went first, her stomach lowered to brush the ground. It was always better to present a smaller target. Wendl, to her credit, kept her talons from clicking on the stone as she followed.

Where Nighteyes and Wendl descended, the brazier light could not follow. She tracked the scent of paws on rock, stopping only a few times to check side passages. Every time she stepped off the path, she found ruin in the form of collapsed tunnels.

Her mind went back to the Abyssal Depths, and she searched for specks of light to follow. Luminescent fungi appeared to float down another dead end, their pale light too weak to reveal even the walls they clung to. Nighteyes was ready to turn back when her scarred eyes caught a faint flicker around the end of the path casting sharp shadows against the floor, the lick of a crocodile's tongue against its teeth. She approached at a crawl, stopping every time Wendl made a noise.

The path ended, revealing only one, final side passage.

The smell of blood waxed. The dripping waned.

Into the gullet we go.

The assassins peeked around the corner.

A CHAMBER even larger than the Sky Beneath the Earth stretched before them, lit by braziers in every corner. On the left side of the room, a map of the continent as it had been when the temple was built was carved into the wall, flora and fauna of all sorts offering their texture to the map. Nighteyes didn't recognize most of the animals.

Her eyes traced the ceiling, carved to look like the canopy of a jungle, until it reached the right wall. A mural of glyphs representing all of the starling prides, past and present, stretched from jadebeak to stormtail. Either wall, lit by the braziers and hidden beneath the sacred heart of the jungle, would have been the most interesting thing Nighteyes saw on a given day—under normal circumstances.

Today, however, her eyes were drawn to a dais with a vat on top of it. The vat had shattered, large shards of glass glistening in the firelight. Cracks in the temple floor drank greedily of the purple elixir. Knowing even a single vial could buy years of life for victims of bloodbeak, she watched the lifeblood of her pride vanish before her paws, food for fungi too useless to light the correct path.

Balthar's supplies, the salts stolen from the desert, a metal opinicus cage, crates of all sorts, and a dozen other things she couldn't identify were stacked in the back of the room. In front of them lay...something. *Someone*, judging by the green feathers and fur.

"Balthar?" Wendl gasped, rushing to pick up torn strips of leather in front of the bloody body.

Nighteyes recognized scraps of the harness Balthar had worn when he stole the mallard's pouch on the border. She didn't recognize him from the remains.

Remains was the only way she could describe what she was seeing: fur, feathers, and bare bones sticking out from where his foretalons should have begun. The jungle offered up a lot of dead gryphons, torn apart by animals or opinici, but she'd never seen a corpse reduced to an unidentifiable mass before. It reeked of rage and betrayal, and for the first time in her life, she had to look away and cover her nares.

What happened here?

Wendl wept, her grief shielding her from the other horrors of the chamber, but a dead gryphon had the opposite effect on Nighteyes. Her ears perked up as she heard the sound of claws clicking on stone, and she pulled Wendl away from the body.

From behind the vat came the pridelord, looking more wild beast than gryphon. The green of his paws, chest, and stomach were gone, stained red by the blood. He breathed in deep gasps, as though learning how for the first time. She thought he might have a punctured lung, but she didn't see any open gashes or fresh cuts.

Maybe he caught Balthar unaware? Or maybe Balthar wasn't much of a fighter.

"P-pridelord?" she ventured.

He blinked a few times, his eyes finally focusing on her and Wendl, before spitting out blood and feathers. "Nighteyes."

He must have been exhausted, because his pheromones came seconds after the word. She was overwhelmed by the intensity of citrus, and her mind left her body as it had with the altruism.

Whisper did warn me this would happen, Nighteyes recalled. *If he tries to kill me when I'm like this, will I regain control, or just watch my body die?*

Idle thoughts went through her mind, paired with scents. It took her a moment to realize what was happening. The pridelord was pulling the past two days out of her, but he was getting a sanitized version of events. Whatever Whisper had done, it was saving Nighteyes' life. The pridelord seemed satisfied she wasn't a threat.

Glass clinked against the wet, stone floor. She couldn't force her head to turn, but she managed to get her eyes to look left. Among the red and purple stained glass from the vat was an intact vial, a hint of orange on its rim.

The pridelord stood in front of Wendl, and the stench of obedience coming off him flattened Nighteyes, soaking her white stomach in purple sludge and green mold. Wendl, however, didn't bow her head, didn't mantle to him, and didn't answer his questions. The contest of wills lasted only two minutes before the pridelord, disgusted, relaxed his pheromones for a moment.

Wendl pounced, pinning him with her talons and reaching into her harness for a piece of broken glass with her beak.

The pridelord's musk of alarm overwhelmed Nighteyes, and her body acted on its own. She barrelled into Wendl, sending her friend into the stone of the map wall. The scholar slumped down, and while Nighteyes' heart ached to check on her friend, her body turned to do the same to the pridelord.

"Pridelord, are you hurt?" her beak asked on its own, while her paws checked his neck and chest for lacerations. All she felt were old scars across his stomach, spreading out in several directions, nothing new.

"Bring her." His olfactory command came a moment later. Nighteyes dragged Wendl by the scruff to the opinicus cage in the back, pushing her inside.

Was this scavenged from the Nighthaunt's ruins? she wondered. Once Wendl was secured, the pridelord locked the cage, fumbling with the key. Nighteyes didn't think her paws could do any better. She was honestly surprised he knew how to work an opinicus mechanism at all. She doubted she'd be able to figure it out.

Wendl remained prone, but she was breathing, which was the most Nighteyes could ask for. She would come back for her friend once the faux-altruism gave back her body. The pridelord stumbled across the room, forgetting for a moment to order her to come with him.

The citrus finally came, and she continued in his wake, listening to the clicking of his foreclaws against the wet stone. He passed Balthar's remains, not bothering to look at his kill.

Nighteyes had always thought Balthar resembled Wendl, but in death, he wore a stranger's face. His scent was Balthar, however. Strong, unmistakably Balthar: as though on the opinicus's death, the pridelord had purged his scent from the murmuration, drenching the corpse in the traitor's pheromones. It reminded her of the way Whisper had forced Nighteyes to emit a strong scent when helping Clamshell.

"Pridelord?" her body asked as they passed the remains. Even with Whisper's dissociation, this version of Nighteyes was herself, just one who had never thought of treason.

"Leave it," he commanded. "We have no room in the murmuration for opinici who aren't loyal. Nor gryphons."

The citrus came a moment later, leashing her behind him. *Nor gryphons?* she wondered. *What does that mean?*

As they left the corridors and the Sky Beneath the Earth behind, his pheromones sent the murmuration into a frenzy. Nighteyes could almost imagine a thousand gryphons beating their wings and lifting the temple off the ground to fly away with it, but it remained grounded.

He raised and lowered his own wings a few times, but perhaps he had been injured in the struggle, or perhaps he had developed a flair for the dramatic as he began the slow ascent to the top of the temple by paw.

31

SWARM

Nighteyes trailed behind the pridelord. His first few steps up the crumbling stairs winding around the temple were weak, as though his paws were numb from killing Balthar, though he found his footing as he went. This close to him, his scent was like unripe citron, but as it dispersed, it attracted more and more of the murmuration.

Most jadebeaks filled the skies or clung to the ruins of the city below, but one landed beside Nighteyes. Iri the First, eyes vacant, followed behind the pridelord. The leaders of smaller starling prides began trickling in soon after, adding new shades of green to the city.

The pridelord's slow pace gave Nighteyes too much time to think. Despite the separation of mind and body, she felt the ache in her spike-impaled paw at having to traverse so many stairs, wishing they'd just flown. Still, the long walk bought time for the other prides' leaders to gather.

Talli the Second's arrival caught Nighteyes off

guard. From what she remembered from Wendl, only one of The Six was a pride leader. Their Fourth was dead; Balthar's remains rested as far beneath the temple as they were above it. Kism the Third wasn't a pride leader, and if he were smart, he'd have already have fled the Emerald Jungle.

Nighteyes sniffed Talli. Her pheromones told of a small pride whose leader suffered from an affliction that made emergency flights impossible, so he'd sent his trusted friend in his stead.

The starlings above the temple were so numerous, they formed a second canopy. Stray sunbeams spilled down from the rare cracks between gryphons to reach the ground below. Every pride was now represented.

No, that's not right. Where are the Newmoon and Stormtail Prides?

She tried to remember how Whisper had taught her to process pheromones and teased apart the subtle threads, pushing past the citrus. The susurration had been ordered to guard the northern border. The stormtails were being told...*something.* She'd never experienced these scents before, and she couldn't make heads or tails of what was going on, just that they were restricted to Lightningmaw.

Four new starlings landed, so dark in the shade they were nearly black and not green. They stood in front of the pridelord, ready to amplify his message to the murmuration.

Nighteyes had been to several gatherings of the starling prides before, but this was the first time one had begun with words instead of smells.

"Extinction." The pridelord's word echoed through the ears and nares of his gryphons, forcing them to settle down, the cacophony of stars becoming silence. "Once, we were disparate prides, dying at the claws of wild animals and hunted by opinici. We faced our own eradication, our own expulsion from the continent, and it was only by binding our wills together that we pushed back the inevitable. Individual gryphons were hunted and killed. Individual prides went extinct. But not the murmuration. The murmuration thrived, becoming feared and respected."

Nighteyes couldn't remember a pridelord ever giving a speech before, only orders. The assassination attempt must have shaken him.

He continued, "At the time, we spread out, filling the jungle and pushing past the naze and mountains. The pridelords of old saw that we could, one day, control the entire continent. But they weren't cruel, not like the opinici. Nor were they blinded by self-interest like the other gryphon prides.

"In his selflessness, in his kindness, in his *altruism*, a pridelord of old set borders around the Emerald Jungle to keep it safe. With the help of alchemists, he allowed visitors, opinicus and gryphon alike, to come and petition. He taught them to make glyphs to show their borders; he made pacts the Emerald Jungle has followed closely ever since.

"But the outsiders have broken their pacts. The Abyssal Naze seeks to use us as another pair of talons to rend away their foes, letting starling blood turn their fields fertile. The Ashen Weald guard their borders like jailors, as though they didn't owe their continued very existence to the grace of past pridelords.

"Outsiders send their silver sickness across the Jadebeak Mountains, hoarding the cure for themselves. Outsiders try our borders, forgetting the ancient pacts. Outsiders poison our prides, disconnecting starlings from the care of the murmuration. Blasphemy!"

Something about the pridelord's words were wrong, but Nighteyes couldn't place it. She'd never heard so many words from the leader of the starlings before. Her physical form was enraptured, watching the pridelord as he continued.

"And now they send their spies and assassins at me. They changed opinici to look like starlings, but I have smelled the truth. I pulled it from their souls before I killed them."

The pridelord nodded to Iri. Though her eyes were still blank, she signaled to her pride, who dropped the bodies of dead blackwing soldiers on the ground at the foot of the temple.

These must be the dead blackwings everyone back home was talking about. But weren't they dead before they crossed the Emerald Veil?

"When Balthar and Wendl arrived, with their deformed paws and fear, we welcomed them as we would any other starlings. We gave them prides, mates, friends, food, and shelter. But they weren't here because they wanted to join the murmuration. They were here to spy on it.

"Balthar and Wendl were from an opinicus pride called the Blackwing. This...*eyrie*...believed they could destroy the murmuration through subterfuge. They believed they could stand against the Emerald

Jungle, the true rulers of Belamuria. They are about to find out how mistaken they were."

In her time with the Ashen Weald, Nighteyes had seen speeches elicit talking, grumbling, cheering, and hisses. The starlings remained silent, awaiting orders.

"Return to your prides," the pridelord commanded. "For the next week, feast. Eat all you can. When the moon is full, we will show this pride of *blackwings* what happens to opinici who make enemies of the Emerald Jungle."

Nighteyes shivered in spite of herself. The starlings from the ground erupted into the sky, the little light disappearing in an artificial eclipse that turned the temple to darkness. When it ended and the sun returned, it blinded her.

The only gryphons to remain were the pride leaders atop the temple. The city below had never been so empty.

"Pridelord, what of the Stormtail and Newmoon Prides?" Nighteyes was surprised to hear herself speak, partially because it was the same question she'd been wondering from her place of altruism. If she were the pridelord and she'd nearly been assassinated, she'd want all of the prides here to defend her. Especially Whisper, who had always seemed to be his most loyal vassal.

The pridelord looked back at her. "The Newmoon Pride must watch the border and keep the Ashen Weald at bay. We cannot risk their sickness infecting other prides. The Stormtail Pride...are no longer part of the murmuration. I was too kind, thinking their *cancer* would stay contained, that Whisper could fix them before it spread. I am no longer willing to take that risk. The infection must be cut out."

As soon as he said it, Nighteyes felt it. The sense of where all starlings were, the pheromone map of the jungle, suddenly went dark along the southern coast. Even the one bright spot in the Winter Jungle vanished.

The pridelord was still talking, pulling her out of her shock. "I will not have starlings I cannot control near me. Clearly, that's how the blackwing reeve sent his assassins after me in the first place. An opinicus pride who can create false starlings cannot be permitted to live. I will scourge his *eyrie* from the maps the same way I have removed the Stormtail Pride as a warning to others."

The only things Nighteyes could think were profanity, though thankfully, her beak didn't say those out loud. She was left with one final thought.

What now?

32

SPARKWING DENMOTHER

The next few days passed like a raging storm, but Nighteyes knew they were the opposite: the calm before the typhoon, the retreat of the waves before the tsunami. The borders within the murmuration had weakened.

A dozen starling prides now moved through her lands, bringing food to fatten up her pride. The gryphlets and fledglings delighted at getting to try saltwater fish, strange new birds from the southern jungle, berries they'd never heard the names of.

She'd struggled to feed them without enough hunters, and hearing their joy at eating a ripe eggfruit pierced her heart. Yet this week of feasting could be the last of their brief lives because none of the gryphons with bloodbeak would survive a long migration. They'd die in the air, falling to their deaths, if the pridelord demanded they come.

As might Talli's pride leader.

Nighteyes didn't know where the Blackwing Eyrie was located. She hadn't paid much attention to maps beyond memorizing where the Ashen Weald had once held territory before the Seraph King defeated them. She got the impression it was far away, and she wondered how the pridelord would find it.

Though most of the intrajungle border glyphs had vanished under the week of feasting, not all had. While her sisters watched over the pride, Nighteyes took advantage of the chaos to roam the Emerald Jungle. She went northeast first and found the jungle ended where the Newmoon Pride's glyphs used to begin. She stared at the vegetation, seeing only a matte of green and brown, no idea what was beyond it.

Just like Whisper's hidden path through the Stormtail and Jadebeak Pridelands.

When a sunshower came down from the mountains, she thought she could smell mallow root. When the winds shifted, she tried to imagine her thoughts as scents, asking for help with her pride's sicker members. She received no answer.

Then she travelled south, hoping to catch a glimpse of Lightningmaw. The border there was similarly impassible. Clamshell's Grasslake Pathway had vanished, invisible even from the sky as her starling brain rewrote everything south to be endless jungle.

He's cut us off from the southern shore. We'll need that food when we return. The pridelord wasn't stupid, but he was, apparently, cruel. She suspected he'd find a way to force the Stormtail Pride to leave when the other starlings weren't around to see it.

She reached the border of the Winter Jungle, putting a paw in the salt water, but couldn't pass the glyphs where Talli's pride ended. If anyone was out there, she was blind to them. She was certain now she'd felt the Gourmand disappear, but she hadn't sensed any starlings on the island Whisper claimed was beyond the Winter Jungle. Perhaps the water obscured its inhabitants.

Nighteyes resisted the urge to use Whisper's fish on Talli, who rightfully worried about her leader's health, instead moving on with her travels. She crossed into Kism's home pride, but all his pridemates could say was that he'd vanished. None had sensed his death, lending credence to Nighteyes' theory he'd fled.

Good on him, I guess, but he can't stay away forever. Her body shivered as she remembered what it had been like to take Wendl's elixirs month after month. She gave him four months before he'd be a danger to any gryphons or opinici he came across.

She surveyed the borders of King's Reach and Alwren. If Slate was correct, fleets of ships were hidden beyond the Emerald Veil, just out of reach to both her and the Abyssal Naze. The Seraph King could be fifty yards away, staring back at her, and she'd never know.

The last place she visited was the old Sparkwing Pride's nesting grounds. It was on her way back from the border with Alwren, and she'd never seen it before. A massive tree had once existed here, long before she'd been born. According to legend, it had no twin on the continent. It was called the sailtree, which made some starlings think it was like the spine of a sailfin monitor rising out of the jungle. The word *sail* in *sailtree* was a much older variant, similar to the opinicus word for the sail of a ship.

Regardless, the tree was long dead. A rot had cut it off at the base. The trunk, slow to decay even in the humid jungle, had become a popular place for sparkwings to build burrows. She'd spotted it from the sky, which had given her the idea to land. She walked from the top of the fallen tree to its base, where the old stump had become the Sparkwing nesting grounds.

With most interior borders gone, several old sparkwings returned here. Where broadleaf trees had begun to encroach, they cleared out the canopy, letting light fall upon the stump. If the nightsky were a pride of twilight and stars, the sparkwings were sunbeams and leaves. At first glance, with her impaired vision, she thought she was seeing a green pond sparkling in the light. Only when they chirped at her arrival did she realize they were gryphons.

Her landing earned her some harrumphs and squawks. The sailtree's rot left pockmarks on its stump. Old nest moss had once filled these indentations, eroding to dirt after the pride dissolved. Someone had come in and planted squirrelbrush in the old nests, a mountain plant that needed plenty of sunlight to grow in the jungle. It reached for the bright skies, and had Nighteyes stood on her back paws, she'd have required twice her length to touch the top of the plants. It must be several years old at least. Perhaps the sparkwings had left seeds in their wake to be remembered by.

Nighteyes was about to leave when the sound of scratching near the base of the trunk caught her attention. An elderly gryphon pawed at the roots of an even older broadleaf tree, sniffing after she scratched.

"Is everything okay?" Nighteyes asked. "Did you lose something in there, perhaps lunch?"

Squirrelbrush was accurately named. In its native mountain home, it provided cover for ptarmigans and baby goliath birds. Here in the Emerald Jungle, however, purple and gold squirrels poked their heads out of holes and threw acorns at the sparkwings to try to fend them off.

"Just looking for someone," the elderly gryphon said. "I misplaced him, but his scent is strong. I'm sure he'll come back here."

Happy to help, Nighteyes sniffed at the roots and vines. Her sense of help*ful*ness transformed to help*less*ness when she realized who the sparkwing was waiting for. Though the foliage here smelled sweet, the bitter hint of thornvine mixed with gryphon filled it.

Her mind flashed back to the remains beneath the temple. "I'm afraid Balthar's not coming. He died recently. I'm sorry for your loss."

The sparkwing stopped pawing at the vines.

Nighteyes nuzzled the other gryphon, unsure what to do. "Was he a friend of yours?"

"Of my daughter's," she replied. "Well, I suppose they were all my children. But you remember the ones you can help, don't you? They hold a special place in a denmother's heart."

Nighteyes nodded.

"Balthar was her best friend," the sparkwing continued. "She had a hard time making friends, so it took an outsider to win her over. Tough not to like a gryphon who takes a cassowary kick for you. Eventually, they became mates. After she died, I started to lose my memory of her. But whenever I could smell him, I could remember her. I'm not sure what I'll do now."

"Why don't you gather your things, and you can come back with me?" Nighteyes asked. "There's a gryphon who can help you remember."

While the denmother tried to retrieve her belongings from the squirrels up above, Nighteyes stared at the thick roots. With the long scratch marks coming down them, the dead sailtree smelled faintly of kashow sap. After seeing Balthar's remains drenched in his scent, though, the thornvine smell had lodged in her brain, and it lingered behind the roots. Weirdly, in the recesses of Whisper's gifted memories, Nighteyes could remember what he'd smelled like as a blackwing.

She was a lot stronger than the elderly sparkwing, and she pushed and gnawed at the roots and vines until she revealed stone behind it. Then she tracked Balthar's scent until she found a break in the stone and pulled herself inside.

The vines sealed behind her, closing her off from the sun. She could smell old rushlights, but she didn't have a way to light them. Instead, she sniffed around the hidden chamber. Balthar had obviously spent a lot of time here, but she also detected the whiff of dry herbs and chemicals Wendl used in her medicines.

Nighteyes almost gave up and left, but beneath some clay jars came a smoky aroma. Wendl enjoyed cooking with fire and even drying out meat or herbs, but this was different. It smelled of oilbirds and bristlespines. It smelled of cave gryphlets rescued from flameworks.

It smelled of a saltpeter explosion that left Nighteyes stunned while Balthar stole the satchel of opinicus secrets and fled with it.

She scratched at the hide-woven satchel with her paw, then licked, coming away with the taste of ash and duck. Once she located the pile of stolen parchment, she felt around with her beak for one of the coarse medicine bags opinici loved so much and put the flameworks documents into it. There was no sense bringing all of the other smells with her.

She stumbled over a crate and sent glass vials rolling throughout the lair, though thankfully none broke. It was one of a dozen crates of opinicus supplies, and she couldn't imagine where he was finding all of this. A boat from Alwren must have shipwrecked on the coast. She wondered if Wendl knew about it, then quickly put Wendl from her mind—just for now—and found the flameworks satchel.

Once Nighteyes had nuzzled her head through the strap, she pushed her way out through the roots and vines to meet up with the sparkwing denmother.

Here's hoping I can make sense of the documents. There's little hope of getting them to the Abyssal Naze at this point.

THE NIGHTSKY PRIDE didn't think anything of their new sparkwing arrival, not with the constant influx of jadebeaks and other prides bringing them food. It was only once Nighteyes asked her sisters to find their guest a nest that the youngest one spoke up.

"She's too green to stay," her sister said.

Nighteyes rolled her eyes. "Wendl was green. It's just for the night."

"Yeah, well, look what happened to Wendl." Sheen glared at Nighteyes from across the nesting grounds. If not for her wounded leg, Nighteyes half-expected Sheen to challenge her next.

Once, I wished any member of my pride had that kind of spirit. Now, I need to stay in control until I can set things right.

In the dying light, her protégé shone more blue than purple, almost the same shade as Rudder. Emotions pulled at Nighteyes' heart, but she denied them purchase. Unlike Rudder, Wendl was in *immediate* danger. Nighteyes had managed to fly by the temple once on her journey, her scent masked by a flock of jadebeaks. Her brief glimpse showed her the entrance to the Sky Beneath the Earth filled in with rocks and a nasty stinkbug scent that screamed *stay away*. She'd been unable to find another way down there, and she had nightmares of Wendl starving in the dark.

After Wendl, Nighteyes' own pride was in danger. She needed to find a way to save those with blood-beak. And, selfishly, she wished she had a way to stop Sheen from coming along. Sheen was strong enough to fly, but with a broken leg, she wouldn't fare well against whatever awaited them at the Blackwing Eyrie.

That left Rudder and the Stormtail Pride to fend for themselves. If they were smart, they'd get out of the Emerald Jungle before the murmuration returned. Still, for the moment, they were an afterthought. Unlike every other starling in Nighteyes' life, they weren't in any immediate danger.

Sheen continued glaring, and Nighteyes' sisters hemmed and hawed, so Nighteyes finally invited the sparkwing denmother to stay in her island den for the night.

33

POTTERY

The long flight had worn out her elderly guest, and it was well after dawn before the sparkwing could fly again. Nighteyes hoped Whisper would take her in, but there was no telling what the newmoon would do. Nighteyes was getting desperate. Tomorrow, the war migration would begin. She was out of time.

Before they reached the Newmoon Pride border, Nighteyes landed with the denmother and offered her the medicine bag. "I found this behind those roots. I thought Balthar's smell might give you comfort."

The sparkwing thanked Nighteyes but also sniffed suspiciously at the bag, catching the fiery scent of its contents.

Look, whatever's in the bag is safer with you than me. Nighteyes had spent the early hours of the morning trying to figure out the papers. She understood a lot of opinicus glyphs courtesy of her time at the Ashen Weald and asking Wendl questions when she returned home, but the documents were mostly numbers and locations. Someone was moving things out of various flameworks and silkworks.

Why that was important, Nighteyes had no clue, but she didn't want to bring it with her and have it fall into the talons of an opinicus. Her border with the Abyssal Naze was patrolled by the Alabaster Eyrie, so she couldn't just toss it over the Emerald Veil. If she'd had a safe way to get it to the Ashen Weald, she'd have done that, instead. This should safeguard it for when she got back.

Nighteyes and the denmother reached the newmoon glyphs and found a surprise waiting for them. Though the jungle was a blur of vegetation, someone had drawn a clear line of salt along the border. They'd carved out a circle that intruded upon Nightsky territory. Inside the circle was a clay jar.

"What's this? It's very pretty. Did an opinicus make it?" The sparkwing reached out a paw, but Nighteyes caught it, carefully stopping the fragile denmother.

From across the barrier, she smelled a nocturnal flowering vine. The Newmoon Pride were clearly watching to see if she could figure their gift out.

Nighteyes sniffed at the salt on the ground, careful not to inhale any. It was the same type Whisper had used to create the path for the infected. The jar looked to be some sort of Redwood Valley design. She walked to the edge of the salt circle, but there was a faint message on it. Nothing quite clear, but she got the distinct impression that she, personally, should not cross the line.

She twitched an ear while wracking her brain to figure out why Whisper had given her pottery. Had Rudder been here, he'd have teased her about her ears, but that was because his own were so small and round he couldn't rotate them the way she could.

"Do you get the distinct impression we shouldn't open the jar?" she asked the denmother, who shook her head no. "Okay, well, just open it a little so we can see what's inside. Be careful, though. Don't break the salt line, and don't do anything rash."

The sparkwing crossed the line of salt and pulled the lid off the clay pot. Thankfully, it was sturdy because it hit the ground hard. She reached a paw in where Nighteyes couldn't see and licked it.

"Just salt," the denmother said. "Probably the same salt used to make the circle. Hmm, there's flecks of something in here. Ow! Something bit my tongue!"

Oh no. Nighteyes had asked Whisper for a plan, and Whisper had, indeed, come up with one. What Nighteyes had failed to intuit was the lengths a newmoon gryphon would go to in order to solve this problem.

"I'm going to need you to step across the glyph line and into Newmoon Pride territory," Nighteyes ordered the sparkwing. "You're Whisper's ward now."

The denmother looked confused, but a new scent came on the wind, and suddenly the elderly gryphon chirped a hello to someone Nighteyes couldn't see and vanished beyond the glyphs.

The Nightsky Pride's leader stared into nothing. And then a piece of bark materialized through the air and hit her upside the head.

"Hey!" she protested. "What gives?!"

She looked down at the bark, which was carved with glyphs. They were the glyphs denparents put above the eggs while they slept. The message roughly translated to *all children are safe here.*

Nighteyes looked at the clay jar. Deliberately infecting members of her own pride with the parasite seemed like a step too far, but she was desperate. Once they were infected, they'd become part of the Newmoon Pride, leaving behind their home, possibly forever.

But they'd live, and that's what was important.

I hope Whisper knows what she's doing.

Nighteyes went to retrieve the pride's children, praying that she could convince enough of the adults to help her carry them to the border.

NIGHTEYES LISTENED to her sisters critique everything wrong with her plan without offering any good alternatives. Nobody disagreed those with bloodbeak would die if they had to fly across the continent, they just disagreed with the idea of deliberately infecting anyone with the parasite.

"It's not fair for you to decide for them," her youngest sister said.

"Great!" Nighteyes replied. "We'll let those with bloodbeak decide for themselves. Anyone want to die flying out of the Emerald Jungle, or is everyone pretty happy to go spend the next few days in safety being fed pumpkins?"

Though some of the gryphlets were young and not particularly bright, everyone was happier being fed and alive. While the adults without bloodbeak still grumbled, they helped fly the youngsters to the newmoon border.

The jadebeak food deliveries continued, though there were now many fewer gryphons at the nightsky nests.

"Sheen, I need you to come with me, too," Nighteyes ordered.

The indigo fledgling bristled. "Why? I can't lift anyone. I want to stay here."

This would be easier if I could tell her I didn't kick Wendl out of the pride. Nighteyes looked around for a denparent, but they were all mid-transit. "Because I'm your pride leader, at least until your paw heals and you overthrow me, and I think it's important you be there."

To her surprise, it worked, and Sheen begrudgingly flew to the border with the rest. There was a brief moment where the dense, unidentifiable foliage seemed to give her pause, a gift from Wendl's treatments, but she quickly shook it off. Unfortunately, just getting her here was only part one of Nighteyes' plan, and part two would be much more difficult.

Sheen sniffed at the salt but stayed well back. The Nightsky Pride's denparents were carefully putting each gryphlet or fledgling's paw into the jar, then lifting it out and letting the grains of salt sift between the pads. When the young gryphon let out a yelp, they were moved to the border, where they vanished.

We're bending the rules here, but none of this technically goes against the pridelord's orders.

A few gryphlets tried to fake being bitten, but when they couldn't cross the newmoon glyphs, they were sent back in. Soon, everyone infected with bloodbeak had disappeared.

"Hold up," Nighteyes ordered the denparents. "Some of you may have the parasite now. We can't risk spreading it. Walk towards the Newmoon Pride's lands. If you can see the newmoon gryphons, cross over, and you can help take care of the fledglings."

"Will we be able to return to the Nightsky Pride after the fighting with the blackwings is over?" a denmother asked.

"I don't know." Nighteyes didn't see any reason to honey-coat it. "But if you can see the newmoon gryphons, you're probably infected. I'll do what I can to get you back when we return, but I can't promise anything."

Half the nightsky denparents vanished. The others crossed the salt circle, then flew home.

"Now it's your turn," Nighteyes said to Sheen.

The fledgling continued showing off her impressive bristling skills. "No. My paw will heal on the flight to the air-ray."

"*Eyrie*," Nighteyes corrected. "And I won't risk you dying. We don't know why you're okay, but what if the only way to save all of your sick pridemates is lost because you get killed by an opinicus? Is that what you want?"

It felt like a very sensible decision to make in her head, and so she was surprised when Sheen declined.

"The pridelord has spoken," the fledgling protested. "It's not our place to say no. I understand why you sent the bloodbeaks away, but it would be wrong for me to stay back when I *can* fight. I trust the pridelord to take care of the murmuration."

There was a lot Nighteyes wanted to say, but there was always a chance the pridelord would find out through Sheen, so she kept her beak shut. She should be proud of Sheen, but instead, she was ashamed of what the murmuration had become.

If she dies, she won't die thinking I'm ashamed of her, Nighteyes decided. "That's very good of you. You may return to your nest. I just need to close the clay jar and speak to Whisper privately before I return."

Sheen trilled a little, forgetting she was mad at her pride leader, and began the flight home.

Nighteyes looked at the clay jar. *Of course, there might be a way where she doesn't have to die.*

The scent of cooking mallow root intensified as she approached the circle of salt. There was still a warning there, *Nighteyes-stay-away*, but she ignored it. With a broadleaf in her beak, she crossed the line and siphoned away just a little of the salted mites, careful to keep them from touching her skin. She wrapped the broadleaf with other leaves, again and again, until she was fairly certain that even if the little bugs escaped, they wouldn't get out.

She didn't want to find out what would happen to her pride if she got infected. Most likely, they'd go the way of the sparkwings, especially now that she'd sent so many of her pridemates to the Newmoon Pride.

Still, they're not going to miss one more gryphon.

She bowed her head in the direction of the scent of mallow root for the kindness of the susurration, then rejoined her pride.

34

MURMURATION

The day of the war migration, Nighteyes woke up two hours before dawn. The pridelord had sent out the calming scent of cassia and mint, and the Emerald Jungle entered a deep sleep. Many enterprising squirrels would pad their nests with gryphon treasure tonight.

For two gryphons Wendl had dosed, the mint wasn't strong enough to quell their anxiety. The cassia, too, only served to remind them of the opinicus's absence and draw them to her nest.

Nighteyes poked her beak into Wendl's hideaway. "Sheen? Are you in here?"

The fledgling squeaked. "Sorry! I just...the cassia smell. It made me miss her. I'm worried she hasn't come to say goodbye."

"I'm worried, too," Nighteyes said. Though Sheen bristled, she continued, "I have something to tell you. The fight with Wendl was staged. We needed to talk to the pridelord privately. We hoped to plead our case and convince him to let us seek outside aid to help with bloodbeak. Wendl had some ideas that might work, but the pridelord wouldn't see her. This was the only way to get her an audience."

The lie worked, and Sheen relaxed. "I knew it! At least, I thought I knew it? But then you slashed her and flicked the blood, and I didn't know. But I sort of knew? Then I heard rumors she'd tried to assassinate the pridelord and been killed!"

"Unfortunately, the pridelord has her working on something top secret, so the lie was necessary." Nighteyes hadn't gotten any hint Wendl was dead, but she didn't know if the pridelord could hide a starling death. If so, maybe Kism wasn't *missing*, either. There was no sense worrying Sheen, though.

Sheen pawed at Wendl's bedding, mindful of her hurt leg. "I miss her. I hope I survive the battle so I can come back and see her again. She promised to make me a bracelet."

"Aw, that sounds nice." Nighteyes put a wing over Sheen. "Say, you know what else might be nice? I have some sugar beet paste I was going to give Wendl. We should light some of her incense and eat it together, just to remember her before we go."

At first, she didn't think Sheen would go for the bait, but the younger gryphon finally agreed. "Yeah, I'd like that."

"Great," Nighteyes said. "Do you think you can get this rushlight lit? I'm rubbish with flint and tinder fungus. I'll go grab the sugar beets."

Once she was out of the hideaway, she watched the ventilation holes on the top until a wisp of smoke came out. Wendl had left a bit of emergency incense, the sort used to knock out gryphons for several hours while she experimented on them. After half an hour, no more white smoke drifted out of the roof.

Nighteyes didn't trust herself to go inside, but she slowly unwrapped the salts. Then she used the last broadleaf to funnel it down through the ventilation hole in the ceiling, onto the unconscious Sheen.

The nightsky leader wasn't positive it would work, but she thought it was worth a try. With any luck, Sheen would wake up hours after the war migration, infected, and Whisper would come retrieve her.

Nighteyes went back to her burrow one last time. Before she'd become pride leader, nests had been an ethereal thing for her, something she wore out and replaced. She'd slept in every corner of the nesting grounds at some point. Once she had a burrow of her own, though, she found she quite liked it.

She'd spent good times here—with her sisters, with Rudder, with Wendl, even with Sheen when the indigo gryphon had brought her rhea eggs. If Nighteyes never came back, she hoped its new owner loved it as much as she had.

She sat atop her home and waited for the sun to rise, thinking on the last two weeks. She'd tried to do a lot, and she'd failed at many of those tasks.

Failure is a strong word. I have...not yet succeeded. She'd written the glyph for Wendl across the mallard's documents sent with the sparkwing. She hoped Whisper and Sheen would be able to locate Wendl, that Wendl was still alive. Rudder and Clamshell should be smart enough to see what was coming and flee the jungle. She'd miss Rudder, but better safe than dead.

The only thing she regretted was that they hadn't

arrived in time to stop the pridelord from killing Balthar. If she didn't think of something when she got back, she'd lose more and more gryphlets to bloodbeak until they were all dead. That was part of her equation in leaving them with Whisper. Now bloodbeak was a Newmoon Pride problem, too.

For now, I have a new purpose. I must lead my pride to war.

The sun, still hidden behind the Jadebeak Mountains, lightened the sky. To the west, she saw the start of the murmuration. Sparkwings sparkled in the light, drawn away from their fleeting homecoming. Talli's pride, Kism's old pride, and a dozen smaller prides filled the skies.

As they flew over Nighteyes, they brought the smell of citrus with them. Her body was pulled out from under her, Whisper's protections kicking in and making her a passenger in her own mind.

The Emerald Jungle emptied, a migration the likes of which had not been seen in several lifetimes. Squirrels looked up from their squirrelbrush homes, curious at the gryphons' strange behavior. Caimans and crocodiles lazed about. Lost cassowaries chased off a flock of rhea.

The jungle was empty.

Almost.

Back home, a single nightsky slept as tiny mites awoke from their saline slumber and burrowed into her fur.

In the northeast, the Newmoon Pride remained hidden behind their glyphs.

In the southeast, a heavy debate ensued between

the leader of the Stormtail Pride and its denparents, who wished to flee east.

Beneath the submerged Winter Jungle, a monstrous creature hunted saltwater crocodiles, indifferent to the plight of the drypaws who lived on land.

And then there were two more starlings, one who hadn't seen light in days, and another who dreamt of pumpkins.

Just beyond the Emerald Veil, on the Abyssal Naze side of the border, was one final starling...waiting for just such an opportunity to return.

35

SATRA BLACKCREST

O utside the ruins of the old kjarr nesting grounds, a golden-crowned kinglet stalked the river, her crestfeathers dyed a much darker shade to hide her from assassins.

This time of year, sunshine and blizzards were equally as likely, and the refugees living in the taiga had seen both—sometimes on the same day. Snow covered the abandoned homes of the kjarr nesting grounds, but there'd been enough warm spring days to melt the Kjarr River coming down the mountain, though ice clung to its bank.

Satra Blackcrest's paws grew damper and colder as she inspected the bodies of several flamingos splayed out along the river's shore. Even with chilled nares, she could smell the iron tang of blood in the air. Sail-fins and goliaths would arrive soon—for the crates of dried fruit and seeds littering the path north to the Crackling Sea's brackish farms if not for the bodies themselves.

"I don't get it," one of her Ashen Weald rangers

commented. This particular ranger had been Satra's bodyguard for three years now, and her long neck bore more scars than the Kjarr's at this point. "Why are they dragging all this food out into the middle of nowhere and just leaving it? Is it poisoned? It's got to be some sort of trap."

The Crackling Sea Eyrie was too far away to see from the ground, but Satra looked in its direction, expecting the pink reeve's army to descend upon them at any moment. She couldn't look at the eyrie or the Clover Ranch without feeling Jonas's gaze upon her, his voice in her head. "Take the food to the caves. We'll test it on the scout Blinky caught first. If he's not afraid of it, we'll run it by the medicine gryphons."

Across the frozen Kjarr River, a harpy eagle gryphon tried to land next to a red wingtorn, but his muscular legs were too heavy, cracking the thin layer of ice atop the snow and burying him up to his chest. The red wingtorn, her wide paws and light form giving her purchase above the ice, shook her head and hid a laugh. Only once Merin's offspring begged for help did she dig him out.

Satra's bodyguard secured the lid and signalled for Blue Jay and Cardinal to come and retrieve it once he was free of the snow. "Blinky's prisoner seemed pretty skittish. If he'll eat it, it's probably good. Why take medicine gryphons away from their bloodbeak work if it's not poison?"

"It might be red fern." Satra longed to visit her old home, but the flamingos had trapped all of the abandoned nesting grounds. Though Jonas was gone and many of his loyalists with him, there seemed to be at least a few ex-rangers teaching them bog traps.

"When we were held prisoner, they'd dose our food with contraceptives to keep the gryphon population down. Often at doses high enough to cause sterility."

The bodyguard flinched. While Satra had been kind by not specifying who *they* had been, the great blue herons who had joined the Ashen Weald had done so out of a sense of guilt, though Grenkin had forged it into purpose.

She put a cool, damp paw on her bodyguard, letting her know the past was forgiven. Then Satra turned to leave. Better she not present herself as a target if this were a trap. Whatever was going on with the food in general probably was, but Cardinal and Blue Jay had caught this set of pinks off guard and alone.

Snow burrows worked as well as sand burrows— better, even, without crabs or mud—and several of Merin's offspring had hidden under the bridge, ready to strike when Card gave the order. The wingtorn and harpy eagle were arguing over the best way to move the crates, shooting Satra looks that told the Kjarr they'd prefer if she'd stayed in the taiga.

"Satra," the bodyguard began before correcting herself. "Kjarr Satra, I mean. What's that, to the west?"

Like most of the herons, the bodyguard hadn't been at New Eyrie during the Ashen Weald's original assault. In fact, even when the Ashen Weald took the Crackling Sea Eyrie, this opinicus had been locked up. She'd been caught bringing food to the wingtorn. Though she'd been told it would ruin her career as a ranger, it had made her an obvious choice when Grenkin selected bodyguards to protect the new Kjarr.

Satra, however, had seen this once before. When

the commander of New Eyrie had nearly murdered her, a swarm of green had risen out of the bog, a storm of infected starlings that had nearly wiped out both the Ashen Weald and the last of the Redwood Valley survivors.

"Fly! Now!" she ordered her bodyguard. "To the caves, leave the food!"

Cardinal stopped dragging a barrel of seed and sprinted for the mountains. Blue Jay was right behind her. He whistled, and she leapt into the air, letting him carry her the rest of the way.

Satra dove to the nearest hideaway. No one here had seen an Abyssal Naze gryphon in two years, but before their disappearance, Chert had helped the Ashen Weald map out the cave systems along the taiga and Poisonmaw.

Satra waited at the entrance, next to the weather barrier, as the swarm descended upon the pink reeve's farms. The seeds were clearly for the starlings. If it was a trap to catch the Ashen Weald out in the open, it had failed.

Strange way to set a trap. How could they know the starlings were coming?

Though her spies inside the eyrie had all been killed or forced to flee, the diving petrels kept tabs on the city from the inland sea, hiding in swarms of crackling jellies. There were reports that the eyrie had been fitted with heavy barriers on every balcony. At the time, she'd thought it an extreme reaction to the sea's storms, but it seemed they were trying to keep something else out.

"Satra, we should close the weather barrier." Her bodyguard put a talon on Satra's shoulder, leaving it there a moment too long. "This won't be enough to stop them if they see us."

The Kjarr waited a few moments more. The murmuration seemed without end, but it stayed north of the bog and kjarr. That meant two things: they weren't infected, and they'd learned to avoid the parasite.

That'll keep our home and food safe.

Still, a sense of dread came over her. The parasite kept the wetlands south of the Crackling Sea safe, but what if they were headed to the weald next?

"Seal the barrier," she said, brushing off her body-guard's misguided touch. "But have Cardinal run to the nearest exit and find a messenger. The free prides need to know this is coming."

36

THE FAMOUS GOURD THIEF

A snowstorm raged along the Darkfeather Highlands, submerging them in several feet of snow. The blizzard had come down from the north, coating the glacier peaks and Poisonmaw along its way. The warm air off the desert kept it from the sea, but stray gusts reached the outposts guarding the new goliath roads from the Crackling Sea to Blacktalon.

"Oi, get those pumpkins inside!" Alabaster Eyrie Captain Eckle shouted to his underlings. "This keeps up, we're gonna get frozen inside and might need to eat them."

Eckle did not enjoy guarding the first outpost north of the Crackling Sea, and his displeasure was compounded by the fact he'd picked it himself. He'd distinguished himself as a King's Guard when the Blackwing Eyrie had attacked the Alabaster, and he'd been given his pick of outposts to lead.

Unfortunately, his fierce defense of his home had come from a place of terror, and nightmares haunted him ever since. Thus, he'd picked this particular outpost to guard because it was farthest on the route from the blackwings, whom he hoped to never see again.

What's more, it was stationed along the mountains. Certainly, that would give him added defense against wingtorn gryphons, whom he believed burrowed under the ground like worms and could appear anywhere the dirt was soft.

Thus far, he hadn't run afoul of any blackwings, trashbirds, or longears. Every other outpost along the route had been hit, and over time, they'd sent their valuables to his location: Crackling Outpost One. His stores had filled up with pumpkins and salt, two of the most precious goods here in the south.

When the cellar and spare rooms had reached capacity, he'd been forced to stack things outside. That had brought in feral goliath birds, so fences were built. He sometimes worried at having so much food and salt in one place, but as the year continued, the other outposts reported sightings of thieves and padfoots, but he remained safe.

Safe and sound. I'll bet no one wants to be this close to the Crackling Sea Eyrie. I made a good choice.

Well, a mostly good choice. His outpost was high enough that he suffered from occasional narebleeds. It was also far enough from the Crackling Sea that mountain storms sometimes dropped an avalanche of snow upon their heads.

Just like now. We're going to have to dig out the supplies after the weather clears, I suspect. Ah well. Maybe I can petition the pinks for a larger stone structure.

He gazed out at the storm, admiring the shape and flow of the snow. It would be beautiful to watch from behind a pane of Crestfall glass with a lit brazier next to him. As it was, he could no longer feel his beak, and he wasn't the one trying to get supplies inside. His underlings were in even worse shape.

The captain ran a talon over his head, dislodging the snow, and turned to go inside when something caught his eye. Not all the snow was falling. Some seemed to hang in the air, long globs of it, as the storm raged around them.

What...? At once, they fell like icy comets, striking the ground around him and cutting him off from the door to the outpost.

"Hello," a spotted, snowy gryphon with a long tail said. "I suppose you know who I am?"

Eckle chattered as he spoke. "You're t-t-the gourd thief."

Younce bowed his head. "Famous gourd thief, thank you. We'll be taking these pumpkins. They're winter squash, as you know, and thus belong to the Snowfall Pride. There's no need to keep them at such a low elevation, though I do appreciate that a few appearances by our sandy padfoot friends was all it took to convince you to put all your precious goods outside and unguarded."

Eckle reached for his metal talons, but the famous gourd thief pounced him.

Younce held him down with giant paws. "Shh, quiet there, don't speak, and there won't be any need to hurt you. Ah, there are my friends from the Hoarfrost Pride, ready to help. Just a few more moments, and we'll be out of your feathers. My goodness, I've never seen such a haul of pumpkins. Were these grown at Blacktalon? My compliments to the farmer."

The snow lightened for a moment, and the gryphons turned to look southwest. "Deracho, Cielle, grab the others and leave. We'll meet outside Dark-feather."

As suddenly as they'd attacked, they were gone, leaving Captain Eckle on his own. His chest felt cold. Where the warm paw had once rested, there was now a single pink feather.

I suppose that could have gone worse. I'm alive, and they left fully half of our supplies here! Not much of a gourd thief, is he.

Eckle went to check on the other guards, all of whom were unharmed but just as confused as he was.

"Maybe it's a gryphon thing, only stealing half?" one guard asked. "Gryphons are a superstitious lot, you know."

Eckle did not know anything about gryphons, and he suspected his underlings knew even less. "Well, let's head back inside. We can always inform the king we held off an attack of fifty gryphons with just us four. If we tell it right, it's not a defeat, it's a startling victory against a much larger force."

Even as he said it, he wondered what the gryphons had been looking at. His talons and paws were turning numb, but he stared southwest, where the Crackling Sea Eyrie was hidden by the storm.

The white snow was drowned out by dark shapes. His first thought was ash, but the longer he watched, the greener they looked. By the time he realized the starling murmuration was upon him, it was too late for him or the remaining pumpkins.

37

THE SABERBEAK'S NEW MATE

East of the storm, the rimu tree canopy of Poisonmaw Valley strained beneath the weight of thick, wet snow. In several places, the treetops had given way, providing light and snow purchase along the forest floor.

In one such nascent glen, a gryphon with sabers on her beak stalked a monitor lizard even larger than she was. The reptile nuzzled its way into an old ground parrot nest, unaware gryphons had already stolen the eggs and birds, unaware it was being hunted.

The saberbeak, overly eager, stepped on snow-covered rimu needles. With the *crunch* of paw-on-snow, the lizard flipped its head back and hissed a challenge.

In response, she reared back on her hind legs, spreading her wings to appear larger than she was. The monitor lizard was not impressed by a gryphon smaller than it. It whipped out its blue tail, bashing the gryphon across the chest in an attack that would bruise heavily before the day was through.

The saberbeak stifled a growl, keeping herself calm. When the lizard attacked a second time, she flattened herself against the ground. The lizard's tail hit the nearby redwood. Unfortunately, the impact didn't faze the lizard.

The saberbeak raised her tail, the light tuft at the end distracting her quarry. It bit several times, catching a bit of her fluff but exposing the soft skin of its stomach. She barrelled into it, knocking it down and digging her sabers through its thick hide and shaking it back and forth until it went limp.

Then the saberbeak gryphlet carried the lizard over to where Grax and Hatzel were watching, beaming at her first monitor kill.

"You did well!" Hatzel proclaimed. As was customary, the pride leader took a little of the meat, though with her giant beak, she ended up eating more of the lizard than she intended. "When I was a gryphlet, this would mark you as a hunter of the saberbeak pride. You're now old enough to hunt for yourself. You no longer need Pink Paw to feed you."

The baby saberbeak sniffled and looked like she was going to cry, and Grax of the Strix snorted, hiding an owlish laugh.

"But I suppose you've got a lot of growing to do if you want to be bigger than me, so it'd be a shame to stop feeding you now." Hatzel patted the gryphlet on the head, her large paw making the tiny saberbeak vanish beneath it.

The gryphlet ran off with the rest of the lizard,

looking for Squirrelbane to gift it to and leaving Hatzel alone with Grax.

"Do you think she'll grow as large as you?" the owl gryphon asked. Among the weald owls, brown was a rare color. According to the Darkfeather University, one of the headmasters of the previous Redwood Valley University had been a brown owl, though there was no indication he bore any relation to the gryphon who sat before Hatzel now.

Grax had served several roles in the Strix Pride, going from lead hunter to personal denmother of Squirrelbane, Sound of Snow, and Marshmallow. Finally, when Ninox flew off to search for Cherine, Grax had taken over as ruler.

Ninox's disappearance had been inconvenient, but Hatzel understood the sentiment. She worried about Zeph, and Kia's siblings had sent several messengers to ask if anyone had heard anything. When Hatzel took Grax as a mate, she'd expected Ninox to return at any moment, Cherine Metalbeak in tow, and reclaim her pride. If the saberbeak had thought Grax would still be a pride leader going into spring, she'd have picked a different mate, as she had for the past few seasons.

Grax cooed something, breaking Hatzel from her thoughts.

"Sorry," the elder saberbeak said. "Just snowgathering, as the taiga gryphons might say. You asked about the gryphlets' size? I don't know. The saberbeak pride were always bulky. We had to be to fight weald monitors, but my parents were a lot shorter than me. I'm sure one of your darkfeather scholars would say something about stress and eating wild goliath birds leading to larger saberbeaks, but who can say that these gryphlets will grow up in safer times? I just don't want the saberbeak pride to be forgotten."

"Are you thinking of splitting up the copperhawks, magpies, and saberbeaks again?" Grax asked. Despite her calm demeanor, she sometimes asked questions as though she worried Hatzel would vanish the way Ninox had. When Hatzel had approached Grax about being mates, she'd said yes immediately. Only later did she admit confusion as to why she'd been chosen.

Hatzel laughed. "Good luck splitting up the magpies and copperhawks. I think Xavi and Pink Paw are joined at the tail. I just hate the idea of the old stories fading with me. Seeing three seasons of saberbeak gryphlets hatch in Poisonmaw got me thinking."

Though Sound of Snow had gone with her mom to find Cherine, Marshmallow and Squirrelbane stayed behind. Marshmallow was enrolled at the Darkfeather University continuing his father's legacy of food science, but Squirrelbane had been spending a lot of time around Poisonmaw and Snowfall. Hatzel had finally asked Grax if Squirrelbane was looking for a new pride, but Grax had just laughed and explained that Squirrelbane was trying to put together a team of the best hunters across all the prides.

Judging by the way he currently praised Hatzel's tiny doppelganger, so far his teambuilding attempts were limited to gryphlets and fledglings.

"It's good to see our prides getting along," Hatzel said. "I always liked Ninox. I hid her from Merin's offspring when she was a fugitive. I feel like

Poisonmaw and Darkfeather go together like matching fur and feathers."

Grax purred at the analogy, and they might have gone off to steal some time together while Squirrel-bane babysat the little saberbeaks, but Cielle of The Wrecks chose that moment to crash through a break in the canopy, bringing the snowstorm down with him.

"Pride leaders!" he chirped. He began to bow but seemed to forget what he was doing mid-process and shook off all the snow instead. "Oh, sorry!"

Grax groomed some of the snow from Hatzel's face but didn't speak herself. Though the owl gryphon's common was excellent from her time with Cherine, she was shy around the other prides.

Hatzel had spent her gryphlethood being poked and prodded by medicine gryphons, so shyness had never been part of her life. "Cielle, for a gryphon who brags about his flight skills, perhaps you should spend more time working on your landings."

The fisherfolk laughed, a chirpy sound. He'd lost the fluff of youth, and it was like his ears had grown three times longer now that they weren't covered by feathered down. "I apologize, but there was no time. I came ahead to warn you. The starlings are coming."

Hatzel looked up through the break in the canopy, and she caught a glint of emerald between the flakes of snow.

"Notify the scouts," she ordered Grax, then she turned to Cielle. "If you think you can get ahead of them, make sure the glacier pride know they're coming. We'll head to The Crawl. Thank you for the warning."

Hatzel charged through the thick foliage and snow, catching the saberlet in her beak, careful not to hurt her. Squirrelbane disappeared, as owls were wont to do, and the inhabitants of Poisonmaw vanished into canyons and crevices as the skies overhead filled with starlings.

38

KHALIM THE EIGHTH

Outside Blacktalon, Lei wandered through fields of wheat, tall and green in the spring heat, calling out for a missing capybara. The humidity on the plains dripped off him, a far cry from the cool mists of his redwood home.

The emerald peacock, soggy as a sandgrouse, zigzagged through the field, careful not to destroy too much of the crop. Once he was sure no one was watching him, he slipped into an abandoned farm on the edge of Vilessa's fields. The previous inhabitants had fled when the Seraph King's forces took the city two years ago.

He went through the stables to the ranch's common area and groomed his tailfeathers dry. Ever since finding out that, when it came to the peafowl birds, only the males had colorful trains, he'd taken pride in keeping his clean, though his crush, Lemmy, teased him about it. Piprik had hinted that they may need to take their salt trade into Reevesport to do a favor for Ninox, and Lei couldn't wait to see all the wild peafowl birds guarding the apple groves.

Once dry, he made his way to the kitchen and down into the root cellar. There was, of course no lost capybara.

"Ah, the red reeve finally graces us with his presence, Iony." Reeve Rybalt Reevesbane emerged from behind a stack of empty barrels. His orange feathers and black fur glistened where the light struck them. "He looks just like his mother."

Two long, grey ears perked up from behind an empty crate, followed by the rest of the glacier gryphon. One ear had a metallic wrap covering the missing section, matte so it wouldn't catch the light. "Na, he's messing with you, chick. Snaky Brev never had nearly that much muscle. What've you been doing while we've been gone, picking up goliath birds for fun? Dropping capys on the alabasters?"

Lei rolled his eyes, though he was secretly pleased. None of his sisters had been anything except dainty, and he'd been the smallest of the red reeve's offspring, suffering from malnutrition after his home eyrie burned down. "Ranching is hard work. We have to feed the city of Blacktalon *and* the king's garrison stationed there. Maybe you should do something about that."

"I thought they grew out of the bratty phase," Rybalt quipped. It was strange to see the Reevesbane without his torn shackles and hood. He still had them, or at least something resembling them, because rumors of someone wearing that outfit attacking alabasters reached Blacktalon weekly.

Lei was pretty sure Rybalt just had his assistants

dressing up as him. "I'm not a brat, I just don't like having you here. You're putting us in danger."

"It's true. I mean, we don't care, but he's not wrong." Iony licked at an idle paw.

"Is Pip coming?" Rybalt asked. "Not that I don't enjoy our chats, but his message said he had information for us."

Lei settled down, his long train disturbing the dust of the cellar, ruining the good job he'd done of preening it clean moments ago. "He'll be here soon. We wanted to make it look like he was coming to find me."

Minutes passed. When Rybalt didn't have something snarky to contribute, he was as still as a snake overlooking the Summer Falls, waiting to catch ground parrots come to drink. Iony continued grooming, ever the gryphon. Lei tried not to look at the owl's ears, but the one with the metal cuff hung slightly lower and didn't wobble the same way the other did.

By the time Pip joined them, Iony had finished his grooming. Lei had thought his guide and surrogate parent old when they'd first met at Luminaire, ages ago. Of course, everyone seemed old when he was a fledgling. Even as he grew, though, he'd seen Pip as a greyfeather, an elderly fisherfolk. It was only meeting Pip's mate and son that made Lei realize how many years the salts had stolen from his mentor.

Pip came down the ramp, looking around. "Ah, good, you're here. I thought you would be. I have news, but first, what's going on outside of our little ranch? Have you heard anything of Tresh and Rorin?"

"How would we know anything about the weald?" Rybalt asked, but Iony poked him. "Fine. Our splotchy blue merchant friend says they're doing well. Your monster hunter managed to acquire large sums of whale pheromone, and your pet shark has taken to tagging any ships that venture east of the Emerald Jungle with it. They're becoming quite the ocean explorers."

"Good, good," Pip said. "And what of the Seraph King?"

Here Iony spoke up. "We're still working on that. For the moment, he seems content to sit pretty and build up his navy. We've had reports of ships going south from Duckbill, and reports that Reevesport has something planned, but that's it."

"Reevesport?" Lei perked up. He was still pretending to be a wayward heir of one of their merchant families. "Am I in danger?"

"I should be asking you that," Rybalt replied. "Word on the wind is one of the merchant families has acquired the last surviving daughter of the Redwood Valley reeve, and they're working hard to petition the Seraph King to reclaim the burnt eyrie and put her on the red throne. That's not you, is it?"

"No," Lei bristled. "But...is it one of my sisters?"

Rybalt shrugged. "How should I know? I never met your siblings."

"You seem very keen on lineages," Lei countered, "and when you took the serpent necklace and cobra talons from me, you said you weren't sure my siblings were all dead. What does Bario say?"

In addition to being a prized possession of both his mother and the blackwings, Bario the Phoenix had set off the saltpeter that levelled the island fortress where Lei's siblings had hidden from Satra during the Ashen Weald's assault on the Crackling Sea.

"He wasn't there when the explosion went off," Iony replied. "Now, if you want, we could take you to Reevesport, and maybe you could tell us. Thing is, it doesn't matter much. The Portmaster wants to control another eyrie. Six apples to a dozen, it's just one of her berserkers she dressed up nice and green."

Lei had never been particularly close to his birth family, and he declined the offer to travel across the desert to watch someone impersonate his sister. They'd get there sooner or later doing the favor for Ninox, and that would give him a chance to get a look at the false red reeve. Even if it was one of his sisters, it would be too dangerous to make contact with her.

"If that's the last of your news, here's what we've learned." Pip pulled out a sheet of vellum covered in ink stains. His cover, using stolen documents, had been as an alabaster spymaster managing contacts in the region. He'd taken advantage of that position to spill disappearing ink on important papers, offering to replace them, and stealing the soiled versions. "The alabasters have built some sort of storm shutters all around Blacktalon. At first, I thought they were expecting a storm from the northern blood coast. But instead of bringing food inside, they've been gathering barrels of seeds and produce and leaving them in the market square. They're claiming it's so any blackwings who are hungry can eat, but it's a *lot* of food, and a week ago, they were punishing thieves. They've also brought in new wagons and goliath harnesses with saddlebags. I think they're up to something."

Rybalt looked at Iony. "Poison? That's the only reason I'd bring in a lot of food within reach of my enemies."

"It is sort of your thing," Iony confirmed.

"The padfeet have managed to steal some, and nobody who's eaten it has gotten sick." Lei stood and stretched his legs. "If it is a poison, it's a slow-acting one."

He walked around the room, careful not to touch the pitohui, while Pip and Rybalt offered up theories. Much as he once enjoyed this sort of planning, Lei had taken to ranch life. His mom would have had him attend the university to learn to do something important and grand to bring honor to the family, but he was perfectly content with the capybaras and goliath birds.

And Lemmy.

He wandered upstairs, calling out the names of capybaras in case anyone wandered by. He looked south, where his boyfriend and Vilessa were keeping the rest of the family busy so they didn't stumble upon Rybalt and Iony.

Years ago, two dehydrated pitohui and a bloody glacier gryphon had stumbled onto their ranch. Pip and Vilessa had seriously considered letting them die, but ultimately, every enemy of the Seraph King was a chance to set the world straight again, and she'd sewn up Iony's ear and nursed the reevesbane and stargazer back to health.

It was a devil's bargain. Lei held no love for either, but the blackwings felt differently about Rybalt than the reds did. They didn't *like* him, per se. Mostly, they didn't like pitohui in general. Lei's first fight with his boyfriend had come when Lemmy called one a *trash-bird*. But they thought of Rybalt as a monster on their side, a weapon that struck down reeves no matter how large the army defending them.

A storm was brewing to the south. Strange, as the wind currents usually brought rains from the north, especially here in the wet season. Memories stirred in Lei, memories of clinging to Zeph while they fled the Battle for New Eyrie.

"S-starlings?" he whispered. Then, turning back to the root cellar, he shouted it again. "Starlings!"

Pip came out first, confirming. "We need to get everyone to safety! Go fetch Lemmy; I'll find Vilessa. Rybalt, you and Iony can stay here."

The Reevesbane had frozen, staring out at the murmuration descending upon Blacktalon. Lei knew better than to think it was fear, however. Some sort of calculation was going on in Rybalt's twisted brain.

Finally, the reeve of the pitohui spoke. "Iony, go warn the Blackwing Eyrie. I'll find the stargazer and meet you there."

Lei had a vague memory of a third opinicus with the duo when they'd arrived at the ranch nearly dead. Some sort of astrologer or cartographer. Why anyone would want to face off against a horde of starlings with a mapmaker, he had no clue. He only had one concern: Find Lemmy and get him into the hidden chamber beneath the ranch.

39

EMERALD SKIES

Days ago, the murmuration had begun its migration across the Jadebeak Mountains, following the sawgrass marshes below the Crackling Sea. The spring air was cooler here, and the tang of salt and seaweed filled every starling's nares, kindling a desire to land and hunt whatever strange turtles and crabs hid in the rough grass.

The pridelord reined them in, keeping them from consuming the Clover Ranch and a dozen new ranches that had sprung up. The murmuration had consumed half its body weight in food before leaving, and it obeyed, leaving the goliath birds and capybaras alone.

The first pangs of hunger hit near the blue eyrie. Most of the starlings had never seen the Crackling Sea before, but one member had, a nightsky, and she found it strange that there were no opinici or gryphons around. Here, the pridelord stopped the murmuration, and they descended upon fields full of crops, eating their fill.

The purple starling thought the vegetables still tasted a bit brackish, but she couldn't convince her body to go to the barrels of seeds, though they gave her something to think about on the flight.

The murmuration slept in fields, the pridelord at their center. From up close, he was invisible to outsiders, a blade of grass on the plains, identical to all others. An observer in the sky, however, might divine a different conclusion. He was the origin point for fractals that spread out in a mosaic around him.

When they awoke, they finished off the nearby farms and turned north, not continuing into the weald, much to the joy of the purple gryphon. Most outposts between the sea and the mountains were closed and shuttered, and the murmuration ignored them. One was not—and had opinici outside. The pridelord tried to take control of the murmuration, but the altruism was too strong. They killed the opinici, raided the outpost, and filled themselves again.

One member of the murmuration saw a taiga gryphon fly northeast, and despite the pridelord's protests, altruism pulled them over the Darkfeather Highlands and into Poisonmaw, where the taiga gryphon had vanished. They sniffed around, finding only a few stray ground parrots and lace monitors. By then, the altruism had worn off, and the pridelord regained control.

The murmuration returned to the strip between the inland sea and the mountains, pushing north, into the farmlands of the Blackwing Alliance. Blacktalon smelled of alabaster opinici, but it had been boarded up like the Crackling Sea Eyrie. The white-tailed kites and blue peafowl who hid within had not warned the red-winged blackbird farmers.

The southern farms were consumed by the murmuration. The northern ranches lost most of their goliaths and capybaras, but the opinici hid in stables and root cellars.

The murmuration gorged itself on barrels of seeds in the market square, then it slept. The pridelord, exhausted from the flight and having to control so many starlings, fell into a sleep so deep that no one could wake him. He dreamt of fields east of Blacktalon, of terraces guiding waterfalls from the mountains to the ocean.

When that happened, the pattern spreading out from his form frayed at the edges. Starlings wandered, and the purple starling's body returned to her.

NIGHTEYES' mind had spent days in a place of only thinking, and when she regained control of her body, she had no idea what she'd been in the middle of doing and walked beak-first into a goliath bird trough.

She shook off the water and looked around. Her travels with the Ashen Weald had taken her through a few eyries, but she hadn't really spent time in an opinicus city that wasn't trying to be something grander. The Redwood Valley had been ash and ruin, the Crackling Sea wet stone, New Eyrie a new fishing settlement. Though the fortress blocking the city's view of the desert was relatively new, the city was old.

A circular common area was the main feature. Merchant stalls had been knocked down to make room for crates of grains, seeds, fruits, and other produce. Around the outside of the courtyard were paths large enough to fit several goliath wagons across. The birds' heavy talons had packed it so hard, it felt like stone on her paws. Yet it had seen enough use that there were well-worn wheel grooves.

Buildings rose along the roads. Some were secured shut, others had been wrecked by starlings, and ominous bloodstains kept Nighteyes from looking inside the rest. The murmuration had napped in several groves of trees on the way up the eastern coast of the Crackling Sea, and the wood of the buildings smelled different from the aneda, redwoods, and other trees she was used to. It was a far cry from the heavy, bitter smell of a fallen spiketrunk or broadleaf.

The sea was the last landmark I recognized. This wood must have come from somewhere else, brought here just to make the buildings. It was a small thought, but it reminded her of how far away she was from gryphon lands.

Despite the Ashen Weald's large opinicus population, the kjarr and weald had felt like *gryphon lands*. Even the Crackling Sea's cliffs housed fantails as well as opinicus herons, and the nearby sawgrass marshes were a second home to the wingtorn who had once been held captive at New Eyrie. The ones who had taken to the salty marsh like they were born there became known as *saltlicks*, as their fur was often frosted with evaporated salt.

Blacktalon was not a gryphon home. She'd seen no gryphons on the flight over that weren't in the murmuration. There'd been no sign of nests, no pride markers letting her know whose territory she entered, not even scent markers. The last thing her brain remembered, territory-wise, was crossing the Jade-beak Mountains into Ashen Weald lands.

Really, Satra the Kjarr's lands, according to the black and gold glyph.

While a part of her brain said she was still in kjarr-owned territory because of the glyphs, what her eyes saw told her otherwise. These were opinicus lands. And not an isolated red or blue eyrie trying to hold back civilization: This was a city and farmlands that stretched beyond her sight and smell, and it unsettled her. She wasn't sure she could find her way home to the Emerald Jungle from here.

The journey had been long. The murmuration flew over a week to get here, exhausted the whole time by the pridelord's control. A silver hawk could have made the journey in better time, she was sure. A silver hawk also wouldn't have skirted the Crackling Sea, instead flying above it or following the northern coast. That was what made her realize how strange their route had been.

What's going on here?

The pridelord had specifically avoided cutting through the Argent Heights, Whitebeak, and the desert. Nighteyes had been worried he meant to take out his anger on the Ashen Weald, whose crimes were bested only by the Blackwing Eyrie's in his speech, but they'd stayed out of the bog.

Perhaps he fears the parasite. He didn't say anything about me sending my infected members to Whisper.

Then Nighteyes had thought that the Ashen Weald might be helping the murmuration, with the fields and barrels of seeds and grain left out for them.

But the smells were all wrong. Nighteyes knew Satra's pheromones inside and out, as that had been her job. She even recognized what all the individual prides smelled like. None of the crates of food left out for them held the aroma of a taiga gryphon or parrotface. Instead, the scent had been something opinical with hints of alabaster and silver opinicus mixed in.

It was possible the Ashen Weald had lost the Crackling Sea Eyrie since Nighteyes last travelled through their lands. If that were true, who was feeding the murmuration?

And where exactly are we?

She looked for her pride to see if Wendl recognized this land, then remembered Wendl was lost, possibly dead. Her heart ached, and she tried a new strategy, tapping into the memories Whisper had inadvertently given her. Within them were the pheromones of what Wendl and Whisper had been like as mothfeathers, what they'd smelled like together doing fieldwork as scholars. Nighteyes held that scent and sniffed around the buildings.

Nothing resembled Wendl's true essence, really. Not enough for her to think she was in Wendl and Whisper's home city.

Nighteyes sniffed around the fortress on the western side of the city, and *that* scent she recognized. There were alabaster opinici inside, the Seraph King's favorites. That didn't make sense, though. The glyphs guarding Alwren and King's Reach were old, and the reeves there had met with the pridelord in old times to renew the boundaries. The pridelord had no direct contact with the Seraph King or Alabaster Eyrie. Why would they feed starlings?

Nighteyes checked on her pride, but despite the pridelord's deep slumber, they were still under his sway. The smell of alabaster opinicus left their minds abuzz. Nighteyes went to inquire on the other prides and found some of the jadebeaks had wandered off.

Hmm, jadebeaks. She went south to where the farms had been unprepared and found dead black-wings. *Okay, so we're in Blackwing Alliance lands, but alabaster opinici control the fort. So Iri or Talli might know where we are.*

She queried some jadebeaks. They were in a dream-like state, but one said Iri had gone to fetch their lost kin, pointing his beak west, past the fortress. Talli had last been seen tending to her pride leader, who was not faring well on the journey.

Heat pulsed off the desert in waves, endless sands with only cacti breaking up the red expanse. It could take her hours to locate anyone in there. She back-tracked and searched the farms for an herb garden, finding one with a patch of lavender. Wendl always said it helped gryphons sleep, so Nighteyes carried several beakfuls to the inert pridelord, surrounding him with the flowers. He sniffed a few times, sneezing once, then rolled onto his back, the sun highlighting the star-like scars across his stomach.

Hopefully, that buys me some time. Though he's going to wake up to such a tummy burn!

Her first leap into the air after carrying all the lavender sent spikes of pain into her joints. She sympathized with Talli's leader. Nighteyes had never had to fly so far for so long. Even her journey to the temple had been relatively short compared to the ground they'd covered on the war migration.

This city around a fortress resembled New Eyrie, if New Eyrie had been granted resources and a real architect. The southern walls sported long spikes, hinting that perhaps Satra's wingtorn had once reached this far north. The western walls were tall, but they weren't spiked at the bottom, perhaps serving instead to keep out some sort of desert creatures.

On the thought of *desert creatures*, Nighteyes caught up to Iri and the missing jadebeaks, who were not as far into the sands as she'd worried. A small stable with water troughs marked the start of a goliath trail to the various outposts along the wasteland. The jadebeaks had eaten the birds, and that had attracted some sort of sand-burrowing monitor lizard from the desert. The lizard was too small to be a threat to so many gryphons, and they were playing with it.

"Iri," Nighteyes said. One of the jadebeaks looked up, red on her shoulders. "Do you recognize this place? Do you know where we are?"

Iri shook her head, resisting the pridelord's dream for a moment, but lost herself again. Nighteyes tried a new plan. She had Whisper's fishbone scent lure. Thankfully, her murmuration-self hadn't divested itself of Wendl's stolen medicine pouch, occasionally sticking interesting plants or lizards into it to eat later.

Nighteyes got between Iri and the others. When the lizard ran off and the other jadebeaks followed, Nighteyes held Iri back. Once they were gone, she pulled out the wrapped fish and put it down in front of Iri.

Iri sniffed at the fish, and at first, nothing

happened. Then her eyes came into focus, and she yelled.

"Whoa, wait!" Nighteyes said. "I just want to talk!"

She was too late, and Iri shoved Nighteyes off, leapt into the air, and fled deeper into the desert. Nighteyes hissed with annoyance and followed.

THE DESERT NORTH of the Crackling Sea was, as far as Nighteyes had been told, a desolate wasteland full of sand swimmers, scorpions, and padfeet. That was true, she imagined, most of the time, but it did not reflect what she was seeing after half an hour of flight.

A forest of cacti offered up flowers in a dozen colors. The empty riverbeds were full of raging rapids, and wherever water went, life spread like veins across the desert's dry skin.

Nighteyes nearly lost Iri, she was so busy gawking at the wildlife. Griffinflies the size of sand gryphons flew along the riverbanks, pollinating cacti. Frogs hidden in the dry creeks chirruped their burly songs, poor imitations of birds, seeking mates. They ate until their bellies were full, and then allowed the griffinflies to perch on their heads.

Nobody is going to believe this. I wish I could show the rest of the Nightsky. Or Sheen!

Nighteyes pushed those thoughts from her mind. She couldn't do anything more for Sheen or Wendl. She had to trust Whisper would help them. But Nighteyes *could* find out what was going on with the murmuration. Something was wrong, and Iri might have answers.

Unfortunately, the red-winged jadebeak was fleeing deeper into the desert. If she went too far, the sand gryphons would get her. Nighteyes had no idea if the fish protected against altruism, but the strength of starlings was in their numbers. She did not want to try to fight a sand gryphon pride with just the two of them.

Nighteyes' quarry finally landed to drink, and she approached Iri slowly. "I know it's tempting to dive right in, but please don't. You might wash off the scent. I promise, if you'll just talk to me for a moment, it'll wear off."

"Nighteyes." Iri the First recognized her at last. "Is that one of Wendl's elixirs? You had no right."

The nightsky gryphon stayed on the other side of the thin creek, hoping the running water would keep Iri at ease. "No, it came from Whisper. She said it'd let me speak to one of you briefly, then you'd forget. I don't think we have much time, and we need to get back to the murmuration before the pridelord wakes."

"Pridelord…" Iri shook her head a few times. "I remember. We're on a war migration to the Blackwing Eyrie."

"Your home," Nighteyes pushed.

Iri looked down at her reflection. "A long time ago."

"But you still have family there, right? You can't want them to die." Nighteyes took a step into the creek. "We need to find a way to stop this. The pridelord thinks the blackwings tried to kill him, that their dead bodies were some sort of incursion. That's why he killed Balthar and Kism. Does the pridelord know you were involved? Does he know I was involved?"

Iri looked confused. "What're you talking about?"

"Kism got the incense for you at the border." Nighteyes felt like she were walking through mud trying to get Iri to remember what was going on. "You were supposed to meet Talli and set the incense along the entrance to the temple. Did anyone see you doing that?"

The ex-blackwing's expression seemed to be genuine confusion and less mind fog now. "Yes, we had a plan to make you pridelord, but that was just an idea. You're telling me Balthar actually tried it? That's why this is happening?"

That can't be right. Kism definitely knew what was going on. Though...Talli wasn't near the temple when Balthar said she'd be. Nighteyes wracked her brain, trying to find the right questions to ask before Iri forgot this conversation. "Wendl said Kism was there on your behalf, waiting for her. Are you telling me he never talked to you? Are you telling me Balthar never reached out to you? This was about four days before the announcement of the war migration."

"I don't know what you're talking about." Iri looked up from the reflection. "No plan was put into action. I would have told Balthar it was a bad time, anyway. I'm sure Talli doesn't know anything, either. If he wanted to make you pridelord, he was acting on his own. Or with Kism, I guess. Goliath scat, this heat. I'd forgotten how much I loathe Blacktalon. To think they want to call themselves an eyrie when they're hardly a dovecote."

Acting on his own.

If Iri and Talli weren't in on it, then whatever Balthar was planning, it wasn't for Nighteyes' sake.

She thought back to Balthar's remains, the way his body looked, or what was left of it. The dead eyes. The missing forelegs.

She looked down at the water, seeing Iri's reflection. With the scarlet cactus blossoms behind her, the red on her shoulders didn't look so strange. Her face, in fact, looked familiar. She had the same four-star pattern across her beak that Wendl did.

But Balthar's dead body did not. Wendl's words came back to Nighteyes about how she could remember who she was because she'd keep her scars. *When Wendl tried to kill the pridelord, I saved her, but then I checked him for injuries. His stomach was littered with scars, as you'd expect from a hunter of the Sparkwing Pride...or from someone who was kicked in the stomach by a cassowary while trying to protect his mate. The pridelord, however, never had to hunt a day in his life. He'd have no scars.*

In her mind, she saw the sleeping form of the pridelord covered in lavender, rolling over to warm his scarred stomach in the sun, and it all clicked into place.

"Balthar's not dead. Balthar's the pridelord!" Nighteyes shouted, but her words were lost. Whisper's magic fish had worn off, and Iri flew back to the murmuration, back to the *hardly a dovecote* she'd called Blacktalon.

40

A WEEK EARLIER

Whisper waited until the murmuration had left the Emerald Jungle, then she crawled out from the Newmoon Pridegrounds and searched for the Nightsky's nests. From behind the veil, she'd watched as Nighteyes stole away the salts, and she had a good idea what they'd been used for.

I just hope she hasn't caused an outbreak.

Whisper had stolen jars of salt ever since she'd seen the way the outsiders used them to put the mites or their eggs into hibernation. She figured a path of salt would reduce the chance that her wards would spread the parasite before she could cure them.

The jar she'd left for Nighteyes had been unusual, an accidental acquisition. Whisper checked every clay jar before stealing it, but some Ashen Weald opinicus in the bog had mixed up the jars, leaving one with the mites still in it next to a bunch of containers of just salt.

She'd had every intention of destroying the jar and its sinister contents. She knew The Six would probably suspect her of more nefarious intentions, but she'd stolen the jar thinking there'd be an easy way to kill the parasites once she got them back home.

Destroying so many had proven a difficult task. Unlike Wendl or Balthar, she didn't have an easy way of making a bonfire to burn the mites. And once she had the eggs, she didn't know how to ask anyone else for help. When she was beyond the Emerald Veil, she sometimes forgot to prioritize the pridelord's will. Once she was back home and the jar was tucked away somewhere safe, she remembered what would happen to her if the pridelord found out what she'd brought back into the jungle with her.

Nighteyes wouldn't do anything stupid with it. Right?

The nesting grounds were abandoned, which made Whisper more worried. She'd been sure Nighteyes was going to infect the indigo fledgling. If that hadn't been her purpose, Whisper had no idea why she'd steal a leaf's worth of bugs. She looked around a second time, seeing a small hideaway that smelled of cassia.

This must be Wendl's nest.

The pridelord's speech had eventually reached the newmoon leader, hidden away in the scents of his subjects. He'd claimed Balthar and Wendl were dead, but Whisper hadn't felt their deaths. That didn't mean anything definitive, but perhaps Nighteyes was hiding Wendl here. The note on the satchel suggested Nighteyes wanted Whisper to look for Wendl, at least.

Whisper opened the door to the tent and found the fledgling inside. *Ah, I was right the first time.*

Sheen, or so her scent claimed her name was,

stank of the parasite. As the only warm thing in the tent, they'd all come to her, which was good. It meant enough pumpkin would kill them. Whisper's stores were running low, but she could check on Flicker's stash. Pumpkins kept pretty well, hence their popularity with farmers, and her old mate probably had a few stored around for the seeds.

"Hello, little one." Whisper nudged Sheen with a paw. "Are you able to fly?"

Sheen yawned so big she resembled a crocodile about to swallow a capybara whole. She looked around a few times as though she'd forgotten where she was and wiped at her eyes with a splinted paw. Whisper watched this closely. There was no silver—yet.

"Where'd everyone go?" the fledgling asked. "Oh! I need to fly to catch up to them!"

"You're too late. You won't be able to catch them." Whisper blocked the way out. "Your pride leader infected you, and you'll need a few days of treatment before it's safe. Will you come with me?"

Sheen looked like she wanted to say no, but the pridelord's edict meant Whisper held sway over all infected. The newmoon leader shook off a little citrus, and Sheen calmed.

"Sure, of course," the nightsky said. "Can I bring my things?"

Whisper led Sheen out of the hideaway. "I'll come back for them. Let's get you to safety first."

"Wait, the parasite? Am I going to die?" the fledgling asked. The young were even more superstitious than their elders about silver eyes.

Whisper added in a bit of mint. "No, no. It's only

been a day. I've cured many starlings further gone than you. In fact, if we get some pumpkin into you soon, you should be fine to go back to the Nightsky Pride when they return."

Sheen stumbled a bit trying to get into the air, struggling with just three good paws. "Back from where? I'm going to miss it all."

Wherever they're going, you don't want to be there, Whisper thought. Out loud, she said, "The Blackwing Eyrie. Trust me, it's not a great place to visit. You'll hear the stories when you return. For now, let us get you full of pumpkin, like your pridemates. We got to them fast enough the itchiness and eye goo weren't a factor. If you're lucky, you won't even end up silver-eyed."

IN WHISPER'S ABSENCE, Moonlit Blossom had been overzealous in the application of pumpkins. It had been a long time since Whisper had brought in more than three infected at a time, and getting a whole patch of youngsters—who were also suffering from bloodbeak—had left him an anxious mess.

Whisper looked at where her pumpkin stockpile used to be and sighed. "Are there any left?"

"Er..." Moonlit Blossom looked down at his pointed silver paws, nearly losing his flower in the process. "No, sorry. When they started running around, I freaked out and ordered them to all eat pumpkins. I'd forgotten how the infected respond, and they went into a frenzy."

"Frenzy!" the jadebeak with the metal talon hat confirmed. "Pumpkin frenzy!"

Whisper considered it a minor success that Taloncrest was talking again. It was usually a bad sign of cognitive function when one of the infected started wearing weird objects as hats. Thankfully, it appeared this starling's strange sense of fashion was not a result of tiny bugs.

Not everyone has my skill with eyeshine.

"Wait...does that mean I'm going to die?" Sheen yelped.

Moonlit Blossom was so quick with the mint that Whisper didn't need to take control. Despite her earlier joking, he really did seem ready to take over as pride leader if anything happened to her—assuming he'd learned his lesson about rationing pumpkins.

Whisper pulled her medicine bag from her fluff, dusting it off and pulling out some bog blossom paste. "You'll be absolutely fine. This paste will suppress the parasites, and my mate will have more pumpkin. She's probably left with the murmuration, so I'll fly down to her place. We'll have you fixed up by morning."

She didn't know for certain if Flicker had gone with the murmuration. There was a fifty-fifty chance she'd gotten caught up planting produce and missed the whole thing. Still, she said she was growing pumpkins to help the infected, so she should be happy to part with one for a good cause.

Whisper guided Sheen to a small nest surrounded by salt in the meantime. Several jadebeaks sniffed around the quarantine area, curious about the newcomers. A ptarmigan, the red marks above his eyes always giving him an angry look despite his jovial personality, let out an *aqesgiq* of welcome.

"That's hello," Whisper translated. "Some infected jadebeaks I was tracking got ahold of him, and I arrived just in time to save his life. Actually, I thought he was dead. I was surprised he lived and *even more* surprised he stayed with us. Snowfeet don't live in prides."

Sheen looked up from her brooding. "I thought all gryphons had to have prides, otherwise they die?"

"Oh, no, we wouldn't have the word *padfoot* if that were true," Whisper answered. When Sheen didn't know the word, the newmoon gryphon explained. "It means a prideless gryphon. Sometimes, padfeet come together to form a new pride. But snowfeet aren't like that. The ptarmigan gryphons live in the Jadebeak Mountains on their own. That's why I'm surprised this one has taken to susurration life so well."

She turned to the ptarmigan and replied with her own polite *aqesgiq*. She added in some pheromones that sent him and the jadebeaks back a hundred feet from the salted area.

"Why did you send them away?" Sheen tried to settle down, but she stumbled a little from putting pressure on her bad paw. "I have so many questions for him about what it was like outside the Emerald Jungle."

Whisper crossed the salts to inspect the wound. "They're all Newmoon Pride, don't get me wrong, but the spotless starlings here with the large tails are descended from bog-starling pairings, so they're immune to the parasite. The jadebeaks, snowfeet, and other gryphons don't share that immunity. I cured them, but you could still re-infect them. That's why we have the quarantine area."

Moonlit Blossom, a little calmer now that Whisper had gotten everyone sorted into salt-nests, approached. "You should get the pumpkins. This one's scent has changed even in the last half hour."

"Hmm." Whisper sniffed. He was right, and she'd missed it, distracted by the ptarmigan. "I need to check one thing, then I'll be off. You're in charge while I'm gone."

"Wanna fight for it?" His eyes sparkled when he spoke.

"No, thank you. Perhaps later." Whisper laughed in spite of herself, then summoned a bit of respectability. "You did well, Moonlit Blossom. Perhaps a bit heavy-pawed on the pumpkin, but this was an unusual situation for any pride leader to face. I'm proud of you."

He beamed as she left, and she went to her hiding spot in the old ruins, where two vials of salts awaited her, both gifts from Wendl. She had no intention of leaving, but with the pridelord and most of the murmuration gone, this would be the perfect opportunity.

Next to the vials was the journal Nighteyes had sent with the sparkwing denmother—who was doing much better now that she had Whisper's pheromones in her head reminding her of who she was and to take care of herself. Whisper didn't have time to go through all of the details, but she'd read enough to know it was some sort of alabaster eyrie document. There were certain words the alabasters used that no respectable blackwing—nor even a mothfeather of ill-repute—would use.

I'll look at this later. For now, I don't want my alabaster pridemates to find it first.

She carried the journal to a nearby spiketrunk. One of the underground monsters had punched a hole in the middle of it, leaving a perfect hole for hiding things. The spikes curved in, discouraging anyone from reaching inside.

She looked at the message scratched into the cover of the book. *Find Wendl.* She traced it with an idle paw pad, her own scent on top of Nighteyes'. Then she put it in the tree, leaving behind a single pawprint of scent in case Nighteyes came back for it and Moonlit Blossom needed to find it.

She stretched, forelegs, hind legs, and then wings. For once, she'd get to fly across the jungle without the barrage of inquiry scents and squirrel updates. The only gryphons in the entire jungle were Newmoon or Stormtail Pride—even the Gourmand was technically a stormtail, though he never left the Winter Jungle.

Nobody here but us. I could get used to this.

And then Kism crossed back through the Emerald Veil ten feet in front of her.

41

THE CRUEL LIGHT OF THE MOON

Whisper rarely experienced confusion inside the Emerald Jungle. With her connection to other starlings, she could sense what was going on across the land from Abyssal Naze to Winter Jungle, from the border of Alwren to the Newmoon Falls.

The history of starlingkind spread through scent, glyphs, memories—it was a tapestry of the past, accessible to her as long as starlings filled the jungle, and there was even a certain predictability to watching how the threads were woven and where they would go next.

She did not often find herself in open-beaked surprise. Her friend appearing through the Emerald Veil in front of her, however, did the trick.

"Kism? Are you all right?" Whisper knew the answer was no. She couldn't connect to him. Or, at least, she couldn't control him. He was using some sort of elixir to keep her out. She could still pick up a little of what he was thinking, but that was it.

One silver-eyed starling trying ineffectively to

assert control over him was probably not his biggest problem, however. Kism the Third wore leather bindings and a leash. His face was covered in a falconry hood, as though someone was worried about his altruism taking over. Behind him, fifty alabaster opinici, their armor shining in the afternoon light, stepped through the veil.

These are the sounds and smells that were agitating the murmuration before they left.

The creature leading the alabasters was something else. Nighteyes' scent memories, echoes from their time in the Abyssal Naze came back to her. Whisper hadn't understood Nighteyes' *feathersnake* then, but she did now. What's more, she could smell enough from Kism to get a name, one that had struck fear in blackwing and mothfeather alike growing up.

"Hi-kun," she hissed.

The Talons of the Seraph King, The Metalworks, The Lord of Whitebeak regarded Whisper. From his muscular, snake-like body, two sets of wings folded, he looked down upon her as though she were nothing more than a squirrel eating the stores from his nest. "You must be Whisper. It seems we've found the Newmoon Pride. You all have your orders."

The light caught his feathers, shimmering with iridescence like a rainbow sparkwing. The feathersnake drew himself up high on his back paws, his metal foretalons glistening. He seemed to expect her to go paw-to-talon against him.

The murmuration may be gone, but my susurration is more than enough to turn you into caiman food.

She dug her paws into the ground and called her pride to her. She could hear the cured jadebeaks rising from their nests, a vicious chittering on their tomia. Spotless starlings came down from the mountains where they'd kept watch over the clawdigger caves.

Hi-kun waited. He smelled calm. He smelled...victorious.

Overhead, a dozen peacock flew across the field. That was when Whisper realized her mistake.

Hi-kun and the alabaster opinici stepped back beyond the veil, pulling Kism with them on his leash, as Wendl's incense bombs rained down upon the Newmoon Pride.

The Newmoon Pride I called to me. This is Kism's doing. I'll kill him.

She tried to send the command to flee, but it was too late for most of her pride. The only two outside the incense were Moonlit Blossom and Sheen. Whisper ordered them to flee, but a bomb landed next to her and exploded into a cacophony of white smoke.

Whisper felt a screaming inside her skull, only realizing after it stopped that it had been her scream. Blood leaked from her nares. When her screaming stopped, only silence was left, the whispers of her pride gone from her mind.

She collapsed.

Moonlit Blossom was showing Sheen the salt pits where the infected had to relieve themselves when Whisper's warning hit.

The first message called the susurration to her. He

would have hurried to her aid, but she'd made it so he could disobey in a limited fashion in order to fulfill her other orders. In this case, keeping someone with an active infection inside the quarantine was more important.

The second message came immediately after, ordering her pride to flee and suppressing their altruism. He couldn't make sense of it. What enemy was so dangerous it required the full susurration? Not even the clawdiggers required everyone. But then...could there be a foe so deadly starlings would have to flee from it?

The wind coming down from the Jadebeak Mountains saved him and Sheen when the bombs hit. They landed, exploded, and white smoke filled the Newmoon Grounds. But the quarantine area was just to the east, and the winds shielded him.

"Can you fly?" he asked Sheen. "We need to get south, to Lightningmaw, before—"

The same way the wind from the mountains carried away the incense, it brought the smell of opinici crossing the eastern veil with it.

A duck opinicus struck, charging on four flippered feet before rising up, slashing with metal-tipped talons that just missed his beak. He'd spent his life fighting squirrels and rhea. He didn't know how to kill a gryphon, let alone an opinicus.

I promised Whisper if something happened to her, I could lead this pride.

At the moment, his pride was two, and he shouted at Sheen to get into the air as he side-stepped the mallard. Two alabasters with nets had marked Sheen, but he wasn't going to give her up without a fight.

His opponent's eyes were on the nightsky fledgling, which gave him the opening he needed. He charged, catching the mallard off guard. Apparently duck opinici did not expect anyone to grapple with them. He clawed at her, catching mostly leather harness, and discovered why that was.

The opinicus stabbed some sort of leg spur into his hip, injecting him with poison. As she did it, she paused, perhaps expecting it to kill him instantly.

Moonlit Blossom pecked as hard as he could, right at her face, with his eyes closed. He tried not to think too hard about what had happened as he felt his beak break through something.

When her body fell, he opened his eyes again. A small army of alabasters were marching through his pridegrounds. Anger rose within him, the smell of pepper oozed from his pores, but no susurration came to his aid.

He barreled into the two white-tailed kites trying to net Sheen. "GO! Get out of here!"

"I can't leave you behind!" she shouted.

He thought she was speaking from a place of camaraderie, but then he realized she meant literally. With Whisper incapacitated, he was acting pride leader, and his scent would entrap nearby starlings to protect him.

How do I turn this off?

A flamingo got a net over Sheen, but Nighteyes had trained the fledgling well. She caught the flamingo's neck in her beak and shook. The flamingo pushed back in alarm, falling but still alive.

Moonlit Blossom isolated the citrus pheromones

he'd started making when Whisper screamed. He toned it down to nothing. "Can you go now?"

She hesitated, and he realized it was both valor and scent keeping her here.

"Get the Stormtail Pride," he ordered. "They're our only hope now."

The peafowl who had dropped the incense bombs were circling back around now that the smoke had cleared, looking for anyone still moving. Moonlit Blossom flew up to distract them, but no matter what he did, they had eyes for only Sheen.

What's so special about that one nightsky?

Something clearly was, however, and he knew it was crucial they not catch her.

Wait...my altruism? Where did it go?

Whisper had explained altruism to him, but he'd given it little heed. Maybe it wasn't real, or maybe she'd done something to him. Even Sheen was missing it.

He had a strange new memory for scents, and he felt it now. It had come with the order to flee. *Smart, we couldn't flee otherwise.*

Without altruism, he was able to take advantage of the enemy's tunnel vision. He got up above the peacocks pursuing Sheen, then dove down, smashing as many as he could.

Sheen crossed over the border into Jadebeak Pride territory. She was leaving them behind. He even thought she might make it.

Then a new shape appeared in the sky, something he'd never seen before, metal and rainbows stretched long. It beat two sets of wings together, using a back set and a long, fanned tail to maneuver.

It's going too fast. It's going to catch her.

He pumped his wings, trying to gain height. Behind the angry rainbow came a familiar sight. Or, if the sight of a starling in a falconry hood wasn't familiar, his smell was.

"Kism?" Moonlit Blossom ventured. He'd developed a sense of who every starling was when Whisper blacked out. She'd sent a warning about this gryphon in particular.

The warning wasn't enough. As the strange being caught Sheen out of the sky, Kism opened a bag, releasing a rain of metal flechettes from the sky above Moonlit Blossom.

He died before he hit the ground.

42

MALLY'S EXPEDITION RUINS

Whisper awoke in a dark cage. The last thing she remembered was a scream and then silence. She clawed at the bars, hissing, until she realized her head was no longer empty.

The faintest of pheremonal whispers came in. Her pride were also in cages. She could sense most of them. The nightsky with bloodbeak were being kept somewhere far away, but still within scent range. Or someone was carrying their scent here to her when they made their rounds.

The spotless starlings who formed the core of the Newmoon Pride were housed somewhere south of her. She sniffed again, and she thought the healthy nightskies were north. To her east were all the gryphons and opinici who weren't starlings but had joined her.

Now that she knew where her susurration was, she let her mind calm and catalogued the other smells. She paired them with her knowledge of the Seraph

King. Alabaster Eyrie's white-tailed kites. Alwren's osprey. Duckbill's mallards. Crestfall's flamingos. Even a Crackling Sea heron mixing jelly toxins.

Then the mystery smell. A Redwood Valley peregrine? No, an oilbird. No, a feathersnake. She inhaled again, loudly, letting the scent move through her. When she isolated the avian smells, she was left with one final, unforgettable scent.

Mally the Nighthaunt.

He'd reclaimed the ruins of his old expedition. This time, instead of walking along behind him, taking his notes and making copies of them for the rest of his research team, Whisper was the starling in the cage.

She laughed, but the sound morphed into a cry of despair.

"Are you quite done?" came a voice from the darkness.

Whisper was so startled, she let out a hiss and leapt up, hitting her head on the low ceiling of the cage.

The void snorted.

"Darkstalker." Whisper needed a moment to isolate her from the rest. Unlike last time, there was a feathersparkle aroma. Despite how innocuous the cosmetic smelled, it triggered a very strong fight-or-flight instinct in Whisper from the time her father caught her wearing it as a fledgling.

The scent grew closer, and talons reached out and held her paw. Whisper was very tempted to bite as hard as she could and take a few digits with her to the grave.

"I warned you," the darkstalker said. "You could have left."

Whisper had a few answers but didn't think that *starlings don't leave* was good enough. "I'm all the susurration has. Without me, the infected die. I keep them whole. You should let me near them so I can keep them calm. They must be falling apart in my absence."

"They are, but the Nighthaunt doesn't trust you near the others. Kism warned him about what you can do." The darkstalker removed her talon weapon and struck a rushlight, the flame too weak for Whisper to confirm the feathersparkle. The opinicus's whiskers had been trimmed since their last meeting, hiding her gryphon essence, though her black eyes would do that long before the whiskers would have. In the flickering light, the markings around her eyes seemed to drip down even farther.

Whisper sensed a hesitation, perhaps because she'd saved the darkstalker's life. "You could let me out of the cage. He wouldn't need to know."

"No." There was the slight scent of sadness in the darkstalker's pheromones, something she hid quite well in her tone. "I won't be helping you escape from here."

Whisper tried a few scents, but nothing worked. Controlling a non-starling was nearly impossible if they weren't badly wounded or afflicted by the parasite, but there was more to it. Whisper had been drugged with something. She preened through her fur and feathers, finding neither were dusty.

"We gave you quite the grooming while you were asleep," the darkstalker said. "You've got a very cute birthmark on your hindquarters. Is that yours, or did it come from the starling?"

Whisper didn't speak.

The darkstalker shrugged. "Sorry, I don't get to talk to many opinici since my own transformation. Or I suppose you're a gryphon now. I'll confirm what you're thinking. You were preened clean, then you were drugged, and your food and water are also drugged. It's funny how something as simple as a dandruff shampoo can render one of the scariest gryphons in the Emerald Jungle as harmless as a fledgling."

The leader of the Newmoon Pride did not answer.

"How do your mates stand it?" the darkstalker asked. "I've washed myself four times and still your scent clings to me. That's why you didn't smell me while I watched you, by the way."

When silence came, Whisper let it, refusing to speak any more words to this opinicus who could help her but chose not to.

Finally, the darkstalker grew bored enough to leave. "Here's your food. Opinicus rations, not the scraps you fed the starlings you imprisoned as Mally's scribe. That's my second kindness to you. The first was the warning. Where I grew up, with the lakefolk, it takes three kindnesses to pay someone back. As is appropriate for your name, the last will be a whisper in your gryphon ear. That's the most I can offer you. Now, eat up. The Nighthaunt wants to see you at midnight."

She blew out the rushlight, leaving Whisper to eat alone in the dark.

TRUE TO THE darkstalker's word, Whisper was let out of her cage around midnight and escorted across the ruins to a set of tents. Four alabaster guards seemed a bit much for a single starling, but they looked askance at her markings and forced her to wear a goliath bird hood, the straps pulled tight around her beak. By the bitter almond smell, it was one of Kism's.

She was glad to be out of the rotting ruins. Much as the current Newmoon Pridelands had given the susurration more room to hunt compared to their old home, she didn't enjoy being so close to where she'd first entered the Emerald Jungle.

She paused and took a deep breath, gathering her strength. The night air cooled her warm neck. It felt good but did little to assuage her headache.

She thought she smelled night-blooming vines through the hood, a scent she'd formerly found reassuring. Her reassurances changed to distress when she passed by the open graves where the starlings who had been killed instead of captured were dumped.

Moonlit Blossom. She dug her claws into the earth and tried to tell the others of his death. Her pheromones were so weak, nothing happened. The guards were unsure what to do, but they gave her a moment. Once her scent reached the cages, a wail began, and the guards yanked her leash to pull her along, shoving her into the largest tent. They removed the hood once she was inside but left her beak bound.

A single lamp burned in the twenty-paw chamber, providing enough light for the alabasters while not offending the Nighthaunt's sensitive eyes. The entire place reeked of the Abyssal Naze.

Whisper would not have recognized her old master by sight or scent. He existed between feather-snake and opinicus, and something in his mannerisms evoked the same feeling the clawdiggers did: this was once an opinicus, but no longer.

The faint rumors that reached Whisper spoke of a pale creature that haunted the darkness, but that was no longer true. His body was a dark red, the red of blood that told of a wound that could not be recovered from. Compared to the darkstalker, even his black eyes had hints of red in them.

He moved like an old, dying opinicus but spoke with the same arrogance as ever. "Ah, my old scribe. Whisper, you call yourself now? Well, I have to applaud you for your resilience. Much like myself, you managed to survive in a world that wanted you dead."

One of the guards untied the gryphon's beak, but she didn't speak.

"I remember you as much chattier. It's good you've learned discretion, I suppose." The Nighthaunt looked through tomes of knowledge, the same ones Whisper had hidden away in her old room. "Ah, I remember this study. Well, that explains your current form. Your quillwork was something, wasn't it? Such flourish, so easy to read! It's a shame you traded talon for paw."

Every time Mally looked down, Whisper's eyes darted across the main room of the tent. There was a cage in the corner with Sheen in it. The other wounded were stored elsewhere, meaning this particular gryphon was of interest to the Nighthaunt.

What would have happened if she'd gone with the war migration? How would he have gotten ahold of her?

Whisper had been blindsided by the attack, but she'd be ready if an opportunity for freedom presented itself. She sent a quiet inquiry to Sheen, getting back a reply that the fledgling was sleeping. She tried again, seeing if she could awaken the gryphon, and Sheen stirred slightly.

The Nighthaunt was going on about old times, and Whisper tuned back in to see if he revealed anything. He was well informed on starling matters for an outsider.

"Did Kism tell you this?" she asked. Clearly, the Nighthaunt had a spy in the Emerald Jungle to know they'd left, and Kism's appearance at the start of the battle confirmed it.

The Nighthaunt looked surprised by her voice. "You've lost your mothfeather twang. If not for the gryphonics, you'd almost sound like you were a city opinicus now."

She didn't reply.

"I'm not here to answer your questions, nor are you here for old times' sake." The Nighthaunt stood, weaving around his stacks of books to reach her. "A team from Duckbill will arrive in a day or two. I've seen what happens if you pull a starling out of the jungle. I've heard you're different, that you can cross the border. If that's true, you'll need to keep your pride in line. If not, we'll just kill them once we're over the border."

Whisper counted the books on the Nighthaunt's

table. If he'd found Nighteyes' documents, they weren't here. "I'll need to be at my full strength to do so. You'll have to stop drugging my food if that's what you want."

"Oh? You'd like that, wouldn't you." The Nighthaunt laughed, a sound that echoed even in the small tent. "No, I'm afraid not. If you can't keep your entire pride under control, just pick the starlings you want to live and help them. We'll kill the others as they turn *altruistic*. I suspect we won't have any trouble finding more starlings to experiment on if we need to."

She didn't care for his confidence. "I'll do what I can. In return, I would like to know: Who killed Moonlit Blossom?"

"Is that the spotless starling with the flower? Your mate, was he?" he asked. "Your friend Kism, I believe. He's handling Wendl's elixirs better than I hoped, but we didn't want to take any chances once he was in the jungle, so we gave him flechettes instead of letting him use his beak and claws."

The Nighthaunt let out a sound that escaped the tent, and a new sound returned to him.

A few moments later, the darkstalker entered. "You called?"

"How are we on time?" he asked.

The darkstalker ignored Whisper but stepped aside as a stabletalon came in to feed Sheen. "The Metalworks has established a base camp just outside the stormtail glyphs. Jonas' mixologist is preparing a new batch of toxin to ease the transportation. Kism seems to be holding it together, though I told him the restraints stay on. The forces from King's Reach will be there soon. It's time for us to head out and the stabletalons to drag the cages closer to the border for pickup."

"Hmm, Hi-kun is ever efficient. I was hoping to get more time here to socialize with old friends." Mally looked around. "Well, send the books back. Then prepare the rest for Duckbill."

The stabletalon in the corner poked Sheen like she was a goliath bird, but whatever she'd been drugged with was strong enough to keep her asleep.

The Nighthaunt returned to his paperwork, and the darkstalker walked past Whisper, bumping the gryphon with her hip.

Then the darkstalker turned to the guards holding Whisper's restraints. "Make sure you take your vitamins. Seems there's a cold going around, some sort of exotic jungle disease. You wouldn't want to get sick."

It took Whisper a moment to realize she'd been given her third *kindness* from the opinicus she'd saved.

Moonlit Blossom never gave Sheen any pumpkin. The attack interrupted me from retrieving it from Flicker's garden. And neither did the darkstalker.

The stabletalon reached into the cage to shake Sheen, perhaps thinking her dead. Whisper summoned all the pheromone and featherdust she could muster, then sent the olfactory equivalent of a scream to Sheen.

BITE!

The fledgling leapt up and chomped down as hard as she could, digging her tomia into the opinicus's foretalons.

Sheen, suddenly awake and confused, let go at her victim's scream, but it was enough. The Nighthaunt laughed, the guards came to help the stabletalon, who shouted a few mean terms for a gryphon at Sheen while being escorted out.

"Well, are you going to stand around all night?" Mally asked the remaining guards. "Take *Whisper* back to her cage. My scribe will need to rest if she wants to save her pride."

As she was escorted back to her cage, she thought she saw the darkstalker watching her from the corner, curious what would happen next. Whisper didn't say anything. Her old master was correct. If she were going to save her pride, she'd need her strength.

Once she was in her cage, she curled up and closed her eyes. The rest of her pride mourned, imitating the scent of their friend. The smell of Moonlit Blossom grew so strong, Whisper could almost imagine him here beside her.

A quiet rage took root in her heart.

43

A FLICKER OF HOPE

Southeast of the Newmoon Pridelands, hidden between the Jadebeak Mountains and the broadleaf jungle, a single red starling woke up, yawned, and stretched her legs.

Flicker's nest was covered in mud and orange goo, as was Flicker herself, but the planting was done. It had taken her a few days to retrieve all the seeds out of the winter squash, with enough left over for her mate to feed to the infected. Come autumn, Flicker would have a nice harvest. Whisper would be over-joyed to see all the pumpkins, she was sure of it.

Say, was I supposed to meet Whisper for something?

Flicker shrugged. There was little she did that was particularly pressing. It was one of the reasons she was always in a good mood. Still, she was overdue for a bath, so she dragged herself to the closest spring and swam until the dirt was gone. Once she felt clean, she returned home to take a post-waking up nap.

Oh wait, my nest is all dirt, too.

She decided to make a day of cleaning. There

were starlings who only cleaned their nests at the start of mating season, but despite how much time Flicker spent in the dirt, she liked to have a tidy place to sleep. When she could remember to clean it.

As she'd made the closest spring muddy, she dragged her nest farther out, to a sun-warmed hot spring. Usually, at this time of day, it was full of jade-beaks. Today it was empty.

Must be something going on with the squirrels. Ah well, I like being alone.

Her nest was made of dry reeds found only along the edge of the mountains. They kept bugs away and had a generally pleasant smell, or so she thought. Unfortunately for her, reeds did not lend themselves to being washed. Once her nest was in the water and rehydrated, the reeds slipped out of their weavings, and soon her entire nest had dissolved and was drifting downstream.

"Cassowary scat," she swore, startling a nearby squirrel. "Sorry, pridelord. I know you have sensitive ears."

The Pridelord of the Squirrels returned to scavenging, oblivious to her plight. Flicker was in trouble now. It took her two weeks to gather enough reeds and dry them out to build her old nest—the jungle was a very wet place. Now she'd have to make a nest the old-fashioned way, if she could remember how.

I'll bet Whisper would know. She probably has a very fancy nest. Yes, that's right, I think. Did I ever visit Whisper? Hmm. I can't remember.

Well, unlike Flicker, Whisper had *friends*, and *friends* were gryphons she could ask dumb questions of without being judged. She went back home, put her paw on the nearest tree to leave the scent of *Here I am!* as Whisper had asked, and flew north.

It wasn't just the jadebeak lands that were quiet, the newmoon hunting grounds were also empty. It seemed like there was a great to-do that had happened here, lots of scratch marks on the ground, lots of square indentations, but whoever was here had left recently.

Drag marks led northwest. She shrugged. Newmoon gryphons probably had their own holidays where they dragged things around. Jadebeaks had their squirrel races, so it stood to reason that the Newmoon Pride was similarly weird. The Dragaway Runabout or some such to-do.

She sniffed around the ruins, but they smelled of death. *Oh, a funeral. Well, maybe I should stay to comfort Whisper. We were mates once. Last week.*

Flicker found some nests northeast of the ruins. The one that smelled like Whisper's, however, was very poorly made. It was sticks and pinecones stuck together, pointy bits still intact.

That poor dear, no wonder the entire time we were mates, she always wanted to stay over at my place.

Flicker was about to leave when the wind shifted, giving her the scent of Whisper once again. It didn't seem likely Whisper had a decoy nest, but it wasn't impossible, either. Maybe she had so many ex-mates that this was a real problem for her. Flicker followed the scent to an old spiketrunk that had seen better days. She reached inside with her paw, retrieving a love note from Whisper.

Or, at least, it was a note with Whisper's scent on it. The note read *Find Wendl.*

Flicker thought back. She hadn't been paying much attention to the murmuration lately, but she did think she'd heard something about Wendl and Nighteyes going to the temple to fight for a pride? Well, that was in Jadebeak territory, so it shouldn't be a problem.

She turned back south and began the slow flight to the center of the Emerald Jungle. Every so often, when she stopped to eat or drink, she thought she heard someone flying overhead. She never bothered to look up and see, as she had a tendency to get distracted if she didn't stay on task, and Whisper was probably waiting for her at the temple, and if she didn't find Whisper, she couldn't have Whisper ask one of her friends how to make a nest without dried mountain reeds.

And, seeing Whisper's nest, I think she'd benefit a lot from that knowledge, too. Really, I'm doing this for both of us.

Plus, Flicker had never had a hidden message from an ex-mate before. Maybe Whisper wanted to be summer friends.

Just think of it! A jadebeak and a newmoon as summer friends. What would the squirrels think?

She continued her journey into the city, wondering where all of the jadebeaks had vanished to.

44

EROSION

Wendl coughed, a sound as wet as the depths. Every so often, she could hear an animal scrabbling through the darkness, chewing at the remains of Balthar. Something no starling ever talked about was how many centipedes lived in the depths of the pridelord's home. If she survived this, it's all she would talk about.

She was starving. It was a simple, inevitable fact her brain refused to accept. She hadn't died of thirst, courtesy of a leak in the ceiling that drizzled water down onto her cage. She wasn't sure why water was moving through the temple, but perhaps the lower levels were meant to house a pond and a leak had developed.

Sour drops landed on her head, each one a reminder of the actions that had brought her here. It wasn't that she had expected the plan to work, exactly. She'd hoped it would, of course, but there seemed an equal chance of failure. It was *how* it had failed that caught her unawares. She went back over the events in her mind again and again, trying to figure out what had happened.

The vats were boiling; I could feel the heat. So Balthar was getting them started when the pridelord arrived and... what? Caught him off guard? But would the pridelord even know what the vats were for. Balthar was my friend, but he was also a liar who excelled at sleight-of-talon. And why weren't Iri, Kism, and Talli there setting up my incense bombs?

She wished the world would turn back time and show her what had happened before she and Nighteyes entered the Sky Beneath the Earth.

Nighteyes, where are you? Did he lock you away in another pit, or are you a mindless drone again? You were meant to be the queen bee.

The pridelord hadn't returned, leaving Wendl to stare at Balthar's dead body until the rushlights and braziers gave out, which had taken days. She'd thrown pebbles to keep the crawlies away from his body as long as the light lasted. In that time, she'd been unable to accept what she was seeing. Not the gore, which had been a lot even after what she'd gone through. But the face.

With the clarity of starvation, in what could be the last moment of her life, she finally accepted it.

The dead starling's face lacked the four-star pattern across the beak that Wendl shared with The Six.

The dead body couldn't be Balthar.

With that acceptance came determination. She clutched a piece of broken glass. After she'd awoken in the cage, she'd searched for anything that might let her pick the lock, without success. She'd kept the piece of broken glass in case she got desperate—or the pridelord returned. Of course, he hadn't. Neither he nor his lackeys had come back down here. He seemed content to let her die in the dark.

In her anger, she clutched the glass too hard, and it cut her talon. She swore and released it. No, she wouldn't use the glass on herself. She was going to sit down here drinking slimy, sour drops of water until she died of hunger, if that's what it took.

The sound of scratching echoed down the corridor. *Of course, I might survive longer with food. And whatever's eating Not Balthar is probably edible itself.*

She let her blood drip down and pool outside her cage while she sat perfectly still, ready to ambush whatever creature hid in the dark.

FLICKER STARED at the door to the lower levels of the temple. She'd already searched up high, flying circles around the fern-laden structure, looking for someone to ask for help. It was empty, and that was strange.

Is today the squirrel races? Am I missing them right now?

Not everyone was interested in squirrels. Surely, the entire pride would not have left without telling her, but she grew anxious. She decided to take a new approach, and she started at the bottom of the temple, sniffing around to try to find any hint of Whisper.

There was nothing, as though Whisper hadn't come here. Flicker went around to the back of the temple, discovering a passage filled in with rocks. Though they mostly smelled of other jadebeaks, the sorts who rarely gave her a second thought, she could just detect a whiff of Nightsky Pride.

Wendl was part of the Nightsky Pride, their greenest member the way Flicker was the Jadebeak Pride's reddest, so perhaps this was a clue. Flicker got to work removing the rocks, wondering why no one was here to stop her. Sometimes, the squirrel races got out of paw, and the rodents fled into the jungle and needed to be hunted down. She sent out scents of inquiry, but no answer came. There were no starlings close enough to relay her message, leaving her a little lonely.

But just a little. She did enjoy being alone most of the time. Though she also enjoyed spending time with Whisper even more and was very curious what awaited her at the end of the scavenger hunt.

It took two hours and required several breaks, during which time she raided nearby nests and stole food from her fellow jadebeaks, but she managed to remove enough rubble to reach the lower chambers.

This is far too dark. The little light that made it down the passage disappeared in a large chamber with wings on the walls. Flicker smelled a few opinicus braziers. Ever since discovering opinicus tools could be used to grow plants, she'd become good with most of them. She hadn't brought any of her own, but she sniffed around the braziers until she detected tinder fungus, then beaked around until she found the matching flint. They weren't easy to get going, but she considered herself an expert at opinicus tooling. Once one brazier was lit, she could see the entire room.

"This is very romantic," Flicker said to the darkness. "This is some summer friends level courtship."

She circled the room, searching the wings for clues, dragging the brazier around with her beak until its outside grew too hot for her to handle. Then she went outside to gather reeds, threading them through the exterior of the brazier and dragging it behind her. The heat still eventually burned them through, but it saved her beak and paws from getting hurt.

"Well, there's nothing here. No choice but to go deeper." Flicker's voice echoed back to her. An ominous chamber in a forbidden temple might dissuade other starlings, but not her. She liked a challenge. It's why she grew her food rather than hunt it.

Maybe that's part of the challenge? Only a starling willing to break a few rules would want to be mates in the summer. Ah, I knew Whisper liked me. I wonder where she's hiding?

The strawberry starling gathered more reeds, creating a stockpile of them in the wing chamber, then dragged the brazier into the depths, hoping to find Whisper or at least some sort of prize at the end of her journey.

45

STRAWBERRY

Flicker ran afoul of a few dead ends, though she found some exciting fungi and bugs, which made the whole experience worth it. In the brazier light, she'd even found a shiny bit of metal, some sort of circle with a prongy bit she thought might make a nice gift for Whisper.

Flicker was about ready to give up, thinking the corridor fully mapped by her pawprints, when she found the partially concealed turn into the final chamber. This one smelled salty, bloody, and wet. While she didn't think these qualities precluded having a good time, they were an odd combination.

Pieces of glass sparkled in the firelight. She reached for one, captivated by the rare treasure, but it bit her. She dropped it and clutched her paw protectively, licking until the bleeding stopped. Every so often, dead blackwings appeared near her pumpkin patch. On two such occasions, she'd recovered bits of shiny glass from their harnesses. That glass hadn't been sharp like these pieces were.

Maybe it's a glass weapon? Or I guess it could just be broken.

The trenches between the stonework made it hard to drag the brazier along. She got an idea when one of her reeds dried out enough to catch flame, and she ran the burning reed to the edge of the room, hoping to find more braziers.

Success!

She managed to start a couple of fires at the room's entrance before the reed's heat reached her beak. The flickering flames revealed what she'd missed on her first trip down.

"Has that dead body always been down here?" she asked to no one in particular.

No one in particular replied, "Yes, at least, it was there when I arrived."

Flicker pulsed an inquiry but received no pheromones back. At the edge of the light was a metal cage, its occupant concealed by darkness. "Why are you quiet? Why didn't you respond when I asked where everyone was?"

She grabbed more reeds, using them to light braziers in the direction of No One In Particular. She skipped the brazier behind the dead jadebeak, not wanting to get too close. She didn't mind dead *things.* She'd even used several dead blackwings as fertilizer for her pumpkins. But she did mind dead *starlings.*

When she reached the metal cage, she saw another jadebeak, this one gripping a chunk of shattered glass in her talons. No One In Particular was emaciated, her eyes both wild and sad. She stared through Flicker, as though sure she was a hallucination.

"Oh, talons, those would have been handy for gardening," Flicker thought aloud. "I should have brought down the flint and tinder fungus. Who're you, and why can't I smell you? Are you Wendl?"

The stranger snapped out of her daydream. "Sorry, I was lost there for a moment. You said you can't smell me? But you're also not feeling, well, homicidal towards me? And yes, I'm Wendl. Who sent you?"

"Whisper." Flicker answered the last question first. "My mate. Well, ex-mate, but the season has only just ended, so that's not strange to say. We're definitely not summer friends. I think a lot of starlings probably make mistakes like that, don't you think? And I don't seem to be like other starlings. Whisper says I need to make sure to broadcast my scent so the pridelord doesn't worry."

Wendl looked at the dead body, then dropped her glass shard. "Well, if you could hold off on talking to the pridelord or anyone else, I'd appreciate it. I don't think I'm in his good graces. If he found me here with you, it could get us both in trouble."

"Oh, the pridelord is off at the squirrel races," Flicker explained. "There aren't any jadebeaks at the temple. Oh! Except you? But you smelled a little Nightsky. That's why I thought you were Wendl, because I was sure there was a Wendl in the Nightsky Pride, and I didn't remember anyone else naming their gryphlet Wendl. That happens sometimes, you know? The sparkwings have a Lusci, then the jadebeaks get a Lusci. And at first, it works out. Sparklusci and Jadelusci. But then the sparkwings get assigned to the jadebeaks, and then they're both—"

Wendl interrupted her. "You didn't find a key on your way down by chance, did you? A small metal thing with a long end?"

"Oh, sure. I was saving it for Whisper, though." Flicker went back to where she'd burned her beak, retrieved the *key*, and brought it over. "I suppose in a scavenger hunt, Whisper probably left this as some sort of clue. I guess that makes it okay to give you."

The green nightsky's talons shook, and she couldn't hold onto it. "I don't suppose you could do it for me? It goes in the lock, then you need to twist it."

"Sure, I got the flint and tinder fungus working, didn't I?" Flicker didn't mention that she'd failed more times than she'd succeeded at that task, though Wendl probably figured that out for herself after half an hour passed and Flicker kept failing to twist the key.

The opinicus reached her talons through, gently steadying them on Flicker's paws. "We can do this together, yes? I'll help shape your paw, and you twist when I say."

Working together, they got the door open. It took another half hour for Flicker to guide Wendl out of the darkness. She insisted the strawberry-colored starling go back up with flaming reeds and light the other braziers. Even then, Wendl was too weak, and Flicker ended up dragging her.

"How do you know Whisper?" Flicker asked, wishing she had enough reeds to tie around her new friend. Reeds could be extremely versatile in the right paws.

Wendl cleared her throat. "Same as you, I suppose. We were almost opinicus-mated."

"Funny thing to do with a gryphon. And we were *actually* mated, so I think I win." The strawberry starling considered this information. She'd heard opinici mated for very long times, perhaps an entire year. That could be a point in favor of summer friends, but the *almost* suggested that was why Whisper had left Wendl. "Did you break up because you both had the same first letter in your name?"

There was a long silence before the opinicus replied, either from exhaustion or introspection. "No, that wasn't her name back then. Honestly, I guess I don't know. We grew apart, but it was probably salvageable. Then she was just so full of joy, and I wasn't, and I think I stepped back. I don't know what would have happened if I'd stepped forwards instead."

"Sounds rough." Flicker could see the daylight ahead. "Though it's like my denparent used to say: there's always another mating season. We can fight over Whisper when the summer ends, if it'll make you feel better. I should warn you that I don't fight fair, though. I bite high and kick low."

Wendl laughed. "No, thank you. I've been considering moving somewhere with less humidity, and I think my time in a wet cage helped me make up my mind. I entrust Whisper to your capable paws. If you're willing to groom the goo out of her eyes every morning, more power to you. Oh, is that fresh air?"

A LIGHT MIST fell upon Wendl's face. Despite her comments about having had enough of the humidity, the cleanliness of it all—mixed with the fresh air and sun—made her a little weepy.

"I've missed this." Her voice caught in her throat, always afraid to show emotion even to her strange savior.

She needed to get away before the pridelord returned, but she didn't have the strength to fly. She hated to depend on Flicker, especially not if that meant she'd owe a favor to Whisper, who would soon find out what Wendl had done if she didn't know already. She didn't see any other options. Before she could ask for help, however, the red starling snapped a gliding lizard out of the air and offered it to Wendl. It was still alive and struggling, tail thrashing and rainbow wings spread in agitation. The opinicus ate it in one bite.

"You should start slow if you were sick," Flicker said. "Otherwise, you'll just throw it up. Now that we've got some meat into you, let's find you some-where soft to rest, and I'll rustle up some gryphtail reeds."

Wendl killed a second lizard and ate it with even smaller bites. "I didn't know gryphtail reeds were edible."

"Anything is edible if you're persistent enough." Flicker guided Wendl down the temple's steps to one of the smaller tributaries. "The caimans taught me that."

Wendl lay in the damp grass, letting Flicker hunt gryphtails for her. The smell of the river, wet and sweet, came over her. Her nares had always been weak, opinical, but she could barely smell Flicker at all. When Wendl tried to remember what her savior smelled like, strawberries came to mind, probably because of the way Flicker resembled the fruit. But when Flicker dropped off a new, fuzzy set of gryphtail reeds for lunch, there was no strawberry scent on her. She smelled more like fresh-toiled dirt, and one side of her face smelled like pumpkin.

"Do you...sense any of the murmuration nearby?" Wendl asked.

Flicker cleared the fuzziness off a cat tail and chewed the stalk underneath. "Nope, you said not to contact any starlings, so I didn't. Honestly, I forget about the murmuration sometimes. Most of the time. That's why I like it better at my garden."

"I see." Wendl imitated Flicker, chewing the stalk and leaving the fuzzy bits behind. It tasted like cucumber. She longed for a cooking fire, but at least it was filling her belly. "You said you were going to take me to Whisper?"

Flicker shrugged. "I would if I knew where she was at. I went to her nest, but it was empty. Thing is, her scent didn't go east. Though I found a hiding spot with a bunch of opinicus stuff in it. Across the top, the glyphs said *Find Wendl*, and so I tried to remember the last time I'd heard anything about you. It was days ago, when you were supposed to go to the temple. So here we are."

Wendl blinked. That sounded less like Whisper had sent someone to rescue Wendl and more like Whisper herself might be in need of rescuing. "What made you say east? Are you saying the murmuration has left the Emerald Jungle? And what direction did her scent go?"

"Oh!" Flicker said. "It went to Nightsky territory.

That must be where she wants me to take you. And...I didn't think to look for the murmuration. Hmm. One moment, let me fly around."

Wendl watched her gryphon companion fly around, sniffing random stone towers, cliffs, and ruins. Her stomach rumbled a bit at the gryphtail lunch. She doubted she'd be flying before the day was through, but at least she wouldn't starve to death.

"Okay, found 'em!" Flicker landed. "Sort of. Everyone else's scent is stronger east than west. I'd guess they all left across the Jadebeak Mountains."

Oh good, so I've got time to recover before they get back. It took Wendl's addled brain a second try to reprocess the message. "Wait, they *left* the jungle? Where did they go?"

"Dunno! Explains why they've all been so quiet, though." Flicker shook off a bit of the mist. "Oh, not Whisper's scent, though. The Newmoon Pride was moving west, probably to your home. Oh! But there were some nightsky smells going east...and others going west. That's confusing. I guess we'd better go check it out. Can you fly?"

Wendl wasn't sure she could stand. "Sadly, no. I need to find a place to sleep. You could go check on them, though, and come back for me."

She wasn't sure that was wise. She had no idea what a starling pride left behind while the pridelord was away would do. Would Whisper act as a new pridelord for them? Would they obey his final orders? She might be better off with her strawberry friend.

"There's...something else." Flicker sniffed at the air, then crawled up the bank and flew to the side of the tower, clinging to it like a cicada, her beak facing southeast. She remained frozen there for several minutes before returning to the soggy ground of the stream. "There are nonstarlings here. I didn't think to smell for opinici, but now that I'm sniffing around, someone has come through here. A lot of someones. Look, you can smell one on this rock I found."

Wendl didn't expect to detect anything, but she did. What's more, she remembered it from the battle over the expedition ruins. It was white-tailed kite. There was only one thing she could think of that the Seraph King might want in the jungle.

"The salts. We can't stay here, it's not safe." She pulled herself to her feet and beat her wings a few times. She could get out of the temple grounds but probably not much farther than that. "They're coming here."

Flicker sniffed. "I don't think so. Since the wind changed, I'm missing something coming off the ocean. Is that...fire? Oh no, the Stormtail Pridegrounds!"

"The jungle won't burn, not this time of year." Wendl hoped that was true. There were moments in the summer when it got so hot the pumpkin-shaped fruit of the spiketrunk trees exploded, injuring many young starlings who didn't know to stay away from the trees on hot days. Still, she was sure Lightningmaw wouldn't burn, with its near-perpetual storm. She didn't know what was going on *there*, but she was certain someone from the Nighthaunt's retinue would come *here* for the salts.

In the early days, Whisper had been more open with Wendl and the others about what she could sense. It seemed a good chance to put that knowledge to use.

"New plan, Flicker. Do you know where the Winter Jungle is? I need you to head down there." Wendl searched her harness pockets, finding one of her orange vials she hadn't managed to consume before her assassination attempt on the pridelord. "You might need this if glyphs get in the way, but don't drink too much. You'll need him to recognize you as a starling."

Flicker took it in her paws, dropping the glass. Thankfully, it landed in the mud.

Whisper searched her pockets for some of the strips of leather she'd been saving to make a bracelet for Sheen and wove them into a smaller version for Flicker to hold the vial against her paw. "There we go. You should find a stormtail in the Winter Jungle. Tell him what's going on, and then head to Lightningmaw. I'm going to go hide."

"What about Whisper?" Flicker asked. Despite her generally forgetful and happy-go-lucky demeanor, the smell of fire sobered her. "If there are outsiders here, she might be in danger. She'll need us."

Wendl didn't see what a wounded scholar and a forgetful pumpkin farmer could do for Whisper if the Seraph King was here. She figured if the jungle had any defenses, they'd be in the Winter Jungle, so she lied. "I'll save Whisper. You look into the stormtails. Now go!"

Flicker flew off, leaving Wendl alone. The opinicus walked up from the creek to the back entrance to the temple, getting winded by that effort alone. Part of her wanted to crawl back into the depths and grab as many of the salts as she could. Khalim had worked hard to acquire those salts, and she still believed she could make the murmuration better with them. Without, there was no hope.

Before she realized what she was doing, she'd taken three steps towards the entrance to the Sky Beneath the Earth. She caught herself, turning and leaping off the side of the temple and gliding away.

Her wings got her from one pillar to the next, then she had to rest. Like a flying squirrel, she was going to have to glide her way out of the temple before the Nighthaunt got here.

The timing is strange. How did he know the starlings were gone? And why go to Lightningmaw? The only thing of note there beyond food and caiman are the Stormtail Pride. Actually, why are the stormtails still here at all? Shouldn't they be with the murmuration?

46

THE WINTER JUNGLE

Flicker did not rush on her flight to the Winter Jungle. She was good at pacing herself, and if she had to fly back up to help Wendl save Whisper, she would need to leave something in reserve.

Spiketrunks gave way to broadleafs. It had been a rainy spring, and the Winter Jungle was mostly underwater. She didn't expect to need Wendl's weird medicine, but along the edge of the water, she reached out to see if Wendl's friend was around, and she was suddenly hit with a warning that she had left the Emerald Jungle.

Her body panicked, turning back to the shore. It was like the time as a little red gryphlet when she'd nearly been swallowed whole by a crocodile. Her body fled for safety, then she caught her breath. In front of her were two glyphs. One was the electric tail glyph of the Stormtail Pride, marking the Winter Jungle as theirs. She'd always liked it since it looked like some of the blue ferns that grew along the edge of the Jadebeak Mountains.

Next to it was a new glyph, one she hadn't seen before. It was a red pawprint with black stars around it. That was the glyph that gave her trouble.

Given enough time and creativity, she could have removed the glyph. She didn't have that time, so she worked the stopper off Wendl's orange vial with her beak and downed some of the orange goo. She was careful to return the stopper.

Oh, it tastes like tangerine not pumpkin. Wasn't expecting that.

Nothing happened.

She tried to move past the glyph, but now that she knew what it meant, her body refused to allow her passage. It was also trying to tell her something she knew was impossible. She refused to believe the Stormtail Pride weren't starlings. That made no sense.

What happened while I was tending to my garden? I wish I had another starling to ask.

She opened her senses as Whisper had taught her, and the message was louder, filling her nares with hostility. But every second, it faded into tangerine numbness.

The glyph cried out in the citrus scent of the pridelord: *NO.*

Her mind started at a *NO* but softened to a *no?* and finally a *maybe.*

She'd never disobeyed the pridelord before. At least, she hadn't deliberately done so. Doing so now gave her a headache, but she walked past the red and black glyph. Once she was on the other side, the headache faded.

Now, time to search the Winter Jungle!

She looked out at this stretch of the jungle and

realized she had a problem. It was all underwater, and she wasn't a great swimmer.

FLICKER CLUNG TO A TREE, holding it with her claws, and crawled under the water. She'd heard of the Winter Jungle, of course, and knew where it was, but she'd never experienced it.

The same thing that made it familiar was what made it so strange. It looked the same as the Emerald Jungle on the other side of the glyphs, full of broadleaf trees, ferns, and plants—but they were underwater.

The branches of trees that usually housed squirrels now hosted red crabs that waved their pincers at her in warning. Where cicadas would cling to the broad trunk, there were snails and water bugs. Instead of birds flittering between the trees, there were colorful fish.

This is amazing. I could stay here forever.

That thought lasted for about ten seconds until her lungs reminded her to return to the surface to breathe.

Okay, not forever.

She couldn't search an entire underwater jungle, not from beneath the waves, not twenty seconds at a time. She retreated to the coast while coming up with a new plan. Unfortunately, her brain was too excited by the interesting plants and animals. Little bugs hid on branches overlooking the water, while tiny fish sat below them, waiting to see if they'd fall.

Or, in the case of one black and white fish, getting

into position and spitting a stream of water to knock the bugs into the water. Meanwhile, blue and green kingfishers dive-bombed the fish, impaling and pulling them into the sky. Animal warfare waged across land, sea, and air.

I think the kingfishers have the right of it. I'll fly over top and look for signs. There are enough broadleaf trees that aren't fully underwater yet that they'll give me a dry place to rest.

She took to the air, leaving the wildlife behind, and began her survey of the Winter Jungle. As she flew from tree to tree, she was struck by how strange it was that no one came here, even in the winter. She'd heard this was the original home of the Stormtail Pride before Lightningmaw, but none of them ever returned.

Maybe it has saltwater crocodiles. That thought gave her pause. What she liked about being a jadebeak, even a bright red jadebeak, was that there were a lot of stormtails between her and the crocodiles. She'd been born when the coast was Jadebeak territory, back when jadebeaks had a coast, and her fear of crocodiles was practical. Even ghavials gave her pause. It was why she liked growing plants instead of hunting. Plants didn't try to eat her.

It was no coincidence her garden was along the edge of the mountains. She wanted to put as much distance, vertical and horizontal, as possible between herself and crocodiles.

She'd heard a rumor, though, that the Stormtail Pride had killed most of the crocodiles in the Winter Jungle, so that was good. She kept telling herself that fact as she flew between vast stretches of ocean.

A sense of anxiety grew as the salinity of the water did the same. She couldn't see the shore any longer, just the last tree. If a storm came through and visibility decreased, it would be very easy for her to get stranded out here, clinging to the top of a broadleaf, praying no crocodiles still lived here.

She shook her head. Wendl had given her a task. Whisper needed her. The stormtails might be in danger from outsiders. She could do this.

Do what? There's no sign of anyone out here.

She sighed and landed on a grove of broadleafs sticking out of the ocean. Where usually she only had one tree to cling to, many of these were above the water level. She searched the tops of trees, finding a few bugs and crabs to eat. The currents must have been rough, because there were long scratches along the side of the tree.

She sniffed at one. The scent was definitely starling, though not one she'd met. *I'm on the tail! Er, on the trail! On the trail of the tail. Trailing the stormtail's tail.*

From the sky, a grove of trees only halfway underwater had been reassuring. Down below their canopy, with no ground beneath her except dark water, she felt less reassured. She heard a splash and stiffened.

It's probably just a stormtail. They live in water, right? Love water, love swimming? Of course they'd splash. Big splashers, those stormtails.

She glided between the trees, following the sound. Sure enough, she found more scratches and stormtail scent. By the pheromones, this gryphon called himself the Gourmand. She climbed the tree, thinking her soon-to-be friend might have a nest, but she found only kingfishers.

They weren't happy to see her here, but they still provided her with her next clue. Several of their nests were made with gryphon feathers.

Look how long it is! This must be a tailfeather, surely? A blue-green feather the size of her foreleg, curled by age, was full of twigs and nesting material—and king-fisher eggs. She wanted to take the feather and examine it, but she didn't want to get attacked by birds, so she returned down below the canopy, into the salty damp.

She continued following the trail, hearing the occasional splash. At least, she thought she was following a trail. After half an hour of searching for scratch marks, she made a startling discovery regarding the existence of her first two clues.

All of the trees had scratch marks on them, and the scent was strong on each. It didn't make any sense. Flicker couldn't think of any reason for a gryphon to mark a bunch of trees. Was this *Gourmand* really so worried someone else would come out here and steal his trees?

A loud splash echoed from across the grove.

"Okay, that's it," she grumbled. "I'll pull you out of the water by your whiskers, if that's what it takes."

She climbed the canopy and flew to the other side. There were ripples near one of the trees, but no sign of what had caused them. She beat her wings, expending energy to let her take a close look around, and then she saw it.

To the left of the ripples, below the water, was a reptilian face, its snout just out of the water. Flicker traced the body as it wrapped around the tree. It looked almost like a snake.

Wait, that's not a reptile. That's a juvenile serpentine—

The jet of water hit her in the chest, knocking her out of the sky. True to its shape, the whale slithered through the water towards her, lashing out with a toothy bite. Flicker managed to flap enough to get out of the water, evading becoming the beast's next meal, but was too wet to stay aloft and fell back down.

The serpentine whale circled back around, building speed, and Flicker's heart raced in her chest. Then the sun vanished, a giant in the sky interposing himself between her and its fiery glare.

A large stormtail, his kingfisher form now obvious, plunged into the ocean, his spear-like beak stabbing through several layers of blubber before poking out the other side. The whale thrashed wildly but couldn't get its head at the right angle to bite the gryphon, who used a massive paw to push it away.

Whatever the beak had gone through inside the creature, its twitching stopped.

Flicker stared at the dead whale and gryphon. Then the kingfisher pulled his beak from his prey and turned to look at her. Having the beak pointed in her direction made her nervous, even as foreshortening hid that it was as long as she was tip to tail. His body disappeared into the dark water, concealing his true size in a way he'd probably picked up from the whales he hunted.

Rough, ragged feathers worn by saltwater framed his eyes in dark blue with splashes of orange. Judging by the stains on his cerulean face, his salt ducts were working overtime. He tilted his head slightly, revealing a bevy of scratch marks on his beak that did nothing to dull how sharp it was. Considering whales and crocodiles had probably left them, she was amazed they were so shallow. His beak must be hard as stone.

Also like his prey, he had a way of remaining still while floating that didn't cause ripples, and she imagined he would be easy to miss in the underwater jungle.

I had no idea gryphons grew so large. I'll bet those claws could till my garden in a quarter of the time it takes me.

"Oh, my manners," she chirped. "Thank you for saving me. Are you the Gourmand?"

The kingfisher didn't seem to recognize her words, reminding her she had other options. She sent her unique pheromones, identifying herself and her pride.

His grizzled features relaxed, though confusion set in. With the distance of Wendl's elixir, she could feel the individual scents and what they meant. It took longer for Flicker's brain to tie them back together and understand what he was saying.

Oh, the stormtails are still in their prideground, but they were kicked out of the murmuration. Why would the pridelord do that? I'd like to have this beast of a gryphon on my side in any fight.

The Gourmand barked, a deep rough sound. When she didn't reply, he tried again, eventually finding his voice. "You, garrumph. Grab whale tail. Can't let blood stay in water. Or adults come."

The kingfisher latched onto the dead whale and

began dragging it out to sea, leaving her to try to find its other end. Even once she had it, she couldn't get it out of the water, and ultimately, she decided to just hold on and let the Gourmand pull them both to his den.

THE GOURMAND'S ISLAND WAS, perhaps, the last dry land before reaching the southern ocean. The sand wasn't blue, but the way the sun reflected off it had hidden it from Flicker's view when she flew above the final bit of the Winter Jungle.

His home was more like the lair of a beast than the nest of a civilized gryphon. The same way Flicker would sometimes decorate her little nest with flower petals or sweet-smelling bark, her new friend decorated his home with the bones of sea creatures, especially skulls.

She hadn't gotten a good look at him as he swam, and even now his tail dragged into the water, but he was larger than a saltwater crocodile and not too much smaller than his prey. She'd gotten glimpses of the other starling prides when they came to visit the pridelord in Jadebeak territory, and while their colors varied, they were of a similar stature...except for this one, who dragged his prey past a rather interesting skeleton.

"Is that a two-headed crocodile?" she asked, unsure if he'd combined the skeletons of two different reptiles into one or if it had come that way. When he barked the affirmative, she continued, "It's very nice.

If I had one, I'd definitely put it over my nest to scare away ghavials."

The Gourmand considered her, then nudged the skeleton towards her. "Yours now. What you offer in trade?"

"Pumpkins?" she asked.

He stopped chewing the whale, and she wondered if she'd offended him. "Twenty pumpkins."

"Five," she countered. "They kill parasites, and I need to make sure I have enough to save any infected."

"Garrrrrrrumph." He bit off a flipper and tossed it to her. "Deal. Now eat. We leave soon."

True to her earlier worries, the skies had turned cloudy and cool. While she didn't want to stay on a small island during a big storm, she'd rather be here than over the whale-infested groves. "What if we wait out the rains? How will we find our way back through them?"

"Grrrrumph," he repeated.

She realized she hadn't been broadcasting or listening to scents. Apparently, anyone showing up was enough for him to assume an emergency. She did as Whisper taught her, letting her nares and scent glands work as intended, and was filled with as much information as she shared.

"Opinicus-made fire," he said, analyzing what she shared and pushing the smell of smoke to her. "A trick, hides scent. Means they'll attack. I attack first."

Flicker liked the idea of handing off a problem to a gryphon who appeared to be very capable. "Sounds good! Once we get back to the mainland, I can go rescue Whisper."

When he didn't reply, she pushed the scent of cooking mallow root, and he perked up.

"Newmoon leader. Good. Fixed Desert Rose. Will fix us." The Gourmand stood, stretching his wings. Despite having come from the sky to save her, she hadn't seen him fly since and had forgotten he even had wings. "Garrumph. Help me drag this into the tree so the beasts don't get it. Keep safe from sharks if not octopi."

The thought that there were octopodes large enough to try to consume even a baby serpentine whale cemented within Flicker a deeply held belief that she would never return to the ocean as long as she lived. Still, she did her part, holding up the tip of the beast's tail as her stormtail companion did the heavy lifting.

The sight of a whale carcass draped over a large broadleaf on a tiny island sticking out of the ocean was something to behold. Whisper would not believe her.

She must have broadcast the mallow root smell again, because the Gourmand spoke.

"You come with me. Can cross glyphs." He shook his feathers, spraying blood and saltwater all over Flicker and making her begin defensive preening. "If opinici use fire, hide just out of reach, they know stormtails out of murmuration. Can use that. You strike from Emerald Jungle, where they won't expect. Drive them to me."

Flicker was impressed the Gourmand's speech improved so quickly, though she had a much better plan and held up her paw to show him the vial. "This will let you cross, too. It suppresses the pridelord's will temporarily."

"Unusual for a jadebeak to have." His eyes narrowed, and his body became as still as the crocodile skeletons that littered his nest. "Still, cannot protect the Emerald Jungle if I can't enter it. Garrumph. Finish your preening. We leave for Lightningmaw."

Though her red plumage hid blood rather well, she got herself into flight shape again. As she did so, she couldn't help but look around the parts of the island she could see. There were several opinicus rafts, along with the bones of sailors. The whale was not unique here, and the bones of its kin lined the tree where it hung. Suddenly, the scent marks on the grove made sense. They'd been a way to lure the small whales to a specific location.

There were other, stranger things. On the largest broadleaf were glyphs carved into the bark. The scratch marks that made them required large claws, and the Gourmand was the most likely culprit. None of them looked like starling glyphs.

One had a hooked beak that resembled no gryphon beak she'd ever seen. Most starling beaks were fairly straight, though some were longer than others.

"That's a weird glyph," she asked. "Who's that from?"

"The Merinkin left it," the Gourmand said, as though she'd have any idea what a *Merinkin* was. It sounded like the name of a squirrel. "Before he went south."

"South?" She looked out at the expanse of water.

There were no groves beyond the Gourmand's lair, no leaves sticking out of the water, no sign of land. "What's south?"

The Gourmand, strangely quiet for a beast so large, had already left to fly northeast. She hurried to catch up, thankful she was a lot lighter than he was. As they passed over the nearest grove, she could see shark fins where the whale had died.

Blood in the water, she thought. *It turns the largest of predators into prey.*

47

FLICKER AND WENDL'S EX-MATE

Whisper's paws and beak ached from trying without success to bend the iron bars. The tinny tang of metal filled her mouth every time she ran her tongue over her tomia. She did not like being stuck in a cage.

Her only consolation was that, though the Nighthaunt and darkstalker had left, the opinici from Duckbill had not arrived on time. The scout sent to find them, a small silverhawk, reported that she'd been unable to locate any sign of the missing mallards.

The alabaster opinicus in charge shrugged. "More food for the Naze's spider. Go back to Duckbill and ask for more. Wait until morning, though. No sense flying over the abyss at night. Probably about time we gave it another good burn."

I owe Silky and Bristlespine a rhea, I suppose. If the ducks had gotten us, we'd be dead before my plan has a chance to work.

Whisper owed a thanks to one other gryphon. Or,

rather, opinicus. Her body was adjusting to the chemicals put into her food, and she could sense all her pride, including Sheen. The ex-nightsky was recovering from her infection, which meant the darkstalker had made sure to put pumpkin into her food.

The black-eyed opinicus had waited, though, until after Sheen had bitten some of the stabletalons to do so. And that's why Whisper thought she had a decent chance of getting out of here.

A stabletalon stumbled into Whisper's tent, nearly dropping a bowl of grub. His beak trembled as he set the food in front of her.

The Nighthaunt had insisted Whisper be kept away from the others, kept in the dark. He'd underestimated her. She didn't need her eyes to see what her pride was doing. Trails of pheromones shifted with the wind, keeping her informed. But it wasn't just them.

As the stabletalon pushed the food into her table, she reached out her forepaws, quick like she was catching a squirrel, and held his face in them.

"Hello, hello," she whispered.

The opinicus chittered a little when he spoke back. "Hell-o, hell...Oh."

Whisper licked a paw, wiping the barest hint of silver out of his eyes. "That won't do, not at all. We can't have the others noticing, can we?"

She flooded him with citrus and got back rage. That was the bugs speaking. Though she suspected the parasite itself was separate from the bugs, that the tiny mites were either its victims or co-conspirators, she couldn't help but see their tiny, red forms when she spoke to the infected.

"Calm." She punctuated her words with mint. She pulled the opinicus in close, resting his head on her shoulder, and placed her paw against his belly. He was fed, but the parasites inside of him told his brain he was starving, that if he didn't consume the closest meat he could find, he would die that instant.

She chipped away at that feeling inside him. It took some work. The parasite had a way of shifting, of trying to elude her. She worried if she overused mint, it'd build up a resistance to it. Instead, she gave this opinicus the smell of cooked goliath bird, emphasizing that this was how he felt. He relaxed a little.

The red bugs shifted. Now, he felt like he was in danger. He had to peck and claw to free himself, otherwise he would be eaten alive!

She clung to his head, keeping his beak away from her important bits. His talons dug into her, but she suppressed this feeling, too. With a little more citrus, she regained control, and his beak stopped chittering.

"Remember to wipe your eyes," she told him. His expression was blank. It was mostly the pheromones that controlled him. The chemicals from the bugs hollowed out part of his brain, letting her come in and fill it with mint and orange. "Then tell your friend to come visit me."

She released him, and he stumbled back. He opened the flap of the tent, staring out at the sun for a few moments, then found himself and left.

The stabletalons all slept together in a makeshift goliath bird stable, which made it easy to suggest they bite their neighbors in their sleep. The tricky part had been to keep them from infecting the goliaths. Whisper had come across infected wildlife in her time, and her skill set didn't work on them, just gryphons.

And opinici.

She curled up to sleep, conserving her strength, but the scent of the silverhawk returned.

From outside her tent, she heard the scout say, "They'll be here tomorrow morning. Had to go the long way around. They've got some extra carts, so we can load everyone up and take the high road all the way to Duckbill. They'll firebomb the Abyssal Naze at the same time to keep the blackeyes out of our feathers."

Whisper sent out a scent to calm her pride, old members and new. *Not long now. We'll be out of here by tonight.*

GENERALLY SPEAKING, it was ethically unsound to use the stabletalons to kill their former friends. At least, Whisper assumed they were friends. Maybe she was wrong, and the Seraph King's expedition just needed stabletalons and hired some from the local ranch. Either way, that kind of killing left its own mental scars.

Instead, when the sun went down, she ordered all of her pride to exude mint. Not cooking mint, gold mint, or even gryphmint. Instead, she borrowed the smell of what the Ashen Weald's witches were calling *opinimint.*

It worked. The opinici in the camp were all a little weird that night, saying things they wouldn't normally, talking about how much they liked each other, and then they slept.

The advantage of knowing the stabletalons was that she'd been able to query their remaining memories, learning all she could about her jailors.

Many of them had been chosen by Hi-kun for their ability to follow terrible orders without questioning them. Others had been chosen by the Nighthaunt because they took a certain joy from hurting gryphons, which was something he believed would be required.

But there were a few, perhaps four, who had just been assigned to the Emerald Jungle. Whisper was perfectly willing to kill anyone who stood in the way of her susurration, but perhaps her time with Nighteyes, Flicker, Wendl, and even the darkstalker had dulled her edge.

She whispered to her pride, and the susurration whispered back. They knew where all four—she hesitated to use the word *good* but settled on *not definitively evil*—opinici were located. It seems they were particularly susceptible to opinimint and had all gone skinny dipping at a nearby pond.

What a good way to get eaten by caiman. Though I suppose, in this case, it saved their lives.

She woke the infected stabletalons. The opinimint hadn't hit them as hard, as the bugs still struggled for control of their minds. She ordered them out of the stables and into the camp, where they freed the red-beaked nightsky sick, the black-plumed Newmoon Pride, and the rest of the susurration.

While she longed to be free, this was a numbers

game. If the Alabasters woke up, she needed enough of a force to overwhelm them.

They ordered us underfed so we'd be too weak to fight. She had some choice words for them. Thankfully, she'd convinced the stabletalons to butcher a goliath bird to keep everyone fed.

Once her pride were free, she had the stabletalons fly the Nightsky gryphlets deeper into the jungle. Then she drew the adults to her tent.

When the flap opened, her pride stared in, all except for Sheen, who was being kept in the leader's tent, under orders from Mally that he needed her alive.

Whisper didn't order her susurration around the way she had the stabletalons. She instead gave them calming scents, memories of good times, reassurances. One by one, they all confirmed they were ready.

The command to kill wasn't citrus, nor mint, nor cassia, nor any of the usual scents of control. It was a cool breeze on a bright night, the floral perfume of a vine often pollinated by moths.

Moonlit Blossom.

The Newmoon Pride descended upon the remaining tent.

THIS HAD BEEN the hardest spring of Sheen's admittedly short life, and it didn't seem to be getting any better. Her pride leader had abandoned her to the Newmoon Pride, who were all weird. Her fellow hunters, just starting to like her, had flown off in the war migration.

She'd broken a paw, which still ached, though she could put a little weight on it now. She'd nearly been blown up by a duck. And the adult who liked her the most, Wendl, had been declared a traitor and killed—or, worse, kicked out of the murmuration.

Sheen did not think herself special, but she did think herself especially unlucky. Thus, she was surprised when a creature called The Nighthaunt knew who she was.

His voice was like a crocodile, a caiman, a shark, a cassowary. It wasn't gryphonic. It wasn't even opinical. It resonated in her skull, as though her mind were full of bees.

"Ah, Wendl's pet," he'd hissed when he saw her. "Excellent. The rest of the jungle may yet die, little violet, but you will remain safe with me."

She didn't know why the Nighthaunt had taken a liking to her, but the answer wouldn't be anything good. The way he spoke of Wendl worried her, too. How could such a monster know a starling?

Around then, a fever had taken her, and she'd lost consciousness, coming in and out of it to find herself biting someone or the other. All the while, she could just barely sense the Newmoon Pride dancing at the edge of her perception. She'd overheard someone saying her food was drugged.

Then, over the last two days, the dosage had decreased, and she could hear Whisper in her mind. It wasn't like talking, it was emotions and memories. If she could translate them into speech, they would have sounded like, *Oh good, the bugs are gone. Welcome to the pride, little one. I'm coming to save you. Stay safe and conserve your strength.*

It was a strange message as Sheen was in an opinicus cage, a contraption no gryphon would be able to figure out, and she was guarded by some sort of pride-sub-leader opinicus and several burly peafowl wearing metal to guard their chests.

Sheen did not have high hopes for being rescued. Even when the leader and peafowl began to act a little goofy, she thought it was a sign they knew they'd already won.

Two guards usually stayed awake with her at all times, but they dozed off tonight, leaving Sheen to sulk. She'd heard the leader warning the others that starlings lost their minds when they left the Emerald Jungle, so to be prepared for it.

Whatever the Nighthaunt needed Sheen for, apparently it did not require her mind to remain intact.

Sheen shivered with fear, cried slightly, and then caught a strange scent on the wind. The leader had kept incense lit around her, apparently thinking Whisper could be warded off in such a manner, but he'd fallen asleep early, and it had burned down.

The indigo gryphon sniffed at the air. *I don't remember any flowering vines in this stretch of the jungle.*

There was a rustle near the entrance of the tent. Then several Newmoon Pride stalked across the floor of the tent—the size of the common area in the nesting grounds—the soft fur of their stomachs scraping the ground in silence as they walked.

The Nightsky Pride hunted prey that was best caught from above, thus they didn't need to be stealthy. At most, they would lie in wait on game trails, then pounce.

By contrast, the Newmoon Pride were shadows at dusk, crossing the open paths in darkness and silence, absorbing the light of the room with their spotless fur.

Somehow, they were even scarier without their eyeshine.

The shadows reached the opinicus leader and peafowl, smothering them. They didn't move, but as the shadows pulled back, blood stained the ground.

The pride parted, allowing Whisper to approach the cage. Unlike the others, she'd acquired eyeshine from somewhere, though her stripes and crescent moon had faded during her incarceration.

"There's no way out of the cage." Sheen had resigned herself to her fate. "Just leave me behind, get out while you can."

Whisper ignored her. She stood on her back paws to reach part of the cage, then extended one claw on each paw, forcing them into the mechanism. Where Sheen's claws had been cut short, the others hadn't been.

After a few moments, there came a click, and the cage door opened.

"How..?" Sheen began to ask, but Whisper retracted her claws, put both paws on Sheen's cheeks, and stared into her eyes.

The Nightsky fledgling filled with smells, memories, and knowledge. For just a moment, she saw in front of her a mothfeather opinicus—and *mothfeather* was now a word she knew.

"I learned how to pick the Nighthaunt's locks

before the expedition left," Whisper said. "I didn't think this knowledge was something my pride needed to know, but I see I was wrong. This is the enemy you face, and this is what he did to me...and what we did to you."

The tent filled with strange smells, and several of the nightsky starlings fell over, overwhelmed. When they stood again, they all saw Whisper for who she was...*not* Whisper.

Then, the scents adjusted. Each starling emitted the smell of cooked mallow root, accepting her once again. It took Sheen a few tries to learn how to make that scent.

"I had to take the stabletalons to save us," Whisper said. "I think, without the pridelord here, I should not try to replace him. Instead, the susurration will make decisions together. What do we do with them?"

The smell of pumpkin filled the air, and Sheen added her assent. If their minds were not yet gone, they should be allowed to live.

Sheen stumbled out, the three-paw walk of the wounded, and discovered the stabletalons outside the tent, staring up at the sky. Several of the Newmoon Pride, of her new pride, disappeared into the medical tent, returning with vials of orange goo. The stabletalons took the elixir, then Whisper put them to sleep.

"Pride leader," Sheen said. "The Nighthaunt said he needed me. I'm putting us in danger."

Whisper looked at her, her eyes reflections of the moonlight itself. "Nightsky are too loud."

Scents and memories flowed through Sheen. Some were Whisper's, some were her own. Sheen saw a small purple bath, stormtail blood, and everything Wendl had made her forget.

An anger rose within her at the betrayal, but the smell of mallow root grounded her. Then she heard the conversations Wendl spoke while Sheen soaked.

"I hate that it has to be this way," Wendl's ghost said. "But I know I can save you. I can't let you die, Sheen. I haven't saved any of the others, but I think I can save you. Just hold on there."

Sheen shook her head. "But they said I wasn't cured, so she was wrong."

"Wendl is very good at what she does." Whisper spoke, leaving the scents behind for a moment. "She's diligent, smart, and if you set her off in a direction, her mind flies there before your paws have even left the ground. But she sees a problem and a solution and views her success or failure from that angle."

The pride slunk into the jungle, but Whisper remained with Sheen, who had to hobble along on three legs.

"She wanted a cure, and she didn't get it," Whisper continued. "She's always been more opinicus than starling, so she's limited in ways I'm not. She thought the stormtails were key, that they were immune to bloodbeak, and that she could pass that immunity on to your pride."

Sheen's confusion remained. "Is that not what she should have been doing?"

"It would be nice," Whisper confirmed, "but that's not what nature has provided us. The stormtails aren't immune. She thought since no stormtail has died of bloodbeak, they must be. After all, my old master caught stormtails, too, and tested and released them.

So the Stormtail Pride, like the Nightsky and Spark-wing Prides, must be ravaged by bloodbeak, yet there were no deaths."

"Right! So they're immune. Or Mally failed," Sheen added.

Whisper shook her head. "Neither. Bloodbeak ravages the Stormtail Pride. I can smell it when I purge the parasites out of them. Same with the jade-beaks who had stormtail parents. It's not about curing bloodbeak. Something about their blood bonds with the iron and gets rid of it."

"Iron is....the red?" Sheen asked.

"Yes. It builds in the body, destroying the parts of an opinicus that make pigment," Whisper said. "And as it hits toxic levels, you see it in the feathers and fur before an opinicus dies. But stormtail blood stops it."

In the distance, an opinicus called for help. Some-where, within the information Sheen had acquired, she remembered that a few of the opinici had left to go swimming and must have just returned.

"There's no cure for bloodbeak," Whisper contin-ued, "But there's a treatment. The Stormtail Pride has always been different, new. I wonder if they evolved to fight bloodbeak the same way we evolved to combat silver eyes? I don't know if the timing works. But I wish Wendl had worked with me instead of against me."

Ahead, in a part of the Nightsky territory Sheen had flown over a dozen times, there were some spiketrunks she'd never seen before, marked with crescent glyphs. The Newmoon Pride slipped between the spiked branches and onto a trail of salt.

"I shouldn't blame Wendl," Whisper continued. "I

didn't see it, either. I was so caught up in helping the silver-eyed, so worried about the pridelord, I missed the obvious. At least now I have a chance to make up for lost time."

Whisper pushed to the front of the pride, Sheen in tow. Being around so many Nightsky Pride stirred something inside of her. There was a sharing, an inquiry of wellbeing, a sense of encouragement that followed her. She'd need to ask Whisper how to turn it off.

Next to her, one of the old sparkwings let out a hiss, and the rest of the pride took added their own. When Sheen looked forwards, she saw a green shape, unidentifiable, but clearly marked as an outsider. The altruism welled up within her, feral and angry, but then mint filled her nares and she calmed, the hiss sounding more like a deflating eggfruit than a war cry.

"I didn't think you'd be able to stop them from tearing me apart, but I figured it was worth the try." The outsider's voice was familiar, but only when Sheen closed her eyes.

Whisper nuzzled Sheen, leaving a scent behind. When she opened her eyes, Wendl stood in front of her.

"Wendl!" Sheen ran over and hugged her friend, who wrapped very weak wings around her. "I thought you were dead. I was so worried!"

Whisper's reception was cooler. "It was kind of the pridelord to spare your life, but you're not part of the murmuration anymore."

"You were just saying you wished you'd helped Wendl," Sheen bristled. "You were saying you should tell her how stormtail blood can treat bloodbeak."

"Is that true?" Wendl asked.

The newmoon leader's silver eyes were unreadable. "Yes, but this is a starling concern, and you are no longer a starling. The pridelord has taken your green, Wendl, and your altruism with it. It is a gift, and you should take it and leave."

"It wasn't the pridelord." Wendl started to fall, but Sheen leaned against her. "It's Balthar, I'm sure of it. And Kism was in on it, too. The murmuration has left, and it's going east. You may not give a damn about our home, Whisper, but I do. Do you really think Balthar would agree to destroy the Blackwing Eyrie but leave Mothfeather untouched? We need to stop him."

Sheen tried to emit a scent that she agreed with Wendl, hoping the other Newmoon Pride would echo it the way they had the pumpkin, but the others were mostly confused or uninterested.

Whisper rolled her eyes. "I will take care of it *after* I save the Stormtail Pride. You should just leave. Go find Khalim and become a gry-fish-on."

"Fisherfolk," Wendl corrected. "And hold on, the Stormtail Pride aren't part of the murmuration anymore. If you're really concerned about an Emerald Jungle for starlings alone, there's no reason you should help them and not me."

"They're starlings..." Whisper began, before Wendl interrupted.

"Kingfishers!" the opinicus let out. "Are there no birdwatchers among gryphonkind? They're *kingfishers*. And I was just helped out of an underground dungeon by what was clearly a strawberry finch. I'm sorry, but the Emerald Jungle may have started out with only starling prides, but it's evolved past that. Look at your own pride—that's some sort of frost chicken. Are you going to tell me the distinction matters? I'm not asking as someone who looks like a jadebeak starling, I'm asking as someone who was one of your closest friends."

"What if she joined the Newmoon Pride?" Sheen asked. "I mean, then she's a starling again?"

Whisper looked past Sheen to Wendl. "Your altruism will return."

"Fine," Wendl said. "I'll do it to save Nighteyes and my family. Besides, you could probably find a way to stop altruism entirely if you tried."

"It serves a purpose," Whisper protested.

Wendl held up a talon. "I'm sure a smart gryphon like yourself can figure a better way to solve that problem, too."

Sheen had seen Wendl lose a fight to Nighteyes, and she was afraid she was going to see her friend lose a fight to Whisper, too, when the Newmoon gryphon rushed Wendl.

There was a burst of scent, but when it faded, Sheen was flooded with memory after memory from Wendl. Some of which were embarrassing and about Whisper.

"Was that really necessary for me to become a newmoon?" Wendl asked.

Whisper shrugged. "Who knows? My pride needs to know everything it can about opinici. Now, if you're done, it's a long walk to Lightningmaw."

"Oh, the skies are clear," Wendl replied. "I kept watch while I was waiting in your hidden trail. You're safe to fly. There's even a hidden spring where you can stash the fledglings. I can walk them there while you do your thing. Just don't forget me."

Whisper stared into Wendl's eyes for so long Sheen thought they might start grooming each other, but then the scent changed, and the pride ran to a gap in the spiketrunks and flew off, their own small murmuration rising to the defense of the Emerald Jungle.

48

THE PERPETUAL STORM

R udder had been hunting saltwater crocodiles with Clamshell and Desert Rose when his link to the murmuration was severed. Considering how temperamental crocs were under ideal conditions, it was a bad time to suddenly feel a lifetime of rules and restrictions vanish and another lifetime of memories flood back in.

Stranger still, he was in a much better position than either of his hunting companions, who still suffered nightmares from having been disconnected in the past. He snapped out of his stupor before they did, and his brain sought refuge from memories of killing gryphons and opinici in the Jadebeak Mountains by doing math.

Six saltwater crocodiles along this shore. One had been wounded and fled, probably shark or whale bait by now. Four others were dead and dragged to shore, a meal for the pride. That left—

He twisted in the water as a crocodile a few inches longer than him bit at where he'd been floating, nonplussed, a moment earlier. He said thanks to whatever had kept the crocodile at bay while he'd stared off into space. Perhaps the crocodile was having its own existential crisis.

He couldn't imagine what the other prides were going through if they'd been cut off from the murmuration, too. He had no way to reach them without scents. He was lucky he was a stormtail because he could lean back on the noises they used when hunting underwater.

He let out a bark and whine, snapping Clamshell out of their stupor. They knocked into Desert Rose, bringing him back around, too.

Desert Rose was not his original name, but he said he liked Whisper's moniker for him, so the others had taken to calling him that, too. In a pride of Clamshells, Rudders, Seaweeds, and Lilypads, a name like Desert Rose was about as cool as it got. It was certainly better than Spatterdock, a name Nighteyes had forbidden Rudder from naming any of their gryphlets.

The side effect of having a cool name was that the pride leader sent Desert Rose out to kill crocodiles until he lived up to it. Just another ninety-six before the name was made official.

Ninety-five if they could kill the saltwater crocodile circling back around for another attack. Enough time had passed since being severed from the murmuration that the stormtail trio were back in their hunting calm. Generally speaking, crocodiles thought of themselves as the reeves of the jungle. And, it was true, no gryphon wanted to go up against them. Unlike ghavials or caiman, they were nasty and ready to pick a fight with anyone.

The reptilian advantage of being an armored pair of teeth was greatly reduced when more than one stormtail was added to the mix. Crocodiles didn't work together and didn't have an easy way to flee. Gryphons did.

While Rudder and Desert Rose harried the crocodile from below, nipping at it with their beaks, Clamshell swam to the beach and shook the saltwater out of their feathers.

Once they were dry enough, Clamshell flew into the air, waiting for the crocodile to surface. When they saw the scales of its back, they dove down, spearing it behind the neck.

Rudder checked the area for any crocodiles they'd missed while the others pulled it up on the beach. When he got back, the weight of what had happened settled over him.

Desert Rose spoke up first. "I...can't feel either of you. I can't really smell anything at all. I need to find Whisper before I hurt someone."

"It's the same for me," Clamshell confirmed. "Not quite the way it was before, but I can't feel anyone else."

It made sense these two would think it was just them. When Rudder told them he, too, had lost the murmuration, their reaction was guilt.

"Did you catch it from us?" Desert Rose asked. "Whisper said we couldn't spread it. I'm so sorry. Look, she's creepy, but she fixes things like this. We should find her fast, before the pridelord catches on.

There's a spring we can use to get into Jadebeak lands."

Memories of entering the bog through faded glyphs cycled through Rudder's mind, and he needed to lie down for a moment until his head cleared. The practical part of him wanted to take the five crocodiles back to Lightningmaw. It was a lot of meat. The wounded animal in him wanted to take them and hide and see if he got better on his own.

Seeing two friends who had already gone through this got him back on his paws, and he groomed the salt out of his feathers. "I have a better idea. Whisper has a hidden path by the Grasslake Pathway, the one with the bad spatterdock. We can wait there."

THE TRIO of stormtails ran into a small problem at the start of their journey: the rest of their pride. For some reason, stormtails had taken to the skies, perhaps looking for them. Their pridemates' flying was certainly erratic.

"Do you think the pridelord ordered them to kill us?" Rudder asked. It had happened to several other stormtails who had found themselves outside the murmuration, and it was why Rudder had hurried to find Wendl when Clamshell started showing symptoms.

"Probably." Desert Rose had, smartly, insisted they eat one of the crocodiles before leaving so they wouldn't need to hunt in Jadebeak territory. "We should wait until night."

The agitated stormtails flying to and from Lightningmaw didn't relent, and the trio was forced to take the worst waterways to swim their way up north. The ones covered in leaves with water that tasted of tannin. Several times, they ran into gatherings of stormtails and had to backtrack, then work their way around.

"This is getting us nowhere," Clamshell said at last. "All of the rivers and lakes are full of stormtails, as are the skies. What if we hit the ocean, go west, then swim up one of the big rivers? Stormtails think to search water, but the other prides don't, and a lot of rivers combine around the temple. We're not part of the murmuration, we don't have to mind the glyphs."

I don't like the idea of being so close to the pridelord, Rudder thought, but it made sense. If the pridelord had their pride searching for them, he wouldn't expect them to move towards Jadebeak territory.

"What if they're looking for us to help?" Clamshell asked.

It was a possibility Rudder had wondered, too. "Then they'll take us to Whisper, right? It's the same end result, but if we're wrong, they might kill us. It's safer this way."

"It's a lot of swimming upstream." Clamshell ran a paw over their beak, cleaning their whiskers. "I'm sure I can do it, but you two? I dunno."

Desert Rose barked a challenge. "Spoken like a dry and itchy jadebeak! All right, let's see who gets tired first. To the ocean, then to Temple Run. We can use the rivers from there to reach Whisper. Wait, where did Rudder go?"

Rudder was already in the water, drifting to the ocean, as the others wriggled to catch up. This would be the easiest part of the journey, and he hoped to catch a nap before the freshwater turned to salt.

TEMPLE RUN WAS the combined tributaries of several rivers flowing from the pridelord's home to the Winter Jungle, and it was not an easy swim. The current was strong, but they dared not leave the safety of the water lest someone smell them. Rudder might not be able to sense other starlings, but he didn't trust that they couldn't detect him.

Thankfully, crocodiles rarely came up Temple Run, preferring the ocean, and other large reptiles tended to stick to the calmer pools formed during rainy seasons. At this point, it had been a few days, and they were forced to stop and hunt before they reached the Jadebeak Pride markers.

"I don't like this." Clamshell shook their head, spraying cool water everywhere. The jungle was rife with underground springs and rivers, several of which fed into Temple Run, making this section of the rapids downright frigid in places. "It's weird that it hit all of us at once. Something's wrong."

Desert Rose shrugged. "If worse comes to worst, we can hide in the bog. I only got caught because I was infected, and that happened because of the weird mummy. My plan to stick to fish and clams was a good one, overall."

Rudder wasn't ready to abandon the Emerald Jungle. He didn't want to abandon his pride, and he worried for Nighteyes. He enjoyed going to see her every autumn, spending time with her until spring.

He didn't want to leave that behind to eat clams in a stagnant bog with his two most obnoxious friends.

I love them, and I am impressed Desert Rose lasted a long time on his own. But add in Clamshell and me, and the bickering will probably bring the Ashen Weald down on us within a week.

They moved off Temple Run to catch carp in the side pools and take turns napping. It would be better to cross the center of Jadebeak territory at night, which meant they'd need to start swimming in the afternoon. Being so close to the border at night made Rudder nervous.

So nervous that after the naps, when faced with the glyph on the jadebeak border, he couldn't bring himself to cross it. "I'm, uh, having trouble here. Can someone else cross first?"

Neither Desert Rose nor Clamshell made a move.

"Friends?" Rudder prompted.

Clamshell held out a webbed paw but paused at the glyph on the tree. "It's not just you. I can't cross it."

"That means we're still connected to the murmuration, right?" Desert Rose ventured. "Otherwise, we'd be free to cross. It's like...we've lost all of the good parts of being a starling, but we still have the bad parts."

"What does that mean for our altruism if we head to the bog? Will we even be able to cross the glyphs to leave?" Rudder followed the border with the jadebeaks, taking it back east with his companions in tow. While the skies had been full of stormtails on their journey here, his pride usually stayed away from the border itself. Jadebeaks were ornery.

"I don't get it," Desert Rose said. "If the pridelord

knows where we are enough to stop us from crossing the border, why doesn't he just come get us?"

Clamshell cleaned their whiskers, a common stress response for stormtails. "Do we really want that? He killed most of the other stormtails like us."

"Of course not, but it feels like he's just playing with us." Desert Rose reached down, picking up a good clamming rock in his long beak, and flung it at a glyph, breaking off most of the pattern. Despite the lack of visual marker, he couldn't cross.

Rudder tried to replicate the act. "I can't *smell* the glyph, but I can't cross it, either. I think we need a new plan."

"There's still the river that connects to Greenscale Springs. That'll get us across, unless it's been re-glyphed," Desert Rose suggested. "We shouldn't run into any stormtails along the border."

That's true, Rudder thought. *But what about jadebeaks?*

The foliage beyond the glyphs was vague in a way he'd seen before, where Nighteyes had found Whisper. It was like the Stormtail territory was the Emerald Jungle and the Jadebeak territory was the outside world.

Oh, no, it's like the opposite. Rudder didn't like that thought, not at all. Suddenly, his coastal home felt like a prison. *What if we follow this all the way to the Jadebeak Mountains, then find we're closed in?*

It was one thing to live somewhere because he wanted to, it was something else to be forced to. There was no reason to think that was the case, but once he'd had the thought, his brain wouldn't let it go.

"Everything okay?" Desert Rose asked.

Rudder decided not to tell them what was on his mind. "Yeah, let's keep going, find that spring of yours."

The trio continued their journey, though he couldn't shake the feeling he was being watched from the other side of the glyphs.

RUDDER, Clamshell, and Desert Rose reached the point on the Stormtail territory where Greenscale Springs came out, but there were new glyphs here.

This was particularly odious to Desert Rose because the new glyphs were on the Stormtail side of the border. "That's my favorite spring! They can't just put glyphs on our territory. There are rules about prides and territory."

"What now?" Clamshell changed the topic. "Do we continue to the Jadebeak Mountains, or do we return to Lightningmaw?"

They both looked to Rudder, who had no idea. He'd led the crocodile hunt, and so they'd continued to leave him in charge. He had a bad feeling about returning to Lightningmaw. He had a worse feeling about the Jadebeak Mountains.

"Let's go back," he said at last. "If the skies look clear, we'll try to get a read on Lightningmaw. If things look dicey, we'll search for some islands. There's no way to close us off from those, right?"

Clamshell agreed islands were preferable to living in the bog. Desert Rose protested, apparently enjoying the bog, but wanted to stay with the other two.

They were searching out a good tributary for sneaking south when the smell of smoke reached them.

"What's that?" Clamshell stood up on their back legs. "A forest fire? In the jungle?"

It was nice to smell anything, even if it took something as pungent as smoke to get through to Rudder's nares. He inhaled, trying to train his brain to remember how to smell again. It did not oblige.

"Now's our chance to head to Lightningmaw," Desert Rose said. "It won't be in any danger, but smoke will draw out the others. They'll want to help."

Already, in the air, Rudder could see the distant shapes of his pridemates rushing off to the source of the fire. They reached the edge of Stormtail territory and stopped, one nearly falling to the ground after becoming disoriented by the border.

It's not just us. Rudder took to the sky, shouting behind him, "We need to help them. They're disconnected, too!"

The pride was west of their current position. Fifty stormtails stopped at the border, disoriented, and landed. Rudder longed to be with them, feeling foolish for not going back earlier.

"It's all of us," he barked to his friends. "We'll be okay if it's all of us, right? We can live happily as a pride, even if we can't leave the coast."

"Rudder!" Clamshell called after him. "Rudder, that's not a good thing!"

Rudder ignored the worry in their words, pushing onwards, flying as fast as his wings could take him. Swimming was one of his top two favorite activities, but he'd missed flying. All this skulking around was silly, leave that to the newmoons. He'd reunite with his pridemates, and they could leave and find an island together.

A glimpse of something white and silver appeared in the sky, then a rain of sparkling objects fell upon the fifty stormtails milling about at the border.

The screams snapped him out of his daydreaming. He landed to find his pridemates with small, glistening bits of metal embedded into them. He worried they were dead, but when he put a paw on the pride leader's chest, he could tell she was still breathing. He reached to pull the metal out of her, but Clamshell grabbed his tail and pulled him back.

"Stay back," they said. "It must be poison."

Desert Rose looked up at the sky. "I saw something, before the poison rain. It looked like...Oh! That!"

The trio dove for cover, landing under an old lightning-felled broadleaf. The sound of sharp metal hitting the trunk echoed like heavy drops of rain.

Rudder looked out from their hiding spot, and he was greeted by the sight of a force of opinici crossing the border.

Outsiders? Here? But...how?

He didn't have to wait for his answer. At the head of the party was a starling in restraints, though no one held his leash. Seeing a gryphon wearing anything was strange, but seeing one in restraints was even stranger. Without access to his scent library, he couldn't place them.

An opinicus wearing shiny rock armor stepped into view. At least, he looked like an opinicus when it was just his head poking through the strange glyph veil. When the rest of his body came through, Rudder had no idea what he was.

"That's what the mummy must have looked like when it was alive," Desert Rose whispered. "The witches called it a mummified *opinithing*."

The opinithing spoke with a voice that resonated. "Our guide seems fine even this deep. I suppose the Nighthaunt's elixirs are working. Remove his hood but leave the bindings in case that changes."

Two ducks came forwards and removed the hood, revealing the starling beneath.

"Who's that?" Desert Rose asked. "A jadebeak?"

"Kism," Clamshell replied. "In the winter, I sometimes hunted mussels with his pride along the edge of the Winter Jungle. I'd peel them off the trees and fling them over the border. He doesn't look like the rest of his pride."

But Kism did look like someone else Rudder knew. Without scents to depend upon, he looked at Kism and saw Wendl's face. Not just Wendl, but also the jadebeak pride leader, Iri.

Something was wrong, but Rudder couldn't put his tail on what was bothering him. The opinithing ordered the others around. Teams of ducks and peafowl appeared and disappeared across the border, pulling unconscious stormtails behind them. Every so often, he caught a glimpse of a single great blue heron with a fishy badge.

"We need to warn Lightningmaw," Desert Rose whispered.

Rudder was about to agree, when Kism sniffed the air loudly, then turned and looked right at their hiding spot. His worries about other starlings still being able to detect them were confirmed.

"He's here, the other one the Nighthaunt needs." Kism inhaled again, then looked right at where Rudder was hiding. "Dark blue, called Rudder. Get him!"

A peafowl in black with long talons slashed at the bushes, but Rudder had already turned and started fleeing, diving into a fast-moving current heading into the heart of the perpetual storm, Desert Rose and Clamshell right behind him.

49

LIGHTNINGMAW

When it came to hurricanes, the *eye* referred to an area of relative calm where one half of the storm had passed, and the other half was yet to come.

Lightningmaw was the exact opposite of that. For reasons unknown to Rudder, the air currents coming off the Jadebeak Mountains and the Emerald Jungle collided over a large lake, swirled together, and created a lightning storm that only disappeared in winter.

There were many stories of how Lightningmaw and the Winter Jungle were linked, but they were mostly silly tales to tell while eating clams. Even in Rudder's lifetime, there'd been years when Lightningmaw's storm had lasted weeks longer than usual, but the Winter Jungle had already dried out.

Still, there was something comforting about swimming through the swift moving currents and into the nesting grounds where he'd hatched, even if he was here to tell them to flee.

"Rudder!" one of the gryphlets shouted from atop the egg stone, a large oval-shaped stone sticking out of the damp island in the middle of Lightningmaw. She was in that awkward phase where she wasn't quite a fledgling yet, but her tailfeathers were starting to grow through her long tail, and she chewed at it constantly. "I heard you were eaten by a crocodile!"

"I saved him," Desert Rose replied. "The crocodile had already eaten him, so I swam inside, fetched him, then swam out."

Clamshell continued the story. "Then they were both eaten by an even bigger crocodile, and I had to save them both."

As Clamshell led the gryphlet away, Rudder asked Desert Rose what that was about.

"The little floodlings panic easily," Desert Rose explained. "If we're going to get them out of here, we can't have them hiding. I'll speak to the denparents, see if we can move them somewhere safe."

Rudder was ashamed he hadn't thought of that. "Underwater, though. Kism will sniff them out otherwise. You need to get them as far from here as you can, but not on land."

"Are you sure? Once you get offshore, there's no storm to hide them from a flying opinicus or...whatever their leader was." Desert Rose barked at some of the gryphons napping in their nests, telling them to rouse the others. Another advantage of getting the gryphlets underwater was that their squeaks wouldn't be overheard.

"I'm sure." Rudder searched around, seeing that it was mostly wounded here. Everyone healthy had rushed to stop the *forest fire*, if there'd even been one.

He gathered all the adults he could find at the far side, out of hearing from the gryphlets. "There's opinici coming here, and they've got poison. They captured the others. We were nearly to them when it happened. I think our best bet is if we all flee in different directions while someone hides in the coves east of here with the gryphlets."

"Why not have the floodlings spread out, too?" an old barker asked. "We could each take one. They're good at hiding."

Rudder remembered to show deference in his answer. "Because they're good at hiding for an hour tops, and I think they may need to hide for days. I *hope* these outsiders will leave quickly, but I'm not going to count on it."

"The storm will hide their barks. Muffle their scents enough to stop an opinicus, too," one of the wounded said.

"They've got a starling sniffing us out for them." Rudder watched the others deflate. "He's a drypaw from a western pride, so the storm will slow him, but he was able to detect me from a good distance away. I worry that if we spread out with gryphlets, they'll search until they find everyone."

An idea came to him while the others were here. The outsiders already had the healthiest of the gryphons. The opinithing had said they wanted Rudder in particular. If he went in one direction while the gryphlets went to the cove near the mountains, would the opinithing's forces follow him?

The catch was he'd have to buy enough time for it to work. If everyone spread out, the opinici would search the entire coast, and they might find the gryphlets.

He couldn't find the words to ask the wounded and elderly to fight, but the old barker did it for him.

"I think we should stay, form a distraction. Lightningmaw is a scary place to outsiders," the greyfeather said. "If we concentrate them here, that'll keep them from searching until the floodlings are safe."

Rudder cleaned his whiskers in agitation. "There's something that's not a gryphon or opinicus with them, and it's in charge. It told Kism, the sniffer, they needed to capture me alive. When it looks like we've lost, I'll fly west to buy the gryphlets more time."

The wounded, the elderly, and a few gryphons who had just stayed behind to nap found hiding places, preparing for the attack. Rudder approached Clamshell and Desert Rose, walking them through a few possibilities.

"I'll explain the plan to the denparents," Clamshell said. "You should go with them, Desert Rose, in case they need to cross into Ashen Weald territory."

Desert Rose shook his head. "They won't be able to. Some of the hunters tried it while we were playing tail-chase around our borders the past few days. We're trapped in here. Whatever the glyph says, they didn't get far enough south to cross it. You know the coves better than me, it should be you or Rudder."

Rudder, lost in thought, looked at them. "About that. I need to stay, because I think they're chasing me, though I don't know why. I leave the gryphlets in your capable paws, Clamshell. You should all swim there if you can, don't leave a scent trail for Kism. I'll fly as far west as I can go, into the Winter Jungle. Hopefully, that buys enough time."

Clamshell left with the denparents, careful to remain cheerful around the floodlings, who departed with them. Anyone older and healthy had already been captured or was absent.

Hopefully, they stay hidden.

Desert Rose looked north, but the storms hid the sky. "How is this possible? How could the pridelord let this happen? They're not coming across the mountains or from the ocean. They're coming from Jadebeak territory, but the jadebeaks aren't attacking them."

"Something's wrong," Rudder agreed. "I don't know what, but maybe all the other starlings are gone, or dead. Either way, we don't have time to find out. We've weathered a lot of storms in our time. This is just one more."

"A storm of poisoned stone." Desert Rose looked out at the gryphons meant to defend the nesting grounds and his whiskers drooped. Rudder couldn't blame him. He didn't know what would happen to the poisoned stormtails, but the gryphons here may be better off dead than captured.

RUDDER DIDN'T BELIEVE in spirits the way other prides did. Where a sparkwing might stare up at the sky ocean and dream of spirits looking down, stormtails looked up and saw lightning. They didn't need the ocean of stars, as they had the actual ocean.

The closest he got to stargazing was when he looked into Night's eyes, and he reminded himself that her stars were scars. He would leave thoughts of the afterlife to drypaws. Thus, he was rather surprised that Desert Rose believed.

"The sky is on our side," his friend said, emphasizing sky in a way that did not mean air.

Still, it also worked in a literal sense. The storm above Lightningmaw intensified, a near-constant rumble of thunder making it hard to hear the barks of the defenders. Black clouds turned day to night, while lightning blinded anyone looking in and filled their nares with ozone, hopefully protecting them from Kism.

Lightning struck four times in quick succession, leaving Rudder with the afterimage of a small number of gryphons working hard. The wounded worked like crabs, digging holes in the mud across the pridegrounds, a mix of shallow and deep, to give them hiding spots. A team of five healthy gryphons pulled fallen spiketrunks up to the lake overlooking the nesting grounds.

When Lake Notagain was but a young puddle, it had probably sported a much fancier name. Where many starling prides hunted during the winter season, stormtails took advantage of the clear skies to build dams during the dry season.

The dams were simple things. Fallen broadleaf trees, rotting leaves, mud from particularly gooey springs. While Lightningmaw would never be dry, they didn't want it to wash away, either. These dams redirected the water to a lake and then around their home. Nighteyes had joked that it didn't work, she was always up to her ankles in water, but *without* the dams, she would have been up to her tail in it.

Over time, the mud and leaves cemented trees into place. But the new dams were fragile and sometimes needed a few rounds of repairs in the wet season. In fact, the pride leader had been complaining that one of the larger dams was fragile and a safety hazard if it gave way.

So yes, perhaps it had once been called Bounty of Fish or Sparkwater. But the tendency of the dams to break and flood the nests once or twice a year was where Lake *Not Again* got its name from. For all the trouble it had given stormtails over the years, its penance was that it would now direct its mischievous ire towards the outsiders. Behind the fragile part of the dam, the healthiest gryphons had secured the nastiest, pointiest fallen spiketrunks.

"It's not enough," Desert Rose said. "The outsiders have their own tricks, and we don't know their numbers or motives. We've spent too long making our home safe to suddenly turn around and make it dangerous now."

Rudder preened Desert Rose's face. "The fact we've had to make it safe to live here is why we can defend it: we know how to make it dangerous again. If things get too bad, take the others and flee directly south. I hear drypaws get nervous over deep water."

Lightning struck all around the pridegrounds, and once again he was grateful for Wendl's lightning rods. Several of the old barkers had red, fern-shaped scarring from electric strikes, something much rarer these days.

Wendl's lightning rods!

"Say," Rudder began. "What happens if we chew down the lightning rods?"

Desert Rose's eyes widened with excitement. "I don't know, but we'll find out!"

Rudder knew better than to wish them good luck, but he hoped they'd be smart about it. Between strikes, he heard the sound of the metallic lighting rods falling over. As the last one fell, and the lightning began to strike new locations, he caught sight of opinici following the riverbank in their direction.

He barked a warning, and his pride fled to their hiding spots.

THE FIRST TEAM of white-tailed kites to enter Lightningmaw came by ground, smart enough not to fly through the storm itself. To Rudder, they looked like elite warriors, champions of their pride. They moved as a group, protecting each other and watching behind them. It was only when they reached the heart of the nesting grounds that they relaxed a little in their confusion at the lack of resistance.

They stood in the center of Lightningmaw, the flat nesting grounds usually covered by broadleafs, and were in deep conversation about what to do next when lightning struck. As Wendl had often explained, lightning was hungry for shiny rocks. Whenever an opinicus expedition left behind any of what she called *metals*, she brought it down south and set up a new lightning rod.

These stupid opinici had made their armor of it,

and Lightningmaw devoured them whole. They lit up like lightning bugs, then exploded.

The enemy's second set of forces, mostly mallards, were just coming down from the direction of Lake Notagain when it happened. They froze, stripped off their armor, and then backed away slowly, afraid to anger the storm.

This bought the stormtails a period of reprieve, though they didn't dare leave their hiding spots. Every so often, they'd hear screams from inside the jungle. Where they were paired with lightning strikes, it was obvious what had happened. Some poor bird hadn't learned not to be the tallest thing in a clearing. Where there was no lightning, Rudder assumed Desert Rose or one of his pride had caught someone off guard.

I never thought I'd wish for more crocodiles around Lightningmaw, but they'd sure be useful about now.

While Desert Rose had been smart enough to hide Wendl's lightning rods, some of the outsiders were located where the poles had been situated, and in time, they brought their own metal and set them up again.

The opinici were cautious. They took their time and didn't seem worried the murmuration might return at any moment. Only once a full hour had passed without any strikes on Lightningmaw itself did the next team of outsiders arrive. These were peafowl, and they wore leather armor and long, wooden claws.

The leather armor looked borrowed from stable-talons, and the wooden claws' original purpose seemed to be as a training weapon, though they'd spent the hour sharpening them to a point. The lightning didn't strike the peafowl, and they grew confident. They started destroying the nests, including the rocky outcropping that kept eggs off the ground, thankfully free of their prize.

A black peafowl whose feather dye was running stumbled through some of the puddles in his haste to stomp on the ruins of the last shelter. He scoffed at the nests. "Looks like they turned tail and fled. Hi-kun will be angry. We have Sheen, but it might not be enough to save the Nighthaunt. We need this *Rudder*, too."

As he spoke, his tailfeathers rested over one of the deeper pools. Just beneath the surface, Rudder listened to the peafowl's speech and decided if they waited much longer, someone might detect their hiding spots.

He leapt from the water, catching the opinicus's thin neck in his long beak, and pulled his opponent's face underwater. The peacock struggled, but his wooden claws were caught in the mud. The rest of the Stormtail Pride attacked, latching onto the peafowl and drowning them, all except Desert Rose, who was hidden farther north.

"If they keep coming in with small teams, we might win this," an old barker said.

Unfortunately, the next set of forces were already on their way. Standing atop the riverbank at the edge of the nesting grounds, their leader watched the proceedings.

Hi-kun.

Rudder preened his feathers. "This is it. See the long one? If you get a chance to kill him, take it."

He barked to Desert Rose. With the intensity of

the storm, there was no way of knowing if his friend heard him, but Rudder hoped for the best.

The stormtails didn't flee this time. Instead, they held their ground as a mix of white-tailed kites, peafowl, and mallards descended upon them. The opinithing remained back, though he'd smartly removed his shiny rock armor.

In a one-on-one fight, the army had the advantage. The stormtails fought fiercely, but once they started dying, Rudder barked a final order to Desert Rose, and the newest segment of the dam collapsed, sending twenty fallen spiketrunks and a wave five gryphons high crashing down upon the nesting grounds.

The stormtails dove into their deep puddle hiding spots, clinging to stone, seaweed, wood, or whatever they could latch onto while the wave came overhead.

Once the wave—and spiketrunk logs—passed, Rudder swam up, letting the rest of the water push him out of the nesting grounds, latching onto a tree and preening his feathers from soaked to damp as quickly as he could.

The wave had hit like lightning and passed like thunder, but before the nesting grounds dried out, the opinithing landed atop the egg stone in the center.

He made no sounds, the way a crocodile has no dialogue with a rhea who has come to its lake for a drink. Rudder leapt off his tree and flew west, Hi-kun in fast pursuit.

50

HI-KUN THE SKY CROCODILE

Rudder was a gryphon who prided himself on his ability to run away. It was what separated stormtails from crocodiles, after all. They knew when to flee and return with greater numbers. While a stormtail could take a comparable-sized crocodile in a one-on-one fight, most crocodiles were larger than stormtails.

Unfortunately for him, not only was the many-winged *crocodile* chasing him larger than he was, it probably still had friends left. The only advantage Rudder had over Hi-kun the Sky Crocodile was that he knew this territory well and could fly in a storm.

He flew over alarmed mallards and a pawful of osprey opinici, his opponent right behind him. He tried to lure Hi-kun near the lightning rods without luck. When the rains came down harder, the sky crocodile vanished entirely, rising above the storm.

Well, that's no good. I can't lure them away if they aren't following. Although...

The Stormtail Pride often said a good plan that

definitely won't work wasn't nearly as useful as a terrible plan that could possibly work. If the sky crocodile was above the clouds and expected Rudder to go west, and Rudder's allies who were hopefully escaping had gone south or east, there was always the direction the opinici had come from.

How many troops can they still have up by the jadebeak border? A few? A dozen, tops?

He changed direction and headed north. He didn't know what he'd do when he hit the jadebeak border, but he thought he might survive longer than if he continued west where Hi-kun was surely waiting in the skies to swoop down and grab him like a fish.

He did not want to be a fish.

Rudder finally broke free of Lightningmaw's perpetual storm, the rains fading to moody clouds and finally sun. He flew north from the coast, towards the jungle proper, a raincloud in his own right, shedding stormwater as he flew.

Fortunately, Hi-kun was not there to catch him like a fish.

Unfortunately, the bad plan was bad, and twenty white-tailed kites were guarding a set of cages filled with his pridemates. The pride leader's body, covered in blood, lay unmoving nearby, and his heart ached to see her like that. A blue heron of sorts was guarding vials of poison, perhaps what was used on the light metal they dropped from the sky, with Kism next to her.

Maybe they won't notice me?

Rudder didn't think he was pungent, but Kism's head snapped up the moment he flew over.

"There, that's the one! That's Rudder!" the traitor shouted.

Rudder's body recoiled from the northern border, refusing to let him fly over it. He resisted the urge to fly east, to the Jadebeak Mountains. He had a sunbaked plan to skim the border with the Ashen Weald and perhaps lure some of the funny drypaws from the bog over.

If we're going to have a party here in the Emerald Jungle, we may as well invite everyone.

But if that plan failed, he'd be leading them towards where the gryphlets were hiding. The white-tailed kites were starting to rise up, and before he could switch to going west to try to reach the Winter Jungle, the sky crocodile crashed down on him from above.

I'm the fish after all.

A BLOW from above by an obviously skilled flyer like Hi-kun should have killed Rudder, but thankfully, they wanted him alive for some reason. Instead of wicked claws rending his flesh, a closed talon hit him across the face, and while he was disoriented, one pair of wings wrapped themselves around him and forced him to the ground, knocking the air out of his lungs.

"Stupid sky crocodile," Rudder mumbled between gasps, earning him a confused look. The blow to his head must have knocked something loose, because he could see past the Emerald Veil for a moment.

Drypaws always looked at the ground or the trees,

sometimes at the sky. Rudder would happily concede if he'd looked up, perhaps he'd have seen the opinithing sneaking up on him and wouldn't currently be face-down in the mud at the moment.

He squirmed a little, managing to move his head before Hi-kun's talons tightened.

Unlike drypaws, stormtails looked to the water. He'd learned to see the signs of crocodiles and ghavials. When the rare snowstorm hit, they'd stick their little noses above the water. But knowing the difference between carp ripples and crocodile ripples was the difference between eating and being eaten.

Thus, though the jadebeak lands and skies looked normal, the only thing Rudder saw was a large shape lurking beneath the Grasslake Pathway running past the outsider's makeshift camp.

"That's a large crocodile," he mumbled, then looked at Hi-kun. "Not you."

"Metalworks," the blue heron began, "would you like me to knock this one out, too? The pink reeve sent us more than enough jelly toxin."

Hi-kun the Metalworks looked down from his tall neck. "No, we can't risk an allergic reaction."

The nearby opinici all turned to look at the stormtail pride leader's prone body, and Rudder refused to consider what that meant.

"Is the Nighthaunt really that important?" Kism asked. "Wouldn't it be better if he were gone?"

The voice of a jadebeak helping the opinici sparked a frisson of disgust in Rudder. It was the same feeling he got the first time he'd seen the silver-eyed, infected corpse of a dead starling. He moved his head to get a better look, and Kism looked comically small next to Hi-kun and the great blue heron. For all his pompous tone, he was a squirrel trapped between two gryphlets, unaware they kept him alive just to play with him.

Nor did his comment help. Even dazed, Rudder could tell that was the wrong thing to say by the way the other Alabasters glared at the jadebeak.

Though the Emerald Veil had returned, the water not-crocodile had passed through it now. He crawled on his belly, coated in spatterdock, approaching the camp from the north, where they didn't expect a stormtail to come from. The gryphtail reeds were long enough to hide even his massive form.

Just how're you doing that, old friend? Rudder wondered.

"The Nighthaunt has earned his treatment." Hi-kun's tone was flat. "But even had he passed, we'll need these to treat the outbreak of bloodbeak. We can mix it with seraph blood and continue uplifting the chicks and fledglings."

Rudder didn't know what *uplift* meant. He twitched his tail, trying to get the pride leader's attention, but she didn't move. He waited thirty seconds but never saw her chest rise or fall, and then he knew the truth. The others were still in cages with long strips of heavy leather attached to the top, enough for four opinici to fly them away. Apparently, there were too few metal cages, and they'd been forced to build flimsier wooden ones to hold half of the prisoners.

"I think we're done here," Hi-kun said at last. "We have the two Mally wanted. We have extras for him to test. Wrap up 'Rudder' here and let's—"

The Gourmand pounced, nearly snapping Hi-kun

in two, but the opinithing—*seraph?*—was too fast. Two pair of functional wings lifted him into the air while the large gryphon slammed his muscular tail down, crushing the blue heron mixologist.

"Rudder," the beast growled. "Flee north."

Rudder stood, putting a cage between himself and the nearest alabasters. "Can't, old buddy. My brain won't let me."

"Garrumph," the Gourmand replied, a word Rudder had never been quite clear on the meaning of. "The little strawberry has a bit of elixir left. Call for her when you can't move any farther."

Rudder didn't know what that meant, but he figured it would make sense when he got there. While the Gourmand smashed the wooden cages with his tail and plowed through white-tailed kites like a crocodile through a flock of rhea, Rudder ran north shouting "Strawberry, strawberry!" until something happened.

That something was a little red starling who shoved a glass vial into his beak, then shoved her paw in after it, shouting: "Wait, you can't eat the glass!"

She got her paw and the glass out, and when he gagged, she wrapped her paws around his beak to keep it closed. He tasted something bitter, but it didn't have an immediate effect.

"Please let go of my beak," he mumbled.

"Sorry!" she said. "I'm Flicker. I'm here with the Gourmand to help him save the stormtails. I'm not great at fighting. I'm more of a gardener."

The Emerald Veil lifted, and he could finally see beyond it. He could flee north, so long as the elixir lasted. Behind him, however, were fifty of his pride, drugged and in the unbreakable metal cages.

I'm not going anywhere.

He hurried back to help the Gourmand, Flicker shouting after him that he was fleeing in the wrong direction. The blue heron, somehow still alive, had thrown a small net over the monster stormtail, and the alabasters were scrambling to put on metal talons.

Kism ran for the bottles of jelly toxin, and while Rudder wasn't sure anything could stop the Gourmand, poison might. Rudder caught Kism by the tail, pulling him away.

"You stupid stormtail!" Kism screamed, which felt like a rude thing to say during a battle.

Rudder crouched low. Against Hi-kun, he didn't have much of an advantage out of the water. But he felt pretty good about his odds fighting a jadebeak.

The traitor realized his mistake and backed up. "Hey, Rudder was it? I've heard Balthar talk about you. You know Balthar, right?"

Rudder did not. He had a hard time remembering any jadebeak now that he couldn't smell them. But he did recognize someone trying to trick him.

He pounced before Kism could reach the bottles of poison, twisting his entire body to fling the jadebeak away. Kism crashed into a metal cage, attracting the attention of the Gourmand.

If Rudder could take Kism in a fight, the Gourmand could swallow him whole. Kism obviously felt the same way, and before the Gourmand's crocodile-length beak could snap him in two, Kism closed the cage door with himself inside.

Huh.

"Open the metal cages," the Gourmand ordered Flicker and Rudder. "I will hold them off and break the remaining wooden ones."

One of the white-tailed kites had escaped towards the storm, calling for help. Rudder grabbed a cage with his paws, trying pry the bars apart without success. He tried to wedge his beak between them, but they didn't budge. His unconscious pridemates snored quietly, similarly imprisoned in unconsciousness by the jelly toxin.

Rudder turned to the strawberry. "Surely they have a way to get the cages open again later, right? Do you have any idea?"

"Oh!" Flicker said. "Wendl showed me how. There's this little bit of metal, and you put it in the... uh...hole part. The lock. It's called a key!"

Flicker searched the crates and table where the poison was kept while Rudder rifled through the harnesses on the alabasters. Both came up empty.

"Garrumph," the Gourmand exhaled, causing both of them to look south. The peafowl and mallards were coming back to camp.

Rudder ran to Kism's cage. He tried to poke the traitor, but the bars were too close together. "Hey! Where's the key?"

"What's a key?" Kism asked.

Even without access to pheromones, Rudder was pretty sure Kism was lying. He tried to stab again, and then he saw it: the shiny metal thing hanging from Kism's harness.

"Toss that here!" he ordered, but Kism just laughed.

Rudder's mind raced like floodwaters. Kism had

the key inside a cage. They couldn't reach Kism to stab him or get the key. If they waited, the outsiders would reach them.

For once, he found himself at a loss. He had no idea what to do. Three mallards attacked the Gourmand, slashing at him with their metal talons and their weird foot spikes. By the time they disengaged, two were dead, but the third's talons dripped blood, and the Gourmand was slowing.

Rudder turned to Flicker. "I need to help our friend. Can you figure out the cages on your own?"

"No!" she replied. "I need Wendl for this."

When Flicker spoke, the air was punctuated by her scent. The elixir she'd given him had weakened the pridelord's grip enough that he could just barely sense other starlings again. Her fruity scent, Kism's nutty smell, and the aroma of mallow root.

Mallow root?

Flicker let out a cheer, and from a strip of spiketrunks nearby, a stream of black starlings flew out of the woods to the Gourmand's aid, their silver eyes sparkling in the last light of day. Their leader, Whisper, landed in front of him and put her paw on his face.

"Come back to us." She removed her paw, and citrus flooded into Rudder.

Flicker's elixir had dulled his senses, but he was suddenly aware of the stormtails in the cages, each member of the Newmoon Pride, Flicker, Wendl, and even Sheen hiding in the spiked grove. With it came the knowledge of what had passed since the territory was closed off.

"Whoa." He tried to inquire about Nighteyes, but

everyone was busy chasing off the outsiders. His head still swam, so he went to check on Sheen, who hung back with her wounded paw. Included in the information was the fact Wendl had taken his blood to save this single Nightsky fledgling.

"Hey," was all he managed before he found himself at a loss of words. What could he say to someone who was saved because of something stolen from him? Theirs was a strange relationship, in the sense that there was no direct line from Sheen to Rudder except by blood.

But he knew how important Sheen was to Nighteyes. He knew how much the gryphon he loved in turn loved this fledgling. He thought of his memories of Nighteyes and turned them into scent form.

Sheen nodded in agreement.

Wendl and Flicker were having a different moment, something about a lost key. The red starling took it and flew off, leaving a weakened Wendl in the spike grove.

"What happened to you?" he asked her.

She looked up. "Did Whisper not share that with you, too? I suspect we'll all know each other's secrets if nobody teaches her discretion. You look like you're doing better than I am, can you help me over to the cages? Flicker's terrible with her paws. It'll take her an hour per cage to get everyone out."

He didn't like to part ways with Sheen, but most of his caged pride had only superficial wounds. If they could wake them up from the toxin-fueled sleep, they could join the fight.

Rudder ran behind Wendl, then slipped underneath her, lifting the opinicus onto his back and balancing her between his wings.

"Oh!" Wendl laughed. "That's not what I expected. I feel like a sack of potatoes."

"Potatoes?" he asked, and he was greeted with the scent of something savory, fluffy, and filling. "I should like to hunt a potato someday."

Once he started running, Wendl held on tight. Most starlings had small, compact bodies that didn't know how to wiggle as they ran. It's why they were bad swimmers—no wriggle, no swimmle, as the denparents taught floodlings.

Rudder had excellent wiggle, which his rider showed her appreciation for by clinging to him for dear life. He dropped her off by Whisper, who had used a strong scent to try and rouse the unconscious stormtails through the bars without success. Between her, Flicker, and Wendl, they freed the rest of the stormtails, going cage to cage until they reached the peculiar prisoner.

"Not him." Whisper stared into Kism's eyes. "Leave him in the cage. I will decide what to do with Moonlit Blossom's killer later."

Kism, who had seemed certain the reinforcements from inside the storm would save him when he first entered the cage, looked less sure now.

The Gourmand collapsed, filling the air with the pheromones of exhaustion. The newmoon gryphons had chased the rest of the outsiders back into the storm, but then retreated, unwilling to get wet.

With Whisper's help, the caged stormtails were back on their feet, though they milled around their leader's dead body.

There'll be time for grief later, Rudder thought. *We need to catch the remaining outsiders before they can flee.*

He turned to Whisper. "We'll take it from here. Thank you for your help. Once you finish, come meet me at the nesting grounds and we'll talk about what to do next."

Whisper, as dry and dusty a gryphon as had ever set paw in their territory, replied with a terse, "No."

"Afraid to get wet?" Flicker asked.

"No," Whisper repeated. "Well, yes. All three times I have nearly died it was because I was clean. But now that you're safe, we must head northeast. The murmuration needs us."

Rudder looked away. "Does it? They seemed happy to cast us away days ago."

"That wasn't the pridelord," Wendl explained. "It was Balthar. He quarantined your pride so Hi-kun could come collect you once the jungle was empty."

"How're we supposed to save the murmuration?" Flicker asked. "It's very big and we're relatively few in number."

Whisper licked a paw and used it to groom Flicker's face, a very personal gesture outside of mating season. "Wendl and Nighteyes' original plan. We kill the pridelord."

"I'm in," Rudder said before his pride could reject the idea outright. "Nighteyes and the rest of our friends are going to die if we don't do something. Win or lose, the Seraph King isn't gonna want the murmuration around. Two of the smaller prides just kicked his tail. He'll order them to fly over the ocean until they collapse and drown, or he'll poison them in their sleep. We have to do this. Just let me clear out the shore and give word to Desert Rose and Clamshell."

With his piece said, he turned and left. The waking stormtails were tracking down the last of the invaders. Whisper and Wendl would figure out the details of their trip to wherever the murmuration had gone. He was just happy that, against all odds, he'd managed to defend Lightningmaw. The stormtails owed Whisper, Flicker, and Wendl a great debt.

All he wanted now was to catch a fish and take a nap, but first he needed to make sure his friends were fine. Unfortunately, as soon as he was away from the safety of the others, a shadow appeared in the sky. The shape was so strange, the flashes of sunlight against it so bright, he couldn't tell what he was seeing. His ears perked up with curiosity as his hackles raised of their own accord, aware of what was coming before his conscious mind figured it out.

A meteor with four wings crashed into him. In one talon, a small flechette with the jelly toxin on it was driven into his chest, the warning about allergic reactions no longer holding sway.

As consciousness left him, Rudder felt himself being pulled into the air, the opinithing carrying him to King's Reach before anyone even realized he'd been captured.

I'm the fish again.

51

MOTHFEATHER

After the pridelord's collapse and temporary loss of control of the prides, their pace slowed over the plains and forests east of Blacktalon. Nighteyes felt like a locust moving from field to field, consuming any crops that weren't locked down. Most of the places they arrived at were hastily abandoned but smelled of their recent occupants, but not all. The first exception came when they arrived at an abandoned eyrie.

Long needlegrasses, their tufted tops raised six feet in the air like the tails of saberbeaks, grew along the goliath bird trail, shrouding much of it from view. Abandoned dwellings clung to the trail, and the starlings devoured anything edible left behind.

The migration was now a crawl, and wherever the farms were plentiful, the murmuration paused so their leader could rest. When the pridelord recuperated, the various prides spread out. Jadebeaks chewed on flaxseed plants topped with blue flowers and the verdant sprouts of various sages. Talli's pride rolled in fleabane, which was supposed to have medicinal properties, though Wendl had always turned her beak up at such folk remedies.

The Nightsky Pride was particularly interested in the fringed sagebrush, rolling around on it, crushing the small green growths beneath. To Nighteyes, it smelled of Sheen, left behind in the jungle, and she wondered if her pride's behavior was their way of showing they missed her, too. Nearby, a sparkwing nearby choked on last year's bee plant: dry, dead, and already picked clean by birds. He eventually took the hint and found a saltbrush to lick instead.

The farm density grew heavier and heavier leading up to the next city. From the sky, the dry eyrie resembled the bog pride's sunken home—farm terraces like steps, going down into the ground, as though someone had built their nests in a sinkhole. Nighteyes wanted a chance to explore while the pridelord slept, but she was ravenous. Thankfully, her time with the Ashen Weald had taught her a thing or two about ranches and opinical ways.

While the other prides explored empty storehouses, she roamed farther. When she heard the *mronk*s of a proper, if abandoned, goliath ranch, she signalled her pride. She felt sorry for the birds, but they filled her stomach with little effort and gave her time to explore.

The pridelord's sleep here was shallower than before. Perhaps he was just being careful, or perhaps some of the starlings had escaped at Blacktalon. The latter thought was worrying. With their altruism, she didn't think they'd fare well in these lands. They wouldn't even know how to reach home again.

Most of the murmuration avoided the eyrie, letting Nighteyes explore it unobserved. Not because they feared it, just because it didn't smell like food. The heavy stone buildings were dusty, sunbaked, and abandoned. When she walked past boarded up homes, she left footprints in the white chalk. She'd seen similar along the Jadebeak Mountains, light grey powder left behind after the snow melted.

Do they get snow here? It's cooled down considerably since Blacktalon. Even the jungle gets snow from time to time. I'll bet nobody has walked these halls since midwinter at the earliest.

Up near the trails, above the ground eyrie, she saw a stone stable with walls around it to direct goliath traffic. That one had been boarded up recently and smelled like blackwings. She left it alone, not wanting to disturb its occupants. She also didn't trust her own ability to keep her altruism down.

A walkway cleared of snowdust led down from the giant stables, past something the opinicus markers called a bathhouse, to a sort of domicile covered in paw and talonprints. Unlike the smooth walkway, this building was made from rough, colorful stone. She put her paw against a wall and licked. It was compressed shells. She looked around, not seeing another structure like it. Above its barricaded entrance was a teal scarab. Hanging from the over-hang were strings of shells, perhaps whole versions of their crushed cousins used in its construction.

She stood to the side of the door and sniffed where she thought opinici would put their talons. There were blacktalons and perhaps another type of opinicus, along with hints of something acrid and insectoid. She went through the scents she knew: flying insects, click beetles, even memories from her gryphlethood of a megapede crossing into Nightsky territory. Nothing matched.

Not wanting to spook the inhabitants if they were peeking through the cracks in the barricade, she went around to the alley behind the building, stacked full of empty boxes. She beaked through a few, but there was nothing edible. When she accidentally knocked one down, teal beetles scurried in every direction, and it clicked: Reeve Rybalt Reevesbane, an assassin Satra had warned her about, wore this scarab as his icon.

She licked her paw a few times to get her scent gland going, then stamped the outside of the shell-stone building, warning her pride to stay away.

Poison was her official reason. The way the building was secured, she suspected its occupants, like those in the one barricaded stable above, were cowering until the starlings left.

Fine by me. She left them behind and flew down, searching for a sign of why the rest of the eyrie had been abandoned. At the deepest point, she found a giant seal, as though this were the Abyssal Naze in miniature, and the pitohui and blackwings above were its jailors.

Or guardians?

She traced the inscribed metalwork, looking for a way to open it. She started by trying to see how it had been closed, but she couldn't figure it out, not until she had an odd thought.

Perhaps it seals from the other side. That conflicted with the other opinici being jailors. She thought back to the drawings on Wendl's wall, in her newly recovered memories. Holding Whisper's memory of how she and Wendl smelled in her mind, Nighteyes was finally able to unlock the scents coming from the edges of the seal.

This was Mothfeather, the Sleeping City. Hidden behind this seal were the mothfeather opinici, closed off from the rest of the world until their hibernation ended. Winter was gone, though, and spring was here. How much longer would they sleep?

Nighteyes searched past conversations with Wendl. The opinicus had commented once, in passing, that she'd never seen the Jadebeak Mountain bee plants when they were small and without flowers.

The purple gryphon hadn't paid them any mind on the way here. She flew up, not wanting to accidentally alert the murmuration to what slept below. She dove into a pile of sage, flax, and golden astor, searching for any bee plants. They remained elusive here where the grass and sage was thick, so she searched out a spot of free dirt and waited for a sleepy ground bee to emerge from its burrow.

She tracked the bee as it flew around, stopping at some flowering cacti that looked like they belonged in the desert, then moving south and locating a familiar sight.

The Mothfeather Peak bee plants looked the same as the Jadebeak Mountain variety, about knee-high to a starling, and the first ones were showing the barest hint of purple flowers.

She returned to the air, her wings protesting, and looked around. She could just make out some mountains, perhaps part of the same range as the Redwood Valley, now curving east. To the north, she could only see deep forest, trees of types that didn't grow in the jungle.

What she wanted to know and had no way of finding out was how much farther they had to go. Because if the bee plants were starting to bloom, then an entire eyrie worth of opinici would soon rise from below like ground bees, and the murmuration might get ambushed on the way back.

She looked in the direction of the desert, seeing endless grasslands and the occasional trees sticking up, lost from the forest north of them or the mountains south. Just out of view, she saw a flicker of something white. When the wind changed, she could smell it, too.

White opinici? She'd smelled them all around Blacktalon, which had been fortified even better than the blackwings and pitohui here. *Have they been following us?*

She started to fly west to investigate, but the pridelord awoke, and her mind drifted from her body as she rejoined the murmuration on their migration east.

52

REEVE RYBALT REEVESBANE, REVISITED

Nestled in the Blackwing Eyrie, Reeve Rybalt Reevesbane sat inside a war council and listened to the reeves of eyries he had forgotten existed try to come up with a good plan for dealing with a murmuration of starlings. A great variety of plans were presented to the blackwing reeve, few of them good. Though of the bad plans, some were exquisitely poor in quality.

"Perhaps we can bribe them?" a vibrant orange opinicus suggested. She was not a reeve herself, as her home eyrie was far north of here and its reeve smart enough to stay out of the line of combat.

Iony, his ceremonial ear cuff glistening in the light the way his everyday version never did, suppressed a laugh. "How're you gonna bribe a starling? They're like drones when they get like this. The only one you can deal with is the leader."

"Then speak to the leader, the queen bee," she countered. "Just find the one wearing a crown and strike a deal."

Iony and the motmot representative shared a look suggesting they were reconsidering the choices in their lives that had gotten gryphons onto this council. The glacier gryphon in particular looked as though he wanted to ask the opinicus if she thought insect queen bees wore tiny tiaras.

Rybalt had done a lot to make this council happen, so he felt he should take some of the pressure off his four-pawed peers. "Ah, unfortunately, their leader looks the same as the others. Jadebeaks, I believe the largest swarm is called. You can't spot him out of the crowd. Sometimes you can see where he's been if they're moving. Had there been a way to locate the pridelord easily, we would have killed him by now."

The orange representative did not seem convinced, pointing out that even the glacier gryphons put shiny things on their leader's head so they could recognize him.

Thankfully, before Iony could start a fight, a black and blue jay opinicus spoke up. Despite his diminutive personality—and lack of a crown—he was, in fact, the reeve of a small eyrie. His home was on the other side of the mountains and in the path of the swarm, so he had wisely opted to come here personally.

"Can we scare them off?" the jay asked. "Perhaps if we were to launch a counteroffensive on the way, to kill several of them, they could be persuaded to just...give up?"

"No." The motmot representative did not elaborate. The motmots were allowed a representative, but she was officially part of the Pitohui Eyrie, and so Rybalt, once again, was forced to explain for her.

He tapped a talon on the stone floor to redirect attention to himself. "As my island neighbor was saying, they're more like...a swarm of bees. One-on-one, starling-to-starling, they're quite pleasant, I hear. The same as any gryphon, really. But when they come in contact with non-starlings, they..."

"Lose their minds," Iony interrupted. "Just completely feral little biters, all claws and tomia. They're small, but there's a lot of them, and it's amazing the damage a small gryphon with no sense of self-preservation can do."

The blackwing reeve had remained silent for most of the meeting. It wasn't like him to refuse to weigh in; he certainly thought very highly of his own opinion and liked to hear himself speak. But he'd also been humbled by the loss of his main army trying to take the Alabaster Eyrie. Many had lost loved ones in the conflict, and few had returned home.

Rybalt's sister, Stripes, was among the missing. None of her motmot bodyguards had returned, either, suggesting they'd died trying to save her. The last Rybalt had heard from his spies at Blacktalon, she'd managed to kill Impir before disappearing.

That's not nothing, but it feels like it. This sort of war did not allow for pacifists. Stripes wasn't his first sibling lost to the war, but she was the only sibling who hadn't wanted to be on the front lines.

As the conversation continued and the worst of the ideas were rejected by the alliance's leader, Iony kept shooting glances at Rybalt. In the grand scheme of things, they both wanted the defense of the Blackwing Eyrie to succeed. They just didn't want it to succeed too quickly.

That doesn't seem to be a problem here. We may be taking refugees back to our island. I wonder how the black-wings will feel, having to be guests in our home for once. If we could just get these dullwits to understand that this is no longer a war we can win on the battlefield, this'll go better for all of us.

The plan, in the end, was rather simple. Evacuate everyone who could be evacuated, sending all the boats south to the port near the glacier peaks—a remote and chilly destination even in spring, but Cielle's warning had given them time to prepare—and everyone who could fly would head north, to the orange opinicus's eyrie. Had her reeve been here, he would have made excuses and suggested an alternative. He was not, and that was that.

The only eyrie missing from the council was the Mothfeather representative. There'd been no time to evacuate The Sleeping City, so they had to hope the seal held. At Rybalt's insistence, none of the winter caretakers had been warned, either. He trusted his own pitohui to be smart. The blackwings, well, he could take them or leave them.

Once the orders were given, the lesser reeves exited. The motmot looked like she wanted to speak to Rybalt, but Iony ushered her out. For the first time in a very long time, the blackwing and pitohui reeves sat in a room alone.

"I can't believe this is how it ends," the blackwing reeve stated. "Ultimately, it'll be gryphons who raze our eyries, not even opinici."

Rybalt wasn't used to small talk. "I wouldn't count

us out just yet. We have Bario, if you'll let him back into the flameworks. We could even send word to the Ashen Weald. And for what it's worth, I can't imagine the swarm is staying. I've never known starlings to spend long outside the jungle."

"Hmmm." The blackwing reeve paced. Unlike many leaders Rybalt had killed, this one's leaf tiara, bracelets, and even his harness were subdued. He made up for it by dying his feathers red and orange to match his shoulders, but he was no pink reeve. "What do they want, then? What brought them here?"

Rybalt had a few ideas. "I think they were lured. Do you know about the rains on the Argent Heights?"

"Just that they fall rarely. Are you going somewhere with this?" the blackwing asked.

"I am." Rybalt found a bowl of water, took it to the engraved table, and gently tipped it over so the water fell into the cracks before dripping to the floor. "You can't hold a storm in your talons, but for most of the year, the heights see no rain. The hot springs are nice for a quick dip to rinse off a bit of gore, but the water is full of dangerous minerals, so you can't drink it. Instead, they slow and redirect the water through limestone and moss so it reaches their reservoirs at the base of the mountain, weeks or even months later."

The blackwing reeve didn't right the water bowl. "I see. Someone cut a groove from the Emerald Jungle to here, and the storm of starlings flowed through it. If that's the case, we should have evacuated earlier. Whoever's pulling the strings won't be able to redirect the swarm easily."

Strange to see you become a good strategist in your old age.

"Unfortunately, we didn't see this coming. Who could have spies among the Emerald Jungle?" Rybalt quipped.

"The Nighthaunt appears to, if your pitohui are correct," the blackwing answered. "I suppose we're seeing the fruit of his labor now. I wish we'd killed the red when he first came here. Then we'd never have had to deal with bloodbeak or starlings."

For once, Rybalt agreed with the reeve. "But the Seraph King would still remain. There are many intelligent scholars out there, though none as motivated as the Nighthaunt. I do not believe either you or I would have been so lucky as to see Emin die of old age."

The blackwing reeve made a noncommittal sound, and Rybalt took the opportunity to steer the conversation in a new direction.

"I know you trust your forces to guard the gates to the Waterfall Palace, but eventually, they will be breached." He stated it as a fact. "When that happens, you will not need adept aerial combatants like the motmots, nor troops who work best in a formation like your blackwings. Within the corridors leading to the chambers behind the throne, you will want, no, you will *need* pitohui."

The blackwing took a vial of antitoxin out of his harness. "What reassurance do I have they won't poison me when the battle begins? None of the blackwing troops I send with you come back."

"I'm not one to offer guarantees." Rybalt preferred to keep things straightforward. "But you mix your own antitoxin, and I believe you have a secret passage from these back chambers across the mountain, though how you had that built in secret, I haven't a clue."

The blackwing reeve wasn't surprised to have his secrets laid bare. "Something the Reevesbane doesn't know? How fascinating. Well, here's some trivia for you. The reason the chambers aren't atop the Waterfall Palace but are down a few stories is because of the secret passage. The palace was designed around it, and it already existed before blackwings came here. I don't believe in myths or legends like our white-feather friends, but if their stories of seraphs are true, I suspect the plan was to have goliath passages throughout the mountains before something inter-rupted them."

"A joy to learn something new," Rybalt commented. "Or so my sister used to say. Where does the tunnel come out?"

"The quarry eyrie across the mountains, though there's supposed to be an exit at the Goldtree Gardens," the blackwing replied. "With our luck, some daft minor reeve stacked barrels of mead in front of it or secured it shut, not realizing what it was."

The term *minor reeve* was a bit of a silly one, used by pompous rulers of cities too small to be eyries to try to puff up their own importance and used by rulers of actual eyries to belittle any eyrie whose population was ten opinici smaller than their own. Their enemy's equivalent was a dovecote, a nod to the small cities that sprung up across the Seraph King's countryside after the destruction of the pigeon reeve's eyrie.

Rybalt had caught some of his pitohui attempting

to count *minor reeves* in their totals, and he had made it very clear that he would not accept any *minor reeves-banes* among his ranks.

The two-opinicus council sat in silence for a few moments more, and Rybalt thought his plan may have died on the vine until the blackwing reeve finally said, "So be it. Grant me twenty of your finest assassins."

"Fifteen," Rybalt replied. "I'm afraid I'm low on assassins at the moment. But I'll throw in ten glacier gryphons who are immune to batrachotoxin, and Iony and myself will personally guard the two largest ways into the palace."

"So be it." The leader of the alliance must truly have expected to lose the battle to agree to the terms so quickly. "And I've already ordered your redwood phoenix freed. Any chamber marked with a teal cross, he's to avoid blowing up. Anything with a red circle is fair game. Now leave so I can brood in silence."

Rybalt bowed low, one final gesture of kindness, and departed the council chamber. He leapt off his favorite balcony, the one he'd first exited from when freed, and pretended to scout the city until Iony found him.

"Our motmot friend is waiting at your nest," the glacier gryphon said. "You should stop in before she gets too anxious."

Rybalt slowly turned, gliding back down to the pitohui embassy. He didn't spend much time there, as he didn't like to wake up to assassins. "Fetch the stargazer and secure him inside the palace. Send a team through the reeve's passage and see if you can locate me someone who knows the architecture of

Goldtree Gardens. Then go find Bario and make sure he's at the flameworks."

"Bario? You think he's gonna want to be around us?" Iony did not sound convinced.

"No, probably not. It was a mistake to tell him pitohui killed Impir." Rybalt would have kept that information from both of their remaining Redwood Valley scholars, each of whom had become prisoners in all but name after Impir's betrayal.

The cockatiel forger, Headmaster Neider's old pet, had redoubled his efforts to make himself useful, creating all manner of falsified alabaster documents. It was much easier to keep a spy network hidden when they weren't being arrested for having the wrong paperwork.

Bario, however, was a skilled chemist. Unfortunately for Rybalt, though it was possible to be a good chemist and also an idiot, the Redwood Valley phoenix had figured out what was going on. After Stripes' flirting had sent him to the hospital, he'd tested his rations and discovered someone was secretly dosing him with a mix of chemicals to make him particularly susceptible to pitohui toxin.

That opinicus, of course, was Rybalt, but it had only been meant as a precaution, not a serious assassination attempt. There were some scholars where, should the need arise to murder them, he didn't intend to give them the opportunity to down a hidden vial of antitoxin.

"Still, Stripes liked him," the pitohui reeve continued, "and I don't trust the blackwings to keep him alive. Don't take him into your confidence but see if you can find a way to make sure he survives this. If he dies, he dies, but at least if I've tried I won't be haunted by my sister's ghost."

Iony didn't respond. He still held out hope that Stripes was alive somewhere, hiding in the king's lands. Communication across the desert had become difficult since the king controlled both Blacktalon and Whitebeak, but difficult didn't mean impossible. Four motmots should have been able to smuggle her home if she were alive. It was easier to think of her as dead.

He landed on the balcony, letting Iony retrieve the stargazer, who was currently sleeping in a giant shipping container on the docks. His friend quipped that all the opinici they safeguarded ended up smelling like fish in the end. While Rybalt would have liked to take a few hours to sleep, at least his next conversation would be brief. The motmots were always direct.

This one sat on his nest, napping. She hopped up when he came in. "You should assign motmots to help your pitohui. We can use the poison, we just don't secrete it. Or we should all leave here and let the blackwings fail on their own."

He laughed, then saw she was serious. "Now, now, what sort of opinici would we be if we let our allies die?"

"Live ones," she said, and he knew he was in for a long night if he didn't want his long-beaked allies to abandon him before morning.

53

DAYTIME DIPLOMACY

Ahot northern wind brought the smell of salt and marsh across the sawgrass to the cypress tree where Erlock Chartail perched. Her dark green plumage and chestnut fur were better camouflage among the coastal redwoods of her home, but they did an adequate job in the bog. Her long, feathered tail trailed behind her, disappearing into the leaves and moss. So long as she stayed low to the branches, she could remain hidden here for hours.

As long as her stomach didn't betray her. The flamingos at New Eyrie had resumed fishing since the starlings' migration passed, and the smell of turtle meat made her queasy.

You eat one bad turtle, and you never forget it, Biski had told Erlock in between feeding her kashow bark tea. The mismatched blue and orange medicine gryphon—and occasional legal advocate—often served as Erlock's mate each season, though only after making a big production of bragging about all her suitors.

Biski's confidence wasn't unearned, either. She'd stopped the parasite from spreading across the taiga and into the weald, leading to many fisherfolk in Sandpiper's Dune naming their children things like Biske or Biskers. She also wasn't wrong about not eating dead turtles, though the culinary variety of the southern bog left something to be desired.

Erlock's innards grumbled a second time in protest.

"Need something to settle your stomach?" Cielle offered her a salted fish bar from his fisherfolk harness. After the *starling incident,* the taiga prides had supposedly sent him to report to the Ashen Weald. More likely, he'd volunteered to help the Ashen Weald to be closer to Pumpkin, who had dyed Cielle's usually fluffy white feathers a tan color that matched the color of dead sawgrass.

Erlock declined the food, continuing her watch of the Jadebeak Mountains. Satra had assigned Cielle to the fantails since he was descended from both the taiga's Williwaw Pride and a group of fantails who fled the Connixation.

A lot of strangers were claiming they were part fantail or feathermane recently, though most of those were opinici feeling guilty about the weald fires. She turned most of those away, letting them apply to join the Ashen Weald as part of Grenkin and Mia's Crackling Sea Pride. Cielle was a special case because his tail made his fantail heritage hard to deny, even if names like *Golrin Goldpaw of the Fantail Pride* had long been lost to time on the mainland.

An iridescent green bird flew out from the mountains, and Cielle crouched down, ready to pounce.

Erlock made a clicking sound to tell him to relax, forgetting he didn't know the Ashen Weald's bird and animal codes. "It's just a bird starling, not a gryphon starling."

The bog was getting overrun by avian starlings as gryphons ate the other types of birds. Word of the Nighthaunt's theories, backed up by their sand gryphon allies, had made gryphons nervous about eating starlings lest their gryphlets hatch with green plume. It made Erlock laugh when it didn't make her angry—her own brown and green colorations had faint white spots.

Comments about not eating starlings had gotten worse the past few days. Seeing the murmuration made the Ashen Weald nervous. Wingtorn had been pulled back to the sunken eyrie, and only the fastest gryphons and opinici were allowed north of the Jade-beak River.

Of course, some of the Ashen Weald were better at following orders than others. From beneath Erlock's tree, a pile of moss hooted up at her.

"Hey," Blinky repeated. "Biski wants to know if you have seen anything yet."

Erlock rolled her eyes. It was just like Biski to send an owl gryphon to spy for her. And by *send*, Erlock really meant *spent some of their hidden fish stash to bribe*. "Nothing yet, darling. If there is, I'd have flown back or sent Cielle. You really here on Biski's behalf, or did you get bored and come visit on your own?"

Blinky did not reply. Instead, she slowly hooted at Cielle until his scarred ear began twitching. He tossed her a fish bar to make her stop. Some of the fantails may think of him as an obligation, but the owl gryphons' suspicious natures melted away at the sign of salty fish.

North of the bog, pink shapes flew crab traps to and from New Eyrie.

"The mingos are out again," Cielle commented. "They all hid before the starlings came last time. I think that means we're safe, right?"

"Maybe." Erlock had not become leader of the fantail pride by assuming nothing would go wrong. She'd also spent more time with the starlings than anyone else, enough to know that nothing that had happened recently was normal—or safe.

She shifted her perch. Cypress wasn't the best tree for supporting a gryphon of her size, and her back paws were falling asleep. She swished her tail, knocking some of the moss from Blinky's head.

The owl gryphon glared quietly.

"Blinky, you can go," Erlock insisted. "We're fine here. If anything happens, we'll let you know."

The owl gryphon's head snapped west. "Something comes."

Erlock's vision was good, but it was several moments before she saw what Blinky did. Unlike before, where most of the mountain range had erupted with starlings, this time a small group flew in tight formation out from the Jadebeak Falls.

"I see Whisper," Blinky said. "She is leader of the infected and the one who stole your scent. She sent us the message."

Cielle shifted.

Erlock clicked to settle him down. "Count the starlings. Satra will want to know how many there are. Blinky, look for anyone you recognize."

The black starlings gave way to a red one, several blue, and then a menagerie of different colors, including what looked like a frost chicken with angry red eyebrows.

Behind them, struggling to stay aloft, was a gryphon Erlock knew well. Rather an *opinicus* she knew well. "That's Wendl. I'm gonna go talk to her. Cielle, you stay hidden unless they turn south. If that happens, flee and raise the warning."

Blinky hissed her disapproval, but Erlock's starling ancestry meant she shouldn't trigger the altruism the way other gryphons did. She flew up to the swarm, coming in from behind. They ignored her, which was a good sign. It was easy for the fantail to match speeds with Wendl. Erlock's old friend looked like she'd gone through hell.

"Wendl!" she shouted. "What're you doing out of the jungle?"

The opinicus broke out of her daze. "Erlock! Can you take over? I'm too tired to think and fly at the same time."

Wendl beat her wings, rising, then folded them in while Erlock caught her harness. She weighed little.

"We saw the murmuration pass by here a week ago," Erlock tried. "Why weren't you with them? Where were they going? Why did the pink reeve leave out food for them?"

Wendl took a moment before answering. "I don't have energy to answer all of that, friend. The murmuration is going to the Blackwing Eyrie, and we need to stop them. I'd ask the Ashen Weald to come with us, but I fear the murmuration we chase would attack you as readily as the blackwings, though Whisper seems to be keeping her lot's altruism suppressed. If you know a fast way to the Blackwing Eyrie that avoids the alabasters, though, I could use the help."

"That's not an easy proposition, considering who currently owns the sea." Erlock weighed her options. Strange spring snowstorms were hitting the eastern coast of the Crackling Sea, slowing down opinicus and starling alike, but the western side was clear—although controlled by the Argent Heights and flamingos these days. "The forces at New Eyrie are skittish. If they see starlings, they'll hide, fearing there are more of you. If you head north, we can meet up with the Padfoot Pride. They've got a hideaway not far from here. They use it to attack the supply caravans."

"The desert? I don't think I can survive that heat," Wendl protested.

Erlock knew the feeling. She hadn't enjoyed either of her trips to the desert, though she'd heard Triddle was hard at work making Crestfall Eyrie hospitable. "If you fly at night, it's not so bad. With Sponge's help, you won't dry out, either."

The gryphon Blinky had identified as Whisper fell back. Her silver eyes elicited a visceral reaction in Erlock after her rescue operation in the bog.

She reminded herself she was a pride leader and trusted Wendl's calm to guide her. "Er, hello. Whisper, I presume?"

"The weald starling," was all Whisper said.

Erlock felt a tingling in her nares, the scents starlings used to communicate that smelled to her like a Blue-eyed Festival dish gone awry. She reiterated the offer. "Let us help you. Without the Blackwing Alliance, there's nothing stopping the king from controlling the entire continent. We have a fraught relationship with them, but we'll help if we can."

The air filled with the faint aroma of mint. Wendl went limp, and for a moment, Erlock thought the opinicus might have died. Thankfully, her snoring confirmed she was just sleeping.

Whisper didn't look to be in much better shape. "I am not enough for what needs to be done. I need Wendl's help at the eyrie. If we go to the desert, do you think you can carry her across?"

"Not a chance," Erlock laughed. "But if we can find Sponge, I think you two can work something out. Now...to get you up there, do you think you can keep your gooeys from biting my friends, darling?"

Whisper nodded, then returned to the front of the flock to redirect them north. Erlock let out a quetzal cry, summoning Cielle up to help her fly Wendl the rest of the way.

WAVES OF SUNBAKED sand crashed across dunes above, obscuring the entrance to multiple underground burrows. Just several feet below the surface, the temperature was much more pleasant, if still hotter than an owl gryphon would have preferred. Or, at least, than a weald owl would have liked.

Ninox shook a piece of torn parchment in her beak, scattering sand everywhere, before laying it flat to read it. Once she was certain it held nothing of value, she tossed it into a box to pass along to the Darkfeather University. "No sign of Cherine."

Sponge, the only source of humidity in the cave,

cooed encouragement. Though Ninox had taught her damp friend to read, the sandgrouse had a way of making ink run, so handling any communications was up to Ninox and her opinicus daughter, Sound of Snow.

The owl pride leader had not liked leaving her home behind, not after she'd worked so hard to establish the Darkfeather Highlands. At first, she'd told herself that Cherine would return any day. Then the cave gryphons stopped coming. Then she'd found out there'd been no word at all from Zeph or Kia, either.

She begrudgingly missed Zeph and Kia, but she greatly missed Cherine.

I told him not to go, but he went anyway. I warned him I would not come to look for him if he became kidnapped, but he did not listen.

This is his fault.

She could feel her hackle feathers rising when Sponge put a damp paw on her back. With it came a coo of encouragement.

"You are correct." Ninox replied, stealing a sip of water from Sponge's hydrated ruff. "This is Cherine's fault."

Sound of Snow made a *tsk* sound that felt like something an opinicus would do. Moody gryphon fledglings would have just hissed or tried to bite something. She would have to ask Sound of Snow's father if this was normal behavior for a female opinicus or if she should encourage her daughter to do more hissing and biting.

Ninox let a hunting calm fall over her. She could not let herself be distracted by Cherine's foolishness or Sound of Snow's irritated preening. *He said she would develop slower than her brothers, but he did not say that the annoying adult feathers phase would last twice as long, too.*

I am doing it again. Hunting calm. Stalk the words, find the prey.

The prey, in this case, was any sign of an easily kidnapped, know-it-all golden eagle opinicus. The desert was the first place she looked, as it was where he'd gotten lost the previous time. At first, it seemed like it would be easy. A desert pride of blackpaw gryphons reported seeing an opinicus with a metal beak north of Whitebeak.

When he is near opinici, he gets captured. It is simple. I do not have to locate Cherine. I just need to locate whoever is holding him prisoner.

Unfortunately, no one knew where the Seraph King held his prisoners. Hence her current alliance with her sometime-rival for Cherine's affections, Sponge.

Though I am winning.

Ninox continued searching through the papers, nuzzling them over to her daughter when she was done. Courtesy of the darkfeather scholars, Sound of Snow had learned to read very young, and she sometimes caught things Ninox did not.

A roadrunner gryphon poked her head down the entrance and chirped a warning. "Ashen Weald guests. And guests have guests."

The sand gryphons in the burrow, mostly burrowing owls, fled to the nearest escape tunnel. Despite being part of the Ashen Weald since joining Hoppy's pride, they didn't like visitors showing up anywhere except Crestfall Eyrie.

Ninox finished with the last page, tossing it to Sound of Snow in frustration. *Where did that stupid opinicus go? Does he not know that I need him to be safe so I can be great?*

Cherine was smart, but he couldn't read her thoughts, so she felt safe calling him stupid there, despite knowing that he could be very smart about a limited number of non-gryphon things. She sighed, earning a *tsk* from Sound of Snow, and poked her head out of the burrow.

A taiga gryphon, a fantail, and a bunch of starlings had begun their descent.

"What could Chartail want?" Ninox asked.

Sponge cooed an intelligent, well-spoken reply.

"Makes sense. If true, you will need to call your offspring," Ninox replied.

The champion of the sand gryphons cooed a bit more, before finishing the last bit in owlish.

"Fine," Ninox conceded. "Your territory, you should greet them. I will gather your offspring myself."

Once Sponge was outside the burrow, Ninox turned to Sound of Snow. "Go fetch Oasis, Thundercloud, and Rainy Season. Tell them to fill up first."

"Fine." Sound of Snow somehow managed to get a *tsk* into the word fine. "But he likes to be called Sound of Sand now."

Ninox forced her hunting calm to return. "We are not calling him that. We would not have called you that if Cherine had not been kidnapped when you hatched."

Sound of Snow *tsked* as she left the burrow, leaving Ninox to once again think back to a time when she wanted to have as many offspring as possible.

Once her daughter was out of hearing and it was just her and several sleeping burrowing owl gryphons who had not fled, Ninox could admit she was glad Sound of Snow had come along. She could have let the Strix Pride denmother raise her children. She could even have had Grax do it.

Grax's ability to handle my three gryphlets—er, offspring—is why I knew she would be good at ruling a pride.

But the annoying fledging phase would end, and then Sound of Snow would be a smart owl gryphon— o*pinicus,* she reminded herself—capable of writing, of speaking common, and of killing things that annoyed Ninox.

First, though, Ninox needed to find Sound of Snow's father. He still had things to teach their children. And to do that, it might benefit her to know a few starlings who owed her a favor.

Daytime diplomacy. I am good at this.

She exited the burrow to greet the newcomers.

54

THUNDERCLOUD, OASIS, AND SOUND OF SAND

Whisper had done everything she could to reprogram the starlings left behind. Every time she thought she'd completely suppressed their altruism, it would pop up again. It was tiring work, especially when she was also leading the susurration. In the past, she had someone to take over control while she did this work.

Moonlit Blossom.

Back in the Emerald Jungle, the Gourmand was giving stormtail gryphlets and sick nightsky gryphlets rides out to his island. It was the only place they were fairly certain Kism hadn't told the alabasters about. While the Gourmand moved the stormtails to their new island home, Clamshell searched the Emerald Jungle for any gryphlets or late-hatching eggs.

Once Whisper knew what she was smelling for, she was able to examine the scents left behind by the new pridelord. Balthar was clumsy and loud, and commanding young starlings required finesse. She was fairly certain the first years wouldn't have made it across the Emerald Jungle, and she hoped against hope that crocodiles or opinici hadn't caught them.

The stormtail and newmoon denparents went with Clamshell. There'd been talk about dividing the remaining flight-worthy, *fight*-worthy starlings into two teams, one to defend the jungle, one to leave it. Ultimately, both Whisper and Desert Rose—serving as pride leader of the stormtails—agreed if the murmuration returned with Balthar in charge of it, it would spell doom for the Emerald Jungle.

Having a second pride leader here helped keep his kin under control. Unfortunately, the susurration didn't listen to the stormtail, so Whisper had to try to fix everyone while also keeping her pride on task, and it was wearing her thin.

I should be grateful for this Erlock Startail offering us a way to catch up. I know she was Nighteyes' friend. That said, I don't know how I'm going to survive the desert.

The sand gryphons refused to discuss things with the starlings at the burrow. Apparently the Ashen Weald had protocols for dealing with sand gryphons, all of whom wished to be treated as reeves. They were redirected to an oasis where the sand gryphons would meet them.

Before they reached the oasis, Wendl had woken up again, though she was still weak and needed hydration. Flicker asked a sand gryphon about water and squealed with delight upon finding out the sand-grouse were drinkable.

Seeing how wet Wendl and Flicker got trying to drink a gryphon convinced Whisper to wait for the oasis, which was just in view. They landed, and waiting for them along its palm-laden banks was a small black and red gryphon. She resembled Blinky, except without the scars and with a long tail and expressive ears.

"Hello! I'm Sound of Snow." Her accent was Redwood Valley without the opi trill, and a quick glance down revealed she was an opinicus, not a gryphon as she'd appeared at first blush.

Whisper wasn't sure how to greet weald gryphons. *Opinici,* she corrected herself. Based on her only other experience with one, she slow blinked.

This was apparently the correct response as Sound of Snow continued. "Sponge has gone ahead with my mom to get approval for you to cross the desert, but her kids are here to help guide you across. May I introduce you to Oasis?"

Oasis came out from behind a palm tree. "Hello!"

Whisper had been briefed about giant teratorns by Erlock on the way over. This gryphon was a tiny teratorn, the same size as Sound of Snow. His fur and feathers were a pretty blue, though he was vulture-like in appearance. Despite the similarity in appearances with Sound of Snow, Whisper estimated Oasis was a year younger.

The teratorn gryphon wasn't an owl gryphon, but Whisper tried a slow blink and was rewarded with one in turn.

"Next, we have Sound of Sand," the owl opinicus added, summoning forth a miniature version of Sponge from the sand in front of her. "We're courting."

"Aaaaw, they're summer friends." Flicker reached for Whisper's paw.

The newmoon pride leader swatted the red starling's paw away, but Flicker just wrapped the end of her tail around Whisper's.

"It is nice to meet you, Sound of Sand!" the strawberry finch chirped. "It's a good name. Very...wooshy. I'm Flicker."

"Thanks!" Sound of Sand beamed. "You should tell my mom that. I like your name, too."

"It's Whisper's pet name for me," Flicker said before the newmoon leader could stop her.

"Didn't you say you were introducing three gryphons?" Wendl asked, looking a little better after eating and drinking.

The water of the oasis rumbled like the Gourmand had surfaced, but a gryphon even larger than the Dread Beast of the Winter Jungle rose from the oasis, dripping water down upon them like a rainstorm.

The large sand gryphon cooed a happy noise, and Sound of Snow cooed back up at him. Though he had the vulture-like appearance of Oasis, Thundercloud's plumage was the soft dune color of his mother and Sound of Sand. Depending on how absorbent it was, Whisper was unclear how a gryphon could fly with all that water weight.

"Hello." Whisper resisted the urge to step away from the small rainstorm falling from the newcomer. "I did not know there were *giant* giant teratorn gryphons."

Flicker lowered her voice so only Whisper could hear. "I wonder if we could get him to fly over my garden?"

"If you needed more rain, you should not have planted so close to the mountains," Whisper replied.

"Thundercloud will carry Wendl and provide water for the trip," Sound of Snow explained. "It's hard for him to get airborne, especially when wet, so he'll go get started. Once he's up in the sky, though, he can soar across the entire desert without stopping. The sun's beginning to set, so we should get going. First, we're going to fly to the border of Blackpaw territory, then stop while Sponge gets permission from the other desert prides to go through their lands. We'll eat and drink on the wing, but we'll sleep during the hottest part of the day underground. If you absolutely need to stop for any reason, tell me, and I'll relay the message. Unless any of you speak sandgrouse?"

None of the starlings did. Whisper thought it was strange enough a version of common had lasted for so long in the Emerald Jungle.

With everything settled, they followed the Sounds of Snow and Sand to the nearest canyon to help Thundercloud get airborne, then joined in. Though they'd been encouraged to fly under the massive gryphon to dissuade any teratorn birds from coming after them, she didn't care for being dripped on and stayed back where it was dry.

Despite her annoyance at Flicker, who tried to find the silver lining of any bad situation, she appreciated her ex-mate's ability to chat with Sound of Snow while Whisper continued trying to fix the stormtails and newmoon gryphons.

Flicker even nudged Whisper when someone was speaking to her, like when Sound of Snow asked about eyeshine.

"So is that the same dye on your eyes and fur?" the

weald owl asked. "I'd love to do something with my feathers, but my mom says it'll look weird if I dye them while I'm still fledging. Like the dyed ones might come out, then the adult feathers wouldn't be dyed. She wants me to do dark red, but dark red and black is a weird combination? I feel like you have the right idea with silver. Oh, I know that cactus. Let me tell Thundercloud to land. The roadrunners get really prissy if you fly over their territory without permission, so we should wait here for Sponge."

Prissy did not seem like the right word, but Whisper didn't correct their guide. The newmoon was doing her best to stay cheerful. If not for the sand gryphons, this would be a much more dangerous flight, but she didn't want to get too attached to new friends until after the murmuration was saved.

If I can save it. We have not had a new pridelord in my lifetime, not without using the salts to swap Balthar in. What if it doesn't work? What if the different starling prides can't agree on someone?

Or, even worse, what if we kill Balthar just to replace him with Iri?

THE BLACKPAW PRIDE'S outpost was similar to the one near the sand owl burrows. Whisper used mint to hold her pride in place while the new sand gryphons sniffed at them, then let go once their hosts vanished into the dunes.

Small, round cacti spread out from a central rock formation in the shape of a disgruntled turtle. From a distance, or perhaps with heat stroke, it would have looked like a matamata covered in spatterdock. In a move that would have given most gryphons a panic attack, Thundercloud dug beneath the turtle's stomach and squeezed into an underground burrow, complete with water.

Erlock Startail waited beneath the turtle's head. Nearby cacti had long beak punctures in them, suggesting the Blackpaw Pride didn't have their own sandgrouse refreshment. Whisper watched her pride squeezing beneath the stones and decided she'd rather wait outside a few moments. Though Sponge remained absent, presumably smoothing things over with other sand prides, the weald fantail was chatty.

"We just missed the rainy season," Erlock explained. "Otherwise, there wouldn't be enough water here for two prides."

Whisper nodded, unsure what to say, but content to let the new smells wash over her. The sun was coming up, and she'd never experienced cactus before. It was a mix of floral, wet, and alkaline.

Erlock stretched her wings reflexively to sun them, then thought better of it. "We'd better head in and check on your friends. Sponge should be back soon. Blackpaws and roadrunners are allowed in each other's territory, but this deep into the desert, they're all suspicious of strangers."

To Whisper's surprise, the caverns beneath the rock turtle stretched in every direction like an oversized anthill, and there were even a couple of Ashen Weald scholars working down here. Thanks to the opinici, weak rushlights kept the chambers from complete darkness.

The scholars liked Wendl and took quickly to

Flicker, who pelted them with questions about dirt. They squeaked with fear, however, whenever the more unusual starlings got too close to them, which just encouraged Taloncrest. It took Sound of Snow promising to keep guard outside their nests to stop an incident.

Once the starlings ate and drank their fill, with Erlock begrudgingly offering to reimburse the sand gryphons since the starlings had kept her fed for months when she was in the Emerald Jungle, Whisper and her susurration were escorted into sleeping caves on the deepest levels. She'd only slept a few hours before barking awoke her, and she followed the smell of wet stormtails to Desert Rose and his pride still playing in the aquifer, ducking underwater when she tried to tell them they needed to sleep.

She ultimately enlisted help from Sound of Sand and several sandgrouse, who lured the stormtails back to their nests with promises to keep them from drying out while they slept.

The previous stormtail pride leader would not have allowed this to happen, Whisper grumbled to herself. By all accounts, even Rudder had done a better job of keeping them under control. At the thought of Rudder, she realized she'd need to tell Nighteyes what had happened to him.

That thought followed Whisper into her dreams, where she had a restless slumber. Only exhaustion kept her from finding Flicker or Wendl to talk to, and when Sponge finally arrived at dusk to let them know they had permission to cross the desert, Whisper wished they could have spent a few days under the stone turtle. Only thoughts of the murmuration lying dead in Blackwing Alliance lands roused her to action.

Once the sun set, they departed the outpost.

THE DRY, cool air of the desert at night gave it a timeless feel that varied little on their journey. This went on for night after night, endless sands beneath them. Whisper and her charges slept during the day in burrows and flew in the cold light of the stars. The wayward children of the Emerald Jungle grew nervous without the smell of trees or rivers to anchor them.

The only time the scent changed, becoming almost salty, was when they stopped off at the ruined palace to sleep in the chambers beneath the plateau during the day.

The Palace of Fire and Ice was a place of myth to a poor rancher. Whisper had grown up on stories of the Pink Reeve's Daughter, of decadence hidden in a wasteland. Functional glass was a rarity inside Mothfeather, decorative was unheard of. The sun's rays glittering on the shattered remains of the pink throne was like visiting the corpse of a dream.

Most of the susurration slept in the depths in what had once been a storage area, but Whisper's nares pulled her higher up. She was quickly joined by Wendl, whose curiosity was even stronger still.

"I wasn't sure if I'd be able to sense him." Whisper's soft voice echoed against the sandstone walls of the laboratory. "The sand gryphons say this is where the king brought him, to the source of the salts, to finish his experiments. I can smell the dead shrimp and poisoned hot springs, but I can *feel* the Nighthaunt in these halls."

Wendl offered an apple, squishy after being left in the heat. "I guess I knew we were continuing his work by searching for a cure. We were doing it for the right reasons, though. I never would've guessed his scarlet talons could reach into the jungle itself."

"I thought Kism, Balthar, and the others wanted to go home, to the Blackwing Eyrie. I never considered they'd follow in Mally's pawprints." Whisper twitched an ear. Somewhere nearby, one of the Blackpaw Pride fought with some monitors who had moved into the palace. Their motto was, *We don't let friends die in the desert, only enemies,* which was reassuring.

"Someone must have found Kism when he used my elixirs to escape all those years ago," Wendl ventured. "Or perhaps Balthar was sneaking into Alwren the entire time he was with the sparkwings. I'm not sure we'll find out the truth; I just worry Iri and Talli are in on it."

Whisper didn't comment on Kism. She'd left him food and water like a pet, but his cage was surrounded by the members of her pride whose minds were too far gone from the parasite to trust away from the jungle. "If we keep up this pace, we'll reach Black-talon soon. The weald owl says there's a place on the border where we can rest, eat, and rehydrate before leaving the desert. There might be an opportunity to contact your family if you think they're still living there."

"They will be," Wendl replied. "If the alabasters

didn't destroy the farm, they'll be there. It meant too much for them to abandon it. But is that a good idea? Altruism and all."

The newmoon pride leader reached out, taking in the scents of the sleeping starlings beneath them. "So far, the altruism hasn't come back. The real test will be what happens when we leave the desert. The sand gryphons here all smell like starlings after spending so much time with us. The sandgrouse smell especially fishy after cuddling the stormtails every time we stop to sleep."

"I'd feel better if you came with me." Wendl's request was reasonable, but Whisper didn't know if she wanted to be around mothfeathers.

"Will they even be awake?" Whisper's question remained unanswered, and she finally gave in. "Fine. When we near Blacktalon, I'll go with you. But we're not stopping to visit my family at Mothfeather. Now get some sleep. There's more desert ahead of us."

55

LAKE TRIDDLE

I f Crestfall Palace was abandoned and reeked of sand swimmers, Crestfall Eyrie was lively and beautiful—after Sponge sounded the all-clear.

The Seraph King had decided that if he held New Eyrie, The Crackling Sea Eyrie, and Blacktalon, he no longer needed to worry about the desert and its blood-coast-fueled storms or giant teratorns. Reeve Pride Leader Hoppy Padfoot was still being careful, remaining hidden when anyone came near, but beneath the sand-blasted exterior was a bubbling metropolis of Ashen Weald and free prides.

Despite Whisper's warning not to wander, word of an underground pool reached the small, round ears of Desert Rose, and the stormtails followed the sand-grouse gryphons to find Lake Triddle. When Sound of Snow mentioned her father had left some research in his quarters, being a sand gryphon by initiation, Wendl wandered off to see if there was any mention of bloodbeak.

Back with the Blackpaw Pride, Erlock had

cautioned Whisper that sand gryphons rarely worked for free, a warning that seemed ominous until the fantail explained sand gryphons accepted payment in many forms, including knowledge and experiences. Food was good, recipes were better. If someone could entertain a group of twenty or more sand gryphons, that was a string of beads that would never run out.

In Whisper's case, she sat in the throne room of Reeve Pride Leader Hoppy Padfoot and recreated the smells of the jungle for him and Sponge. The newmoon gryphon didn't usually work this way, creating aromas just for entertainment, but she had a trick to making it easy: she only chose the smells of gryphons she knew.

She wrapped her wings around Sound of Snow, thought of Desert Rose, and when she released her owl guide, the fledgling ran off to see Sound of Sand, who squealed with delight.

"You smell like desert flowers!" he said with a nuzzle.

The Ashen Weald had two representatives here, and they had clearly been tasked with finding out as much about the Emerald Jungle as possible. Fortunately, they were easily distracted, especially with Flicker's help.

"They say they're co-consorts of the Feathermane Pride," the red starling whispered. "It's all very modern and opinical, if you ask me. But! The blue one is why there's so much water here, and you should thank him for the underground pools on behalf of our stormtails. Apparently, if you see a ground parrot wandering around with a tiny vest on it, it's some sort of pet, so don't eat it. The reddish-brown one with the black bars is called Askel, and I heard Wendl say he's a bit of a firehawk. Maybe make him smell like smoke?"

Whisper had a better idea. She wrapped her wings around Triddle, enveloping him in the smell of a freshwater spring spilling down from the Jadebeak Mountains. Then, after taking a moment to recover, she wrapped her wings around Askel, thought very hard of the spiketrunks, and stepped back.

Triddle sniffed his mate. "You smell like...vegetables?"

"Oh!" Flicker exclaimed. "Spiketrunks make a fruit that looks just like a pumpkin. They call them sand pumpkins."

A story is a type of currency that never runs dry, Whisper had been told, and now she'd put it to the test. "The smell of a ripe sand pumpkin is one of the rarest smells in the jungle to experience, because it happens on the hottest, driest days of summer. The fruit becomes extremely dry, then suddenly gets a surge of water from the branch, making it heat up quickly."

"Then it explodes!" Flicker added, miming the seeds flying off in all directions. "Before the jadebeaks took us in, my pride lived where the spiketrunks were most plentiful, and *everyone* hid during the hottest days of summer."

This gift pleased the firehawk.

"Should come back," Hoppy declared. "Starlings good at trade. Not sure why spend so much time in jungle."

Whisper let Flicker take over the conversation as the red starling could match Hoppy's excitement. He promised to show her the stockpiles of stolen seeds and opinicus farm equipment. Apparently, the chaos between the blackwing and alabaster opinici had provided many opportunities for theft but few buyers.

The newmoon leader took advantage of the distraction to check in with her pride, first via pheromones to tell them not to eat Boomer the Ground Parrot, then by wandering Crestfall Eyrie. Sound of Sand and Thundercloud kept watch on the eastern skies to make sure no one was disturbed, so Whisper wandered the outside of the eyrie. The dunes rose before the canyon that housed the eyrie, shrouding it from view. On the ground, it was possible to be a hundred yards from safety and not realize it.

Riverbeds, though currently dry, crisscrossed the rocky portion of the desert like green veins, full of life. Oasis, the tiny teratorn, flew overhead to warn Whisper that some giant teratorns had been spotted in the area.

The newmoon leader beat her wings to get aloft, motioning with her beak at the riverbeds. "Where do they go?"

"Most empty into the Crackling Sea," he explained. "Some disappear beneath the ground, and we try to redirect those to Lake Triddle. Others just dry up."

Oasis returned to the eyrie to bathe, leaving Whisper to explore the south gates. Inside the city, there were goliath birds, though not many. A desert trip would be hard on the birds, but more likely, they'd get attacked by alabasters or blackwings once they were out of the desert. Judging by the harnesses hanging on the wall, these had been liberated from the alabasters. Beyond the stables was a cave marked with glyphs. She stopped a passing roadrunner and asked what they meant.

"Guest cave!" The sand gryphon swished her tail back and forth when she spoke. "You can stay if you want. Used to be for cave gryphons, haven't seen any in years."

She looked at Whisper expectantly, and the starling put a paw on her, giving her the scent of craneberries. She ran away with a happy trill.

Is it clawdiggers or darkstalkers that keep the cave gryphons in the Abyssal Naze? Whisper wondered, remembering her own cave adventure with Nighteyes. The newmoon gryphon decided to head back to the eyrie and find the stormtails, who were playing in the underground pools. It was much colder down here, which she appreciated, but also a lot damper. Every so often, a sandgrouse gryphon would run up and offer themselves to Whisper. She'd take a cursory sip, leaving behind black featherdust, which the sandgrouse didn't seem to mind.

For a gryphon home, there were a lot of braziers here, giving the place a smell of fish she suspected stormtails found reassuring. They splashed and swam laps like floodlings. A longer pool filled the main chamber, but several smaller pools on different levels fed into it. There was even an area where the stone had been worn so smooth that gryphlets could slide down.

Thundercloud had the second largest pool to himself and purred happily, churning the water around him. Taloncrest and the ptarmigan seemed to enjoy the relaxing vibrations and cuddled up to their new large friend. Oasis and the Sounds of Snow and Sand chased stormtails through the main pool. Though the long, semiaquatic gryphons were fast, occasionally the sand-and-weald trio were able to corner one and tag them.

Desert Rose hesitated before a dive, and Sound of Snow grabbed onto his tail with her talons. Rather than pulling him up, however, he pulled her down into the depths. Sound of Sand, whose tail was intertwined with hers, was also pulled under, leaving behind a dumbfounded Oasis.

Whisper inspected the stormtails as they surfaced to bark a greeting at her. Despite her worries the water would rinse her featherdust off them—which had happened—her scent instructions had taken root enough that there were no signs of altruism.

That was a relief, but it reminded Whisper of the weight of what lay before her. All at once, she slumped down against a dry rock overlooking the pools. With the drop in her mood, every starling stopped and stared at her.

She tried to send a reassuring scent, but Flicker beat her to it, and the others returned to playing and making friends.

Flicker settled down next to Whisper, taking the newmoon paw in her own red starling paw.

Strawberry finch. Whisper remembered Wendl's comment. Without the pridelord's influence, it was easier to see. *And the stormtails are all kingfishers.*

Now that she knew what Wendl had done to Sheen, Whisper saw the wettest starling pride with new eyes—or, perhaps, smelled them with new nares. She'd assumed their color variations from teal to dark blue were just part of their natural plumage, and there was probably some truth to that.

But when she sniffed the darkest blues, she could detect a *tang* in the pigment she suspected was a byproduct of their bodies neutralizing the toxic iron buildup from bloodbeak. If she was right, risking them in battle was reckless. They could be the key to solving everything.

Yet the existence of kingfishers and finches in the murmuration was its own conundrum. Her pride had a collection of stolen gryphon species, even a few starlings, but the core of the Newmoon Pride were definitely starlings. Probably, the murmuration had begun with starlings, but pridelords of old had grabbed new prides.

Her mind went to the murals in the Sky Beneath the Earth, which she hadn't gotten a good look at in the light until recently. She'd taken a moment before they left to check if any salts were left beneath the temple, but the Nighthaunt and his acolytes must have stolen them away to Alwren or King's Reach while she was busy saving the stormtails.

Does the darkstalker splash and play with the opinici from Duckbill? Or does she put on all that feathersparkle and sit in the dark, alone?

Salts aside, the trip down had been worth it just to gawk at the carvings on the walls. There were creatures she'd never heard of. Along the southern jungle section of the mural was a carving of a beast that was half stormtail, half toothy capybara fighting off a crocodile. Another carving depicted a bipedal monster whose body evoked clawdiggers.

Those were what the murmuration of old had to deal with.

Thundercloud stood, displacing large amounts of water and sending stormtails scrambling onto the edge of the underground lake. He tried to squeeze out of the chamber, but he'd soaked up too much water. He backed in again, then shook himself, soaking walls and ceiling. Like an early spring rain, water dripped from the ceiling while the sand gryphon made his escape.

Whisper flicked water out of her ear. The Emerald Jungle felt a lifetime away at this point, and part of her wondered if she could hold the altruism at bay forever. She'd spent so long with starlings near death, giving them any sort of life after the parasite, that she'd forgotten what real happiness looked like.

"I've never seen starlings so content," she told Flicker. "I'm used to watching the infected, the altruistic. Seeing them play with owl opinici and sand gryphons, it's so strange."

"Were you not happy with me?" The strawberry finch's concern was etched into her ears, posture, and pheromones.

Whisper chose her words carefully. "You gave me a bright spot in a hard life. Moonlit Blossom was the same way. He added a levity to what we did, a kindness, like when he'd joke about my nest. And... compared to the life I led at Mothfeather, I'm much more content with who I am here. I love being a gryphon. But the world around me, it was not a happy place."

Flicker wrapped her tail around Whisper's, and the newmoon pride leader felt safe, secure. Anchored.

The *anchored* feeling lasted a full ten seconds before Flicker pushed Whisper into the pool.

Black and grey featherdust, plus some stray silver eyeshine, drifted up into the pool. She was cut off from the pheromones of her pride, and a deep panic rose, which she pushed down. The stormtails had already been swimming for an hour and were fine without her. They'd be fine if she washed off a layer of dust, too.

The last three times Whisper had been clean, she'd nearly died. But here in the least hospitable desert on the continent, the one sandwiched between opposing armies, dangerous jellies, and toxic algae blooms, she decided to take a chance and be happy and wet.

But I won't be wet alone.

She pushed off from the bottom of the pool, splashed out of Lake Triddle, and pulled Flicker in with her, startling a ground parrot in a vest that had wandered in to see what all the noise was about.

56

DARK TALONS, DARK GRYPHONS

While Hoppy took Flicker and most of the susurration to eat frogs and griffinflies in a verdant span of the desert, Sound of Snow and a small team of Blackpaw Pride smuggled Whisper and Wendl past Blacktalon.

Once they were north of the fortress, the sand gryphons disappeared, leaving Sound of Snow to explain. "They're going to scout around. When they find where the alabasters are stocking supplies, they report it to the burrowing owls, who dig a tunnel there. We'll fly back after dark, when the alabasters hide. My mom has made them very superstitious."

Despite it being daylight, Blacktalon looked abandoned. The fields were torn up, the stables empty, and there were no guards posted in the towers.

"I thought this was supposed to be the front lines of a big war," Whisper commented. "Where's the army?"

"Guess the battle lines moved." Sound of Snow picked at a downy feather poking out of her shoulder, light grey against a sea of black and red plumage. "This is supposed to stop after two years, isn't it? You grew up an opinicus, right?"

"You can speed it up with warm baths and feather oil," Whisper said before realizing Sound of Snow probably meant Wendl. "But yes, it does end."

Wendl stepped in to cover for her ex-fiancée. "We grew up together, Whisper and I. Different opinicus species molt in their own way. You might ask your father."

"If Mom ever finds him, I will." Sound of Snow's tail twitched with annoyance. "Figures I'd be the only opinicus. It's not fair. My brothers have already molted, and they're bigger than me."

"Being an opinicus isn't so bad." Wendl looked to Whisper for affirmation.

Whisper didn't rise to the bait. "Shouldn't we be finding your family?"

They circled around to the north, using the cover of the forest. Unlike around the fortress, there were farmers, goliath birds, and capybaras roaming these lands. None were close enough to get a good look at the trio. The gryphons kept Wendl behind them with her starry greens. Hopefully, from a distance, there was just black and a hint of red on Sound of Snow.

As they neared their destination, Wendl paused suddenly, staring past an abandoned ranch to one that looked lively.

"This is not a good place for a rest," Sound of Snow snapped. "There's no good place to hide if we get spotted."

Along the ranch, an alabaster and a blackwing chatted happily, while a younger blackwing played with a peafowl. Whisper sent an inquiry, and it took her a moment to interpret the scent Wendl replied with.

Khalim?

"We'll come back later," Whisper replied, though she hoped they wouldn't need to. There were only a few more ranches to skirt before they reached Wendl's home.

A PAIR of blackwing stabletalons led the goliath birds away from the ranch, giving Whisper, Sound of Snow, and Wendl the opportunity they needed.

They slunk into the main domicile on their bellies. The owl calibrated her hoots as quietly as her starling guests could hear, and Whisper made sure she could tell where Wendl was located, sending her a reminder she was no longer a mothfeather.

"Your family will not recognize you," she said softly. "If we can get one alone, maybe we can restrain them until you explain the situation."

Sound of Snow kept watch on the stabletalons, hooting down reports, while Whisper and Wendl searched the ranch. Ultimately, they went down into the root cellar, which was full of occupied nests.

"It's...not First Morning yet." Whisper was surprised she'd forgotten. "It would have been a great help to have friends in this land, but we cannot afford to wait for them to wake. A war migration moves on its stomach, but we are days behind."

Wendl reached down, caressing the sleeping face of an opinicus who might be her mother. "She looks so much older. I was thinking they wouldn't recognize me, but I almost didn't recognize them. So much lost time."

Owl hoots sounded, and Whisper used citrus to force Wendl to leave. Her friend's history of elixir use meant it wasn't enough to compel her, but it did snap her out of her depression, if only for a moment.

They started to circle back when they reached the earlier ranch and Wendl asked them to stop. "We need friends and information, right? Khalim has both."

Whisper tried to focus on Khalim's scent, but all she could smell was Piprik, the Eyes of the Seraph King, which raised her hackles. She could still hear the original Piprik's voice, his *arrogance,* even up to the moment of his death.

Unlike the others, as Mally's scribe, she'd actually met Piprik several times before she knew who he was. She'd been a naive little apprentice, and when the Nighthaunt told her Piprik was a friend bringing them food and medical supplies, she'd believed him.

The Nighthaunt had even used his real name, Piprik, trusting that a dumb little farm opinicus from Mothfeather wouldn't know who the Eyes of the Seraph King was or what an Alabaster Eyrie badge looked like. The anger within her that had faded to embers after the expedition's failure was rekindled upon smelling him again.

"Down girl," Wendl said, as though Whisper were an unruly goliath bird. "Piprik is dead. That's Khalim. He's a friend."

"Your friend," Whisper hissed. "Not mine."

Wendl must've thought very hard about mint. It

wasn't enough to let her actually make much of the calming smell, but Whisper understood what she was going for. "He's my friend. Do you need to look into my memories and see how kind he can be?"

"No." Whisper realized her tone was overly emphatic. "There's no time, I mean. How do you lure him away from the others?"

Sound of Snow's ear twitched. "No need. The peacock with the Redwood Valley accent saw you and is headed to the ranch nearby to check it out. Sounds like he's expecting you to be waiting down below."

Wendl perked up. "That's right! He had an assistant when he was pretending to be a salt trader. Lei, I think the fisherfolk's name was? He'll relay any messages to Khalim for us. Let's go."

"Sound of Snow, will you keep watch?" Whisper asked. "I don't like this."

The owl hooted and disappeared into the trees while the starlings crawled into the abandoned ranch.

"It smells like blackwings in here," Whisper complained.

WHISPER WAS USED to taking the lead since the pridelord left, but in retrospect, her silver eyes were probably not the best thing for Lei to see when he came in. He saw her eyes and immediately turned to flee.

"Wait, Lei!" Wendl shouted after him. "It's me, Wendl!"

The peacock *did* turn around, though he took an interesting fighting stance.

"Is that pitohui grappler?" Whisper asked. "Does that work if you're not poisonous?"

"It does." Khalim came down the stairs. Or, rather, Piprik came down the stairs, but even through white-tailed kite vocal chords, he sounded like Khalim. "It's been a long time. If I remember from what Wendl told me at the Jadebeak Falls, you're—"

"Whisper," she interrupted rather than risk him using her old name. And, while she was at it, she added, "And they're the Newmoon Falls now."

"Noted." Mally's top assistant in the jungle looked at her strange markings, stripes, and eyes. "That does seem to suit you better. How did you escape from the swarm? Have you been fleeing west for days now?"

"Murmuration," Whisper muttered, but Wendl stepped in front of her.

"No, we were left behind in the jungle," she explained. "The Six, me included, tried to overthrow the pridelord. The Nightsky, Sparkwing, and other prides were suffering from the bloodbeak Mally gave them, and the pridelord wouldn't let us talk to medicine gryphons or opinicus scholars to see if you'd found a cure. He was turning paranoid, so we tried to kill him and use the salts you gave me to swap in Nighteyes."

Sound of Snow poked her head through a hole in the cellar roof. "I like Nighteyes. She visited the Darkfeather Highlands when I was a chick. She's the purple one with the sparkly eyes, right?"

"Right," Wendl said.

"Well, she'll make a good pride leader lord thing," the owl continued. "She seemed like she was pretty smart about diplomacy stuff, even if she wasn't owl-smart."

"They did not succeed," Whisper corrected. She wanted to join the conversation in a non-hostile way, but it had been a long time since she'd had to interact with opinici who weren't also starlings.

Wendl nodded. "Right. We thought the pridelord had gotten wind of our plan and killed Balthar, who was preparing the salts, but now I'm not so sure. I think Balthar saw an opportunity to steal the pridelord position for himself."

"It was not an opportunistic move," Whisper interrupted. "Kism had already left the Emerald Jungle and warned the Nighthaunt. They had armies at the border. They just wanted you two out of the way while it happened. And they wanted access to your incense bombs so they could disable my pride and steal Sheen and Rudder."

"Sheen and Rudder are gryphons? Why're they special?" Lei asked.

"They're just like any other starling," Wendl began, "except something in their blood pulls out iron and converts it to a blue pigment stored in their feathers."

"What?" Sound of Snow asked. "What does that mean?"

Khalim, ever the scholar, understood first. "It doesn't cure bloodbeak, but it would stop the effects of it. Do you need to use the salts for it to be effective, or could you just take some blood from one of those gryphons and give it to someone with bloodbeak to treat them? And it's only two gryphons in the entire jungle?"

"We don't know for sure," Whisper said, "but it's possible some of the bluer stormtails are the same as Rudder. Sheen was Wendl's first secret experiment, and it worked. She turned indigo instead of violet as her body purged the iron."

"Okay, well, we need to experiment, then," Khalim said, the cadence of his speech returning to a time before his plumage had been white. "You haven't tested a blood transfusion? What've you been doing in the Emerald Jungle?"

Whisper settled on her back paws to look Khalim in the eye, Piprik's eyes. The Eyes of the Seraph King. "Revolution. We've had a lot to deal with, and we have no resources for such a thing. A blood transfusion, in a jungle? How? And in case you missed it, Rudder—whose blood we *know* works—is gone. The Nighthaunt got him."

"What about Sheen?" Khalim asked.

"Safe," was all Whisper would reply, "but we're not here for this. We need to know where the murmuration went and what you can tell us about them. We answered your questions. Now answer ours."

Wendl looked from one colleague to another. "Without a friendly pridelord, you won't be able to interact with the stormtails. I promise, our goals are aligned. If you've got a metalworks that can make needles small enough to do this *blood infusion*, we can work together...after this is resolved."

It wasn't Wendl or Whisper that seemed to ground Khalim, but Lei. Wendl had described the peafowl as a salt-trading assistant, but Whisper recognized the look of a father who did not want to disappoint their son. She'd seen it in reverse, back when she hadn't wanted to disappoint her own father.

"The murmuration has been gone for days, but they were moving very slowly, from field to field," Khalim explained. "The free prides were tracking them from the mountains and got a message back. You might be able to reach them before the Black-wing Eyrie, but it's a long shot."

"We can but try," Whisper said.

Khalim nodded. "Lei, will you take Wendl and the Strix gryphon and tell them all you know? Then find out what they know, as fast and thorough as you can?"

Lei departed with Sound of Snow and Wendl, leaving behind Whisper and Khalim. Whisper expected her old colleague to try to pressure her into giving him a stormtail or something like that. Instead, he spoke not as a scholar, but as a parent.

"If it's not an imposition, will you...speak to Lei?" he asked, and Whisper had no idea what he was referring to.

The newmoon gryphon twitched her tail nervously. "About what?"

"The salts did this, right?" He gestured at her body. "With your modifications? I've got a vial stashed away. That might help Lei. I wasn't sure what to do. He seems happy, but how would I know if he wasn't?"

Oh! It took Whisper a moment to understand that Khalim wasn't talking about her wonderful, fluffy, or stylish gryphonic form. He meant her *female* gryphon form. "Not everyone needs this."

"But you did?" he asked.

Whisper nodded. "I did. I will talk to Lei. When the murmuration has settled and the lost starlings have been returned to the jungle, I will come here. Or you may come to me."

"Leave a message at the Newmoon Falls?" he said, using the correct name.

"Yes." She willed her tail to stop twitching. It had been so long since a friend had asked a favor of her, even longer since she'd promised to fulfill it. Moonlit Blossom would be proud of her. "Now, we have little time. I must gather my pride and hurry. Even if the murmuration takes the Blackwing Eyrie, I do not think Balthar will let them live. I think our lives are the price he will pay to become a seraph."

Khalim grumbled. "Being an alabaster is over-rated. I sunburn now, do you know that? White feathers do nothing to keep the sun off my head. Speaking of alabasters, though, watch yourself. The armies of the Seraph King were two days behind the murmuration. I think they intended to perform the coup-de-grace after the starlings are dead."

I do not have enough gryphons to stop a king's army, but if I can reach the pridelord in time, if enough of the murmuration is left... Whisper kept her thoughts to herself. There was a point where planning became worrying, where worrying became panicking, where panicking became waking nightmares of imagining Moonlit Blossom killed by flechettes.

There was a sliver of hope left, and she would latch onto that hope with all the might of her beak, tomia dug in, and refuse to let go so long as she held breath.

BLACK SKIES, CHARRED EARTH

The murmuration continued across the continent, consuming everything in their path. They passed eyrie after eyrie, all abandoned.

Mostly abandoned. Nighteyes looked down at the dead bodies of opinici who had tried to hide inside this nameless mountain eyrie. The architecture was glorified goliath stable, its entryway resembling the small outposts dotting the trail between the Redwood Valley and Crackling Sea Eyries.

Framing the entryway were carvings of trees with golden leaves, presumably what the nearby groves of green trees would look like come autumn. The whole eyrie was blocky but sturdy—the sort of place that could probably withstand rockslides. Judging by the indentations and scratches, it had.

The starlings probably would have passed it by had the pridelord not ordered them to stop and search. While most of the jadebeaks wandered off, rolling in sage or licking flaxseed, the pridelord directed others to search for a way inside the stone structure.

The main entrances had been secured but not barricaded or trapped. To Nighteyes, that suggested it would be empty inside, that someone had just closed the entryway on their way out. It gave her some reassurance that eyries were fleeing. That meant fewer lives lost.

Fewer, but not none, as the bodies at her feet attested to.

The starlings hadn't searched these out specifically, but a few dozen opinici had attempted to hide where the food was stored. Once the starlings sniffed their way down a ventilation shaft, altruism hit, and now there were dead bodies littering a granary, ignored by the starlings pecking away at the wheat and other goods.

The pridelord ate his fill first, then entered a deep sleep. Once Balthar's sway lessened and Nighteyes' body became her own, she searched for a way to take the dead opinici outside. She was too sore to even attempt to fly them up the ventilation shaft on her own. Instead, she followed the opinicus scents to locate the front gates. From the outside, she hadn't seen a way to open them. From the inside, courtesy of her time spent with in Ashen Weald cities, she could see how the mechanism worked.

Looks heavy. Guess I need help after all.

It took an effort to get her request past the citrus in the air, but she persuaded some of her hunters to stop digging up poorwills to snack on and help release the giant latches and drag the bodies out.

She didn't know how these opinici consecrated

their dead, so she left them beneath the stars, figuring someone else would come by and know what to do once the murmuration left. Judging by the carvings and paintings, the trees here held some significance to the inhabitants, so she placed each opinicus beneath a different tree.

Weirdly, the pridelord had not leaned into the altruism on their way here. They'd passed over small outposts she was sure were populated, that had signs of habitation or lacked signs of evacuation, but he'd kept the starlings on task, always going east. It was only eyries and agricultural centers where he forced them down.

The murmuration was tired, but except for Talli's pride leader, it wasn't exhausted. They'd eat their fill here, rest a day, then leave in the morning. While a migration took time, the journey from the Emerald Jungle past the Crackling Sea and up north was rushed compared to the pace post-Blacktalon.

It seemed like a kindness, at first, to get to stop and eat. Now, though, Nighteyes wondered. Opinici depended upon crops and ranch animals to feed their massive eyries. When the murmuration left, what would happen to the owners of this strange land?

Her pride chirped behind her, anxious to be away from the dead bodies. Balthar and the jadebeaks slept below. If she was going to do some scouting, now was her chance.

"Go on, go back to digging up poorwills," she told her pride. If their scents stretched across the countryside, it wouldn't seem out of place if hers did the same. The inhabitants of the unnamed eyrie had left the old, dusty stalks of sage atop the new growth. She rolled in them, hoping to dull her vibrant purple to obscure it from opinicus view, and then started to explore.

NIGHTEYES STUCK CLOSE to the eyrie so she didn't wear herself out. She didn't trust the new pridelord, currently deep asleep within the granary, not to let her fall from the sky tomorrow if she was too exhausted to migrate in the morning. But she wanted to get a message to the Ashen Weald, and she thought these might be their mountains.

At least, she saw redwoods, the very trees the Redwood Valley had been named for. She didn't know the name of this mountain range. The southern stretch was called the taiga, after the prides who lived there. Then she remembered Poisonmaw and the Darkfeather Highlands, both places she'd visited. Those felt...more temperate than here. Wetter. The ferns were a lighter green, and sage was only found atop the mountains, not down below.

She was starting to have doubts. The same range, probably. But far north of the lands she knew. There were no ground parrots in these mountains, which was the most telling sign. Even the trees were too far apart. She sniffed, smelling pine and ash, but no aneda. That didn't reassure her. Still, someone might come to help. She had to leave a message for them.

She glided back down the mountain to the eyrie entrance. Her pride had been busy playing at the front gates when she left and appeared to have acci-dentally shut them again, forcing the few waking starlings to come in and out of a ventilation shaft. Thankfully, starlings were good at squeezing into small places. The designers had probably never expected someone to crawl down such a small opening.

We're lucky nobody got stuck.

A couple of her pride were still out hunting poorwills. They were a rare treat back when the Nightsky Pride's home bordered the Jadebeak Mountains, the only bird she knew that hibernated. Wendl had always considered it bad luck to eat poorwills, a fact that made a lot more sense after seeing the sketches along her hidden workshop's walls. Wendl's family or friends, whoever was in the pictures, had the eyes and plumage of common poorwills.

That explains The Sleeping City.

Nighteyes continued her search outside the eyrie. The stables were empty of goliath birds, so no free meat this time. There were drag marks and talonprints heading northeast, along a trail. A few empty crates remained, broken down and past the point of surviving a journey.

One of her pride pecked at a line of seeds, probably goliath feed spilled as the occupants were packing up the birds to flee. Nighteyes nuzzled her pridemate. He smelled strongly of sage.

Maybe they miss the Jadebeak Mountains. I don't suppose there's any chance I can convince Whisper to let them go through her territory to visit.

That thought gave her pause. What was going on back home? What had happened to Wendl and Whisper? Or Rudder, even? She shook her head. There was no use speculating. The best she could do is hope she was a lot closer to the Darkfeather Highlands than the flora was telling her.

She scoured the outside of the eyrie, endless tree ornamentation, searching for something useful. She'd need to sleep soon. She was just about to give up when she came across some crates piled next to the ventilation shaft. These had a red circle on them and were intact. She sniffed at one, but it smelled bad, like cave guano and salt.

Still, that would let her leave a message. A smell that distinct would catch the nose of a starling, maybe even a wealder. It took a few trips, but she went down to the western side of the eyrie, where someone following her might go, and left a warning to any friendly gryphons who may come through later—be they free pride, Stormtail, or Newmoon.

The lord of the pride is not himself, seek out the Ashen Weald.

That would do it. Hopefully, anyone following who got this far would have found a way to deal with the altruism.

"Simple enough." Nighteyes wiped her paws off in the dirt, disturbing sleeping grasshoppers, but the smell wouldn't come off. It felt familiar somehow, but from a part of her mind that still slept. She tried licking her paw, but the taste was bitter salt, and she spat it out.

It reminded her of the time she'd walked through the fields outside Orlea's flameworks, then groomed herself.

Wait.

She'd spent so long thinking of the pridelord as her enemy, Balthar as the greatest worry, that she'd completely forgotten about the mothfeathers and blackwings who lived here.

An eyrie with only one way in, exactly large enough for starlings to crawl in but not escape easily. All valuable crates removed, then several brand new crates brought in.

In the skies above the forgotten Eyrie, as the sun descended, she saw the stars burning. Stars carried by vibrant, tropical gryphons with long, flowy tails.

The gryphons dove, twisting away at the last second and dropping torch after torch atop the crates.

Nighteyes didn't have time to warn anyone before the first crate exploded, collapsing the ventilation shaft and trapping the pridelord and murmuration inside.

58

BURROWING BEES

Whatever happened inside must have knocked the pridelord unconscious, because no one fought Nighteyes for control of her pride. Which was good, because her pride was the only one outside the blast, and their immediate reaction would have been to fly into the sky and search for the source of the explosion and try to kill it.

The strange, long-tailed gryphons—similar to Erlock Chartail's fantail pride, though with dongles alongside their feather tails—had vanished, so her pride's altruism didn't kick in.

That meant she could give them a simple order, and she ordered them to hide. She had a memory of a place nearby with sage plants and squirrelbrush, and she gave them the scent of it and ordered them to flee there. They put up a token resistance but ultimately obeyed. The squirrelbrush was as much to keep them from seeing anything that might trigger their altruism as to keep them from being seen.

Nighteyes herself grabbed one of the torn hides by

the stables, then concealed herself in a crate. She hoped the combination of the two would keep her hidden from view. Sure enough, when no starlings appeared to escape, the architects of destruction flew down to check on things.

A scarlet tanager opinicus wearing a Redwood Valley harness with a blackwing badge landed atop the stables where she hid. Next to him were several of the fantail mimics. Nighteyes always forgot the Blackwing Alliance had gryphons with them.

"A motmot did well, picking this target," the opinicus said.

The gryphon, presumably a motmot, nodded her head. "We go back now. Rybalt will be upset. He told us to keep you safe. Come, Bario."

"Not as upset as the Goldtree Gardens reeve if he finds out this was us." The phoenix, Bario, hesitated. "It's strange. Sending the starlings after us was a smart move, nothing we'd ever see coming. It's the kind of thing Mally was known for, playing two sides against each other. I know our spies reported the Nighthaunt was near death, but he must still be alive. I wish we had eyes on the king's eyries."

"Stripes will be back soon," the motmot stated.

"Stripes is probably dead." There was a hint of hesitation in the opinicus's voice, though Nighteyes didn't know what that was about.

The motmot scoffed. "Mally must be alive, Stripes must be dead? Stripes had a motmot, a motmot, a motmot, and a motmot guarding her. She is alive and well. The Nighthaunt has no motmot guards. He is dead or will die soon."

Bario laughed, a songbird sound that reminded

Nighteyes of the Redwood Valley's inhabitants. "I suppose you're right. Okay, let's get out of here. I'm surprised you were willing to listen to my plan when Rybalt wouldn't. You should be careful about upsetting your reeve."

The motmot escorted Bario away, the conversation going on about how until a motmot served as reeve of the Pitohui Eyrie, they saw Rybalt as more of a partner than their leader. To Nighteyes' starling ears, this was all foreign. The idea of disobeying a leader would have been impossible to her a few years ago.

Now, though...I guess I've changed. Wendl's elixirs and my time with the Ashen Weald made me someone new. Once the motmots vanished into the moonlit sky, Nighteyes called her pride out of hiding. *Strange that Rybalt wouldn't have wanted them to set this trap. Does he have something else planned for us? Bario nearly eliminated us in one explosion. None of us thought to check this eyrie for traps; it looked like all the others.*

She flew around to the main gates of Goldtree Gardens. Though they were shut, she'd unlocked them from the inside. She ordered her pride to come out of hiding. "Okay, which one of you closed these doors, and do you remember if there's a way to open them from the outside?"

Her pride, purple in the moonlight but drenched in the bitter-herb smell of sage, looked at her blankly. She thought back to her time with Whisper in the Abyssal Naze, and asked again, this time with citrus.

"Show me how you closed the door," she commanded. If the pridelord was still unconscious, this might work.

One of the hunters, the one who got into trouble

for hiding squirrels in the nests of his hunting group, stepped forwards. "I thought it'd be funny to lock the jadebeaks inside. It's this thing here...you have to kind of get under and over and twist it?"

The gates, which had closed so easily, took hours and the entire Nightsky Pride to get open again from the outside. When they opened, the rest of the murmuration spilled out, angry and spoiling for a fight, but the motmots were long gone.

There's an opportunity here. Nighteyes slipped past the flood, through the halls of the eyrie, and into the granary. Between Whisper and Wendl's plotting, Nighteyes had forgotten that if a pridelord died, the murmuration could select a new one. Each pride leader's vote held equal weight no matter the size of their pride. They'd certainly kill the assassin, but anyone would be better than Balthar.

She made it to the pridelord's body, her claws out, when Talli and Iri appeared from the shadows.

"Good to see you live." Nighteyes retracted her claws as subtly as she could. She nearly told them about spying on Bario the Phoenix and the motmot pride outside but thought better of it. They'd ask why altruism hadn't taken her. "We were hunting poorwills in the forest when we heard the explosion. Sorry about the delay, but we got the door open. Is the pridelord okay?"

Talli's look was skeptical. Iri hadn't remembered anything about Nighteyes, and it seemed her sister didn't, either. "I bandaged him up. The bags of grain fell on top of him. I think he'll be okay once he awakens."

Beyond Talli were several wounded from different

prides. Judging by their injuries, they'd flung themselves on top of the pridelord to save him, and now they'd be unable to fly.

"What about them?" Nighteyes asked. "We should send them back to the Emerald Jungle."

Her body took control again, and the heady smell of wheat was replaced with citrus as the pridelord stirred.

"A war migration implies a certain number of losses." Balthar stood, leaning on Iri. "I know they'd rather have died in combat, but...getting ambushed is its own type of combat."

How did I not see it was him immediately? The old pridelord never felt a need to explain anything to us.

Nighteyes thought about a possible solution, hoping the shadow version of herself would say it aloud. A few times now, if it didn't rouse suspicion, it had worked. This was one of those times.

"It's unlikely they'll come back and re-trap this place," she heard herself say. "What if we leave our wounded here, with the food? There's more than we can eat. A few will have healed by the time we return home. And even if someone does show up, it might make the enemy wary of us if they think we've left starlings at every past eyrie."

It wasn't quite how she'd have said it in her own mind, but it worked. She could feel the pridelord peel the wounded out of the murmuration. Not enough to cause other starlings to turn on them, but just enough that they wouldn't be compelled to fly when the order came.

Unfortunately for Nighteyes, who thought she'd

have more time to rest after exploring the mountains, nobody wanted to spend more time here.

"We leave now," the pridelord commanded. "We'll rest in forests from here on out. I recognize the mountains here, the Three Talons. We're close, and we should expect more ambushes."

He looked at Iri and Talli as he spoke it, and Nighteyes thought she saw a spark of something in Talli's eyes. She'd turned to look at Iri when a strong blast of citrus made both of their eyes blank.

He forgot he was pridelord, and he didn't want them to know.

That was interesting, as it meant they might not be in on it. Now that Nighteyes believed Wendl's strange opinicus tales, she'd gone through her mind, retracing every time she'd interacted with Iri and Talli. Talli was well-liked by her pride, which might mean she cared about them. Three of the starlings left behind came from her section of the jungle, and she'd want them to be okay.

Iri was less readable. The leader of the Jadebeak Pride was aloof, and Nighteyes still found her predecessor's death mysterious. But Iri's eyes had gone just as blank as Talli's. It was possible, just a little, that if Balthar died and the other leaders all wanted a different pridelord who wasn't Iri that she'd join in.

I wish I'd had more time with her before Whisper's fish wore off.

Citrus shifted to mint, then the prides abandoned the underground eyrie, flying into the mountains. Their path had previously been direct if a little meandering. Now, the pridelord searched the mountains for a hiding spot away from prying eyes and ordered one of the lesser prides to keep watch while the others slept.

The nightsky were forced to nest in a glen of wild-flowers, purple to match their plume. The plants were still young and the flowers small. The buzzing of the bees reminded her of what was coming. The Sleeping City would soon rouse, and when that happened, the starling prides would be trapped between the moth-feathers and the blackwings.

Nighteyes dreamt of the pridelord's unconscious form in the granary, but this time her dream claws did not sheath, and she tore out his throat before Iri and Talli could stop her.

59

ETERNAL SLEEP

Whisper and the susurration found the missing garrison from Blacktalon before they reached the murmuration. A large army of white-tailed kites had set up camp outside the Sleeping City, and the blackwings who ran the stables and the pitohui who kept watch on the vault below had been taken prisoner.

"We should help them," Wendl said. "Those're our opinici."

Whisper had to use mint on herself to get her hackles down. "We're not mothfeathers, we're starlings. I'm not even an opinici, and your family is safely sleeping next door to Khalim."

Wendl glared at her, but Whisper put on her best unreadable ears and scent. Taloncrest joined in with his own stare. The parasite had taken enough of his mind that he hadn't spoken again, but that wasn't a problem for a starling. In his scents, she saw the memories she'd shared with the pride of who she and Wendl really were.

In particular were memories of Whisper as a young opinicus being treated kindly by the pitohui caretaker and of the dead, eaten blackwing whose mothfeather chick was likely sleeping below.

"I would not have shared those if I thought you'd use them against me," she told him. He continued sending her the emotions of family, of protecting those who were lost, of seeking out even non-starlings who had been infected and saving them.

The snowfoot gryphon added his agreement. A side effect of the red markings over his eyes were that he always looked very angry or disappointed. In this case, she thought he might really be disappointed in her.

"Even if I wanted to help, the susurration isn't big enough to stand against the Seraph King's army." She let the smells of the enemy camp wash over her when the wind changed. The Golden Sky Army were the alabaster's largest force, usually led by Hi-kun. Thanks to interrogating Kism, she knew the feather-snake in the jungle was the result of combining frozen seraph with The Metalworks. Though Hi-kun's elite Golden Sky had been absent from the battle.

Nor were they here.

They must be guarding the Seraph King, she thought. Still, the forces occupying Mothfeather weren't small. They'd have a hard time taking the full might of the Emerald Jungle, even with their fancy metal talons, tactics, and armor. They'd also be hard-pressed to take the Blackwing Eyrie, if nothing had happened there since Whisper had left opinicus life behind.

But they wouldn't need to. This was a force large enough to mop up whoever was left after the starlings and blackwings finished killing each other. For that role, there were more than enough white-tailed kites to deliver the killing blow.

"We can't...do nothing," Wendl pushed, but it was clear she had no idea how they could help the Sleeping City. The giant, very visible seal blocked the way into the hibernation chambers.

The ptarmigan continued glaring at Whisper, and while Wendl might not have any ideas, Whisper did have one.

"When I was a ranch chick, we used to sleep in the city for safety." Whisper didn't mention a goliath bird had gotten out and eaten a hibernating mothfeather on her parents' ranch. "I left my favorite toy behind, a stuffed capybara, and I snuck off to retrieve it. One of the pitohui found me outside after the seal had been put into place, and he brought me in a secret way. Here's what I propose. First, we're going to need some dead bodies and a lot of blood..."

WHISPER'S memory of the back entrance wasn't as accurate as she would have liked, but the susurration's sneakiest sniffers located a suspicious cellar door directly north of the eyrie, and Wendl's opinicus talons got it open. While she checked the side chamber to make sure the inhabitants of Mothfeather were sleeping soundly, the starlings scoured the ranches for the second part of Whisper's plan. Not all the locals had come to the city to sleep, and the susurration located several dead mothfeathers covered in chew marks.

"Poor things," Wendl said once she'd rejoined the susurration and confirmed the city was sound asleep.

"Useful, dead things," Whisper countered. She'd come across many *useless* dead things, and she always appreciated when the dead could be put to use. Versus the many infected starlings she'd been forced to bury in salts.

Especially since I won't be letting my wards eat anymore opinici. That's a lesson I don't need to relearn.

They dragged the dead bodies to the very front of the vaults, where the seal would be opened.

"Not...enough," Taloncrest managed to say. The ptarmigan cooed encouragement to him. "Should... kill...more."

He pointed his beak at individual chambers where hundreds of mothfeathers slept, quiet as the dead. Whisper still remembered her shock at learning other opinici didn't hibernate, too. It didn't seem fair.

She looked from the dead ranchers to the live mothfeather bodies. Ignoring the bite marks, the torpor was so complete she almost couldn't tell them apart. One bloody mothfeather looked like another, living or dead.

"Did you find any goliath birds?" She gave them the scent, along with the image of a very large rhea or cassowary. The susurration chittered, and Whisper turned to Wendl. "You grew up on a ranch. Do you think you could get one of the birds down here?"

Wendl gulped. "Alive or dead? A living goliath bird would wreak havoc."

"Either, I just need a lot of blood," Whisper explained. As Wendl prepared to run off and find some goliath birds, Whisper continued issuing orders to the starlings around her. "I need you to *gently* retrieve the sleeping mothfeathers and lay them out on the floor here. All the way down the main hallway, as far as you can see. And open every vault door on the way."

Wendl shook her head as she went but didn't protest. She'd asked Whisper to save the Mothfeather Eyrie, and Whisper was about to do just that. First, though, she needed to get a message to the pitohui vaultkeepers held above. They'd be the ones who had to sell this.

Whisper crawled up on the alabaster camp, sniffing out where the prisoners were kept. Goliath birds from Blacktalon brought wagons full of supplies, and the opinici here slept in tents, much like the alabasters who had taken her prisoner in the jungle.

The moon was low, but she worried about the brazier lights catching her eyeshine, so she wiped it off. Contrary to popular belief, she didn't keep it on all the time. A newmoon needed to learn to trust her scents, and eyeshine helped train the new ones. It also made the infected more at-ease, its original purpose.

She left her stripes on, trusting them to hide her against the long grasses. She could smell pitohui coming from the shabbiest tent. That would make it easy to poke her head inside. It would have been smarter for the alabasters to confine the prisoners in a stone room, but perhaps they didn't trust that there weren't secret escape passages.

Which, as we've just proven, there are. Blackwings and mothfeathers both love their hidden passages.

She let opinimint featherdust fall off her whenever the wind pushed it at the tent, and eventually, the guards relaxed. Once they were caught up in a casual conversation, she went around to the back of the tent and pecked a hole in it.

"Hello?" she whispered. She pulled her beak back just as talons came after it. To her surprise, she could smell the batrachotoxin. The pitohui vaultkeepers usually remained poison free.

I suppose they did just watch a murmuration of starlings fly overhead. Whisper tried again. "I just want to talk to you. I have a way to save the Sleeping City."

An eye appeared at the hole. Seeing Whisper clearly didn't reassure the owner, but her spooky appearance would show she wasn't one of the Alabaster Eyrie's allies, either. She got a single blink out of it, and she sniffed. It was the same vaultkeeper who had returned Whisper through the back entrance as a little chick.

She wanted to tell the opinicus that she knew him, but she didn't think he'd believe it was her. Instead, she stuck to the facts. "I know First Morning is soon, and I imagine you're trying to delay the Alabaster Eyrie as long as you can. *Don't.* Open the vault first thing tomorrow morning. Believe me when I say that everyone is okay, but you should act horrified."

The prisoner's beak must be tied, as he just grunted a response. She hoped he believed her. A lot of lives were in the balance, even if she didn't care for most of them. She slipped through the long reeds to return to the susurration's hiding spot. Though there was no sign of anyone tracking her, there was the faint scent of owl when the winds shifted.

THOUGH SHE WOULD HAVE PREFERRED to leave her homeland entirely, Whisper remained in the vault to see what happened the next morning. She'd located her family and spent a few hours just staring at them and taking in their scent. Since she'd left, her siblings had found mates and had chicks of their own. It was a strange feeling.

Stranger still was finding her old stuffed capybara toy. One of her younger brothers had given it to his chick. She supposed it was good that it saw use. She knew how important it was to hibernate with a good stuffed animal. Still, seeing a sleeping mothfeather clutching *her* toy left her unsettled. It was a reminder that her family would have long given her up as lost in the jungle. Outside of her family's ranch, there was probably a memorial marker with the wrong name on it.

Her father's face was buried in straw, but his harness was unmistakable. The leather was ancient but well maintained, the metal bits oiled and never allowed to rust. The buckles may be scuffed, but they were polished—only her dad would worry about looking his best as he slept. Nearby sat his satchel, which included a university pin. Whisper checked the paws of her family, but none showed signs of scholarly ink stains.

She returned to the dead bodies and blood to calm herself. Or, at least, the bodies that appeared dead. She wanted this to look feasible, and a 'dead' starling would add to the illusion. She covered herself in blood, cuddled up to a hibernating mothfeather lying in the hallway, and waited.

When dawn came, the large seal creaked open. It was a sound like the challenging *mronk* of an impossibly large goliath bird, a sound no mothfeather ever truly heard as the seal was normally closed after Last Twilight and re-opened before First Morning. Despite the impossibility of it, the sound comforted Whisper. It felt like an old friend from a familiar dream.

The sound rang in her ears until the chatter of opinici broke the spell. The alabaster captain sounded pleased that the pitohui had conceded to open the seal. He was mid-sentence when the light of morning hit the bloody scene within.

"The...the starlings must have gotten in!" the old vaultkeeper shouted. Another vaultkeeper, perhaps his mate, cried next to him.

The alabasters stared in disbelief. One of the soldiers took a step in, slipped on the blood, and fell on a particularly rancid dead body—deliberately placed at the front. He let out a scream and ran out.

"Well, I suppose that solves one problem," the captain grumbled. "Still, I always wanted to meet the Mothfeather Eyrie in battle. At the rate we're going, we won't even get to fight the blackwings."

The gore-soaked soldier wiped a wing on the pitohui's coverings. "The starlings...are they too effective? I mean, will we be able to stop them if the blackwings can't?"

"Find your guts, soldier," the captain ordered.

"The armies of the Seraph King do not lose to *gryphons*."

He'd nearly spat the word, but not all of the soldiers seemed to share his sentiment. Whisper remembered the initial xenophobia the Blackwing Alliance had towards the glacier pride and motmots, but they'd still accepted them in and eventually made them full members. Word was that the Seraph King took a different approach to the gryphons living in his lands and tried to eradicate them.

Something the Abyssal Naze took personally, judging by her brief time spent there. The alabasters here must have memories of facing off against the black-eyed, bewhiskered denizens of the deep, as not everyone seemed eager to face gryphons again.

The corpse at the front of the vault stank as the morning rays heated it up, and the captain finally ordered the seal closed up again. Once darkness returned, Whisper made her retreat, catching up to her pride in the forest nearby.

"Did it work?" Wendl asked, happy to see Whisper nod the affirmative. "We should go back and move the bodies. Can you imagine waking up on First Morning covered in blood?"

Whisper let the susurration groom the blood out of her, afraid to wash off her featherdust. "There's no time, and we can't risk them overhearing us inside and reopening the vault. Plus, if *our* opinici wake up early, it's probably better if they wake up afraid and wary. We don't want someone strutting out the front door and finding themselves beak-to-beak with the alabasters. If they're afraid, they'll send someone out to look around first and prepare."

"I suppose." Wendl didn't look convinced, but she wasn't in charge, Whisper was.

The newmoon leader checked in with all of her pride. She just wanted to know how they were doing, if they could fly, if they'd eaten, but the sense she got back from all of them was that they were...proud. They were glad they'd been able to help another 'pride,' even one composed of opinici.

Also, full. While the Newmoon Pride had carried out their grim task, Desert Rose had taken Flicker and the stormtails to a lake to catch fish. His light blue clashed with her deep red as they carried a large fish horizontally between them, dropping it near Whisper.

The newmoon leader had thought she'd lost her empathy because she was a gryphon, because she was a *starling*. Altruism felt like part of the deal. Between Crestfall and Mothfeather, seeing her susurration acting like gryphlets meeting new friends had her at a loss. Worse, it left her unsure of the path she'd taken.

It all happened at the same time: the realization of the work we were doing, getting betrayed by the Nighthaunt, knowing the Blackwing Eyrie would kill us if they found us. By the time I came out of the salts, everything was a blur until we reached the center of the Emerald Jungle.

I guess it wasn't the change at all. I became who I did because of who I was, not because of who the old Whisper had been.

As the starlings found a cave to hide in until nightfall, Whisper struggled with her feelings, wishing she had Moonlit Blossom here to talk to.

Nighteyes is right. The jungle can be better than it is without losing the good parts. The starlings haven't wanted it before now because they haven't been allowed *to want it.*

Despite setting a bad precedent, Whisper pushed her way between the stormtails and newmoons to curl up with Flicker. The red starling was distressed at hearing of the lengths the susurration had gone today, and Whisper was tempted to bathe her in mint, but that felt manipulative. Instead, she conjured up freshly kneaded soil and pumpkin, and Flicker purred softly in her sleep.

Outside, a dark shape detached itself from the nearby trees and flew east. Whisper didn't dare follow, but she hoped the young owl gryphon knew what she was doing.

They were a long way from the weald.

BLOOD FOREST

Cloudy skies obscured the moon, letting the susurration fly unhindered. Whisper was careful to keep everyone as high as the stormtails were comfortable flying, and she skewed north, over the dark forest.

Despite the fact that most of the starlings had never been here before, they chirped nervously and kept looking at the direction of the ocean, though it was over a day's flight away.

"Did you need to give them all our memories?" Wendl grumbled. "They'd fly faster if they worried less."

Whisper couldn't afford to use up enough mint to keep them calm over this stretch. "The blood forests aren't superstition. When the big storms hit the blood coast, they push the algae far inland. The woods are littered with the bodies of dead opinici who fell sick and didn't have the strength to return home. Most of them were looters, headed to the dead eyries. But some were gryphons, pushed out in unkinder times."

"Strange for there to be cities in a place that gets the storms several times a year," Wendl commented.

"Maybe there were no storms back then. Or maybe the storms were different," Whisper commented. "Or maybe we were."

Wendl's family had left for the farmlands near Blacktalon after the Mothfeather Eyrie was made an official part of the alliance—the blackwings had been the largest detractors when voting time came, wanting access to Mothfeather's agriculture without wanting the responsibility of protecting The Sleeping City in winter. Whisper had grown up here. She'd worked at her uncle's ranch to the north and explored the forests in the summer. She'd even gotten poisoned by a storm once.

The algae turned her beak and talons numb. Her face and neck soon followed. She couldn't stand, could barely walk outside to relieve herself. She'd nearly died from dehydration, unable to keep food down.

And she'd been a healthy young opinicus then. As a gryphon now, such a storm would kill her outright.

Her thoughts must have bled into her pheromones because the susurration closed in around her, Flicker closest.

"Keep it together," Wendl warned. "We're surrounded by enemies on all sides. If you lose control of them, they'll die."

Whisper wasted energy to exude a calming mint. She'd always been prone to invasive thoughts when she was an opinicus, but she'd learned to adjust them as a gryphon. Something about these lands was putting her in a place she didn't want to return to. She moved her thoughts from vomit and the dead fish smell of the blood coast to her joy at living in the Emerald Jungle, where there were no blood coasts, and sitting in the rain with friends, chatting away.

Moonlit Blossom was the one who saw I was afraid of storms. He thought he was helping a former lover, not knowing I was a stranger. But he sat in the storm with me and promised the Emerald Jungle was a place where you never had to fear the rain.

He was wrong, of course. Lightning strikes killed dozens of starlings every year before Wendl's lightning rods. But he meant well.

She recentered herself on the thought of pleasant rain, letting it calm her and the pride. So deep was she in her meditation that she believed the drops falling on her head were products of her imagination until one fell in her eye, causing her eyeshine to run.

"Whisper?" Desert Rose asked, water dripping down from him onto stormtails, who appreciated the effort, and newmoons, who did not. "I checked on the road like you asked. We're ahead of the white opinici's forces now."

The alabasters had brought goliath birds, so they were forced to follow the trails, which tended to skirt the forest for fear of wild animals. Not a lot would pick a fight with a goliath bird, but once they were riled up, it could take hours to calm them down.

Of course, navigation from the sky was a lot easier when Whisper could just follow the existing trails. Wherever there was a major crossroads in the Blackwing Alliance, the closest eyrie was required to maintain a compass visible from the sky to help flyers. It always included two extra arrows, pointing to the two closest eyries.

Now that the king's army had been left behind, Whisper ordered the susurration to cross the road and stay south of it, cleaving closer to the mountains. The last thing she needed at this point was a spring storm to pass over the northern blood coast and kill her susurration before they could save their kin.

They slept during the day, always mindful of scouts. The Blackwing Eyrie wouldn't be any friendlier to starlings than the Alabaster Eyrie was.

Still, no one seemed aware they existed. No one was expecting more starlings.

Hopefully, that extends to the pridelord himself.

Wendl picked herbs and flowers when they stopped for the night, recruiting Flicker to help her. Flicker loved finding new plants, and she'd picked up a basic medicine bag somewhere on their travels, filled to the brim with seeds.

Whisper didn't mean to spy on them, but ever since she'd opened up about her past, the other starlings were constantly sending her their thoughts, a subconscious reciprocity that left her feeling honored and embarrassed. She'd had no idea that the taiga starling was such an artistic soul. When he sang *aqecgiq-segiq aq segseg-qig*, he'd composed those lines himself based on a love he'd once lost to his own hubris.

Of course, Flicker took advantage of her flower-picking time with Wendl to unsubtly ask questions about Whisper's past. The newmoon gryphon had worried it was related to who she was before she changed, and it sort of was. Flicker was completely uninterested in Whisper's previous gender and very interested in Whisper's previous species.

Flicker's words drifted by as she and Wendl spotted some early season starberries. "So opinici don't just mate for the entire year, they mate for…life?!"

"I don't think that's true," Desert Rose added, eager to eat a fruit that tasted of stars. "That's a long time. And what if you don't die at exactly the same moment?"

Whisper sighed. She'd picked up on Flicker's hints about *summer friends*, and she wasn't averse to the idea. She just needed some time. Moonlit Blossom had loved someone who looked like her, and it felt disrespectful not to take time to think about that.

Once the starberry bushes were picked clean, the chatty trio flew over again, searching for much deadlier blossoms. Wendl's plan for when they caught up to the murmuration was to suppress Balthar's influence and try to get assassins in to kill him.

Whisper wasn't so sure. She lacked the brute strength of the pridelord, but the right scents at the right time might provide an advantage. They'd have to see what happened when they got close.

One by one, her own scouts returned, brushing up against her to relay their reports via pheromones. Taloncrest, whose deadly hat had been decorated with flowers with a deftness that suggested ptarmigan design skills, reported there were definitely some opinici hiding in the forests, but they weren't soldiers, they were capybara ranchers. The farms along the way had been picked clean, a sure sign the murmuration had come this way. And to the south was an eyrie that smelled of explosives.

That last bit got her attention. She checked in with her pride, told them to stick together, and turned south to investigate on her own. Wendl, able to resist Whisper as well as she had the previous pridelord, followed along behind.

Whisper felt bad leaving Flicker behind but bringing Wendl. "Wouldn't you rather be picking roots for your poisons?"

"They know what I need. If this is a saltpeter mine, we can put it to use," the opinicus said. "Or it could be a flameworks. When Nighteyes was the Ashen Weald's guest, she learned that the Blackwing Alliance *acquired* the Redwood Valley Eyrie's phoenixes."

An unguarded flameworks didn't seem likely, but Whisper remained quiet on the matter. The murmuration probably caught Mothfeather Eyrie off guard, but now that they were a few eyries deep, the blackwing reeve had probably consolidated all weapons at his disposal to guard his home.

She was so lost in thought, she nearly missed the city. She was used to the sinkhole shape of Mothfeather Eyrie, which had been a drainage nightmare during the rainy season. This eyrie looked like a couple of large buildings, but perhaps the rest of it was below ground.

Wendl echoed her thoughts. "Maybe I'm getting old, but this doesn't look familiar. I do recall an old mining town of sorts, but the way the ground rises up around some of the walls, it looks like this is a deep city."

The eyrie appeared abandoned, but they circled it several times, then Whisper flew down to get a closer look. Wildflowers covered the hills around the buildings. There were a lot of trees, but there was a clear difference between the ones near the eyrie, all young, and the old growth farther out. "I think a rockslide or earthflow covered our mining town, and they just went with it."

"Who needs windows and balconies?" Wendl walked around to the stables. "If I lived in an outpost that got buried by rocks, I'd move to the plains. Who would live here after it got buried once already? It must be important. I still vote flameworks."

The gritty smell of smoke hung in the air, along with the guano-salt of black powder. It was starting to fade, though it seemed not all of the saltpeter had exploded.

"What's this?" Whisper asked, finding a message scrawled across the wall in opinicus common, warning them about the pridelord. "I can't imagine Talli or Iri leaving us a message."

Wendl traced the letters, highlighting where a few were drawn backwards in a way that resembled starling glyphs. "It has to be Nighteyes. You did something to her, didn't you? I saw her eyes go blank when we found the pridelord."

Whisper almost laughed at the accusation *she* had done something to Nighteyes, especially coming from Wendl. Whisper's protections had been meant as a temporary solution. If she'd known Nighteyes would be part of a war migration, she would have done things a little differently. She sniffed at a broken crate and recognized the starberry smell. "You're right that Nighteyes was here. No idea why she was hiding in a crate, though."

They crawled around to the front, where carvings of autumn plumage decorated the eyrie.

"This is Goldtree Gardens?" Wendl scratched some ash from the mosaic. "I expected more trees and fewer rocks."

Whisper was quiet, caught up in a strange scent fresher than Nighteyes'. It was like the dust left behind by snow on dry mountains. She amplified it for Wendl.

"That's...Ninox's chick," Wendl ventured. "I guess the Ashen Weald decided to keep tabs on us. Though I'd hate to think what fate the Strix Pride has in mind for us if something happens to Sound of Snow. We should make sure she got out okay."

The smell of jadebeaks, mint and thyme, plus a heavy dose of citrus blocked Whisper's way in. "The murmuration slept here, then panicked. I think they were inside when the explosion went off. This was some sort of blackwing trap."

She went back to where Nighteyes had hid and sniffed around more, blocking out the starling and owl smells. "You're right about the phoenix, too, or a redwood scholar of some sort. And...gryphons. Not glacier. Motmot pride, unless more joined the alliance since we left. The Nightsky Pride were outside, or everyone might have been sealed in."

Whisper had been so busy teasing apart the different pheromones of gryphons and opinici, she'd lost track of Wendl. The fading smell of cassia continued into the eyrie.

The newmoon leader took a deep breath to calm her nerves, but all that came was citrus. She coughed, then stepped into the darkness.

61

MINT LANTERN

Whisper's mind was full of orders and thoughts, left behind in the scents of frightened jadebeaks and the false pridelord. Now that she had some distance, she could easily see where Balthar was clumsy in how he used pheromones. This smelled of the artificial scents of a waxworks. A candle of orange or lemon lacking the zest of the real fruit.

Every time she opened her beak, she could taste rotten orange. When she breathed too deeply, her mind changed the scent to language, and she could hear a frightened Balthar screaming, *Obey me, you must obey me!* with the fear of a chick facing a wild goliath.

"Whisper?" Wendl called back. "Are you okay?"

Whisper coughed, trying to spit out the scents. "Be grateful your nares are weak. This place is difficult to exist in. We should be quick."

Her opinicus friend sniffed. "I sense obedience, but just faintly. Why does that disturb you?"

Because of the fear. Whisper wanted to keep that to herself, but since the attack on the jungle, she'd resolved herself to tell the truth to other starlings, Wendl included.

"He's terrified," Whisper stated. "I don't know what deal the Nighthaunt made with him, but Balthar had no idea what it would take to pull this off. If he'd had a few years to learn what to do, maybe it would have gone differently. Instead, he had a week, and he's starting to lose his mind. These aren't commands, they're pleas for help."

Wendl's breathing turned ragged, as though she were trying to limit how much of Balthar's panic she inhaled.

Whisper spat again, trying to get it out. "I know I've had my reservations about killing a pridelord, but he's losing control. I don't think he'll have the energy to return home. It's just a question of if we can stop him before he takes the murmuration down with him."

"We nearly did this to Nighteyes. A friend, not that Balthar wasn't also one, once," Wendl stated.

"Being a friend doesn't make you immune to consequences." Whisper used up some of her energy to produce a mint glyph, which would slowly erode the citrus and encourage any starlings who walked by it to produce their own calming mint. "I think you're right, though. If you still have any of your salts, I don't think we should risk trying to dip-dye Nighteyes green and use her as a replacement. I think we have to let the individual leaders choose the new pridelord. Otherwise, they'll fall apart like Balthar."

It made Whisper feel better to do things this way,

but it also added a level of danger. Iri may turn out to be just as dangerous as Balthar.

Even with her weak nares, proximity to the glyph was enough to get Wendl producing the smell of mint. She was like a mint lantern against the citrus dark, and it lessened the stench around her, making Whisper's job easier.

As Balthar's fear faded, the scent of owl grew stronger.

"This way," Whisper ordered Wendl. "I don't see any talonprints heading out, so Sound of Snow must still be inside the eyrie."

WHISPER TOOK THE LEAD, unchallenged by Wendl, which was probably a mistake with the stench of the pridelord reeking from every nook and cranny. Once Whisper figured out what the inhabitants of Goldtree Gardens Eyrie smelled like, she separated out their scent and the starlings to see what was left.

The entrance opened up, offering several levels and passages. Ramps led down to an unloading area for goliath birds. The main level had shops and nests for weary travelers. Whatever rockslide buried most of the eyrie had been recent enough that some areas were still closed off, though not so new that most hadn't been excavated. It was, generally speaking, a small and boring eyrie.

But there were a few interesting scent trails. Many traders went into the throne room, probably to pay respects to the Goldtree Gardens reeve who ruled this second-rate hole in the ground. But what really drew Whisper here was the smell of hooded pitohui.

Residents of the island eyrie coming to visit was probably not unusual. Anywhere that had trade eventually drew scarabs. Underground eyries more than others, if Mothfeather had been any indication. *Oh, the hidden passages into the eyrie were probably put there so pitohui could clear out scarabs. I guess that makes sense.* No, what was unusual was that their scents did not come in from the entrance. They went from the throne room back into a long, winding corridor ending at a pile of boxes.

"Whisper, are we lost?" Wendl followed behind with a rushlight. "I don't see any signs of Sound of Snow here."

Oh, right, Sound of Snow. I forgot. Whisper cleared her throat. "I just wanted to be sure. There's something off about this chamber."

The crates smelled normal. Their scent was fainter than expected, but they did seem to be full of the usual salts and spices. Nothing out of place there.

But there were a lot of half-empty crates forming a wall, and the smell of hooded pitohui went from here to the throne and nowhere else.

The rushlight flickered, causing Whisper to look behind her. She licked a paw, then held it up. "There's a slight breeze. And the smell of pitohui."

"We should leave." Wendl backed away from the boxes. "You and I are no match for assassins."

Whisper was smart enough not to disagree. Without the antitoxin, they were at a disadvantage if the Reevesbane's cronies caught up to them.

"Hmmm." She headed back to the throne room. "I

can't imagine any Blackwing Alliance reeve not having their own stash of antitoxin, can you? The pitohui scent goes from the boxes to the throne room, just to the back of it. That means, unless they had another opinicus working for them, the stash should be intact."

Thrones were useful things if you needed to figure out the scent of a reeve. Though it seemed like some chicks had played on the throne, the strongest smell was easy to track. The starlings followed it back into the royal chambers. Once there, they didn't even need Whisper's nares to track down a few vials of pitohui antitoxin.

"Can you make more of it?" Whisper asked.

Wendl didn't look certain. "It's not...impossible. We'd need scarabs. I have Khalim's recipe. Think you can find a chemistry lab in this burrow?"

"I smell..." Whisper sniffed. "Oh, Sound of Snow was here. I got distracted. She came in through the consort's quarters, then she left through this passage here."

They changed direction, following the owl gryphon. Whisper couldn't read as much from a non-starling as she could from her own kind, but she could still track the weald gryphon as she flew across the eyrie.

"The young are quite mobile, aren't they?" Wendl asked. "I wonder if she's part cave gryphon to crawl through here."

Whisper was always surprised at how little Wendl could smell. "She had a portable brazier, taken from the reeve's chambers. One of the so-called scentless ones, judging by how faint it is, but still."

"Right, owl *opinicus*. I'd forgotten." Wendl looked down at her weak rushlight, then back at the royal chambers where the portable braziers had been sitting out.

The pitohui smell vanished, as did the reeve's. The owl's pheromones grew strong, as did the thyme smell of jadebeaks and...wheat.

"What starling pride smells like wheat?" Wendl asked, her nares finally picking up on the scent. "I've smelled sage and fruit before, even the fishy stormtail aroma. But I don't remember smelling wheat."

Their tunnel dropped them off on the top balcony of the granary, five stories above the crates. Many had been destroyed by gryphons or explosions, and the floor was covered in wheat, maize, and other opinicus crops.

Clearly, built for better times, Whisper thought. Down below, Sound of Snow was stuffing her face with grain.

"I thought owls were obligate carnivores," Wendl remarked, as though gryphons and opinici mapped one-to-one with their avian counterparts.

Whisper didn't reply. Sound of Snow, ever the fledgling, had shoved her entire head into a box of wheat, which meant she didn't hear the jadebeaks sneaking up on her.

They crawled along the ground, and judging by the angle of the wings, they were clearly wounded. Their eyes adopted the tunnel vision of altruism, though they didn't start to chitter.

"Get Sound of Snow," Whisper ordered. "I'll handle the jadebeaks."

Wendl flew towards Sound of Snow, shouting a

warning. Unfortunately, that just riled up the jadebeaks, who broke into a sprint.

Sound of Snow poked her head out of the grain, making a *tsk* sound at the starlings. She crouched down, presenting a smaller target, and looked like she thought she could easily take two dozen jadebeaks.

To be young and stupid again. Of course, maturity doesn't preclude making poor choices.

Whisper dove in front of the charging jadebeaks, losing her footing on the spilled maize, but shaking off as much featherdust as she could.

The pridelord's citrus was too strong for her to use her own—the old problem of a whisper competing with a shout. Instead, she mixed in mint with other scents: crocodiles, attacks on the nesting grounds, gryphlets in danger, and the scent stormtails used specifically when flying fish were playing in the Winter Jungle.

The jadebeaks paused, confused. They looked around for fish, crocodiles, or gryphlets.

"What's the meaning of this, Whisper?" the least wounded of the jadebeaks asked.

Oh, we're using words. Whisper felt out with her pheromones. The pridelord had separated out the wounded into their own subpride so they wouldn't feel compelled to stay with the war migration.

"Ah, you were just about to hurt our friend here." Wendl put a wing around Sound of Snow, who still looked like she was going to fight the murmuration with both wings tied behind her back.

Whisper joined in, but unlike Wendl, her wing was laced with dust. Normally, Whisper wouldn't be able to trick other starlings like this. When the pridelord had weakened his hold over them, however, he'd left room for Whisper to work herself in.

Sound of Snow's smell was now coated in such a way that she came across as a starling from a pride that no longer existed but that all starlings recognized as being a starling pride: the Crescentmoon Pride. It was just confusing enough that the jadebeaks' lingering altruism faded.

"Oh, sorry," the leader of the wounded said. "We couldn't fly, so we stayed here. It's all kind of a blur, but I think the murmuration left recently, within the last day or two."

Another of the wounded stopped sniffing Sound of Snow. "Do you know the way back to the jungle? We could get started walking. Most of our wounds were wing-related. The broken paws continued flying north."

"North?" Wendl let the grains fall through her talons. "We're directly west of the Blackwing Eyrie. Why the detour?"

The wounded didn't know the terrain, but she and Whisper both did. The attack here must have unsettled Balthar.

Directly west of the Blackwing Eyrie. Whisper shook off a little more dust on Sound of Snow, then ordered the wounded to follow her back to the strange side chamber next to the throne room.

Whisper forgot the owl gryphon would need verbal commands. "Come along, Sound of Snow. We need to check something."

She sent the pheromones at the same time, but *Sound of Snow* wasn't a name that translated into pheromones nearly so well. Though snow did come down off the mountains when the weather was just right, the sound that snow made in the heat of the Emerald Jungle translated to more like…

"Drip?" The leader of the wounded looked up. "Your name is Drip? The Crescentmoon Pride have strange names."

Whisper tried to correct the name, speaking aloud so her owl companion would understand what she was trying to do. "No, it is the sound of snow."

"Drip," another confirmed. "The sound snow makes in the jungle is dripping as it melts."

Despite Whisper's worries about offending their free pride charge, Sound of Snow seemed content to be included, which was good. Whisper doubted the olfactory disguise would hold if someone drew blood. Once they reached the throne room, she gave Wendl another order, to start lighting the braziers.

"Okay, down this passage there may be pitohui," the newmoon explained. "They're poisonous, but we have a few vials of the antidote. I only smell a few, so we should be able to overwhelm them. They won't be able to fly in such cramped space."

The least wounded helped her drag the crates into the throne room, revealing a dead end. It was only a *visual* dead end, however, and the scents went up.

By this time, Wendl had returned. "I found the medical district. They've got a stockpile of the antitoxin, plus what I need to make a lot more. What've you found here?"

Whisper and *Drip* took turns fluttering to the ceiling, looking for a way to open it. The scent definitely went up.

When Drip did the same, it was obvious she was unclear what they were searching for.

Wendl set down her brazier and pointed at the dead end. "I think there's a switch."

The insignia looked like the Sky Beneath the Earth, wings intertwined, six of them in three pairs.

"There are similar designs in the Ashen Weald's hideaway," Drip confirmed. "Are they all secret passages?"

"The Sky Beneath the Earth wasn't," Wendl said. "Well, it isn't now, I suppose. It's possible the passages were found and opened before I ended up there. Or perhaps Balthar knew of them."

Though the sculpture looked similar, there was something about the design that echoed in Whisper's mind. She heard the words being spoken by a storm-tail. "Go fetch Desert Rose."

"Okay!" Sound of Snow replied, but Whisper grabbed her by the tail and pulled her back down.

"No, *you* need more pheromone work if you're staying with us, *Drip*," she countered. "Wendl can go. Let's get you fixed up."

Whisper put her paw on Sound of Snow's fore-head and tried to understand the smells coming off her. It was difficult to modify the uninfected, especially when they weren't starlings. She'd had to steal a few more bugs from the clay jar to get into Kism's mind. But she wasn't trying to do anything so drastic here.

She looked into the owl's eyes. "You know how, when you meet a new gryphon, you try to remember what they smell like? Do that now, as though you're meeting me for the first time."

Drip's scent changed a little, and Whisper had the opening she needed. When gryphons smelled someone new, they were both trying to remember the newcomer and also sharing their scent.

Whisper adjusted things slightly, giving Drip the hint of a starling who had died long ago. "Try again."

It took a dozen tries, but Drip now passed as a starling, if barely, when the rest of the pride came inside. Thankfully, while Drip's mind was closed to her, she could modify each of the starlings she met to accept her, then spread that acceptance to others.

That'll have to do for now, since I don't see Drip leaving us anytime soon.

62

THE DEEP SKIES

The cacophony of the susurration filled the abandoned eyrie, echoing from every corridor. Spotless starlings laid down scent trails to the granary, sleeping quarters, medicine wing, and throne room.

Whisper chirped a greeting to Desert Rose, who showed up with several stormtails in tow. "I don't need all of them, just you."

"There was thunder, and your pride told everyone to come inside." Desert Rose sniffed at *Drip*, which she took pretty well. He barked at her, and she barked back, experimentally.

"If you two are finished?" Whisper drawled.

Desert Rose barked one last time in defiance. "Sorry, what do you need me for?"

Whisper stepped aside, letting the brazier light hit the seal.

"Oh." He placed his paws against the design. Though it felt solid to her, he seemed to know where the joints should be, and he pushed, one set of wings going in. "Are you sure you want to do this?

The one by the Ashen Weald had a parasite mummy inside."

The cured jadebeaks who had been napping in the corridor all hopped to their feet and stepped back.

"This is the third place we've found with the wing design," Whisper explained. "I think the mummies were just an odd quirk."

Drip's ear twitched. "Just how many mummified opinithings did you find in the bog? And does Satra Blackcrest know?"

"Sorry, what pride did you say you were from?" Desert Rose sniffed at her again. "You seem familiar somehow."

"The South," Drip replied. Whisper nudged her with a back paw. "—ern part of the North. Northwest. Drip of the Crescentmoon Pride, and if you haven't heard of me, you must have lived underwater or something."

Whisper stepped in before a fight could break out. She'd have to find a way to reconcile Drip and Sound of Snow in the susurration's minds later. "I apologize for Drip here. She wasn't well-socialized as a gryphlet. If you could open the doorway, I suspect it goes through at least some of the mountains. If that's the case and the pridelord is going around the long way to avoid ambushes, I think we can get there ahead of the murmuration...while also avoiding stumbling into any traps meant for him."

"Walking?" Drip looked down at her talons.

"The ceiling on the Sky Beneath the Earth was tall enough to fly," Whisper explained. "I suspect—Ah, there he goes."

Another push, a pull, and a twist later and Desert

Rose opened up the way. Or, rather, there was a click above him. Whisper and Sound of Snow pushed up, revealing a passage.

"Brazier?" Whisper called out.

Drip hopped down, grabbed it, and flew back up. Then she flew higher, searching for the ceiling. "It's very tall in here."

"I think this was built as an escape from the Blackwing Eyrie by the feathersnakes," Whisper said. When Drip looked confused, Whisper remembered the owl couldn't get subtext from pheromones, so she wouldn't know the term. "The long things with the four big wings and then weird back leg wings."

"Opinithings," Drip replied. "Seraphs, they call themselves."

Whisper sniffed, but the way was too open, and she lost the pitohui scent. "Nighteyes preferred feathersnakes. This is a long flight with little light. We could use your help, but if you need to go report to your mom, tell her to search the canals around her eyrie for similar designs. Beneath them are mummified feathersnakes, full of the parasite. That seems like information your Ashen Weald would want to know."

"I'm free pride," Drip corrected. "But the sand gryphons can get word to Satra Blackcrest...after I come back with you. I want to learn how to smell like you do."

"Dusty?" Whisper asked.

Drip made a *tsk* sound. "No, the way you hunt by smelling where things are! That would be really useful in my line of work. It would separate me from my brothers, who hunt by sound. If something doesn't move, it doesn't make sound. But scents stick and linger in the silence."

"Hmm." Whisper wasn't sure how much she could teach a non-starling. In theory, a small parasitic infection might let her in. She doubted Ninox would want her daughter to go through that. Still, if Drip didn't want to communicate with starlings, if she just wanted to learn to hunt better, Whisper could probably help with that. "It's a deal. In exchange for you and the sand gryphons helping us back across the desert, I'll help you learn to hunt by smell…if I survive this."

"If *we* survive this!" Drip added.

Whisper put a paw on Drip's head. "You need to tell the Ashen Weald about the feathersnake mummies. I know you're a ferocious killer, but this is a starling fight, and things may get very dangerous for you fast. There are also pitohui ahead. You know them, right?"

Drip nodded.

"Good." Whisper removed her paw from the nodding head. "Then you know that your talons will let you administer the antidote faster than my starlings can. And I don't know what'll happen with the altruism once we get there. If we become dangerous for you, I need you to flee, promise?"

Drip made a sound that seemed like she'd started a *tsk* then reconsidered. "Okay. I promise."

"Great. Go tell Wendl to have as many batches of antitoxin ready as she can by morning. Then we're going to see where this tunnel goes." Whisper chirped down below, and her pride came up, holding unlit rushlights in their beaks. They lit them on the brazier, then went in search of more braziers.

It seemed unlikely pitohui had flown through here in the dark. If they were lucky, something in the passage would be able to provide a little light.

We're probably better off with portable braziers, putting Wendl in the front and Sound of Snow in the back.

Desert Rose climbed up behind them, looking out at the corridor. "Hey Whisper, come sniff this."

The ground was just flat enough that it seemed there'd once been a goliath path through here, and he was searching for a way to open things up wider. She glided down to join him. Beneath the dirt and muck, there was a stone floor. Not just a floor, but a kind of fancy, engraved road like the ones goliath wagons used inside richer eyries. The pattern included a design, but she didn't recognize most of the glyphs. In the grooves, though, she smelled something...inflammable.

"Is it going to explode?" Desert Rose asked.

Whisper didn't know, so they pulled back everyone into the throne room, then she tossed lit rushlights until one landed in the groove.

The design in the road burned, slowly at first, then it spread into the dark. *This clearly wasn't meant for goliath birds, unless there's a breed willing to walk over fire. But this is also very elaborate for an escape path. It looks ceremonial, but the ceremony has been long lost to time.*

Though the walls were rock, the flickering fire illuminated the ceiling, which had the same endless wing designs carved into it.

Wendl poked her head up from the passage below.

"A second Sky Beneath the Earth. I wonder how many of these there are. What should we call this one?"

Whisper watched the fire crawl along the grooves, into the endless dark. "The Path of Flame, perhaps? At least two pitohui knew this existed, so perhaps they have their own name for it. I think the grooves were meant to hold oil, dripping down from above. What we're getting is the dregs. This must be spectacular with fresh oil."

"There are some jugs of lamp oil, but we're down-hill. It could help us on the way back." Wendl examined the grooves, some of which were starting to burn out. "The treasures of the past, looted and repurposed. I keep thinking of the statues, the ones the old pridelord had Balthar chiseling into starling shapes. What secrets did they once hold? How many more mysteries are hidden beneath the earth? What have the cave gryphons seen?"

Cave gryphons. Whisper went to the side of the cave, sniffing as she went. The smell was faint, but it was clear. Clawdiggers had come through here at some point. If they smelled starlings, they might return.

"Wendl, put out the fire," Whisper ordered. "Let's close this up for now. I think it's dangerous to stay here. We should wait until everyone is fed and rested, then we'll fly for it."

So far, two of Wendl's three *treasures beneath the earth* came paired with danger: the mummies and the clawdiggers. If Whisper came across a fourth such seal, she might just leave it be.

For now, she was going to gorge herself on food and sleep while twenty guards kept watch on the passage to make sure nothing dangerous came after them in the night.

THE NEXT MORNING, Whisper lit the pathway, giving the fire time to spread before they began their flight. As the flames crawled up the passage, Wendl and Drip put harnesses on starlings and filled the pockets with antitoxin, food, and anything else that seemed important.

"I like your hat," Drip told one of the jadebeaks. "I have one just like it."

She opened a pouch, revealing swirled metal talons. The design was an old one, having come from the Blackwing Eyrie's forges.

"Hat good," Taloncrest confirmed. "Good to have hat."

"I forget, sometimes, that the Ashen Weald has been at war with both the blackwings and alabasters," Whisper said. "Strange to see you here helping the blackwings now."

Drip put her talons back in the pouch. "I'm not Ashen Weald, I'm free pride. And I'm not here helping blackwings or alabasters, I'm here helping starlings. Though if beak came to claw, I think things would go much better if the blackwings won than the Seraph King, don't you?"

Whisper didn't disagree, though she hadn't forgotten the blackwings had come to destroy the research encampment as much as the alabasters had, believing anyone associated with Mally was suspect. Her loyalty was to the pridelord.

Well, to the previous pridelord, she amended. *To the murmuration, then.*

If they'd been walking the passage, she'd have brought the wounded jadebeaks along. Had the passage been walking-room-only, however, it would have been too slow to get them there on time.

Ultimately, with the king's armies coming any day, they gave the jadebeaks some of Wendl's orange elixirs and told them to head south, following old trails through the mountains, and to try to avoid anyone except the Ashen Weald.

"We'll come get you after," Whisper told them. "Just stay alive until then."

Drip offered her own encouragement. "The Darkfeather University has medicine gryphons who can make sure your wings heal right. Just tell them Sound of Snow sent you."

Whisper was impressed by the starling brain's ability to allow Sound of Snow, Strix Pride owl gryphon, to co-exist with Drip, Crescentmoon Pride starling. The hurt jadebeaks departed first, and Whisper hoped they'd have enough of a head start to escape before the alabaster forces caught up.

By the time the wounded were safely off, the flames in the passage had spread past her vision, and it was time to go. She debated leaving the passage in plain view but decided against it. Desert Rose thought he could get it closed again, and they dragged crates back into the passage once the susurration were all inside.

"Fire and enclosed spaces is a bad combination," Wendl commented. "Are we sure we'll have air to breathe with the door closed?"

Whisper didn't want to spook her pride, but if there were clawdiggers down here, there was breathable air. Instead, she left the question unanswered and used a little citrus to get the susurration moving.

TIME FLOWED DIFFERENTLY beneath the earth, and the subterranean tunnel had its own perils. Where the fiery path illuminated the walls, claustrophobia settled in. Whisper used pheromones to keep tabs on nearby starlings. The susurration thought of crocodile jaws waiting to chomp closed upon them. The stormtails imagined mature serpentine whales doing similar.

Where the way opened up, their fears evolved. No one wanted to step on the flames themselves, but without illumination, they worried they were walking across a bridge with endless pits on either side. She prepared mint but stopped herself when the anxieties lessened.

"It's unlikely there are any big drop offs here," Wendl explained to Taloncrest and the ptarmigan. "You'd probably feel it in the airflow, right? And besides, we can fly. Sure, I wouldn't fly too far, but just fly back up to the light and you'll do great."

Drip flew back and joined in. "There's enough light for me to see here, and the walls are still there. If they disappear, I'll let you know, okay?"

For someone who was used to having to manage the lives of her entire pride, Whisper wasn't used to seeing its members look after each other.

Still, it saves me energy.

Anxieties rose and fell, particularly where the fire had burned itself out in a few places. First, it was sour water dripping from the ceiling, leaving a stale, calcite taste in Whisper's mouth when she licked it. Later, a cave-in had broken the flame's path.

Most of the damage was on the start of the journey. In some places, the build-up of oil had been worn down and the flames wouldn't catch. They used these opportunities to rest while the opinici flew a little farther on and tried to get things lit again. Flicker, still suffering from an overabundance of bravery after her adventure with the Gourmand, insisted on going with the opinici to keep them safe.

The entire journey, Whisper sniffed along the edge of the cave. None of the clawdigger scents were fresh, but they were becoming *more* fresh. Every time the susurration rested, she feared an ambush, but none came.

They flew for half a day, perhaps more, before reaching a waterfall that smelled safe to drink. The susurration drank their fill, but when Whisper put her paw behind the waterfall, she felt long gashes carved into the weak stone.

"What is it?" Flicker's words pulsed her scent.

Whisper jumped. She'd forgotten Flicker was with her, which made her feel guilty. "In the Emerald Jungle, our pride was attacked by large creatures that live beneath the earth. The darkstalker seemed to think the cave gryphons kept them at bay, and when they were forced to retreat back to the Abyssal Naze, these *clawdigger* things took over cave systems across the continent. I can smell them here, too, and they're becoming fresher. You can see their claw marks on the rock."

Drip and Wendl came over, also curious. Drip had to reach up from her back paws just to touch the bottom of the claw marks. "This is larger than a saberbeak."

"Taller," Whisper corrected, though she'd never seen a saberbeak. "It stands on two legs, like a goliath bird. It isn't a gryphon, not exactly. It may be possible to communicate with them, but I don't think we'll have time to figure out how."

Wendl took out some thin sheets of paperbark she'd stolen from the trees by the last eyrie and used charcoal to make a rubbing of the drier claw marks. "It's a tall passage. We can just fly over them if they don't have wings, right?"

"They have wings, but I don't think they can fly." Whisper thought back to the long, leathery wings of the ones from the attack earlier. "I guess we didn't give them much of an opportunity."

Drip's ears pricked up. "Do they sound like cave gryphons? I keep thinking I'm hearing bats, but my dad says bats aren't real."

"What?" It took Whisper a moment to parse the fake bat comment. "Er, yeah, something like that. Not quite the same. More bat than a cave gryphon's oilbird."

Drip's ear twitched again. "I'm going to scout ahead. Stay here."

The owl opinicus vanished into the darkness, leaving the susurration by the waterfall. Though the flow disappeared underground, enough of the splash spread across the floor to douse the flames.

Desert Rose approached from the stormtails. "Do we rest here? It's wet, so it's a good place to stay."

"No." Whisper looked up at the claw marks. "Water means other...creatures...will come here to drink. Let's see if we can find somewhere along the ceiling to rest. Drip is scouting ahead."

"You're sure she's not part stormtail with that name?" Desert Rose asked, oblivious both to her identity and to the irony of a stormtail with his name asking that question.

Whisper sighed but didn't explain the naming situation. There were enough indentations along the upper reaches of the passage to hide her pride, though they had to clear out spider silk and some large centipedes to make room. The spider silk was old enough she wasn't worried about the spinner showing up. Though she did wonder if it had been made by several small, industrious spiders or one very large one.

Or perhaps a lost silkmouth.

They'd just settled in when Drip returned.

"I think you need to see this," she told Whisper.

63

CLIMB

Whisper followed Drip through the darkness of the passage. Now that they were past the flames they'd set, it should be too dark to see, but something bright burned in the distance.

Drip hooted softly, but when Whisper didn't reply, she changed to common. "Stay up high and don't touch the bodies."

The darkness of the corridor expanded into light, a new fire burning from the higher elevation up the passage. When they reached its origin, they found a cave-in blocking the way, a large bonfire, and several dead pitohui.

"Careful not to touch them," Whisper commented before sniffing. "They smell like the ones from the eyrie. Definitely killed by clawdiggers."

In the firelight, she could see that something had been drug away from the bodies. Her first thought was dead opinici, meant to be consumed elsewhere, but her nares revealed the truth: clawdiggers had pulled some of their own to safety.

So pitohui toxins work on clawdiggers. I don't know if that does us any good, except that they might be afraid of the dead bodies.

The scratches on the wall confirmed this was their territory. Having seen several sets now, she was beginning to think they were glyphs of some sort. These matched the newer ones by the waterfall.

"Feathersnakes may have built this road, but it belongs to them now. We should turn back." She hated the thought of losing most of a day to this side venture, but she saw little choice.

Drip hooted to stop her. "The breeze up here is weak, but there's a stronger one below. I think there's a way through the rockslide."

"Hmmm." Whisper sniffed. The clawdiggers had gone north, presumably to their nest. The susurration was going east, through the cracks in the slide. It might work. "If the pitohui didn't enter from the Goldtree Gardens side, they must have come from wherever this lets out. The rockslide looks old, as best I can tell. It looks like they found a way through it, then were...waiting for someone?"

It was speculation, but it fit. Though the more she thought about her plan to use this secret passage, the more problems occurred to her. If the pitohui knew about it, perhaps they'd intended to send an army through to flank the murmuration.

Or slow down the Seraph King's forces. Perhaps they saw the rockslide and reconsidered. She didn't know, but she wasn't willing to turn back if they could keep going.

There were other problems with the blockage. If the pitohui had squeezed through, the rocks would be slick with poison. Wendl and Drip had produced a lot of antitoxin, enough so each member of the susurration had two vials. It'd deplete half their supply to get through the rockslide, but it would be worth it—time was their greatest enemy at the moment.

Drip's ears both turned north. "You're certain these clawdiggers can't fly?"

"No." Whisper only presumed because they hadn't flown when they'd attacked her pride. "They looked like they could climb, though. Especially the claw-gryphlets."

"So are we staying or leaving?" the owl asked.

Whisper let go of the stalactite she'd clung to and glided back. "I have an idea, but it'll slow us down. Hopefully, not as much as backtracking would."

She settled down and ordered the susurration to line up, one at a time. To her chagrin, Flicker came first, happy to trust Whisper's plan, followed by some of the stormtails.

"We have a problem and a solution," Whisper began. "The problem has claws. The solution is…"

"A funny smell?" Desert Rose guessed. "With newmoons, it's always a funny smell."

She was annoyed he was right. "Olfactory camou-flage. I hope you all can climb. Drip, you go up first and find the way through, then keep guard. Once she gives the word, you're going through one at a time, careful not to disturb anything. Drink one of your vials first. The rocks will be slick with poison."

WHISPER STOOD in front of the passage going north, the one covered in long claw marks, and continued to exude the scent of a clawdigger. Specifically, the clawdigger family she'd hopefully barricaded out of her nesting grounds.

Flicker stood next to her, looking supportive and sometimes squeezing her paw. Whisper didn't need the emotional support, but she supposed two sets of nares were better than one, even if Flicker forgot to sniff sometimes.

Behind them, Drip led the susurration through the rockslide. At the bottom level, there was a lot of sand and scree, but higher up, there were gaps between large boulders big enough for a starling to squeeze through.

Whisper's internal sense of time said it had been hours. Her sense of hunger was more accurate at telling time this far into the earth, and it told her a half an hour had passed at most.

I think it's working. We should be through in no time. Whisper studied the claw marks while she waited, both the pattern and the scent. She knew from the Abyssal Naze the clawdiggers used sound like cave gryphons, but the imitation pheromones had worked to fool the clawgryphlets.

"This is a good plan," Flicker said. "I'm so proud of you for thinking of it."

Whisper didn't reply, instead concentrating on the scents the clawdiggers had left behind. If she could memorize them, perhaps it would let her tell whose territory she was in. It seemed a good thing to know if they had to return by this path.

Flicker sniffed along, and Whisper nudged the

scents into her mind, helping Flicker learn them. The newmoon gryphon closed her eyes, as the light coming off the flames gave her a headache.

Her ex-mate, however, saw like a non-starling, thus she asked, "Hey, are they cannibals?"

"What?" Whisper opened her eyes. Off to the side of the cave were the bones of more clawdiggers. Their vicious, serrated beaks, their equally wicked claws. She went over to sniff them, and they were close enough to gryphons she was able to tease out the clan smell from the different corpses.

Looks like these clawdiggers are very territorial. Maybe I can put that to use back home, put up this pride's scent to scare away the other pride. Though if it doesn't work, it might send them into a blind rage.

A gust of wind howled through the passage, and Whisper's first worry was that someone was coming in the Blackwing side. Though...they'd closed the underground eyrie's seal behind them. The air current couldn't go that way, so it was odd there was a breeze at all.

She held up a foreleg, and the fur on the back of her paw felt the wind more than the front. She could almost sense her featherdust lifting off her fur and drifting into the corridor.

That's when her second worry came. *Wait, this group is willing to kill other clawdigger prides. Maybe borrowing the smell from the Jadebeak Mountain clawdiggers was a bad idea.*

"Flicker, you need to go," she ordered her ex-mate. "Get through the rocks."

The strawberry starling puffed up. "No, I can wait for you. I'm learning things here."

"I need you to go, now." Whisper looked up at the starlings climbing through the rocks. They were just about through. In the firelight, she could just make out Drip's ears. It was faint, but they kept twitching in Whisper and Flicker's direction, even when the starlings weren't talking.

"Okay, just you two left," the owl opinicus called down. By then, she seemed to pick up on what her ears were hearing. "Oh! Hurry!"

Flicker started to flee, but Whisper stared into the darkness. The wind was against her, but something was growing there. And then she saw it, a creature so tall she was eye level with its hip.

Shaggy, wheat-gold fur hung off the clawdigger like it was a malevolent bale of hay. The light coat served to emphasize the dark bits: a serrated beak, open in anticipation, and those wicked, burrower's claws that could slice a starling in two.

She swore and dove after Flicker.

The creatures abandoned their silent approach, letting out a slothful roar and falling to all fours to chase the starling pair.

Drip had, wisely, disappeared through the cracks. Flicker and Whisper were not so lucky. One of the clawdiggers, younger and sprightlier than its parent, climbed up, forcing them to turn to dodge its claws. Whisper managed to catch a leg and pull the monster down, but as Flicker reached the crack in the rocks, one of the adult clawdiggers smashed into the stone below.

Whether deliberate or an expression of its rage, the action worked: New rocks tumbled down, filling in the cracks. A stalactite even fell from the ceiling, crashing into one of the clawdiggers amassing on the ground.

"Back, the way we came!" Whisper ordered Flicker. Though the adults were too bulky to climb quickly, the younger ones were on the walls, trying to keep up. What's more, the commotion had attracted a dozen more from unseen passages in the ceiling, who now hung down to try to catch the starling pair.

"Not too high!" Whisper warned.

Long claws reached for Flicker, and Whisper rammed into the beast, knocking it down. It landed in the fire and screamed, which seemed to give the others pause.

The gryphon duo were nearly to the waterfall when new cries echoed, this time coming from passages to the west.

"Flick, slow down, we need to stop." Whisper glided to the waterfall. She leaned over, trying not to think of the abyss it fell into, and got drenched. Then she started shaking off the water.

Flicker joined her. "Weird time for a bath, but you definitely needed it. I didn't want to say anything, but you've been really dusty lately."

"The clawgryphlets were sensitive to smell. We need to change ours." Whisper groomed as quickly as she could, trying to get dry, or at least *dry enough* she could get some featherdust oiled again. She'd tried— and failed—several times to come up with a smell that imitated cleanliness, but the complex scent-stacking involved always fell short of making her seem actually clean, as Moonlit Blossom used to be fond of reminding her.

Once again, I face death unpleasantly clean.

After Flicker got herself dry, she helped with Whisper. "Why not just fly back to the garden eyrie and close the door behind us?"

"It's too far. It took us most of a day to get here, and we were able to take breaks. Plus, we had the oily passage, which we've burned away now, so we'd be doing it in the dark. That *thing* was silent before Drip shouted to us. I think we're better off with the susurration." Whisper had one other thought that she didn't share. The murmuration was depending on them. If it were just her and Flicker in danger, she might try to get back to the underground eyrie. There was more at stake than just two starlings with contrasting aesthetics.

"But the way's closed?" Flicker finished drying Whisper and began pushing against her, trying to get the scent from Whisper's oil glands, an approximation of clawdigger that matched the local glyph's scent.

Whisper had them hide in an alcove above the waterfall, trying to keep watch for any of the younger, climbing monsters. "The wind was going through the tunnel, but it was joined by another breeze. The northern passage goes somewhere. Hopefully, it reconnects with the main path. If not, at least we'll be above ground."

Flicker didn't reply. She did send a flash of calming mint. It was a nice gesture, but Whisper had to warn her not to.

"No new scents from here on out," Whisper explained. "The clawdigger pheromones I'm giving us are delicate. It's more like we're imitating the smell of one of their glyphs rather than a clawdigger itself. We won't stand up to scrutiny if one gets close to us. But as long as we stay away from them, I don't think they'll be able to track us. Now...let's try flying back."

WHISPER WENT FIRST, Flicker in tow. It was her terrible plan, and she didn't want to put Flicker at risk, but she'd seen how fast and quiet the small ones were. Flicker was safer if they stuck together.

The soft, sour smell of the underground passage had changed to something more like pepper and clawdigger. That worked to Whisper's advantage, since it meant their foes would have a harder time smelling them. They crawled as close as they could to the rockslide and watched.

Or Whisper watched while Flicker held onto her large, fluffy newmoon tail.

Whatever keeps her quiet and still, I suppose. While some of the younger clawdiggers hung from the ceiling near where Drip had vanished, the adults filled the bottom of the passage where the susurration had previously gathered, though they kept a wide berth between them and the flames.

And the dead pitohui. Too bad we didn't think to pile a bunch of those in front of the main cave, it could've bought us some time.

There were few cases where she would have preferred Wendl's company to Flicker's, but this was one of those times. With enough fire, they might be able to get through the tunnels unharmed.

Or I'm just fooling myself. Those things are big, and

their claws are long. They could reach out and scoop me up from the darkness.

Remembering Drip's warning about how good their hearing was, Whisper nuzzled Flicker and then gestured towards the cave the clawdiggers had come from. They didn't need to be completely silent so long as they were making the same sounds a clawdigger might make. And didn't get spotted.

One of the adult clawdiggers trying to climb to the top slipped, and its stone-rending claws pulled loose stones down on top of it. As the others went to its aid, Whisper and Flicker snuck into the passage going north.

The light disappeared, and Flicker latched onto Whisper's tail again. A trail of blood and adult clawdigger scent went left, the smell of clawgryphlets came from the right, so Whisper went forwards—and ran face-first into the wall.

She shook her head to clear out the cobwebs, then sniffed again.

Adults left, stone wall directly in front of me, babies right, and...Ah! The smell of the young adults came from directly above her. She stood on her back legs, lifting her forepaws, and could just barely touch the ceiling of the tunnel. She felt around until she discovered a hole.

Her first leap failed, as Flicker didn't let go of her tail. The second time Whisper succeeded, then left her tail dangling below to guide Flicker. The red starling jumped, caught Whisper's hips, and climbed over her to get into the tunnel, putting her in lead.

Whisper was afraid to say anything aloud, so she just latched onto Flicker's tail and let her guide the way. Whisper could feel her ex-mate's scent pulse with excitement, but it was muted enough she didn't think they'd get caught. Something had Flicker's interest, though, and she picked up the pace.

I hope it's the way out. I can't smell anything except her at the moment.

Flicker slowed, going down on her belly, and Whisper followed suit. A moment later, something whooshed over their heads, leaving Whisper to wonder when the tunnel had opened. Once it was gone, Flicker fell into a sprint, and Whisper lost her grip on Flicker's tail. She tried to follow the sound of feathers and fur, but she ended up running into Flicker when she stopped suddenly.

"Flick—" Whisper began, fed up with not being in charge, but Flicker turned around and pushed something into Whisper's open beak.

Beets? She chewed. *It is beets.*

While Flicker stuffed her own cheeks, a practical way to keep from talking, and sometimes shoved things into Whisper's open maw, the leader of the Newmoon Pride sniffed again.

She definitely smelled more vegetables coming from directly above her. That way led outside: to sunshine on her face, to fresh air, to fields of grass and wildflowers and things to eat. It was the path to freedom. She could take Flicker and flee to some hidden grove. Given enough time, she could change Flicker's brain to permanently suppress her altruism on its own. Whisper had worked hard to get Flicker reconnected with the murmuration, but what if Whisper pushed it the opposite way. If any starling could be easily disconnected, it was Flicker.

The other way, beyond the beets, radishes, and pale carrots, lay responsibility and the weight of leadership, a possible assassination, and the endless night of the depths. On the thought of *night*, her brain conjured up the scent of the moon, or at least the flowers who only bloomed in its pale light. It tugged at her heartbones, this smell of a vine that flowered only at night.

Moonlit Blossom.

His pheromones felt real, like he was nearby. She sneezed, a reflex to clear her narcs, but still his ghost haunted her.

Wait.

It wasn't her imagination—it was the susurration's way of reaching out to her, of reminding her of those they had lost to the Nighthaunt's plot.

It worked. Grief and anger made her turn away from the tunnel heading up to the surface. Her ex-mate, cheeks stuffed full of beets, whined a little but allowed herself to be led.

They were just a few feet into the far tunnel when the sound of something large stomping through radishes reached their ears. Then came a roar of anger, and the sound of more creatures charging through the tunnels.

Remembering the way they'd feared the dead bodies of the pitohui, Whisper poked Flicker in the stomach, forcing the strawberry finch to cough out a radish from her full cheeks. Then Whisper took the dripping vegetable, put as much pitohui scent as she could into it and left it behind.

Flicker protested, but Whisper grabbed her haunches and pushed her away from the vegetable.

They delved deep, into the endless depths one more time, following the fragrance of the verdant night sky.

THE TUNNEL WOUND AROUND, up, and then finally led to a hole in the ceiling above the passage again. Whisper had left three poison-scented radishes in their wake before Flicker ran off, leaving the newmoon gryphon behind. In fact, Flicker was so busy running with her radishes, she missed the hole in the passage and yelped as she fell, a sound made extra silly by the fact it was filtered through a beakful of root vegetables.

The starlings clicked their beaks in excitement and happiness when they saw the strawberry finch gliding down to them.

"Mmmmb-beets!" Flicker managed, coughing up as many beets and radishes as she could. The susurration had, for the most part, not been exposed to opinicus produce. It took Wendl's recognition and nibble to get Desert Rose to join in, then the vegetables quickly disappeared.

They looked at Whisper, who tumbled in second, but she'd accidentally swallowed the only produce Flicker had given her. She chewed when she was nervous, and she didn't think that should be held against her. The nibble marks on Flicker's tail from following her in the tunnel also testified to this fact, though if Whisper were lucky, Flicker would assume it was Taloncrest or one of the other cured jadebeaks to blame.

"Where's Sound of Snow?" Whisper asked. The

starlings looked at her blankly.

"Oh, you mean Drip?" Desert Rose asked. "She was here a second ago...maybe the Crescentmoon Pride are afraid of beets."

A hiss came from above them, where the owl clung to a stalactite. "I am not afraid of food. I was scouting ahead. The oil here smells fresh."

The sweaty run down the corridor had worn off most of the clawdigger scent, but Whisper shook out her coat, then shook out Flicker, and they groomed their starling scent back in. The corridor stretched long, and the smell of oil *was* much fresher here.

"The pitohui knew about this passage, though not the rockfall," Wendl speculated. "I think Reeve Rybalt Reevesbane was planning to use it for something. Shall we see what happens if we light it?"

The opinicus worked flint and tinder fungus, then touched them to the ground. An endless trail beneath the earth lit up, and this time, the designs hadn't been worn down by the sharp feet of clawdiggers.

"Feathersnakes," Whisper said. The ground was alive with six-winged designs, flowing together, as though the world were upside-down, and the sky was below her. "Flying around the mountains takes a lot more time. It's possible we've gotten ahead of the murmuration. When we reach the end, stay quiet. There's no telling what's there."

Or if we can even open it. What if it's locked? She shook away those thoughts. If the way was barred, they'd go fight back through the clawdiggers' vegetable storage to the surface. But she saw hope in the flames ahead.

We can do this.

64

THE COURT OF WATERFALLS, INTERIOR

R eeve Rybalt Reevesbane stalked the humid halls of the Waterfall Palace. Nestled in the east-facing cliffs of the mountains along the northern edge of the range, the palace was named well.

With spring's arrival and the melting of the snow, the decorative waterfalls and opinicus-made canals filled to the brim. Outside the palace walls, the roar of raging snowmelt made it impossible for Rybalt to think. Here, inside, water trickled through artificial streams lining the passages and courtyards at a much more leisurely pace.

The throne room near the back was designed to project blackwing power, and it did just that. Obsidian walls rose, their tops decorated with ruby and citrine teardrops, all oriented towards where the reeve sat. The message was unsubtle: all wealth flowed from the blackwing leader. Had this been Rybalt's eyrie, he'd have turned the room into a garish closet, because the palace's true beauty lay everywhere else.

A moat of fresh glacier water covered in glass surrounded the throne room like liquid sapphire. The original architect took inspiration from the nearby forest rapids, covering the walls in cyan and green tiles. A slate blue walkway guided guests from the moat to open indoor streams, no longer covered, their babbling filling the corridors.

Carved turquoise beads hung like raindrops from the ceiling, silvery threads holding them in place. Cascades of these formed waterfalls to block off private gardens and meeting rooms, often with their own ponds. Frogsong spilled from one such room, the nervous whispers of a clandestine tryst from another. Outside, in the corridor, a fish splashed to the surface, narrowly missing a water scorpion who scuttled to safety.

Then there were the small grey birds the Waterfall Palace was best known for. Belamurian dippers, called water ouzels by the glacier pride, swam in from the balcony beneath the waterfall, diving into the water and exploring the interior streams to catch their own meals.

One hopped up with a minnow in its beak and tilted its head at Rybalt with a whistling *pijur pijur*, perhaps curious what the reevesbane was doing here. Rybalt stared back. The little birds had always fascinated him. Having spent years studying the philosophy of his enemies, having seen the Nighthaunt's theories borne out in his alchemical experiments, Rybalt was left wondering why the palace wasn't populated by little dipper opinici.

Perhaps a pride of water ouzel gryphons, fish in their

beaks, were pushed out. Or perhaps the blackwings have always been here and these little birds are the invaders.

The bird swallowed its fish and returned to the stream in search of another snack, leaving Rybalt to check on Iony and their companions. His fellow assassins certainly seemed to enjoy the luxury of being able to wander the palace at will, something the blackwing reeve had never previously allowed.

Though it appeared the palace staff felt differently about their presence. An angry groundskeeper approached the pitohui and glacier gryphon duo to complain that one of his pitohui had washed their talons in a pond and poisoned the fish below.

Iony's ears wobbled, a sign of suppressed laughter, until the groundskeeper turned and railed on the glacier pride leader.

"And the *gryphons* are just eating them outright!" the irate blackwing spat. "You think it's bad inside? There are no fish in the pools outside. None! Zero! The motmots have eaten them all. Who's going to replace them?"

Across the enclosed courtyard outside the throne room, a place that felt safe but whose ancient Crestfall glass ceiling would certainly shatter as soon as the fighting began, a glacier gryphon with a wet face looked in at the proceedings.

Iony did his best to shoo his fish-poaching pridemate away while deflecting blame. "Well, have you talked to the motmot pride leader? I'm sure she's got a thing or two to say."

"It was the lead motmot who ate the most fish!" the groundskeeper shouted.

Iony looked to Rybalt for help, and the reevesbane obliged, turning on his threatening charm.

"My dear friend," the Reevesbane rumbled, "our job is to keep the palace secure. The price of a few fish is nothing compared to the safety of your reeve, wouldn't you say? Though if you feel strongly about this, you should take it up with him. I daresay he's in his chambers, just waiting to address complaints such as yours."

The groundskeeper grumbled but left. Apparently, assassins and warriors were safe targets to wear out his ire on, but a 'real' reeve was a step too far.

"He's going to send you a bill for all the fish that're missing," Rybalt said. "Both the ones you've eaten and the ones the motmots have."

Iony shrugged. "Opinici keep sending us words on parchment, but we just toss 'em into the bay. The more you learn to read opinicus, the more opinici want to write to you. It's a never-ending cycle, and I refuse to participate."

"Tough to run a spy ring without paper," Rybalt commented, but they were idle words. In truth, very little was committed to writing. A lot of opinici enjoyed puzzles, and he'd never found a code that worked flawlessly. Hence his dependence upon the flawless memories of stargazers as of late.

Behind them, beyond the court and throne room, his personal stargazer was pretending to write down important missives outside of a forgotten storage room. The wall beyond, part of the mountain itself, had wings carved into it. It seemed the best place to hide him.

Win or lose, we'll need that passage. No sense putting our dear friend in real danger.

Behind the seal, several of his pitohui should be lighting the way. Once the passage was secure, they were to look into the damage at the Goldtree Gardens Eyrie and make sure it was structurally sound. As they hadn't reported otherwise, he assumed everything was going smoothly.

"Shame about Bario and the motmots." Iony caught him looking at the stargazer. "I thought our phoenix was properly cowed enough not to go off and have ideas on his own. Too many Redwood Valley scholars have ideas, y'know? Next thing you know, the cockatiel forger will want to start writing love stories."

Rybalt offered a noncommittal *Mmmm* in way of response. He'd been forced to make it sound like he'd set up the ambush there so he didn't appear incompetent. It did seem smart, trapping the starlings in an eyrie. He'd actually suggested the Goldtree Gardens be evacuated to make sure no one saw him use the passage, so it was only natural they also assumed him the mastermind.

The sky through the sheet of Crestfall glass went dark, and Iony looked up from fighting a water ouzel for the last rainbowfin out of the canals along the edge of the court. "We expecting rain?"

The storm to the north fluttered, beams of light breaking through the never-ending thundercloud.

While much of the blackwing army hid in the hills to the west, hoping to ambush the starlings outside of town, it appeared their opponent had gone north.

"Strange." Rybalt whistled, his call to the motmots

to come in and slick their beaks on the nearest pitohui until they dripped with poison. "I'd understood starlings to be a mindless swarm, like locusts. I didn't think they'd have the intelligence to sneak up on us."

While the motmot pride poisoned their best weapon, the glacier gryphons moved into position, guarding the choke points going into the throne room. Blackwing heralds sounded the alarm.

The last motmot was their leader, the one who was too smart for her own good. She had a lot of ideas about how to best defend the blackwing reeve, and Rybalt certainly didn't want that.

"My greatest defender," the Reevesbane said, loud enough to get a glare from Iony, "I fear much of the Blackwing Eyrie's forces are still waiting in ambush. The blackwing reeve has ordered the fastest flyer in the alliance to notify them. I can think of none better-suited to the task than yourself, a motmot."

The motmot bowed her head, and once she exited, they saw her flying west from the glass ceiling.

"A motmot, eh? She wouldn't even tell you her name?" Iony commented.

"Oh, I know her name," Rybalt replied. "It just would have been rude to say it in front of you."

They sat in silence, content to let the battle begin without them. Though scholars and scouts had reported on what the reds called *greenwing altruism* at length, whoever was leading the blackwing army had opted to discard that information when making their plans.

Tactics intended to intimidate the enemy, to bluff them into fleeing, had no effect on a frenzied starling.

Similarly, a strategy of guarding high value targets was proving ineffective. The swarm attacked based on proximity, not upon where weapons, saltpeter, or important opinici were located.

Rybalt turned to Iony, trying not to look at his friend's torn ear. "It's strange to think we could be watching the end of the Blackwing Alliance. For all the nudges we gave other eyries, for all the armies we took down, it's hard to imagine it ending like this. I expected the king to ultimately be our undoing, if not our own infighting."

"My beads were always on a second Connixation." Iony's face was a little wetter, and the Court of Waterfalls was missing another fish. "War moves so slowly it seemed like a second snowy apocalypse would happen before either side got their wish."

A starling crashed into the ceiling, leaving a streak of blood behind. If it hadn't been dead prior to impact, it was now. Surprisingly, the glass held. The starling was soon joined by red-winged blackbirds. They wore darkened leather and swirled metal talons. Unlike their alabaster counterparts, they didn't have the wing muscles to fly wearing heavier armor.

"Where are you thinking of going when all this is over?" Rybalt asked.

Iony's ears twitched each time a dead body hit the ceiling. "If we lose the Blackwing Eyrie, you mean? I was thinking I'd go to talk to Bounce or Trounce or whatever his name is. Join the taiga gryphons, show 'em how it's really done. They keep inviting me to some sort of joint taiga-fisherfolk festival, so I figure they like me. You?"

"I thought I'd take up fishing," Rybalt replied.

It was his usual retirement answer, and Iony laughed, though there was little mirth in it. They'd been unable to get an accurate count of the starlings, and it now looked like dusk, there were so many in the sky.

Or perhaps sunset, Rybalt revised, as the blood tainted the light coming through the glass.

The next blackwing to hit the glass did so metal talons-first, and the roof cracked.

"If I may?" Rybalt led Iony back to the entrance of the throne room. The pitohui within the palace were all talon-picked by Rybalt himself. The glacier pride inside the throne room had been paw-picked by Iony and had built up an immunity to pitohui toxins. Their less poison-friendly kin were back home setting up nests for the refugees.

"Honestly, I think I'd rather win," Iony mumbled.

Rybalt didn't disagree, but his grand schemes were crumbling before the starling onslaught. He wished the alliance had abandoned the eyrie. It would've been easier to fight this army in bits and pieces, from his island, over a long period of time.

From behind the throne came an unfamiliar sight, the Blackwing Eyrie's reeve wearing battle armor instead of his usual crown of jeweled leaves. "How fares the battle?"

"Too soon to say," Rybalt replied. "A lot can happen. They've travelled a long way to get here, and I'm sure they're tired. And if worse comes to worst, we'll make sure you escape."

The blackwing reeve remained pensive. "I'll leave you to it. A reeve's job is to remain safe for his subjects."

Once he was out of earshot, Iony quipped, "Somehow, despite every member of the alliance hating kings—despite it being founded on hating kings—we ended up with one of our own. Like we're not both leaders. He's not wrong, though. If you've got some grand surprise up your tailfeathers, now's the time to let us know."

"I'm working on it," Rybalt rumbled. He had a lot of plans for after they'd won, but none for this moment.

A cascade of flechettes, purchased at twice their cost from sand gryphons, sliced through the starlings and hit the glass.

"I can't believe it held," Iony said a moment before the bodies of the starlings killed by the flechettes hit and the glass shattered, filling the court with the dead. "Never mind."

Rybalt crouched, ready for the first wave of starlings. The screams and hisses of combat above filled his hearing, and it took a fifth iteration before he realized the stargazer was shouting for him.

"Rybalt!" the astronomer shouted. "We have intruders!"

"I know!" the Reevesbane quipped. Then Iony grabbed his shoulder and pulled him around to where the wall to the escape tunnel had given way, and several green and black shapes were flooding in.

"I've got *this*," Iony said. "You handle *that!*"

If not for the gryphon in the lead, Rybalt would have crashed into all of them, letting his poison do the work. But the starling in front wasn't a gryphon, she was an opinicus, and she had a rusted Blackwing

Alliance badge on her harness and the antitoxin dripping from her beak.

"My name is Wendl, and I'm a member of the Mothfeather Eyrie," she stated. "I think we can stop the murmuration, but you have to let us through."

The pitohui and glacier gryphons looked to him for guidance.

"You lot, guard the courtyard," he ordered his pitohui. Then he turned to *Wendl of the Mothfeather Eyrie.* "You can stay here, but the rest of your gryphon friends need to take a few long steps back into the passage."

Most of them went, but a single weald owl remained. "I am an opinicus."

"Is the Ashen Weald here to help, too?" he asked, recognizing her plumage and pedantic nature. "I don't suppose you've got Cherine tucked away in there somewhere?"

The owl was not as good at concealing her feelings as her mother had been. "No, neither my dad nor the Ashen Weald are here to help, just me. I am undercover as a starling. You may call me Drip of the Crescentmoon Pride."

Why is it that whenever an Ashen Wealder or a free pride shows up, they reply to my question with the dumbest answer? he wondered, though he didn't order her away, instead turning to the green opinicus. "Wendl of the Emerald Expedition, Khalim's friend? I assume you survived the same way he did. How many of you are there?"

Silver eyes watched Rybalt from the darkness, and had they started chittering, he would have reconsidered this little parlay. He'd memorized the names of all of Mally's underlings, alive or dead, who hadn't been among the corpses at the Emerald Expedition. None of his assistants turned up later, but after figuring out who Khalim was, Rybalt knew they might be hiding.

Though he'd never expected any to hide as starlings. Had that gamble failed, they'd have been torn apart. And even success was its own trap, forced to live as a starling.

"It's not just me," Wendl said cagily. "Iri and Talli of the Blackwing Eyrie are also here, one leading a pride, but you can't trust them as allies while the greenwing altruism has hold of them. And then there's Balthar."

One gryphon stood in front of the others in the passage. Her silver eyes were matched by a silver beak. Stains dripped down her cheeks, and she had stripes. If she hadn't spoken first, he'd have taken her to be infected.

"And I assume you're Kism or—" he began.

"You may call me Whisper," she interrupted. "Kism is my prisoner. The Nighthaunt promised him a place among the alabasters as feathersnakes, free of altruism, if he could provide a cure to Mally."

"And you have a cure for bloodbeak?" Rybalt didn't have to ask what a *feathersnake* was. The king's lands were now full of them, though most were just learning to fly.

Whisper hesitated. "A treatment."

Good to know, hard to acquire, Rybalt thought. "And what does this have to do with the swarm outside the palace?"

"Murmuration," Wendl corrected. "Balthar used

the salts to replace the pridelord. He's led them here to die. Hi-kun attacked the Emerald Jungle once they were gone."

Whisper's blank eyes never left Rybalt. A starling wouldn't know who he was, so he assumed she'd interrupted him because she was another member of the expedition. "If you can kill the pridelord, we can take control of the murmuration."

"How?" He liked knowing details.

"The pride leaders will automatically select a new pridelord," Whisper explained. "If it's Nighteyes or me, we can force the murmuration to return to the jungle."

"And if it's one of the others?" he asked.

Wendl winced as a dead starling fell into the courtyard behind Rybalt. "If it's Talli or Iri, they won't want to hurt their homeland. If it's another starling…I don't know. Look, isn't the whole point of being a reevesbane that you believe one kill can stop thousands of unnecessary deaths? You'll never find a more literal, immediate opportunity to prove that theory true. Let our susurration through."

Iony had snuck up behind him. "Our craft has always been a little like dropping flechettes, hasn't it? Let 'em through. Let's see where their steel falls."

Rybalt shouted the order, and the pitohui and glacier gryphons fell into the shadows. There was no corresponding order from the rebel starlings, but the air smelled a bit of citrons or perhaps lemons, and a small force of strange gryphons flooded out of the depths, into the court, and into the battle above.

The only one who remained behind, momentarily, was Wendl. "You're not going to join us?"

"Not my eyrie, not my fight," Rybalt whispered under his breath. He was surprised to see the little starling opinicus sizing him up.

She showed little confidence when she added, "There's a second, smaller army of alabasters setting up goliath supply lines a few days behind the murmuration. Thanks to Whisper, we managed to trick them into believing the mothfeather are all dead, though they're just asleep. They're about to wake up confused and covered in blood."

Wendl looked back into the passage like she might want to say more, but then decided not to. Instead, she reached into her harness pocket and handed him several smoke bombs of some sort. "These'll keep away any starlings while they burn. Just be careful not to use them on us."

With that, she left the court, joining the battle above.

"A curious starling," Iony commented. "Susurration, feathersnake. Got a whole vocabulary lesson outta her and the softly-spoken one."

"Shush, Iony," Rybalt ordered. "I need to watch how this goes. Is there any way to see outside safely?"

The stargazer looked up from examining the strange passageway, now open. "There's an observatory up top. The glass there is thicker. No promises it won't shatter, too, but it's back a bit from the fighting."

Rybalt was running the numbers in his head. If this *Whisper* could tame the murmuration, there was a chance to get his plan off the ground. But if they won too quickly, the timing would be difficult.

"Iony, you're in charge here," he said. "Stargazer, show me the way to this observatory."

65

THE DREADED FLAMEWORKS, REDUX

For days, on the flight around the mountains, Nighteyes had sought another opportunity to save her pride, to save the murmuration. For days, the pridelord hadn't given up control, not even when asleep.

Though he seemed grateful to be alive thanks to her pride, it had also made him aware that she *wandered* a little when he was out cold. At the next eyrie they visited after Goldtree Gardens, he left half the murmuration outside when he went in to get some kind of medicine from the stores.

Whatever he took kept him from sleeping too deeply and Nighteyes from leaving any more messages. She waited patiently for a new opportunity that never came. Instead, they reached the ocean, then turned south. The first few abandoned fishing villages fed the murmuration, but at the third, they lingered.

The foothills from the mountains sloped into the ocean, and the huts and common areas clung to their soft peaks like sea foam. The nicer the shelters, the farther from the water they were. Many of the docks housing rafts appeared new and hastily put together. During her time with the Ashen Weald, Nighteyes had been allowed to visit Bogwash and the nearby raftworks, both locations on the southern shore of Belamuria, and they were built to withstand the summer and winter storms. There was a pride to their construction. Even if the gryphons and opinici abandoned them for a decade, something would remain when they returned.

These docks had no such pride or hope. They had been constructed by opinici who knew their fleeting existence would last only until the next storm. The city had been abandoned for days at most, and already two docks had collapsed, releasing their rafts to the sea's cruel embrace.

The murmuration spread out to scavenge anything left uneaten, but this time, the pridelord kept Nighteyes close. She had no way to interrogate their leader, and the medication kept him in control even when he slept. Instead, she let the pheromones of nearby starlings passively wash over her, trying to suss out anything useful.

The gryphons around her felt as mindless as the infected, like animals. A nearby jadebeak could just as well have been a squirrel trying to break into crates of stored nuts and berries. The only personality she got from any of them was a sense of loneliness from the pridelord, along with something best described as familiarity.

The closer they'd come to reaching this city, the easier time he'd had finding caves and coves to hide the murmuration in. This was the first time since their ambush he let them sleep in an opinicus city, and she wanted to know why.

Her body, however, did not oblige her. It remained close to the pridelord, keeping guard with the other starling leaders. It didn't make tactical sense. The pridelord was difficult to find and kill because he disappeared into the other prides. By pulling one of each leader near him, he created a rainbow target to any onlookers.

It wasn't just his starling sensibilities that seemed lacking. This port city had several reinforced buildings, possibly hurricane shelters. Nighteyes didn't know if they'd stand up to saltpeter, but at least they'd provide some protection. Instead of hiding in those, he chose a single house on the southern side of the village, and he curled up in a nest best-described as abandoned.

Talli sneezed, filling the small building, akin to the fancier fisherfolk huts, with dust. That set off the others. Between the running nares and eye rubbing, Nighteyes was pushed closer to the pridelord's nest, and with it, she finally understood why they were here.

Tucked away, stale behind the smell of trees and spices she had no reference for, was the faint whiff of an opinicus who had slept here for years. An opinicus whose pheromones were still lodged in Whisper's memories, including some she had passed on to Nighteyes.

Whisper's olfactory codex showed Balthar, red-winged blackbird, sleeping on this nest. Nighteyes' nares and eyes showed her Balthar, starling pridelord, sleeping on top of it.

No wonder he was so relieved the village had been evacuated. This is his home. Was his home.

Talli and Iri were unreadable. If they knew where they were, Nighteyes couldn't tell. But she had a growing sense that, even taking into account nostalgia, he wouldn't have stopped and let the murmuration rest if they weren't close to their destination.

When he woke, he pulled the murmuration back into the forests and ordered them south for one last push.

THE BLACKWING EYRIE rose before the murmuration. It was beautiful, in an opinicus way. Nighteyes had never seen the Redwood Valley Eyrie before it became ruins, though Orlea kept a painting of it hanging in her hovel. Nighteyes had seen the Crackling Sea Eyrie, and it felt like it coexisted with nature. It was more seaside cliffs, very wet and at the mercy of the elements.

Not the Blackwing Eyrie. The mountain gave way to clean terraces, gardens, and falling water. It ran from the cliffs to the beach and beyond: docks stretched into the ocean with some sort of fisherfolkesque vessels, though not many.

Most probably fled when they heard we were coming.

The waterfalls were the most impressive. Within Balthar's rambled orders, she caught the name of the building where they started: *The Palace of Waterfalls,* and it lived up to that moniker. A clear, ice-like material formed a dome from one spire, then more sat atop a large, square courtyard with water flowing beneath it. The palace was full of balconies, but from the largest, a waterfall spilled several stories then zig-zagged down the mountain in a series of ornamented canals.

There was a mastery to it, but it also felt anathema to what the starlings were about. Water flowed through their lands, too, but they never sought to tame it, to make it do tricks for their amusement. Beauty, at least to Nighteyes, came from letting wild things be free, from coexisting with them.

She felt something similar from most of the other starlings, hidden in their scents. She'd become good at tracking individual pheromones. Iri and Talli were experiencing a kind of nostalgic sadness at being here. Balthar's emotions were too complex for Nighteyes to parse. But for most of the murmuration, something welled up in them, a compulsion to return this place to nature, to wipe the opinicus presence away, to let a waterfall be a waterfall.

It only took the smallest nudge, almost a whim-per, to send the murmuration down to attack.

Nighteyes tried to restrain her pride, but citrus crackled in the air like lightning. She tried to keep herself back, and only succeeded in putting her pride-mates between her and harm's way. She tried to correct things, but it was too late.

The palace is going to be the most heavily guarded. I need to attack somewhere that might let us get away from the pridelord's commands.

Several butcheries were distributed throughout the city, smoke rising from within them, and she ordered her pride to go after one. Smoke meant fire, which was dangerous, but smoke was one of the only things that overrode citrus.

The pridelord redirected them away, and she found she could no longer make the scents necessary to get her pride to go for the butcheries. Her only consolation was that Balthar seemed unaware of what he was doing, which worked in her favor.

The beak and foreclaws of the murmuration, the Jadebeak Pride, crashed into the blackwing defenders. Nighteyes tried to sort out the starling messages from the stench of the city. The butchery was easy, but she also smelled the fish from the docks and the nearby storage warehouses. There wouldn't be any opinici there for her to attack, so the pridelord would override her command.

A few buildings also smelled of food, but something was off. That wasn't just wheat, maize, or rice in the granaries. It took her a moment to place it.

Black powder. They're hiding more of the explosive Bario and the motmot used. She tried to separate out her scents, making sure everyone knew the granaries were bad, but she wasn't sure it got through. *They used food to lure us deeper into the last trap, too. Rigging these granaries to explode means they might be thinking of us like animals, like locusts. Where's a place they wouldn't expect an animal to attack?*

While there was a refined smell to black powder, the saltpeter used to make it had a particular salty-guano scent. She knew it from the Redwood Valley Eyrie, and she was able to locate it here: the flameworks.

It was outside of town a bit, but she tried to think

in pheromones at her pride. She imagined Bario the Phoenix in her mind, the explosion at the underground eyrie, and the scent of the flameworks. The nightsky peeled away to attack, and the pridelord let them go.

I didn't expect that to work. The farther they got from the pridelord, the more control she was able to assert. Not enough to flee the battle, but enough to grant a little autonomy to each of her pridemates.

"Hey," she chirped, trying to force words past the altruism. "Hey, slow. Down."

Her pridemates ignored her. She tried again, this time using their individual pheromones.

She targetted her youngest sister. "Hey. Sis. Slow. Down."

It worked, just the littlest bit. Her sister looked at her, seeing Nighteyes, but then shook her head and turned back to the flameworks.

Maybe when we're inside and the smell of bat guano takes over.

They reached the fields outside the flameworks where the strange leaching process created saltpeter. They landed and crawled low, approaching a weather barrier similar to the ones used in the Redwood Valley.

It would have kept out a lot of gryphons, but Nighteyes had seen the taiga pride work them, and she twisted her paws to get it open. *Once we're inside, I can break them free enough and figure out what to do next.*

When she'd sent the command to hunt Bario the Phoenix in the flameworks, it had been a lie. At least, she'd thought it was a lie. Were their roles reversed, if her pride had a phoenix and no greenwing altruism to worry about, she'd have kept him someplace far away from the front lines.

To her surprise, once the door was open, she found Bario and a handful of motmot bodyguards staring at her, stunned.

"What?" he said, open-beaked. "How did you find me?"

You're a phoenix in a flameworks, you idiot. That's as surprising as finding fish in a lake.

Six motmots moved in front of him, their bright blue and green plumage in stark contrast to the dull environs of the flameworks.

Only the lead one spoke. "We did not have time to glisten our beaks. You should flee, Phoenix. We will hold them."

"But—" he began, only to get interrupted.

"They have no mind to reason with," the motmot explained. "A motmot must kill all of them, or they will not stop hunting you."

Nighteyes resented the comment, but it wasn't incorrect. She'd slowed her pride down by forcing *hunting* on them to overpower the altruism just enough that they were acting like they were stalking a pack of deadly cassowaries and not attacking mindlessly.

The motmots' beaks were long, sharp, and wicked. Nighteyes didn't see a bloodless way to end this, so she tried to minimize her pride's losses.

Attack! she sent, and her entire pride pounced as one.

Each motmot killed a single nightsky starling with their wicked beaks. Each motmot died with that starling on their beak, unable to defend themselves from a dozen others.

A single lizard may eat an ant, but a hive of ants will always eat a single lizard. It was advice Nighteyes' denmother had given her, and she hated to see it in action. When the haze of battle faded, she'd lose herself to mourning those of her kin she'd been unable to save. Until then, her hunting focus saved lives.

Bario fled to the back room, behind some sort of crafted metal barrier meant to survive more than inclement weather. It looked designed to survive an explosion.

But would it?

She couldn't speak to her pride alone in here, not with someone so dangerous one door away—it would take too much time, and Bario was a slippery one. Instead, she ordered her pride to attack a new target, trying to send them back north to find another flameworks. She didn't think they'd succeed, but it'd keep them from the front lines a little longer.

After they left, she inspected the flameworks, finding a barrel of powder. She pecked at it but could just get the very top open. The barrel itself was too heavy for her to move. It was so large, it would need a goliath bird to transport it, which was most likely why it was still here.

Still, I got it open.

She tried to remember what she'd learned from the Ashen Weald. It was early in her visit there, before she'd started shaking from being away from the Emerald Jungle for too long.

Fuse...flint...tinder fungus?

This flameworks was much larger than the Ashen Weald's. While the Redwood Valley produced skilled phoenixes—Felicio, Bario, Askel—it lacked the resources of the Blackwing Eyrie. Work benches full of tools and materials she'd never heard of lined the walls. These, she ignored. It also had an extensive selection of fuses. Those, she did not.

She was good at braiding reeds, and she put her talents to work here, combining two fuses into one very long fuse. She managed to force one end into the barrel, then she got as far from the flameworks as she could get.

Working a flint and tinder fungus was hard with a beak and paws. The fuses were designed to need some fire to light, not just the sparks off the flint. She gathered the tinder fungus on the far end of the flameworks, downhill and by one of the canals so she could dive in, and started hitting one piece of flint against another.

There were a few sparks, but nothing caught. *I wish Rudder were here. I could use his long beak or silly paws about now.*

She was glad Rudder was safe in the Emerald Jungle and not in danger with her, much as she missed him now. Though...he had once taught her a neat trick for getting to the meat of a clam.

She stared down at the flint again, but instead of thinking of them as an opinicus tool, she thought of them as a stormtail's favorite clam-breaking rock.

This is dumb, but nobody is watching, so...

She rolled on her back and imagined herself floating on a river with Rudder. She put one big piece of flint on her tummy, then the fuse, then the tinder fungus. Then she thought very hard about the most ornery, resilient clam she'd ever tried to eat, and she bashed down with the other piece of flint.

Sparks flew.

The tinder fungus caught flame.

The fuse lit.

The flame ran down the fuse, burning part of her tummy, side, and inner thigh in the process.

Nighteyes leapt into the canal to douse the burn.

Seconds later, the Blackwing Eyrie's primary flameworks, their primary phoenix locked inside it, exploded.

Nighteyes dove deeper into the canal as pieces of stone fell around her. She swam to get away, but the canal itself collapsed as the mountainside lurched, flinging her from the water and into a sky full of burning rocks.

66

THE TERRACED CITY

Whisper imagined her pride as a diving kingfisher in reverse. They flew up from the water, or at least the Waterfall Palace, and through the sky. The smell of citrus was intense, and if she'd been left to her own senses, she'd have lost the entire susurration to the pull of the pridelord.

Even with Wendl's elixirs dulling the pridelord's control, Whisper watched as many of her spotless starlings paused in the air, backbeating their wings, then twisting to go into the fray with the murmuration. Despite the worries of some nosy jadebeaks, the susurration had never been meant as a weapon *against* the murmuration. In fact, the old pridelord, had he made a similar decision to attack the Black-wing Eyrie, would have sent the susurration out with the other prides.

Or so Whisper chose to believe. The old pridelord wouldn't have been so...*loud*, for lack of a better word, either. Balthar was trying to control the entire murmuration, trying to force them to take one action:

assault the palace. They'd be much more effective if he'd ease off, give them more control on how they attacked.

Whisper had built up a lot of mint featherdust in the tunnel. She felt it come off her as she flew, but the air was so dense with the smell of citrus, it was like she was chewing on the pith of an orange. She'd never be able to counter this, not in a meaningful way.

The new pridelord was a scream, and she but a whisper.

She hoped to adjust the scent of one gryphon and change the tide of control in her favor. Even as his commands pulled away the susurration, Balthar remained oblivious to her. His pheromones screamed *kill, destroy!* so loudly he couldn't hear who he was shouting at. And when he figured it out, it would be too late.

I hope.

Starlings destroyed the city, swarming in all directions, but the calm at their center, the eye of the hurricane, was the pridelord. Unlike the actual hurricanes that wracked the coast of the Emerald Jungle from time to time, this eye was much narrower, and it glistened with a guard of sparkwings, his first pridemates after he changed.

She had the susurration pass close enough to get his attention. Her mallow root smell caught his attention, and for a moment, the eye of the swarm was like a real eye, and its gaze was on her. Then the sparkwing denmother the newmoons she'd brought caught his eye, drawing it to Wendl and the rest of the swarm.

Whisper felt his inquiries, but Wendl's elixirs

dulled them. She'd feared to take too much lest it stop her own limited capabilities.

Who? How? Why? the questions came, and she answered them in the most unhelpful way she could. She sent back *feather, snake, sky, crocodile, water, crocodile.* It would take him a moment to parse through that, trying to figure out if she were telling him the truth or not. In that time, Wendl led the susurration north, aimed at a single target: Nighteyes.

Iri's jadebeaks fought an army of motmots at the palace entrance. Talli's pride were wrapped up with some orange opinici like the ones found dead at the Goldtree Gardens' storage vaults. They fought claw-to-talon before flechettes rained down upon gryphon and opinicus alike.

Whisper stayed back, but the pridelord, ever suspicious, ordered his sparkwings to intercept. He peeled away more of the susurration, too many too fast, and Whisper sent a new message. *Kism. Infected. Empty. Mine now.*

The realization that she knew his plan caused the Pridelord to lose control for a moment, and Wendl reached Nighteyes, giving her the elixir. Balthar regained control and tried to turn the murmuration on them, but it was very hard to convince a starling to attack another starling when their altruism drew them to other targets.

A starling *wanted* to kill non-starlings. It was just how generations of pridelords had raised them.

Once Nighteyes had downed Wendl's elixir, the pridelord waited for her attack to come, shifting the closest jadebeaks to form a shield between him and the Nightsky Pride's leader.

When he did that, once his back was to her, Whisper took her chance. She flung herself at the pridelord, one small black gryphon against one sparkling green gryphon. There was no time for her to kill him. She wasn't Rybalt or even Ninox.

But, as she'd told the susurration, if she saved her scent for a single gryphon, she could change the balance of power.

The mint gave way, and beneath it she emitted a familiar scent. It was the faint but real pheromone trail of someone she'd worked beside, studied, begrudgingly admired, and gone off on the adventure of a lifetime with. A comrade who had betrayed her.

He ordered his sparkwings back to him as they collided.

She latched onto him and whispered, "Remember who you are," covering him with the pheromones of Balthar the Blackwing Eyrie Scholar, his old scent. She reminded his body how to produce those pheromones, ordered it to do so, the same way she'd helped fix all of those lost stormtails and jadebeaks who'd become disconnected from the murmuration.

Before the pair hit the ground, he managed to detach from her. They landed inside the court of the Waterfall Palace, their iffy landing bolstered by a pile of dead starlings and blackwings.

The old pridelord would know how to fix himself, but this was a tough problem to solve. The new pridelord's body was sending the message, loudly, that he was Balthar the Blackwing Opinicus.

"What...is the point of this?" he asked, forced to use his words rather than pheromones as he tried to fix himself. "I'll have you torn apart for this. I will remove you from the pride the way I did the storm-tails, and the others will..."

He stopped, suddenly realizing her plan. Though the starlings at the far edges of the murmuration continued fighting, the ones nearest him no longer saw him as a starling, they saw him as he truly was.

The sparkwings reached him first. The starling pride who had first adopted him, the ones where he'd found love, friendship, and belonging, tore him apart.

Oh wait, his scent is on me, too. Whisper didn't have time to adjust back to mallow root, so she burrowed into the pile of bodies, hoping it would hide her smell long enough for her to fix it.

She knew it was over when a new scent, one she'd never experienced before, reached her. White grapes distilled into wine too soon, a hint of vinegar on top, and the moment it hit her nares, it also oozed out of her pores. Not just her, all of the pride leaders were emitting that strange aroma, and it was strong enough to protect her. The time had come to pick the new pridelord.

Whisper of the Newmoon Pride crawled up out of the pile of corpses and sent the pheromone signature for Nighteyes.

Nighteyes of the Nightsky Pride did the same.

The acting stormtail leader, Desert Rose, voted for Nighteyes.

Several others voted for the Jadebeak Pride. That was the natural source for a new pridelord, but it still disappointed Whisper.

This has to work.

Iri landed next to Whisper. "This was your doing."

"Fixing things was," Whisper countered. "Were

you part of Balthar and Kism's plan to defect to the Alabaster Eyrie?"

"No, I've always been a loyal blackwing...and my home needs the murmuration now," Iri replied. "Under my rule, we could be allies."

Whisper supposed she should be grateful Iri and Talli weren't in on it. But giving the Blackwing Eyrie an army of starling slaves wasn't much better than what Balthar had planned. "Starlings should be ruled by starlings. They belong in the jungle. *We* belong in the jungle."

Iri the First disagreed and voted for herself, putting her ahead by one.

Crawling out from her hiding place, Drip of the Crescentmoon Pride voted for Nighteyes. The scent was faint, but it was close enough to count.

If the prides tied, another vote would come, and Whisper could already smell Iri coercing some of the smaller prides who had sided with Nighteyes into changing sides.

There was just one vote left, from a pride that generally liked Nighteyes. Unfortunately, there was a reason for their tardiness. Their leader's body, peppered with flechettes, lay limp on the cold floor of the courtyard. They'd been forced to hold another vote first, and their new leader flew up to perch atop the palace.

Talli.

The sisters locked eyes, and Whisper did her best to send scents about everything that had happened in Balthar's absence.

Iri had lived like a small reeve, second only to the pridelord, ordering about the largest pride of starlings, perhaps of gryphons. But her little sister had grown up on the outskirts, serving a pride so small it often didn't even have a dedicated denparent.

When Whisper followed the salt trails through Talli's lands to return the lost, she'd seen Talli sew up wounded hunters with the last of the supplies from her torn research harness. She'd seen Talli visit graves of dead starlings with their offspring, heard the words the green starling offered to comfort them. She'd seen Talli fall in love, and the death of one of her lovers to flechettes today had just made her leader.

The salts had given her the body of a starling, but being separated from her sibling and friends had given her what the Stormtail Pride called *heartbones.*

Talli held her head high and voted for Nighteyes.

Every starling let out a clarion call, and the smell of citrus became berry as Nighteyes took control. Then berry became mint, and the murmuration turned west, abandoning the Blackwing Eyrie.

Iony shouted for some motmots to fly ahead and order the army returning from the mountains to stand down.

The murmuration began its migration home, leaving behind the smoldering ruins of a flameworks, collapsed canals filled with dead starlings, the shattered glass of the Court of Waterfalls, and the body of the only blackwing pridelord.

67

THE VIOLET PRIDELORD

Nighteyes' consciousness expanded as every starling's pheromones and thoughts opened up to her. She'd been asleep her entire life, but now she was awake. She'd become so much more than she'd been. She *was* the murmuration.

Quiet, came a whisper at the edge of her consciousness, one prick of light among a universe of stars. *You are too loud. You're hurting them.*

The Violet Pridelord pulled back a little, and her starlings relaxed. Her body flew of its own accord as it had during moments of altruism, but instead of controlling her physical form, she controlled everyone else's. She had two stormtails fly in front of her, dancing across the sky, their long tails forming streaks in the air.

They do not need you to show them how to fly, the whisper returned. *Try telling and asking, not ordering.*

Nighteyes lowered her pheromones, though they still came out as a shout. But in that shout she formed a question. "Who are you?"

"Whisper." The quiet voice belonged to a spotless starling with silver eyes flying right next to Nighteyes' body. "Your friend, who helped prepare you for this moment, should it come."

"I'm not...in there." Nighteyes located her body using the pheromones of the gryphons around her. "I'm the murmuration. I'm not Nighteyes."

Whisper reached out a paw and ran it along Nighteyes' fuse-scorched chest feathers, a sensation that barely registered. "It's a side effect of the protections I gave you against the pridelord. They're protecting you from yourself now. But I can remove them. You can be Nighteyes again. I can show you how."

The murmuration passed over a camp of blackwings, and Nighteyes felt the altruism well up. Now, however, she could suppress it. "Later. When we get home."

Whisper nodded, putting some distance between her and Nighteyes. "Send quiet inquiries to your pridemates. Have them remind you who they are. That way, you remember they're real and stop treating them like toys for your amusement."

The Violet Pridelord narrowed her focus to a single light blue stormtail, and carefully asked, "Define yourself."

The stormtail did a little twist in the air. "Desert Rose. I was lost in the bog, and Whisper brought me home. I smell like oleander, which I got to see in the desert for the first time on my way here. Rudder and Clamshell are my best friends."

She remembered him again and turned her attention to Wendl.

The opinicus bowed her head. Her message was muted by elixirs, perhaps a hedge in case Iri had become the new pridelord. "I'm a mothfeather opinicus who became a starling to hide from certain death. I cured your blindness, leaving you with the white scars on your eyes. I used to be engaged to Whisper, and one of my best friends is hiding near here with his family. Speaking of family, my own is in danger. They sleep in an eyrie, but the Seraph King's Army awaits without."

Nighteyes switched to a gryphon more unusual than the rest.

"I am the Sound of Snow," the gryphon seemed to say, though her pheromones were shaky. "Crescent. Moon. Pride."

"The sound of snow in the jungle is drip, drip, drip," Nighteyes replied, eliciting a series of hoots that could have been a laugh. "Drip of the Crescentmoon Pride, who are you really?"

Inspired by the stormtails, the owl did a twirl, showing off her opinicus talons, and switched to common. "I am Sound of Snow of the Strix Pride, daughter of Ninox of the Strix, daughter of Cherine Metalbeak of the Padfoot Pride, sister to Squirrelbane, sister to Marshmallow, and future mate of Sound of Sand if he hasn't forgotten about me."

Nighteyes could feel the *youth* coming off this owl opinicus. She could see the work Whisper had done to make Sound of Snow into Drip. Where Whisper had been forced to make subtle changes, a pridelord was not so restricted. She sent a pheromone inquiry, asking for permission, and once she received it, she proceeded to make it easy for

Sound of Snow to change her own scent markers to and from Drip.

You risk Ninox's ire by doing that, Whisper returned. Though her pheromones were weaker than a pridelord's, her nares were strong.

Nighteyes sent mint her way, which annoyed the newmoon leader. *We need ambassadors and diplomats. She'll serve as ours. She's shown her worth to the murmuration, and if Drip were not a true starling, her vote would not have counted.*

Sound of Snow—Drip—looked pleased and went to Whisper to tell her about the change, not realizing Whisper knew almost everything that happened in the murmuration. "I'm a starling now, too! That's exciting. Oh, I forgot to tell you. You smell a lot like my brother when he cooks."

Nighteyes left them, learning how to weaken a scent or message if it wasn't directed at her. When she did that, the entire murmuration relaxed again, seeming happier. It was a good lesson: starlings did not like to be observed.

She continued through the jadebeaks, who mostly talked about squirrels. Then she realized some gryphons were missing.

"Where's Rudder?" she asked. The replies came back full of anxiety.

Feathersnake.

Captured.

Alwren. Beyond Emerald Veil. No save.

Information flowed into her, almost too much to bear. The heart in her body ached for Rudder, but her mind was the murmuration, and it understood there were more important things at stake than one stormtail.

Still, for her body's sake, she asked one more question. *Sheen?*

A jadebeak gryphon named Flicker, once belonging to a mountain forager pride of red starlings, replied. "We saved her. She's with the Gourmand. They searched the jungle to find any lost gryphlets or fledglings who were left behind, and they're all hiding out in the Winter Jungle. The Nighthaunt wanted her and Rudder most of all."

Anger rose in Nighteyes' body, moving into her mind, and the murmuration emitted a pepper smell. She wanted to bite an alabaster opinicus, and she wanted to do so right now.

Calm, Whisper sent. *Are you another Balthar, here to order starlings to fight in opinicus wars for you? We've had three pridelords in a moon's cycle. You must learn from the others' mistakes. Remember why you did this: to save lives.*

The wind from the desert brought with it the scent of the alabaster army Wendl had warned Nighteyes about, and she remembered Whisper's first advice: *Ask, don't order.*

Nighteyes, the Violet Pridelord, *asked* the murmuration what they thought about the Alabaster Eyrie's forces coming up before them. She didn't ask them for the sake of the Blackwing Eyrie, nor the Ashen Weald. She asked what they wanted.

Some wished to hurry home to the Emerald Jungle. Most, however, now understood what had happened to them and who was behind the war migration and the attack on the Emerald Jungle.

Iri's vote was, ironically, first this time. Unsurprisingly, she wanted to attack the alabasters. The others mostly agreed, and despite Whisper's critiques, Nighteyes shifted the murmuration north slightly, going through the blood forest.

"Is this the way to your home, Wendl of Mothfeather Eyrie?" she asked the opinicus.

Wendl's response came quickly. "Yes, Pridelord."

The starlings were used to flying between the trees and vines of the jungle, and they easily kept low, skimming the forest. Nighteyes could feel that they neared Mothfeather Eyrie. The murmuration reached a series of familiar lakes, and they settled down to recuperate. Desert Rose and the stormtails divided the lakes between them, tossing fish to hungry starlings as fast as they could catch them.

Nighteyes looked south. There were gryphons with better eyesight than her, not to mention the owl opinicus's excellent hearing, and she sent them to scout.

"The murmuration is wounded and tired," Wendl tried to warn. "We outnumber the alabaster forces, but they're well rested."

Nighteyes felt exhaustion overcome her, and she released the murmuration. Despite not having felt like she was controlling them, the way they relaxed told her she'd been stricter than she thought.

"Whisper, can you take over if something comes up?" Nighteyes didn't wait for an answer, falling asleep almost immediately. Or she thought she was asleep. She still felt aware of the other starlings, but they came through the filter of dreams—hers and others.

The jadebeaks around her dreamt of the Emerald Jungle, or they mostly did. Iri and Talli dreamt of their families, whom they hadn't seen at the Blackwing Eyrie and hoped were safe. The dreams of stormtails were wet and rainy, the dreams of sparkwings sunny.

Perhaps the strangest came from members of the Newmoon Pride. A ptarmigan, taking a break from the waking world, dug through imaginary snow to locate sugar frogs. Depending on what the parasite had done to their brains, some of the cured dreamt of nothing.

No, that's not right. Nighteyes pushed in further, and in the darkness, she heard a lullaby. Whisper had put a song in their heads so they wouldn't fear the emptiness of sleep. The Newmoon Pride's stranger members were all like that, except one.

For a single alabaster opinicus, the bugs had missed a memory of an eyrie with statues and pagoda-like buildings that reached into the clouds, of gold sunlight coming off the ocean, of skies that were never empty. Though he no longer remembered his name, his family, or his friends, he remembered sitting in a captain's harness and guarding the entrance to the Seraph King's throne room.

The Violet Pridelord awoke with a start and a plan.

"Are the scouts back?" she asked. They gathered around her, perhaps summoned from her dream. "What did you find?"

According to Drip, at the very end of the alabaster's caravan was the Mothfeather Eyrie. The top levels had been destroyed and looted. "There were more weapons than they could use, so they crated up the surplus and put it up top, by the stables, to take back to Blacktalon."

"What about the mothfeather opinici?" Wendl asked.

"The seal is closed," Drip replied. "The back door the Newmoon Pride used has been collapsed by a small saltpeter explosion. The alabasters must have found it. "

Nighteyes couldn't see through Drip's pheromones the way she could the other starlings, who hadn't gotten as close as the owl. "Crates of weapons, a city of mothfeathers. Surely, if they open the seal, the mothfeathers can save themselves?"

"There's more saltpeter by the seal. And above it," Drip added.

Wendl tapped a talon on the ground. "How much saltpeter? Like enough to destroy the seal, or like enough to collapse the hibernation chambers?"

"Why would they do that if they believe the moth-feathers are all dead?" Nighteyes asked, but the answer already came to her through the pheromones. "Oh. Khalim said they tried to steal the mummified feathersnake that was full of parasites. And that there was an outbreak at a prison near Whitebeak, and they bombed it and burned away the remains. They think *starlings* killed and partially ate the mothfeathers."

Whisper, whose idea it had been to cover the hiber-nating opinici in blood, made a grumpy sound. "So they'll just collapse the cave and send in a team to burn it away later to stop the parasite from spreading. Despite there not being a parasite and no reason to think so."

"Well..." Flicker began, before pointing at the

eyeshine worn by several Newmoon Pride. "If any scouts caught sight of us, they'd report on silver-eyed starlings. This is kinda our fault."

"Are the explosives ready to go? If we snuck in fast and light them on fire, maybe just the ones on the seal would explode?" Wendl suggested, but Drip was already shaking her head.

The owl opinicus opened a scholarly notebook, possibly one of her father's, and dipped a quill in ink. She sketched out a map. "If you could just set off the explosives by the seal, it'd open. Any flameworks technician would tell you that. But there's fuses connecting it all. You'd need to cut them first, and the place is crawling with alabasters. Even if the seal comes down, the mothfeathers might not get to the weapons in time. It would be better to wait."

Nighteyes wasn't sure they could stay hidden for much longer. It was probably a miracle that none of the argent hawks had spotted them yet, and it wouldn't last.

She had an idea, though. Something that had come to her in a dream. "Wendl, Whisper: You two stay here. I'll bring the murmuration to the east, to the front of their goliath caravan. When the main force is drawn away, you can sneak in to remove most of the explosives and open the seal."

"Even if you draw them away, there's still going to be guards," Wendl protested. "They're not going to let us just walk up and start messing with their things. Alabasters are very suspicious of any opinicus who isn't a white-tailed kite."

Whisper looked back at one of the white-tailed

kites she'd saved from the bog. "I think I have a way around that."

"Can you control him?" Nighteyes asked. "He just needs to look like he belongs long enough to move a few explosives and light a fuse."

Whisper idly licked at her paw, and a thin line of citrus and something else filled the air. An alabaster stood and walked over to her. "Guess so. You're still trusting the mothfeathers not to turn on us."

"I know mothfeathers," Wendl said. "They'll listen to me. They're afraid of the swarm, but they won't even notice I'm a starling if I'm alone and wearing my harness."

Nighteyes queried the murmuration, and they were still in favor of getting their revenge on the alabasters. That didn't surprise her—she'd just wanted to be careful, as she knew she couldn't suppress everyone's altruism once the fighting started —but what did catch her off guard was that the Newmoon and Stormtail Prides were excited about helping the Mothfeather 'Pride'. In their pheromones, she saw them playing in an underground lake at Crestfall Eyrie and exploring sand owl burrows.

What about you? Nighteyes quietly asked Whisper. *I know how you feel about your home.*

Whisper's eyes were unreadable, but her pheromones were a detailed diagram of her heart and loyalties. *We should do this. I'd like to make sure my family is safe, even if I wouldn't want to live here again.*

With that confirmation, Nighteyes pulled the main body of the murmuration to backtrack. This time, an argent hawk caught sight of them and sped off to warn her leader.

CAPTAIN BOBL

The cool evening breeze outside Mothfeather pulled at the heat rising up from the damp plains. Wet needlegrass, sour and hot, soaked the alabaster opinicus's feet.

White tents with gold trim lined the goliath roads leading in and out of the eyrie. Tall stalks obscured the city from view, creating the illusion this was just a small military camp along a trade route. He knew better, though. The voices told him there was a city here.

He wiped at his eyes, his talons coming away clean, and emitted a confused grumble. The serenade of crickets drowned out the sound. He was certain he'd seen gooey silver a moment ago. It had come with a command.

Go on, a little closer. Be with your own kind, your old kind. The whispers came on the wind, smells of rotting orange hidden between the wet warmth of the grass and the cool crisp of the air.

He grunted and stepped forwards, stumbling a bit.

Someone with different feet was trying to tell him how to walk, and he hissed a protest in pepper.

Sorry, the winds whispered. *Guess I've forgotten how talons work.*

"Mrrrr," he spoke aloud, surprised by the sound of his voice. Memories came unbidden: of him standing tall in a fancy harness outside a huge stone palace, turning strangers away if they looked suspicious. He heard his old voice in his head and tried to replicate it. "Go...away."

Oh? You can speak? Well, that's unexpected. The quiet voice didn't use spoken words, but he understood her commands all the same. *I don't suppose you remember your name?*

"My...name." He thought hard, but thinking was like shoving water into a leaky bucket. Things might get wet, but most of his memories drained away before he could hold onto them. "No...name. Just...scent."

Someone will ask you for a name, the whispers pushed. *We need to come up with a good opinicus name for you. Unfortunately, I've been around gryphons too long, and I don't know alabasters. Let me look around here for a name. Uh, Drip...Wendl...Dripl?*

He blinked his eyes, strangely clear, and saw a golden winged trinket hanging from one of the tall, white tents. The embroidery on the tent was familiar, but his brain tried to remember what the trinket was called. This one had a white bird inside glass, and he remembered that it turned sunlight into rainbows.

"Baub...bob...Bobl," he said at last. "Bobl of... Newmoon Pride."

Okay, so yes, but I'm going to need you to say that

you're an alabaster for this mission, the helpful messages entering his nares told him.

"Bobl of Alabaster Pride." His eyecrests furrowed. That wasn't right. "Bobl of Alabaster Eyrie. I am...Bobl from the Alabaster Eyrie. A guard."

That'll work. Now, the other guards are going to depart when they get word starlings are attacking the front lines. The whisper quieted for a moment. *Looks like the scouts found the murmuration, so soon now. I need you to look like you've been ordered to check the explosives, then remove the ones above the domicile. Once that happens, light the fuse at the seal.*

"Look...busy. A guard looking busy." He did remember appearing otherwise engaged so his superiors didn't assign him additional responsibilities. The voice was doing something with scents, and he remembered things he'd thought lost, along with new memories of how to be an opinicus from a mothfeather rancher.

Confusion grew to a boil, then simmered and combined. He knew there were things still missing, places where he heard a voice and tried to remember who it belonged to but saw only nightmares—the Nighthaunt, a mummified feathersnake, an attack by the Reevesbane, the Ashen Weald, him being knocked unconscious by a glacier owl, waking in the bog, starting to feel sick—

Come back to me, Bobl, the scents on the wind ordered. *I promise, when we get through this, we'll see how many memories we can recover. I thought...well, wrong. I thought I'd recovered everything I could for you. I didn't realize having you out doing familiar things would jog your memory. But first, we need to save the Moth-feather Eyrie.*

He saw the young mothfeather opinicus again, a rancher's chick. He understood they were all sleeping below, and the explosives were up top. He had a map of the city, not quite the same after all this time, but eyries changed. He knew what to do, and he started walking.

Sure you're ready for this? the voice asked, but he didn't need her to tell him how to walk. He went through the high grass, stopping to smudge some mud on his chest feathers, smelling confusion in the pheromones reaching him.

Those scents changed to alarm when he walked right up to another alabaster.

"Are the bath houses open?" Bobl asked an opinicus wearing a recruit's badge. He kept his tone direct. He'd served in the Golden Sky Army prior to being made a royal guard, back before the days of woodpeckers, and he was starting to remember the tone.

"Oh! What happened to you?" the recruit squeaked.

His own memories didn't have an answer, so he borrowed one from the gifted mothfeather's. "Goliath bird."

"Musta been quite a bird!" For a recruit, the tone was unusually playful. He didn't remember one of the new guards ever talking to him like this in his memories. "There's a heated bathhouse down below. It's nothing like back home, but it's warm. Gotta say, I like the selection of feather oils they sell here."

He turned and stared at the words on the wall. His

alabaster memory didn't recognize most of them, but the mothfeather additions knew the way. "I see, thank you."

"You know, if you need help..." she began, before he interrupted her.

"I don't. Back to your post." He took a ramp into a large stone structure with pillars. Mothfeather architecture appeared blocky from the outside, not like the pagodas of home, but the rooms and corridors inside were spacious with a high ceiling and welcoming goliath hide cushions to rest on in every corner. Mothfeathers took their bathhouses seriously.

He heard scents that gave him the impression of laughing. "What?"

She was flirting with you, the whispers came. *You turned her down pretty hard.*

He shrugged. He had a...something. He had something back home.

Scented braziers filled the depths of the bathhouse, fed by a hot springs. There were a talonful of soldiers here, but they were better about minding their own business than the recruit upstairs.

He quickly rinsed off the mud, slathered himself in sage-scented mothfeather oils as he preened himself dry, and then walked over to a pile of discarded harnesses. For the most part, only recruits forgot to remove their badges. Despite believing they had it worse than anyone else in the army, a lot of leeway was given to recruits. New soldiers who lost their badge would get punished—mildly. But at the higher ranks, the consequences were more severe.

Some captains would deliberately leave their badge of rank on a dirty harness as a way of testing to see how competent the laundry team were. He couldn't be sure that was how the captains did things here, but he had a hunch.

"There we go." He pulled a captain badge off one of the harnesses. Though he spoke aloud, he was surprised no voice replied to him. The whispers must be busy, or being inside, hidden behind scented braziers and covered in feather oil suppressed them.

There was a moment where he realized he could just rejoin the Alabaster Eyrie. He played out that scenario in his head and quickly discarded it. They wouldn't know him as Bobl. If he stayed with the starlings, they'd help him recover his memories. He climbed the corridors back to the surface.

Once he was out of range of the bathhouse, something stirred inside him, a sense of gratitude. These weren't *his* memories, but they were memories *of him*. He saw himself in the bog, silver-eyed, attacking someone who was trying to help him, but they were both losing themselves to the parasite.

And then I came. The whispers returned as he reached the top level of the bathhouse. Not whispers, *Whisper* returned. *You were already in the Jadebeak Mountains, but I pulled you across the Emerald Veil. You were too far gone to save without medical care, which you wouldn't get in Ashen Weald territory. Your friend fled, but I caught up to him, too, and saved him.*

The word *saved* tasted strange to Bobl. Was this really what it meant to be saved? Some might call it being damned, though he supposed the alternative was death. His sense of gratitude came from the fact he hadn't killed his companion, that Whisper had stopped him in time.

He exited the bathhouse and walked past the flirty recruit, who only managed an, "Oh, er, Captain!" before he entered a makeshift barracks.

Bobl walked up to two soldiers with light bandages. If they'd been badly wounded, they'd be in the medical tent. That they were in the barracks meant they were capable of basic tasks, if still on the mend.

"I'm Captain Bobl. You two have been reassigned to light duty." He turned and they joined him, not bothering to question anyone with a captain badge. "Turns out, there's something of value hiding in the Mothfeather Vault, and the blackwings are coming to try to keep us from getting to it. That means it's up to us to adjust the explosives a little."

His two assistants didn't question the orders. Whisper wanted him to continue to spin a tale about the incoming attack, but that wasn't how captains worked. The more he talked, the more suspicious they'd become. If he stayed calm and offered up the smallest hook of why their compatriots were about to run off—*the blackwings are coming to try to keep us from getting it*—their imaginations would fill in the rest.

He stood in front of the seal, supervising his assistants. The whispers were persistent, but they were quiet enough now he could ignore them. He knew she could push the citrus and command him, but she didn't. He didn't need a rancher to tell him what to do for military matters.

There was a clarity he'd lacked for years, as though this little excursion had built a bridge to a lost part of his brain that was now coming alive. With it came new grief. He was correct that he'd once had someone back home, but he'd left to join the seraph-retrieval expedition because she'd died, and he couldn't stand to be at the Alabaster Eyrie anymore.

"Captain." The wounded soldiers looked at him expectantly.

He blinked once, snapping out of it. Part of having to guard the throne room was learning to daydream without looking like he was daydreaming. "Good work. Now go report to medical. You're not to fight, but you're to help with the wounded, understand?"

"Yes, sir." They each echoed before flying off. He looked to where they'd put the extra barrels of black powder, and they'd piled them on top of the bath-house. Not the smartest place, but he supposed he hadn't specified where they should go.

Light it, Whisper ordered him. Except it wasn't an order, it was a recommendation.

"Not yet." He smelled the slight pepper of a starling's hiss, but as his brain activity returned, he understood better the goal wasn't just to get the mothfeathers out of the ground, it was to get them to the weapons. Weapons stored in crates next to the well-defended commander's tent.

The cool air tickled his freshly washed facial feathers. He remained still, looking as though he had been assigned to the fuses. Only his eyes moved as a silver hawk flew overhead. He'd never trusted the Argent Heights. The border eyries were too new, and they'd joined out of necessity or force. Thus, their eyes always looked east, wondering if things would have gone differently if they'd cast their lot in with the Blackwing Alliance.

What do you know about their reeve? Whisper asked.

He grunted. "The king calls her twice-bound. She hates the pitohui as much as she loves her opinici, so even if one chain broke, the other would hold her fast."

Silver is a weird name, Whisper pushed. *Do they rename their reeve?*

"She's a commoner." He realized a rancher wouldn't know what that meant. It was unlikely moth-feathers had much in the way of an upper class. "It's meant to be aspirational, but it's the name you give a daughter you know would never be allowed to amount to much. At some point, though, the Reeves-bane killed everyone who mattered, and she was the only one left to put in charge. Piprik and Goldfeather acknowledged her claim as reeve."

The messenger hawk departed, and the camp sprang to life. What Nighteyes and Whisper, neither having been soldiers, were hoping would happen was that the main forces would abandon the supplies by the commander's tent. That wasn't how the king's army waged war. Instead, they always left behind some of the best to guard the commander and supplies. There was only one time he'd seen a commander abandon their stronghold, and that had come at Whitebeak. Commanders and reeves feared one thing above armies.

He waited for his opportunity. A dozen argents ran in and out of the tent, and he slipped in between them.

The command tent glowed white from the outside. Braziers here were covered in Crestfall glass.

Military discipline was good, but when a battle began, it was easy for someone to knock one over. He pushed ahead of the messengers, dislodging a small hawk to make it appear urgent.

"Commander, we just received word that the resupply from Blacktalon never arrived." Bobl kept to the point while letting his tone convey that he felt what he was saying was important. "We located their bodies in the woods, poisoned."

Another captain looked up from his work. "The blood forest? Did a storm come in?"

Bobl appreciated the opi's idiocy, as it let the commander say what everyone smart had been thinking.

"Pitohui." The commander stood. "Rybalt must be preparing to flank us. We need to find a safer position."

All Bobl needed was for them to abandon the command tent so the crates of stolen weapons would be accessible to the mothfeathers, but his assistants' laziness in moving the black powder opened up an unexpected opportunity. "Commander, the local bathhouses are well-fortified with easily defensible tunnels leading in and out. It'll be difficult for assassins to slip inside, plus the water and drainage will help rinse away their toxins."

As the command tent fled to the bathhouse, Bobl slipped away into the tall grasses near the fuse. His body stilled, but his mind returned to the murmuration, becoming a starling once more.

69

FIRST MORNING

An explosion cracked the seal of Mothfeather Eyrie. Whisper had fully expected it to roll away or fall down. As a chick, she'd often held her talons up to it, feeling its weight and sturdiness to the touch. However large it had seemed when she was little, now it simply crumbled.

She and Wendl crawled out from their hiding spot. The susurration hid nearby, but she thought it best they not be the first thing the mothfeathers see— even with Nighteyes trying to suppress their altruism, they were a scary lot. The explosion would be stressful enough.

In fact, it's probably better if I'm not the first thing they see, either. She stepped back, letting Wendl take the lead. There was something calming about a medicine harness. Whisper knew she was the opposite of calming, but she needed her eyeshine and markings for her own mental wellbeing when confronting her old home.

"Hello, Mothfeather Eyrie!" Wendl called out. "I'm

Wendl, a medicine opinicus. I'm here as a friend, but we need to get you moving."

The first opinicus to step through the dust was a grizzled rancher in an ancient but well-mended harness. In Whisper's memories, her dad was young and strong. Finally getting a good look at him in the light of day, exhausted even coming out of the Great Hibernation, made her feel old. The golden browns, charcoal blacks, and other plumage colors had faded to a myriad of greys.

"What do you mean by this?" he demanded. "We were safe inside."

Don't say anything stupid, Whisper thought to herself, but her beak had other ideas. "You weren't safe. The alabasters were about to collapse the entire chamber and bury the lot of you!"

Her accent slipped out, a very slight ranch twang to it. More mothfeathers climbed over the wreckage, and they were all staring at Whisper like she were a monster. In a way, it would be easier if she sounded like the Nighthaunt, a voice almost bestial. Hearing their own rancher accent from a gryphon would be worse.

Wendl cleared her throat. "Whisper's right. The alabasters are distracted by starlings. Now's your chance to flee."

"Or fight," Whisper added. She let her scent turn citrus, ordering Bobl to light the second fuse. The bathhouse exploded. "That's where the commander was hiding. He's dead and the eyrie's weapons are yours for the taking."

"What about the starlings?" her father growled, his voice like an old beast. "If we waste our energy killing alabasters, we won't have any left for killing gryphons."

Whisper's hackles raised. "The gryphons are your allies this day. They won't hurt you. They...*we're*...not monsters."

"They killed my son." He looked Whisper in the eye when he said it, and he seemed to believe it with all his being.

It was the last thing she expected him to say, and her voice cracked when she spoke, making her words unintelligible. "Dad, I..."

"Your son survived," Wendl interrupted. "As did I. You've heard of what the Nighthaunt has done, turning opinicus to seraph? We escaped into the Emerald Jungle, and the starlings took us in. They protected us against the Nighthaunt. You'll get to meet him later. He's the one who had the idea to cover you in blood so the alabasters didn't kill you while you slept."

Whisper's father grunted, his way of acknowledging that a statement would change things if it were true, though he had his doubts.

The dust and smoke in the air cleared a little, and the opinicus chick holding Whisper's old stuffed capybara walked up to get a better look at Mothfeather's two wayward daughters. It was strange to think this might be her niece.

"Where are the blackwings?" her father asked. "Even if the defenders died protecting us, the Blackwing Alliance should be here, not a bunch of gryphons."

Xenophobic as always. Whisper opened her beak,

but her pepper pheromones must have foreshadowed her intent, as Wendl spoke first and fast.

"The main army passed over here first, and we used the blood trick to keep them from lingering," Wendl equivocated. "The Blackwing Eyrie nearly fell, but we arrived in time to save it. What's left here is a secondary army setting up a supply line, hence why they wanted to collapse the vault on your heads."

Whisper's father had never been one to speak quickly, and the silence was filled by heavy winds, signs that at least a hailstorm was coming to the plains. Tumbleweeds fell from roads above, collecting before the rubble of the seal.

Inside Whisper's head, things were not quiet. The murmuration was fighting the alabasters while the susurration wasted time arguing with a greyfeather rancher who hated all gryphons.

She narrowed in on him, trying to read his scent. There was fear of several types in the air, no doubt caused by the explosion. There was also relief, which confused her, until she remembered he thought gryphons had killed his child. She couldn't read opinicus scents the way she could gryphons, let alone starlings, and she found herself staring at his feathers to try to tell what he was thinking. The plumage atop his head was lighter than below from his time in the sun, and the feathers around his eyes were grey and cracked.

He caught her staring at him and returned her gaze, though his words were directed at Wendl, since she was an opinicus. "Fine, but that one is coming with me. You can always tell the lead gryphon because they look the scariest. If it's next to me, the others will stay back. Does it have a name?"

"She's Whisper," Wendl replied. "And you're right, the others here will follow her lead. Now, we need to hurry. The main part of the murmuration is already fighting, and it's just the susurration here to help."

The leader of the Newmoon Pride had just about hit her limit of family time, but she ordered the susurration to clear the bathhouse of any survivors, reminding them to give a wide berth to the mothfeathers. For Captain Bobl and his friend, she ordered them to hide in the woods so they weren't mistaken for the enemy.

You did well, she sent them. *Now rest until it's time to leave.*

No reply came, but white feathers disappeared into the long grass. To be safe, she sent the frost-plumed ptarmigan along with them. With only starlings left, she turned to her father.

"Mothfeather's weapons are in the crates outside the tent. I'll show you the way." She pointed her beak up to where the commander had been. "No idea what's in the other crates, but you may find alabaster steel or flechettes, too."

"Fine. Good." He used his talons to push back his granddaughter, then when Whisper led him to the crates, he slapped her haunch like she was a goliath bird, letting up a cloud of black featherdust. "Dirty animals, gryphons. Does that Wendl never wash you?"

Whisper gritted her tomia, focusing seventy-five percent of her rage at her father and another twenty-five at Wendl, who had choked a laugh down with a snort at the comment. "Emerald Jungle gryphons use scent to communicate, so all that featherdust keeps them calm and prevents them from hurting the Black-wing Alliance."

After much grumbling and opening of boxes, the inhabitants of Mothfeather were well-armed. The Waking City's military was small compared to its population size, and there were enough metal talons and light armor for all of them. Wendl directed the ranchers to pouches of flechettes, instructing them on how to use the metal darts before sending them off to the front lines. Anyone who couldn't fight fled north, into the woods.

Heavy, scattered drops of water fell from the sky. After the stories of the blood forests, Whisper was forced to expend energy to add mint to her pheromones to calm everyone. She was lost in the smells of battle, keeping close tabs on Taloncrest, who had become a target of interest for Whisper's niece, who liked his hat. She suggested Taloncrest's time might be better spent searching the bathhouse. Her father's voice brought her out of it.

"What, gryphons don't get armor or talons?" He picked up her paw like she were livestock and pushed on her paw pads, extending her silver-tinted claws. "Son used to paint his talons the same color after he went away to be an apprentice. Bet he still does now, living among gryphons and crocodiles."

Whisper used mint on herself to keep from biting him. "There's no metalworks or tannery in the Emerald Jungle. Most weapon designs are based around opinicus talons."

"They make metal claws for the glacier pride.

Even saw a kinda metal beak thing on a motmot once." He spoke to her the way he used to speak to the goliaths after a long day of plowing fields. "I hear the gryphon paradise in the south has spiny armor for their lot, too. Should have that Wendl buy you a set to keep you safe."

A softening in his tone gave him away. It was in the way he said Wendl's name this time. Not as a stranger outside the seal, but the same way he'd said it when Whisper brought her home from university to meet the family.

It might have remained subtext if Flicker hadn't crashed into the scene, missing her landing after her paw caught a tumbleweed. "Sorry! We found the enemy pride leader in the rubble. He wants to speak to you about...Oh! Is that your—"

She knew enough to stop herself, but Whisper's dad confirmed her suspicions.

"Yeah, that's me. I thought it was you." He let the words linger, watching as Flicker intertwined her tail protectively with Whisper's. "Guess I did lose a son to the starlings. Nighthaunt alchemy, huh?"

Whisper nodded. "It was the only way to survive, but I knew what I was doing."

The storm picked up, a puddle tinged black with featherdust spreading out from Whisper and onto Flicker. The strawberry finch didn't pull her paws away, letting the water stain them dark. The rain dampened Whisper's ability to smell long distances, but it cleared the shine from her eyes so she could look into her father's.

"I'm glad you're alive," he managed.

Flicker tried to squeeze Whisper's back paw, but

she just ended up stepping on it. "Oh! I meant to say, we found the opinicus pride leader for this bunch of alabasters. He wants to surrender to you."

"To me? Not to Nighteyes?" Whisper asked.

"Oh, no, not *you*," Flicker corrected. "He saw Taloncrest chewing on a captain. He wants to surrender to *Mothfeather* because he's pretty sure the starlings will try to eat him for what they did to the murmuration."

Taloncrest, what're you eating? We talked about this after the blackwings, Whisper sent out. His reply was muffled by the rain, but to be safe, she sent the order for him to stop. Her father cleared his throat, seeming to know her mind had strayed elsewhere.

"I should see this commander, but Whisper, was it? Come visit for your mom's sake...and mine," he added. "Just to visit. Bring your pretty mate, too. She looks like the ranching type."

"I am!" Flicker replied, clearly wanting to say more.

Whisper didn't bother using citrus on Flicker, who had probably closed off her nares. "We will, but if the commander can stop the fighting, you should see him now. If the storm picks up, it'll get harder to control the murmuration."

The rain did pick up, but Flicker was correct: the small army of alabasters were more than happy to take their chances as prisoners of the Waking City than with the murmuration.

With Whisper and Wendl's former opinici safe, it was time to take the murmuration home.

70

THE BLACKWING REEVE

The funk of smoke and rotting corpses clung to the Blackwing Eyrie like a film. The starlings had departed as suddenly as they'd come, leaving behind a wrecked and distraught city littered with their dead.

The flameworks' explosion was so powerful, it had caused a rockslide that wiped out the nicest nests on the entire coast. Burning oil leaked into the empty canals, fracturing the delicate stonework of the original builders. Once tame snowmelt now flooded into homes, markets, and schools.

The palace had it the worst, its courtyards filled with the corpses of gryphon and opinicus alike. None of the royal guard still lived, though the bravery of the glacier pride and pitohui lived up to its reputation. In the final hours of the battle, when all hope had seemed lost, Reeve Rybalt Reevesbane of the Pitohui Eyrie and Iony Silver-Ear of the glacier pride had evacuated the blackwing reeve out of a secret passage that connected the Blackwing Eyrie to

Goldtree Gardens on the other side of the mountains.

During their subterranean flight, strange monsters from the depths had risen. Rybalt and all the pitohui accompanying him had died saving the life of the blackwing reeve—or so the story as told by Iony went. He wore the long claws of the monster who killed Rybalt as a necklace to corroborate his story, not that anyone would doubt it with the blackwing reeve backing him up. It was a tragic loss, and it was time for the leader of the Blackwing Alliance to speak on it.

The remains of a courtyard were cleared out. Without Crestfall, the glass was unlikely to be replaced, though several fish had been donated by the motmot pride so the pools throughout the palace were once again well-stocked.

The throne room was too small for such a public proclamation, and the courtyard allowed Blackwing Alliance survivors to look down from the tops of the palace spires. Several heralds were present to repeat the speech.

The blackwing reeve cleared his throat. It was still a little off, perhaps raspy from the smoke. "Blackwing Alliance, gryphons and opinici, old friends and new. We gather here to mourn the death of one of the finest reeves to ever rule. We gather here to celebrate the life of Rybalt, called Reevesbane."

Iony's head was bowed, though the blackwing reeve had heard that many thought the glacier gryphon was not nearly sad enough for the loss of his best friend.

"In the years since the Pitohui Eyrie joined, Rybalt

championed many causes. He was both staunch ally and rebellious traitor, as the mood took him. Though we often disagreed, there were times—very occasionally—where he was right, and I was glad I heeded his advice.

"If not for him, the glacier and motmot prides would not be among us. While the designated heir of the Pitohui Eyrie is his sister, Stripes, presumed dead, their eyrie has selected a motmot as the new pride leader. May you honor his memory, Reeve A Motmot."

The motmot bowed her head slightly. She would be given two votes on the council, and if the pitohui and motmots split up, each would keep one vote. It was the least the blackwing reeve could do for them.

He continued. "It was Reeve Rybalt's wish that his body be burned. It has been washed and prepared in charcoal, so the poison that followed him in life will not continue into death, in accordance with the customs of his opinici."

Though normally *trashbirds* were required to be covered when in the palace, on this day of mourning, the blackwing reeve had allowed them to stand in just harnesses. Medicine opinici were nearby with the antitoxin if any incidents occurred, but none had.

"He saved my life, and he died a hero. It was his actions that helped overthrow the Seraph King's pridelord and return the Emerald Jungle to starling control. Perhaps, even though he was never able to add a king to his list of *missions accomplished*, he can count a pridelord among them.

"Now, if his loyal assistants would be so kind as to

light the fire? Let his spirit go, and may Reeve Rybalt watch over us, always."

The trashbirds took ceremonial torches and used them to light the body on the pyre. At Iony's insistence, the deceased had been buried in his leather bindings and falconry wraps. The glacier gryphon had been kind enough to identify the body first so there was no doubt it was, indeed, Rybalt.

The blackwing reeve finished his speech and turned to Rybalt's best friend. "Iony of the glacier pride, allow me to express my condolences to you in private. I owe you both my life."

THE BLACKWING REEVE escorted Iony past the throne room and into his private chambers, where piles of missives waited for him to sort through them.

The glacier gryphon waited until the door was closed to speak. "Really, *let us count the pridelord among his successes*? You know as well as I do the shiny starlings deserve that kill. And you need to work on your voice. If Khalim can sound just like Piprik, surely you can work it out."

The blackwing reeve removed the leaf-steel crown and set it on a table before collapsing onto the softest nesting material he'd ever slept on. "Khalim probably knew not to accidentally swallow the salts when he went in. My throat still burns. He also didn't have a problem with his body poisoning itself as it changed."

"I'm no alchemist," Iony replied matter-of-factly, "but maybe we should have brought someone who knew how to use the salts if that's what you wanted."

"We did," the reeve replied. "He was eaten by cave monsters. I suppose it was too much for the starling insurrectionists to warn us about them."

"Shoulda been more polite," Iony said. "Politeness gets you everywhere with gryphons."

The reeve rolled his eyes, taking off the ornate leaf bracelets before settling into a pile of reports from his spies. He sifted through interrogations from Mothfeather's prisoners and reports of missing opinici around Goldtree Gardens, looking for word on what was happening across the desert.

One missive in particular caught his attention, and he tossed it to Iony after finishing it. "There's a report here from the farmlands east of Duckbill. At an orchard, some peafowl were caught harboring blackwing fugitives. The fugitives escaped, but they were led by a red and orange opinicus wearing a red silk veil to keep others from touching her. She had four motmot bodyguards with her."

"Stripes," Iony said.

"Fetch our best assassins. Tell them—" The blackwing reeve paused, remembering himself. "Iony, please speak with the motmot reeve and let her know all of the Blackwing Eyrie's resources are available to her. It is my wish that Reeve Rybalt's sister is returned home alive. It's the least I can do for him after his sacrifice."

Iony rolled his eyes. "Yes, your blackwing majesty. I'll see it done. Perhaps some of Reeve Rybalt Reevesbane's—or was that Pridelordbane's?—assassins would be willing to join me on this endeavor."

The blackwing reeve waved Iony away.

Once the gryphon had departed, the reeve put

down the reports. He'd miss the tropical islands, miss being able to go out wherever he wanted alone. He'd even miss visiting the motmots with their strange, loud festivals. But every pitohui believed the right death at the right time could change the world. The operative word being change.

He coughed, feeling his body's lingering poison working on the blackwing chemistry, and drank more antitoxin before collapsing to sleep. He dreamt of jeweled leaves falling into purple pools, turning them black as the night sky.

71

CONSEQUENCES

There was a hole in the skies of the Emerald Jungle, an emptiness in its rivers, and a missing note in its fragrance. This lacuna had a name: Rudder. Nighteyes should be glad Whisper and Flicker's quick work had saved the Newmoon Pride, Stormtail Pride, and a pawful of younglings who had been left behind during the war migration, but the Violet Pridelord couldn't help but wish to have Rudder by her side.

The starling survivors had returned to their nesting grounds, though they were permitted to roam. It took days to destroy Balthar's glyphs and restore Lightningmaw and the Winter Jungle, days of Whisper and Wendl's constant theorizing and trials, but Nighteyes had accomplished it. By the time the last few glyphs along the far edge of the Winter Jungle were gone, the necessary pheromones were so familiar to Nighteyes that she could control another starling and have them emit the scents for her from across the jungle.

As the pridelord, she was expected to nest at the

central temple. She missed her island hideaway, but when she'd gone to empty out her few belongings, all she could think about was how dry it was without Rudder there. Heartbones aside, her old burrow was too close to the border, too open to attacks by outsiders.

Sheen had also been moved out of reach of the Seraph King's talons and given a nest in the Celestial Courtyard—though the subject of trading with the Stormtail Pride had been suggested, and they seemed interested. The Nightsky Pride had yet to determine who would lead in Nighteyes' absence, but she was certain one of her sisters would fill the role. Gossip put Wendl as the top contender, but the Violet Pridelord had plans for the opinicus.

The Sky Beneath the Earth was sealed off—for now. If there were clawdiggers along the Jadebeak Mountains, there were probably some in the jungle itself. She had ideas for the subterranean lair, but they could wait. There were more pressing matters at paw.

The leaders of the starling prides gathered around Nighteyes. A dry storm came down off the mountains, and the winds blew west, carrying her scents across the jungle. Between the wind and sun, the moss-covered court atop the jungle was as dry as it would get this time of year.

The pride leaders sounded off. A chirp, their name, their pride, and their scent. It was mostly routine, though there were breaks in the flow.

"Sheen, Nightsky Pride, currently leaderless." Whether from stress or something the Nighthaunt had given her, she was more blue than purple now.

When Nighteyes looked at her, she saw hints of Rudder.

"Flicker, Jadebeak but standing in for the Crescentmoon Pride," a strawberry finch of a starling chirped. She wouldn't need to do much, but someone needed to stand in for Drip. After much discussion, it was decided that until greenwing altruism could be fixed, the Crescentmoon Pride would be a way to allow visitors without worrying about elixirs.

It would also give them a small voice in starling matters. That last part had been Wendl's recommendation, a way to dissuade would-be allies from taking advantage of the starlings' peculiarities. As the opinicus had put it, *Give someone a voice if you don't want them acting on their own; give someone an opportunity to be kind, and you may prevent cruelty.*

It felt like something an opinicus would say, but the other pride leaders had agreed, so Nighteyes made it so.

The Violet Pridelord let waves of cool winds and warm sun alternate on her back, calming her mind, feeling the locations of her murmuration.

Talli had spent her life playing second: first to her older sister, then as an assistant denmother, then as a hunter, and finally to a sickly pride leader. After his death, she'd proven herself a surprising and capable leader. She was knowledgeable about everything and had a refreshing humility. It was not lost on Nighteyes that she owed her pridelord status to Talli's vote.

"Are you sure you want to do this?" The Second asked. "The danger is over."

Desert Rose glared at her, a reminder that one of his pride had been taken and the danger to them would remain so long as any opinicus or gryphon suffered from bloodbeak.

Nighteyes considered the course of action before her. "I am."

Though she was better able to exist inside her body when she controlled the murmuration these days, she still preferred to lie couchant while she did it. Whisper may as well have been named Silent at the moment, only confirming the Newmoon Pride's presence, but she'd spent long hours coaching Nighteyes on what to do.

The Violet Pridelord reached out with her senses. The eastern jungle was nearly empty. The few bright scents she felt were warriors guarding her and the other pride leaders at the temple. She had faint echoes of a presence in the Winter Jungle. She couldn't smell them, not with the watery pheromone desert and the wind going the wrong way, but the pheromones read something like *stormtail fledglings and gryphlets were last seen here.*

The bulk of the murmuration were in the northwest and southwest. The starlings chirped and talked to each other, a mixture of boredom and anticipation. Unlike with the Emerald Pridelords, the Violet Pridelord had asked everyone's opinion about whether they wanted to be a part of what came next. Despite Talli's spoken remarks a few moments previous, her scent confirmed she thought this was the right path.

Whisper's advice had been simple: *Feel out the glyphs along the western borders. Determine the owner on both sides, and hold those pheromones in your mind, then imagine the glyph. Then imagine what it would take to erode the glyph. Trust your instincts. If you imagine it, your body will find the scent you need.*

Two sets of glyphs formed a veil on the western borders. Had a pridelord ever looked at them with clear eyes—clear nares?—they would have seen how absurd the boundaries were. The mark of Alwren's reeve predated the Connixation. The opinicus had clearly been long-dead, but Alwren's chemists had replicated her scent to keep the glyphs alive. King's Reach was a similar situation, the pact made with a dead reeve lived on through alchemical necromancy.

Alwren's glyph smelled of fresh whiskerfish. King's Reach was a fruit of some sort, something she could feel Iri and Talli recognize as mango.

Nighteyes tried to think of the opposite of mango, but it didn't work. She pushed the citrus of command, but it made the murmuration stop in place. She tried mint, as had worked to lessen Balthar's control, but nothing. Even pepper just agitated the murmuration.

A claw tapped her back foot, Whisper's way of telling her to be smarter.

The Violet Pridelord let the smells fill her: long-dead pridelord, long-dead reeve. Then something came to her.

The faintest bitter whiff of Argent Heights bark beetle bounced from starling to starling across the Emerald Jungle, but when it reached one near a glyph, they reached up with their paw, and the acrid smell of bark beetle eroded the glyph.

"We hold no oaths with the dead." She spoke as though in a dream. "The only pacts we honor are with the living."

The murmuration all turned west as the Emerald

Veil flickered once, twice, and on the third time, vanished.

Like the floodwaters that devoured the Winter Jungle every spring, the starling prides descended upon King's Reach and Alwren.

The Abyssal Naze claimed that the Emerald Jungle was the armor that shielded the Seraph King. That ends today.

Far in the distance, a fleet of a hundred ships fled north.

The Gourmand caught a straggler and capsized it.

SABERBEAK

EPILOGUE

The redwoods west of Poisonmaw reached into the misty night, and in their boughs waited beak and claw. Where the storm sometimes parted, moonlight turned muddy goliath tracks a sinister red. The only sound was the occasional *skraark* or *boom* of ground parrots, calling to each other after a good rimu mast, oblivious to the conflict enveloping Belamuria.

The untamed forest kept watch as a caravan of goliath birds rolled through the trail. In the month since the failed attack on the Blackwing Eyrie, the king's forces had been in full retreat, and the smarter caravans kept to the coastal road. Heavy rains made for dumb opinici, and when the salt flats flooded, supply runs shifted east, into the mountains, to avoid becoming sailfin bait.

Hatzel, the only—adult—saberbeak, crouched in the center of the trail, right after it wound around the bend. The goliath handlers tended to trust the birds, and there were few things that could stop a fully grown goliath, even the domesticated version.

She was one of them.

To her left was a steep drop. To her right, the mountain rose straight up to the peaks separating Poisonmaw from the world outside the redwood forests. Their thick canopy made it difficult to see if the trail was clear or not, but the rain had stopped, and sound carried through the crisp air.

Other than ground parrots, a squeaky wagon wheel announced the caravan's arrival. Pink Paw, hiding upside down from a much higher vantage point, did her best *skraark* imitation three times.

Once meant everything was good. Twice meant they needed to abandon their ambush. Three times meant something was off, but she was looking into it.

Hatzel remained crouched, pulling her tail underneath her. On one such venture, she'd twitched her tail with impatience, and its light, tufted end had given them away. Embarrassing, as one wagon had escaped.

Not likely with an iffy wheel, but I'd still rather keep my dignity intact.

The squeaking slowed, and the first wagon rumbled to a stop before coming around her corner. Pink Paw's skraarks came in triplicate, and the copperhawk leapt across the trail to investigate, flanked by two more of Hatzel's pride.

Unlike Zeph, Pink Paw was skilled at working with a team. Excellent at it, even. Unlike...

Zeph.

Hatzel pushed her emotions down. Two years with

no word, not even a message. It was a long time for a gryphon. Her pride had searched the cave gryphon hideaways from Poisonmaw to Williwaw, but there were no signs of the denizens of the Abyssal Naze.

"There's something out there," an enemy opinicus called out. "The goliaths smell it."

Pink Paw looked back from her perch, but Hatzel shook her head no. Unless they had trained soldiers with them, the plan stood.

The pride leader motioned to the west, curious who the goliaths had gotten a whiff of. Her pride always came from the heights to the east. It was easier to fall upon prey than to try to rise up and catch it. Fisherfolk may latch onto an opinicus and pull them under, but a copperhawk or magpie couldn't pull a wagon or goliath bird down from below.

"I don't see anything, Captain." A new opinicus, this one with a farmer's drawl. The Alabaster Eyrie had sent quite a few farmers to Blacktalon to take over abandoned farms, and they were some of the last to retreat. The Blackwing Alliance was taking its time reclaiming their western border, perhaps hoping to minimize further conflict.

Or, more likely, leaving it to the free prides and Ashen Weald to do their work for them.

A goliath let out a loud *mronk.*

The captain's voice returned. "There...in the brush. See the blues and whites? It's one of the magpies!"

Hatzel would scold her pridemate later for their poor hiding skills, but she needed to save them first.

The large saberbeak gryphon dashed around the corner, where a dozen alabasters sat atop wagons, affixing metal weapons to their talons. At the head of the caravan, pulling it along, was a nine foot tall goliath bird, a dented metal breastplate with six wings protecting its heart. They were easier to kill from the air, but the same canopy that hid her pride kept anyone from doing much flying.

She roared a challenge, and the opinici balked, but the bird charged, jerking the wagons with it. A beak bigger than her own opened, reaching down to grab her head like it was an eggfruit.

Hatzel's massive forepaws pushed the goliath's face to her left. As it lifted its closest leg to kick, a move that could kill even a monitor, Hatzel launched herself up, flapping her wings, and latched the sabers of her beak into the beast's neck, dug in her claws, and then pulled it off balance and down the steep drop.

The goliath bird fell, taking the first wagon and the opinici on top of it down, too, as they were tangled in the nets securing the goods. The second wagon joined the first, but the opinici atop the third managed to cut themselves loose.

There was one soldier among them, the captain. He rushed her, slashing with his talons like she were a much smaller gryphon. She reared back, taking the slash on her stomach, the metal talons catching on her tough, scarred hide.

Then she stomped down, putting her full weight on the captain's metal breastplate, crushing it. He was dead before he realized what had happened to him.

She whistled, signalling Pink Paw and the rest of her pride to lower themselves into the remaining farmers' view. Every tree along the trail had an upside-down copperhawk on it plus a magpie above.

"Remove your harnesses, leave your supplies behind, and you're free to go." Hatzel growled her words when she gave this speech, but the more time she spent playing with the saberbeak gryphlets, the harder it became to act scary in front of opinici.

She must have succeeded, however, because the remaining alabasters obliged, flying naked to the southwest. At first, the flamingos of the Crackling Sea had sent patrols out here, though they never located Hatzel and Pink Paw. Nowadays, she imagined the pink reeve scolded the supply runs for being stupid enough to cross into the mountains.

"You couldn't have caught the second wagon before it fell?" Pink Paw asked. "It's a lot easier to retrieve the supplies when they're not smashed over the ground."

Hatzel rolled her eyes. "It's a lot easier to pull something off a cliff than it is to stop it from going over. Besides, it's fun. I don't get to break things anymore."

She beaked through the final wagon, letting her pride figure out the logistics of the ones at the bottom of the cliff. Nothing in it was edible. Instead, it was mostly metal—likely whatever they could loot from Blacktalon before abandoning the city for good.

"I'll miss these free gift caravans," she grumbled. "It's like the Blue-eyed Festival comes every five days."

She'd forgotten about the gryphon who had been spotted until someone called for her.

"Pride leader!" a copperhawk shouted—a copperhawk opinicus, just old enough to join these hunts, born of the liaisons after the Redwood Valley Eyrie burned down. "There's something here you need to see."

Pink Paw looked over from managing the fallen wagons, and both she and Hatzel approached the copperhawk opinicus. He pointed to a single white and blue feather caught in the vines. Behind it, almost invisible, was a small cave entrance.

It was one of many she'd investigated when the cave gryphons vanished. It went deep fast, too deep for her to search it, but it would be a tight fit for any gryphon if it led anywhere.

"Fetch the rushlight," she ordered the copper opinicus.

The flame was faint. It revealed nothing until he got it inside the hole, then two black orbs stared back at him.

He yelped and dropped the light.

"Who's there?" Pink Paw demanded.

A charcoal and brown face moved forwards, black eyes and whiskers now visible in the light. Then the face lowered, making room for someone behind it to squeeze out.

"Mom!" Xin shouted as he came out of the cave, vibrant white and blue magpie plumage shining in the moonlight. "I've missed you!"

Hatzel didn't need to guess who the other gryphon was. "Chert, it's been years. Where have you been? What's happened? Where's the rest of you?"

Cave gryphons moved in groups of twenty because to travel with fewer tempted the creatures of the depths. Hatzel had never seen a lone cave gryphon before.

"This isn't, uh, an official cave gryphon exploration." Chert spoke with an opinicus accent despite her gryphonic features. She still sounded young, though there was a new depth to her voice since the last time Hatzel had met her. "In the wake of what happened in the Emerald Jungle, the king tried to burn us out of the naze. Oh, don't worry, we're much to wily for that, but when everyone scattered, us two got separated from the group. So I figured: Xin's probably homesick, what if we just headed east?"

"And no one told you not to," Hatzel added.

Chert nodded, though her tail twitched. "Right, while no one was around to tell us not to. It...well, it didn't go as I thought it would, but we're here and alive! I figured since Zeph and Kia couldn't come tell you what was going on themselves, we were the next best thing."

"Wait," Hatzel interrupted. "Go back a moment. Why can't Zeph and Kia come here themselves?"

Chert groomed her whiskers anxiously. "That's a long story. I'd sort of hoped you already knew."

"I do not." Hatzel waited, hoping to force a reply now, but cave gryphons were fairly patient, and at the moment, she was not. "Fine, you and Xin come back with me to Poisonmaw, and we'll get you fed. But before you sleep, you tell me what's happened."

CHERT HAD DOZED OFF MID-TELLING, but she'd gotten all the important parts out. New nests were hard to come by, but Xavi and Pink Paw had given up theirs for their eldest and his best friend, and Hatzel let the parents move into her cave.

The misnamed last saberbeak stared out at the hatchery where a half dozen small saberlets dozed. All of them had been gifted chew toys by the Darkfeather University, courtesy of Grax, to keep them from biting tails—theirs or others. The toys were made from bone, which the scholars claimed gave important nutrients. Even if that wasn't the case, everyone was happy the saberlets had stopped biting gryphons.

Once Xin and Chert were asleep, Pink Paw slipped outside to meet Hatzel atop the waterfall overlooking Poisonmaw. "I thought I'd find you here. What'll you do?"

"Go," Hatzel said, before realizing that could be misconstrued as a command. "Go to the Abyssal Naze, I mean."

Pink Paw nodded. She'd nearly left a few times herself, hoping to find word of Xin. "What will you do once you locate him?"

"Bring him home." Hatzel felt silly saying it. Zeph wasn't a lost gryphlet, he was an adult gryphon. *Or adult...something.* The point was, Zeph was her friend, and she didn't trust him to know he needed friends right now.

No slight to Kia, but she was an opinicus. *Seraph. Something.* She hadn't been there when Zeph showed up by the Snowfeather River, lost and downy, abandoned by the taiga pride. She hadn't taught him to hunt, to make friends. She hadn't indulged his silly interest in trading parrots, nor had she made sure he was taken care of.

Hatzel shook her head. She'd put a wall between herself and others after Vosk died. He'd been her oldest friend, her favorite mate, and her claws had never felt clean after killing him. She'd been unable to spend more than an hour in Younce's presence since. But in doing that, she'd let other friendships slide in the name of restoring the saberbeak pride's ancestral homeland, Poisonmaw.

Now Poisonmaw had other saberbeaks, tiny though they were. And Pink Paw or Xavi had always been capable of leading a pride. *If they hadn't become perennial mates, I think we'd have seen Xavi lead the magpie pride and Pink Paw lead the copperhawk pride long before now.*

That thought brought Hatzel back to the present. "Do you and Xavi want to be co-consorts, like Askel and Triddle? At least one of you should be in charge."

"Just me," Pink Paw said. When Hatzel raised an eyecrest, the copperhawk continued. "Well, we've talked about what would happen if you died, and Xavi wants to remain denfather. I'll check with him again, to make sure he hasn't changed his mind, but...prob-ably just me."

The wind shifted, and the spray from the waterfall dampened both gryphons. Hatzel raised a wing to block it. *The Pink Paw Pride. I guess it has a nice ring to it. All the lesser prides have found their greatness: Hatzel's pride, Merin's pride, Strix's pride.*

"Grax will miss you," Pink Paw began.

Hatzel stopped her. "Grax already knows about my plans. She was a good mate, but she's even better at training gryphlets to survive. She promised to train the saberbeaks. She was...very good-natured about it all. Though I suspect she's ready for Ninox to return and take over the Strix Pride."

"I'll be ready to turn over the pride when you return," Pink Paw confirmed.

"Don't. It's yours." Hatzel didn't know if she'd be returning. She stretched her legs, sore after waiting in the road for so long. The Redwood Valley opinici who joined her pride after the eyrie fire had designed all manner of harnesses and armor for her, but she'd declined to wear any of them. Still, if she had a long flight ahead of her, she'd need some way of carrying supplies, especially where she didn't know where to hunt. "I'm going to the Strix Pride, since they're up late. There are rumors Ninox's daughter has returned, and she'll know where her mom is. I'm sure they'll want to hear what Chert said about Cherine. Then I'll return and give the news to our pride so they can adjust before I leave."

Pink Paw started to bow and mantle, the leader of the hunt to her pride leader, but Hatzel reached out a paw and stopped her.

"You're going to need to get used to being in charge." Hatzel did her best bow, just barely getting the top of her head below Pink Paw's ears and sinking the sabers on her beak into the water a bit to do so. "Pink Paw of the Pink Paw Pride."

The copperhawk groaned. "I'd name it anything else if I thought my pridemates would listen."

Hatzel let her friend escort her to the edge of the Darkfeather Highlands. She let the beauty of the redwoods, the sounds of the mountain wildlife seep into her, savoring both like a feast.

Stay alive a little longer, Zeph. I'm coming for you.

K. VALE NAGLE

SABERBEAK

GRYPHON INSURRECTION: BOOK NINE

AUTHOR'S NOTE
OTTER SANDBOX

Hello again, fantails! It's been a bit since the last GryphIns novel, hasn't it? There was a charity novel release in there, "Coldbright" from the *Tales of Feathers and Flames* anthology, but I've left you in suspense about Zeph and Kia's fate for far too long, and for that, I apologize—but only a little bit.

After the release of *Starling* in 2019, a lot of fans wanted to visit the Emerald Jungle, and I'm glad I was finally able to grant that request. In some ways, the prologue was a sweet appetizer to tide you over before the claustrophobic feel of being stuck behind the Emerald Veil with Nighteyes, Wendl, Whisper, and Rudder. I did consider a different prologue without Zeph and Kia to draw out the suspense: instead of checking in on the heroes of *Eyrie*, I thought it might be interesting to see a certain newmoon gryphon lurking unseen on the edge of the jungle, whispering to cave gryphons or darkstalkers who came too near.

Ultimately, my husband and early readers demanded to know how Zeph was doing, and I *caved* in. (That's an Abyssal Naze pun.) A brief repose before the jungle itself, a place full of starlings, forests that spend the summer flooded, spiketrunks, and...otter gryphons?

Yep, otter gryphons! The Stormtail Pride has been around for a few books now causing problems for Thistle, and I've had some messages from fans looking to make art asking about the cat half of the pride. The series has had van cats and fishing cats already, two water-loving felines, but the answer is that stormtails aren't cats at all, they're giant river otters.

As a quick aside, thank you to readers who asked if they were flat-headed cats. I'd never heard of these swimming cats with a silly name before, and I delight in learning about new animals.

While I love Clamshell, Desert Rose, and Rudder, giant otters are scary creatures. They live along the Amazon basin, and their Spanish name, *lobo de rio,* means "river wolf" while their Portuguese name, *onça-d'áqua,* means "water jaguar." (Their genus name, in keeping with their pride glyph, means feather-tail.)

They're at the top of the food chain in an ecosystem full of jaguars, anacondas, piranha, and caimans partially because of their size (around two meters or six and a half feet, just over the height of a GryphIns author) but also because they hunt in packs. I'm amazed no one is writing giant otter horror novels. The closest we've got is *The Hollow Places* by Ursula Vernon featuring a taxidermy otter, though I'll call out *The Dragon's Hide* by Dustin Porta and D. K. Holmberg for being an epic fantasy book that acknowledges how scary giant otters are.

Of course, it's not just the fauna that're interesting in the Emerald Jungle. There's also the spiketrunks, based on the real life sandbox tree. Sandbox trees were named after their pumpkin-shaped fruit, which could be used to store sand for use on letters to dry the ink, something that hasn't been done regularly in a long time. It's also a strange aspect of the tree to use as their name since the tree has stabby spines, poisonous sap, and those faux pumpkin fruits *explode*.

I'd have called it a Clue Murder Tree, after the board game, because whenever we'd let my little brother shuffle the cards, he'd accidentally put three weapons, no suspects, and no rooms into the little envelope.

You're probably wondering about the exploding pumpkins. They're just pumpkin-shaped, not real pumpkins. On the hottest days of the year, they dry out, and then the tree pushes a ton of water into them, which superheats, causing them to explode, sending seeds everywhere. Completely normal tree stuff. As Hoppy Padfoot would say, *not weird at all.*

Perhaps the strangest addition were the clawdiggers, warned about throughout *Opinicus* as lurking in the depths, waiting to pounce on unsuspecting cave gryphons. Of course, they were hinted at much earlier, in the common knowledge that pregnant opinici and gryphons needed to be careful about eating certain mammals. The clawdiggers are a mix of three species: pelagornis in the head, giant cave sloth in the body, and spectral bat in the wings. Pelagornis is a prehistoric pseudotooth bird with an impressive, bitey beak. Giant cave sloths have wicked claws, and we see their long scratches in old caves. The spectral bat, also called the great false vampire bat (rude), is the largest carnivorous bat, with a wingspan of over three feet.

We're reaching the end of the Gryphon Insurrection, and it's been fun to stretch the definition of what qualifies as a gryphon. There's still a few new species coming up, but getting to add in the seraphic opinici —*feathersnakes* for any starlings reading this—and clawdiggers has made me happy.

This is normally where I'd answer what's next for the series, but I think it's pretty clear who gets the protagonist spotlight next: Hatzel's the star of *Saberbeak*, which I'll have begun work on long before you read this Author's Note. As has been the case a few times before (*Starling* and *Reevesbane*, *Crackling Sea* and *Opinicus*), I looked at the ending of the story and decided it would work better in a few books than one. To that end, the new bibliographies will show *Saberbeak* as book nine and then...Well, you'll see. No reason to spoil the last titles just yet.

The end is near! But in a good way.

And because readers often write in to check on me when a new book isn't up for preorder, I'm about the same as always. Still undergoing treatment for the autoimmune disorder, pushing the dose up every six months. Still walking Indalecia F. Cat each morning as long as she wants or until she tries to eat grass. Still trying to convince Caliginous Drinkwell (the other cat) to stop hiding moths under my pillow. Still telling silly mystery stories to my husband while we pack books for convention season. Still keeping the Gryphon Reading List updated so gryphon fans can locate new books to read. Still working on converting parts of the yard to native flora (it's a good year for sage, bad year for snakeweed). Still making jokes with James Scott Spaid, my audiobook narrator, as he catches up recording the series.

Until next time, keep your whiskers clean and may your days be full of cats, birds, and cat-birds.

-Vale

ABOUT THE AUTHOR

K. Vale Nagle is alarmingly hard to kill.

After surviving several pulmonary embolisms and multiple organ failure, Vale kicked her writing into high gear and saw her first short story and novel publications. When she's not writing creature fantasy or fighting for her life, she enjoys reading, archery, and exploring the Rocky Mountains with a tabby cat by her side.

She can be found online at kvalenagle.com, via her newsletter at kvalenagle.com/mailinglist, or on Patreon.com/kvalenagle.

patreon.com/kvalenagle

facebook.com/kvalenagle

twitter.com/kvalenagle

bookbub.com/authors/k-vale-nagle

amazon.com/K-Vale-Nagle/e/B07ND33BHW